ABOUT THE AUTHOR

Although born and bred in the city of Melbourne, Lisa has always been a country girl at heart. As a horse-mad teen she read countless books about girls and their ponies and dreamed of a life on a horse stud, far away from her suburban home. After completing a teaching degree, Lisa finally got to realise her dream of a life in the country when she took up a position in a rural school. A flood, a fire, and several encounters with snakes taught her that life on the land wasn't all fluffy sheep and home-baked scones! But she wasn't put off. She loved every minute of life in her new home.

After moving back to the city Lisa's appreciation for all things rural didn't wane. She took to jotting down stories of her life in the bush so she would have a reminder of her time there. Eventually she realised that making up stories was much more fun than sticking to the facts.

Lisa now lives in a small coastal town with her husband, their three sons, and two very spoiled dogs, Millie and Lulu. When she's not writing or reading she spends her time walking her dogs along the beach, pretending to watch her husband surf, drinking copious amounts of coffee at a local café, and cheering on the Mighty Cats at Simonds Stadium.

FEELS LIKE
Home

LISA IRELAND

First Published 2015
First Australian Paperback Edition 2015
ISBN 978 174369306 3

FEELS LIKE HOME
© 2015 by Lisa Ireland
Australian Copyright 2015
New Zealand Copyright 2015

This is a work of fiction. Names, characters, places, and incidents are either the product of the author's imagination or are used fictitiously, and any resemblance to actual persons, living or dead, business establishments, events, or locales is entirely coincidental.

Published by
Harlequin Mira
An imprint of Harlequin Enterprises (Aust) Pty Ltd.
Level 4, 132 Arthur Street
NORTH SYDNEY NSW 2060
AUSTRALIA

Printed and bound in Australia by Griffin Press

MIX
Paper from
responsible sources
FSC® C009448
FSC
www.fsc.org

For Evelyn Faye with love xx

CHAPTER

1

Perhaps wedge heels weren't the wisest choice.

Johanna Morgan wobbled her way across the gravel car park, towards the ring of cars on the perimeter of Linden Gully's football ground. She sucked in a deep breath and tried to prepare herself to go into the fray.

This humble oval held so many memories of her teenage triumphs and tragedies. She'd experienced her first kiss in the clump of cypress pines behind the old timber scoreboard and her first heartbreak in the same location a week later. It was such a long time ago now, but today she felt every bit the awkward teenager she thought she'd left behind.

A roar went up and car horns began to sound. Obviously the Lions had scored a goal. Now was as good a time as any to make her entrance into the crowd.

By New York standards this barely qualified as a gathering, let alone a crowd. But she wasn't in New York now. She was back on Australian soil.

Back home.

Butterflies swirled in her stomach. A warm reception was probably too much to hope for. She'd never truly belonged here. Almost every minute of her childhood had been spent dreaming of somewhere else. Now she was returning as an outsider. A deserter.

It was bad enough that she was Katherine Morgan's daughter — her mother's condescending attitude had done nothing to endear her to the town — but Jo's refusal to settle for a life in Linden Gully, coupled with her recent publishing success and the fact that she was supposedly engaged to a famous American actor, would only reinforce the popular view that she was a stuck-up snob. Tall-poppy syndrome was alive and well in Linden Gully. At least it had been seven years ago.

Jo picked her way towards the boundary fence, eyes down, doing her best to avoid puddles. Despite the chill in the air her palms were sweating. She silently chastised herself for caring. She was an adult, dammit. She didn't owe anyone any explanations.

That was all well and good, but she wished the shy sixteen-year-old inside her would get the message.

'Oi! Don't think you're getting away with it that easily,' a gruff voice accused her from behind.

'I'm sorry?' She swung around, wondering what social faux pas she had committed.

'A kiss is the current entry price for out-of-towners.' Steph's dad stepped forward and held out his arms to her.

Jo grinned. 'I reckon that's a pretty high price, Mick.' She leaned in and kissed him on the cheek.

'Didn't expect you for weeks yet, Jo.'

'I know. Thought I'd surprise Steph.'

'Good to see you home, love. Steph'll be thrilled. And maybe you can settle my missus down a bit now you're here. She's been running around like a headless chook over this flippin' wedding. I think she's driving Steph crazy.'

Jo laughed. Jenny Fielding had been anticipating her only daughter's wedding for as long as Jo could remember. 'Is she here? Steph, I mean.'

Mick nodded towards the other side of the oval. 'Over near the goals, love. She'll be excited to see you.'

The siren sounded to signal half time and the spectators clapped and cheered as the players made their way from the field. Jo squinted into the winter sun and eventually spotted Steph sitting on the bonnet of a large pick-up — no, a large *ute*. Mustn't let the locals catch her using Americanisms like 'pick-up truck'. She'd never hear the end of it.

There was a guy standing in front of the ute, a well-built specimen from the looks of it. Hard to tell who it was from here.

It wasn't Nate, Steph's soon-to-be-husband. Nate was the Lions' star full-back, and she had just seen him making his way into the club rooms with his teammates for the coach's half-time address.

It was a shame Steph wasn't alone, but she could hardly expect a private reunion at such a public place. Jo felt the stares following her as she made her way across the ground. Murmurs of recognition trailed behind her and she noticed a couple of familiar faces turning in her direction. A few people actually pointed. She smiled and waved. No point aggravating the situation. News of her return would soon be spreading around the ground like wildfire.

At least she knew there was one person in town who would be pleased to see her. She couldn't wait to see the look of surprise on her best friend's face. Of course Steph was expecting to see her soon; she was to be chief bridesmaid, after all. But the wedding was a full three weeks away and Jo had intended to fly in just a couple of days before the big event.

Arriving early meant that she could be a proper bridesmaid and organise things that Steph would publicly roll her eyes at but secretly love, like an old-fashioned bridal shower and a huge hen's night.

Jo was here to be the perfect maid of honour. At least that was the story she'd concocted to explain her early arrival, and she'd rehearsed it so much in her head that even she was beginning to believe that her hasty departure from New York had everything do with being a good bridesmaid and nothing to do with being a runaway bride-to-be.

As she walked towards the southern end of the oval, she could see Steph craning her neck, trying to get a look at the outsider approaching her. Jo grinned as recognition slowly dawned on her friend's face and she let out an ear-piercing squeal as she slid off the car's bonnet. 'Oh my god! Jo, is it really you?' Steph pushed aside Hot Guy and ran towards her.

Jo stomach dropped. That was no generic guy.

It was him.

Ryan Galloway was staring right back at her.

Ryan couldn't believe his eyes.

It was Jo.

His Joey.

Here at the footy ground.

Of course he'd known she was coming home for the wedding. He'd known that he would have to sit next to her at the bridal table, that he'd have to make small talk with her and pretend that nothing was wrong. Pretend that nothing had ever happened between them and that he didn't still think about her. Every. Single. Day.

But he hadn't expected to see her here today.

Damn.

He wasn't prepared for this. What on earth could he say to her? Was he just supposed to smile like a chump while she told him all about her fabulous, successful life? Was he expected to be thrilled that she'd found a new love, some Hollywood pretty-boy who'd probably never done a day's work in his life and yet could afford to give her everything she could possibly dream of?

In the movies the good guys always won, but Ryan had learned the hard way that life wasn't always fair.

When Nate had told him Steph had asked Joey to be bridesmaid, he'd figured she wouldn't come. He knew better than most how much she hated this town, and not without cause, he'd admit that much. Now that she was a big celebrity he'd presumed she'd find a reason to stay away.

But when Nate insisted she was coming, flying in for a whirlwind visit, he'd decided he would just have to suck it up. Be polite for a few days and avoid her as much as possible. How hard could it be?

He had it all worked out. At the wedding he'd be cool and suave, show her that he was fine without her. Show that his broken heart had mended without any scars. To prove the point maybe he'd ask Laura Baxter to the wedding. Laura was a pretty woman, and good company. She might not be an international celebrity and maybe she talked a little too much, but she liked him just the way he was, and that was more than he could say for Miss High and Mighty over there. Then again, he didn't want to give Laura any false hope. They'd dated a few times, but she wasn't the woman for him. The wedding was going to be hard enough without creating more problems for himself.

The last time he'd seen Joey he'd offered her his heart in the form of a tiny diamond engagement ring he'd spent over a year saving for. She cried and he'd thought they were tears of joy, but he was mistaken. She'd left the next day, never to return.

Until now.

God, she really was just metres away, laughing with Steph and looking like a movie star. In some ways she hadn't changed too much. The same long honey-blonde hair fell down over her shoulders and she was twirling it around her index finger, the way she always did when she was nervous. But she was thinner and seemed taller than the petite girl he remembered. Maybe it was those stupid high heels she was wearing.

New York had certainly put its stamp on her. The girl he knew and loved would never have turned up to the footy in that get-up. Look at her, with those figure-hugging jeans, ridiculous shoes and bloody enormous sunglasses. And what was with that floppy hat? Did she realise this was a football game, not some fancy-pants art exhibition?

And she was wearing another man's ring — a gigantic diamond — on her finger.

She might be back in Linden Gully but she wasn't his Joey anymore.

There was no time to react. Jo's body seemed rooted to the spot, unwilling to co-operate with her brain's instinct to turn and run.

Steph enveloped her in a bear hug. 'It's so great to see you. I can't believe you're here. Hey, are you okay? You look a little pale.'

'Just jetlagged, that's all. I flew into Melbourne at six this morning and then got on the bus to here.' Jo forced herself to smile. 'It's good to be home.'

'So did you come straight here? Or have you already been home to Yarrapinga?'

'I came to find you before I did anything else. I jumped off the bus, left my bags at the pub and hitched a ride over here with Helen Thompson. She was heading in to Bellington and dropped me off on her way.'

'Oh good grief, listen to you! You sound like a bloody Yank!'

Jo averted her eyes from Ryan, who was still staring, and grinned at Steph. 'Give it a rest. I'm always being asked to say "G'day" back home...I mean in New York. I'm still an Aussie.'

'Well, you sound like a New Yorker to me. And you look so glamorous.' Steph hugged her again. 'I can't believe you're really here.' She paused for a minute and wrinkled her brow. 'Why *are* you here? There's nothing wrong, is there? Is your mum okay? I thought you said you couldn't get away until a couple of days before the wedding.'

Jo tried to keep her voice light. Steph knew her better than anyone and wouldn't be easily fooled. 'I wanted to surprise you.'

'Well you sure did that. Is Zach with you?'

Jo shook her head. 'He's flat out filming a new movie. He would have loved to have come but it just wasn't possible.' Jo glanced over Steph's shoulder. Damn, Ryan was still standing there.

Steph followed Jo's gaze. 'Oh...I wasn't expecting you to be here,' she whispered. 'Not yet. I...I was going to tell you about Ryan being back in town. I was waiting for the right time.'

Jo took yet another big breath and disengaged herself from Steph. She stepped forward and held out her hand in greeting to the first man she had ever loved. 'Hey, Ryan. It's been a long time.'

He smiled and took her hand and she felt like her heart was beating so hard it was going to leap from her chest. He looked the same, but different somehow. His thick, sandy hair was unchanged, and still hung boyishly long on his forehead, occasionally obscuring his blue-grey eyes. But his face was harder, his jaw squarer than she remembered, and it was sporting a very fetching three-day growth. His body, always lean and muscular, had filled out, and his shoulders had broadened. He'd grown into the man she'd always imagined he'd be.

No, no, no.

She would not react like this. He would not turn her into mush with one of his boyish grins. What they'd had was over long ago. Seven years of rebuilding her life, of trying to get over what had happened between them — there was no way she would let him charm his way back in.

'Hey Joey.'

The endearment threw her. How could he call her that after all that had happened? He'd lost that right when he'd taken another woman into his bed just weeks after he'd kissed her goodbye. 'Johanna,' she said coldly. 'People call me Johanna these days.'

He withdrew his hand sharply. 'Sorry, Johanna it is. So, how have you been?'

'Wonderful,' she said trying her hardest to appear relaxed.

'Yeah,' he said, shifting his weight from one foot to the other. 'You look...great.'

Jo was saved from having to reciprocate the compliment by a small curly-haired girl who was running towards them. 'Daddy!' the child called as she approached. She came to an abrupt halt in front of Jo, eyed her suspiciously for a second and then tugged Ryan's sleeve. 'Daddy, I want a sausage. Gran said I had to ask you first.'

Ryan's whole demeanour changed as he turned and scooped the child up in his arms. He planted a kiss on her head and said, 'Ella, this is my friend, Johanna. Can you say hello?'

'Hello,' Ella said, barely even glancing in Jo's direction. 'Well, can I Dad?'

'Of course, sweetheart.' He placed Ella back on her feet and dug in his pocket for some loose change. 'Give this to the ladies at the sausage sizzle, and don't forget to use your manners.'

Jo couldn't take her eyes off the child as she ran back across the oval. She willed the tears to stay away, but only just managed. It was physically painful to watch the product of Ryan's betrayal skipping across the football field.

Jo stood in silence. What did he expect her to say? That Ella was beautiful? That she looked just like him? In fact the child was the living image of her mother, which somehow made Jo feel even worse.

Ryan was clearly as uncomfortable with the situation as she was. He began to back away. 'Tell Nate I'll see him tomorrow, Steph. Nice to see you, *Johanna*.' He turned on his heel and walked away.

CHAPTER
2

After a quick detour via the pub to collect Jo's luggage, Steph insisted on taking Jo back to Kallara to spend the night. She didn't need much convincing. After her long journey and the encounter with Ryan, she wasn't ready to face the emptiness of Yarrapinga just yet.

Jo feigned sleepiness on the twenty-minute drive out to Steph's family property. She wasn't ready to talk about what had just happened. Steph had rarely mentioned Ryan during their regular Skype sessions or emails. Sure, Jo had asked her never to speak of him again, but that was years ago now. Surely Steph should have realised that a heads-up about him being in town was warranted, especially when she knew Jo was coming home for the wedding?

Through half-closed eyes she took in the familiar scenery. Green paddocks filled with dairy cattle flashed by, then towering gums appeared as they skirted around the edge of the national park. When they came to a clearing at the top of a hill, Jo opened her eyes. Kallara would soon be in sight. 'Nothing's changed,' she said.

Steph smiled. 'Seems like just yesterday we were riding through these paddocks.'

A wave of nostalgia swept over Jo, taking her by surprise. It *was* good to see this place again. Funny, seven years ago she couldn't wait to leave.

Last time she had been here was to attend her father's funeral. She'd hardly noticed the place then. Had it really been two years since she and Steph had held hands and walked behind Daddy's casket? The visit had been such a blur. First dealing with the shock of her father's sudden death, and then discovering that her mother had been placed in a nursing home some months earlier. Katherine wasn't quite fifty at the time of her diagnosis of early-onset dementia, a diagnosis Jo had never officially been told about. Her father had tried to protect her from the truth, telling her only that her mother was unwell and having some treatment. Jo had assumed she was depressed, and that the treatment her father so vaguely referred to was psychiatric. The discovery that Katherine could no longer care for herself had been almost as traumatic as losing her father.

Maddock's Gully came into sight, the vision bringing with it a flood of memories. How many times had she and Steph ridden to the top and raced back down? Jo always won. Steph was a natural on horseback, but she didn't have a competitive bone in her body. Jo turned to face her friend. 'Have you still got Sherlock?'

Steph shook her head. 'He died last summer. It was a shocking season. I've never known it to be so hot. Poor old bloke was frail and the heat knocked him about. In the end there was no choice but to...'

Jo touched Steph's arm. 'I'm so sorry. I know what he meant to you.'

'I bought a new gelding a few months back. He's called Shamrock.' She slowed down to cross the cattle grid at Kallara's entrance. 'He's a gorgeous boy but I'm afraid he's not here at the moment. I've got him agisted over at the Callahans' for a few weeks, so Sally Callahan can exercise him for me. Mum's banned me from riding until after the wedding. She insists that it's tempting fate and says I'll end up going down the aisle on crutches.'

Jo laughed. Seeing Steph safely married had always been an obsession of Jenny Fielding's. 'Don't bite your nails, Steph,' she used to say. 'No man will want to marry a girl with fingernails like that. Look at Jo's nails.' Jenny would smile at her. 'You'll make a beautiful bride some day, Johanna.'

And now here they were: Tomboy Steph, about to commit herself to the man she loved, and Princess Johanna, running away from her betrothed. Life hadn't turned out the way any of them had expected.

Steph pulled the ute up near the homestead's entrance. Jo opened the door and breathed in the eucalypt-laden air. The ancient gums that lined Kallara's driveway and ringed the homestead were welcoming her home.

'Jo, before we go inside I want to explain about Ryan,' Steph said.

'Can we talk about this later?'

Steph shook her head. 'Once we get inside Mum will be all over you and I don't know when we'll get another chance to talk properly on our own. I don't want you to be upset, Jo, or angry at me.'

Jo closed the ute's door and stared ahead at the pretty weatherboard house that had once felt like home. 'I'm not angry. I just wish I'd known, that's all.'

Steph nodded. 'Fair enough. I'm sorry I didn't tell you he was back in town. I thought about it when he first came home but there didn't seem any point to telling you. You were in New York, you were happy. I couldn't see any reason to drag up the past for you when you were so far away.'

'But the wedding, Steph. You might have thought to tell me he was here when you knew I was coming home.'

Steph's shoulders sagged. 'I was going to tell you, but when Nate asked him to be best man —'

'Best man?' Jo couldn't hide her disbelief. 'Tell me you're kidding?'

Steph shook her head. 'I'm sorry.'

So there would be no avoiding him. No polite smiles as they passed in the crowd. She would have to spend half the day by his side and get up close and personal during the bridal waltz. 'Bloody hell, Steph, did it not occur to you that I would be less than overjoyed to be partnered with him? A heads-up would have been nice.'

Steph looked crestfallen. 'I know. I was going to tell you, really I was. I was waiting for the right time. I never for a second dreamed you'd be home this early.'

Jo was silent for a moment. This was the absolute pits. Ryan being in town was one thing, but being in the bridal party? He would be involved not only on the big day but in all the pre-wedding events as well. There would be no avoiding him.

To be fair, she only had herself to blame. Years ago she'd asked Steph never to mention Ryan's name in her presence. On the few occasions Steph had broken that pact she'd howled her down. And Steph wasn't to know she would be in town this early. Jo knew she really had no right to be mad.

'Tell you what,' Steph said. 'We can solve this the way we've always solved disagreements.'

'What do you mean?'

'We'll toss a coin. Heads you forgive me. Tails I have to be your slave until you fly back to New York.'

Jo laughed. It was Steph's wedding and she wasn't going to ruin it by acting like a big baby. 'Tempting, but there's no need. Of course

I forgive you. I'm just a bit shell-shocked from running into him like that.'

'But it wasn't too bad was it? I mean, you've moved on now.' Steph stared pointedly at the large diamond Jo was sporting on her wedding finger.

Jo shifted in her seat uncomfortably. This was a conversation she wasn't ready to have. She had indeed moved on, but not in the way Steph was implying. Her relationship with Zach Carlton was over.

She fiddled with her engagement ring and considered confiding in her friend. Steph was trustworthy, there was no doubt about that. But a promise was a promise. She'd given Zach her word that she would tell no one until after the movie's premiere, and with Ryan back in town, maybe that was for the best. If everyone thought she was engaged to Zach then there could be no speculation about her reasons for coming home. She'd had more than enough of being in the spotlight, and had no desire to draw any attention away from Steph and Nate's big day. She would tell Steph, but not until after the wedding and, if she could hold out that long, after she'd done her duty walking the red carpet with Zach at the premiere of *Hollywood Kisses*. 'I've definitely moved on,' she said.

Steph grinned. 'Of course you have. I mean, Jo, you're engaged to Zachary Carlton! It just seems so unreal. Do you pinch yourself sometimes and wonder how a girl from Linden Gully ended up being so famous?'

Jo laughed. 'I'm not famous.'

'Are you kidding? You're a best-selling author and you're marrying the hottest guy on earth. I see your head in the gossip mags every other week. You're like a Kardashian.'

Jo winced. 'I hope I'm not like a Kardashian. And I think Nate would have something to say if he knew you'd called my fiancé the "hottest guy on earth". By the way, Zach has his flaws. What you see up on that screen isn't exactly how he looks when he gets up in the morning.'

'Oooh, do tell.'

'My lips are sealed. Now come on, let's go inside. I can't wait to see your mum.'

'Daddy, I want you to play Monopoly with me.'

Ryan finished scraping his plate into the compost bin and placed it in the dishwasher. 'Not tonight, sweetie. I'm tired.'

'But you promised. This morning you said if I helped by picking up all my toys you'd play a game with me tonight.'

Shoot. She had him there. The last thing he felt like was playing games. He just wanted to kick back on the couch and watch some mindless drivel on the TV. Seeing Joey, sorry *Johanna*, had thrown him and he really wasn't up to being Fun Dad tonight. Perhaps Ella would be open to negotiation. 'Sorry princess, I totally forgot. I'm really too tired for a long game. How about a quick round of Uno and then I'll put *The Little Mermaid* on for us to watch?'

Her little forehead creased in concentration for a moment. 'Can we have popcorn?'

'You drive a hard bargain, missy. Okay. You go find the Uno cards and I'll put a bag of popcorn in the microwave.'

Ryan smiled as she scampered off to her bedroom. She was such a great kid. Nothing ever fazed her. After Carly left, everyone — his mother, his brothers, friends — had tried to convince him that raising Ella alone was foolhardy. 'You have no idea how hard it is, raising a child on your own,' his mother had said.

'You raised three on your own.'

'A girl needs a mother.'

'And boys don't need a father? I've turned out alright haven't I?'

Beth smiled indulgently. 'Better than alright, love. I'm just worried, that's all. This is not the life I'd imagined for you. You're not much more than a child yourself. Bringing up a child is a huge responsibility. What about your future? What will you do about your studies? You can't look after a child while you're at uni.'

Ryan shrugged. 'I'll work something out. Ella is my responsibility. That's all there is to it.'

Six years later he had no regrets. Ella was a delight; the easiest kid on the planet to get along with, most of the time. Sure they'd had tough times, but every day he was thankful for the lessons that Ella taught him, the unconditional love she offered.

Once Uno was dispensed with — three rounds, Ella winning the first and last — Ryan popped the DVD into the player and the two of them settled in for a quiet evening. This probably wasn't most people's idea of a great Saturday night, but to Ryan it was perfect. Or it would have been if he'd been able to get the image of Jo and that bloody enormous engagement ring out of his head.

She'd moved on. He got that. He hadn't realised it at the time, but it was over between them the minute she got on that plane without him.

He and Jo were both born and raised in Linden Gully but they'd always been from different worlds. As love-struck teenagers it hadn't mattered, but he should have realised that Jo was only on loan to him. She had big dreams and a small-town boy was never going to fulfil them.

For seven long years he had thought about what it would be like to see her one more time, to talk to her again, to confide in her about everything that had happened. It was stupid and something he'd not dared to admit, even to himself, but part of him had believed that one day she'd come back to him. Seeing her today had shattered that fantasy. She was engaged to another man and it appeared that he didn't even register on her radar. He'd been a bloody fool to think otherwise. All these years he'd been comparing every woman he met to her. What a waste. The Joey he knew didn't even exist anymore. Johanna Morgan was a whole different person.

The DVD had worked its magic. Ella had drifted off into a contented sleep. Ryan gently lifted her from the couch and carried her into her bedroom. He'd just finished tucking her in when he heard his mother's voice float down the hallway.

'Yoohoo, anyone home?'

'Shhh, Mum. Ella's asleep.'

'Sorry, love. Just coming in to check on you two before I head off to bed myself.'

Ryan motioned for her to go to the kitchen. 'Feel like a cuppa?' he asked.

'You sit down, love. I'll make a pot of tea.' She was filling the kettle already.

Ryan grinned. His mother was a tea connoisseur, and obviously his tea-making skills weren't up to scratch. She never let him make her a cup. He pulled out the china teacup with matching saucer he kept especially for her and set it on the table next to his mug. 'How was the bingo fundraiser?'

Beth rolled her eyes. 'Quite boring actually. I do wish the CWA would come up with some new ideas. Anyway, I'm not here to talk about that. I came to see if you were alright.'

'Of course I'm alright. Why wouldn't I be?'

Beth put down the teapot and looked him squarely in the eye. 'I heard your Jo was back in town.'

'She's not "my" Jo, Mum,' Ryan replied with more venom than he'd intended.

'No, I guess not. She's engaged to that movie star Zachary What's-his-name, isn't she?'

Ryan shrugged. 'So I believe.'

'So you haven't spoken to her then?'

'I saw her at the football and we had a quick chat.' Clearly his mother already knew this information, otherwise she wouldn't be here drinking tea with him at nine o'clock on a Saturday night.

'Oh? How was that for you?'

'Fine. Look, Mum, you don't have to worry. Jo and I had a teenage fling, that's all. Until I saw her today I hadn't thought about her in years,' he lied.

Beth looked unconvinced. 'It was a bit more serious than that, Ryan.'

'Okay, at the time I thought it was too. But it was years ago. I've moved on and clearly so has she. She's in town for the wedding. I don't expect we'll be seeing that much of each other until the big day. It's a non-issue, okay?'

'Really? Because I seem to remember it all being a very big deal a few years back.'

'Well it's not now. We were once an item. Now Johanna's just someone I used to know. Leave it alone, Mum.'

Beth sipped her tea without replying, but Ryan could see the hurt look on her face.

'Let's talk about something else.'

'Actually, if you don't mind I'm rather tired. I might head out to the flat and call it a night.'

Ryan nodded and gave her a goodnight peck on the cheek. He felt like a heel now. He hadn't meant to be so snappy. It seemed he couldn't do anything right today.

With Ella safely tucked up in bed and his mother retired to the granny flat for the night, Ryan allowed himself the luxury of a cold beer. He stretched out on the couch and stabbed aimlessly at the TV remote. It was no use. There was nothing on TV fascinating enough to distract him from his thoughts of Jo.

It was hard to believe that one woman, just by her mere presence in the same town, could unsettle him so much. And it wasn't as if he even knew her anymore. She was no longer that sweet, dreamy-eyed girl who told him stories as they lay in the tall grass staring up at the summer sky. Hell, he wasn't the same either. Back then they'd both been full of hopes and dreams. The trouble was Jo's plans for the future didn't leave any room for him.

He'd wanted her to show him that getting on that plane to New York wasn't an act of abandonment. But when he'd asked for her commitment, her promise of everlasting love, she hadn't been able to look him in the eye. Like a fool he'd hoped that once she was away from him she'd realise what she was missing out on. But after a few weeks the truth became clear. She'd moved on long before his proposal. Just hadn't had the guts to tell him.

That was the thing that really stung — the deception. He'd trusted her and she'd made an idiot of him. That was the part he couldn't forgive. She'd slunk away without having the decency to tell him it was over between them.

He cursed the power she still had over him. Why the hell couldn't he just forget about her? It wasn't as if he'd been a monk these past few years. He'd been with his share of women. Lovely women — some smart, some funny and some exceptionally beautiful. But none of them had meant anything.

None of them were her.

Damn Johanna Morgan for waltzing back in and sending ripples through his perfectly ordered life. The sooner she buggered off back to New York the better.

CHAPTER
3

Jenny Fielding did everything but dance on the well-worn kitchen table when she saw Jo. 'I can't believe it's really you! You look fantastic Jo, but you're so skinny! Don't you eat?'

Jo laughed. 'Of course I do. New York has some of the finest restaurants in the world.'

'No home cooking, then? That must be the problem. Sit down and I'll make you a nice cup of tea. Steph, butter some scones would you, love?'

'Steady on, Jenny. I've brought my bridesmaid's dress with me. I'd like to still fit into it on the big day.'

Jenny waved her hand dismissively. 'One won't hurt. Now tell me Jo, what's he like, your Zachary? He's a handsome-looking young man from what I've seen.'

'Yes, he's certainly good-looking.'

Jenny placed her hand on her heart. 'And that wedding proposal. So romantic.'

Jo winced. 'You've seen it?'

Jenny nodded. 'Steph showed me the video of his proposal on YouTube. I don't mind saying I got a little teary watching it.'

Jo felt the heat creeping into her cheeks at the thought of Zach's proposal. He'd insisted on taking her to lunch at Shake Shack in Madison Square Park. In hindsight she should have realised something was up. A burger and shake — no matter how delicious — was not Zach's idea of lunch. He had joined the queue while she got them a table. Before she knew what was happening she was at the centre of a flash mob miming the words to Bruno Mars' 'Marry You'. Then Zach got down on one knee and pulled out a blue Tiffany box containing the ring she now wore. How could she say no?

The whole thing was over the top and out of her comfort zone. And the fact that there was footage of the event on YouTube was cringeworthy. Until now it hadn't occurred to her that the video might have been watched by people here in Linden Gully. Dear god, what if Ryan had seen it? What would he make of it? Of her?

'What's wrong, Jo? You've gone pale,' Jenny said.

'Have I?' Jo said, picking up one of Jenny's scones as a diversion. 'I'm fine, really. These scones look delicious.'

Jenny smiled her approval as Jo slathered homemade jam onto one of her prizewinning scones. 'Now that you're here, I'll have to catch you up on all the plans for the wedding.'

Steph rolled her eyes. 'Please, Mum, give her a break. She just got off the plane this morning.'

'Actually I am tired,' Jo admitted. 'But I do want to hear all about the wedding. Maybe I can grab a nap and then we can launch into full wedding-planner mode when I'm feeling a bit fresher? I've got some ideas for the kitchen tea that I want to talk to you about, Jenny.'

'Kitchen tea? I don't think that's really necessary,' Steph protested.

Jenny clapped her hands together. 'Of course it's necessary. You must have a kitchen tea! I've been so busy planning the wedding that I've hardly given that a thought. I did tell a few of the CWA ladies to keep next Saturday afternoon free, just in case, though.' She winked at Jo.

Steph groaned, while Jo laughed. 'Well, at least the date's taken care of. I might head off to the guest room and have a sleep for an hour or so. We can discuss the details then.'

Jo woke with a giddy sensation familiar to long-distance travellers. It took her a moment to remember she was in Linden Gully, let alone in the Fieldings' guest room. God, how long had she been out? She groped around in the dark for her phone and clicked it on. Seven in the evening. She'd been sleeping for four hours. The deep-down bone tiredness was gone, but she didn't exactly feel refreshed. Too many stupid dreams. She struggled to remember the details, apart from that last one, where she and Zach were getting married in a marquee here at the Fielding farm. When the minister said, 'You may now kiss the bride,' she leaned in to kiss him only to find it was Ryan kissing her back.

She shivered at the memory and shook her head as if to physically remove it from her head. But the act was futile. Images of Ryan flooded her mind. His blue-grey eyes skimming over her, making her feel naked; the stubble that now adorned his jawline, leaving her in no doubt that he had left boyhood behind; the shy smile that hadn't changed despite all the years; and those muscular arms lifting his daughter into the air.

His daughter.

The image of Ella brought Jo crashing back to reality. She pushed back the bedcovers and swung her feet onto the chilly timber floorboards. She had no business dreaming about Ryan. They didn't inhabit the same worlds anymore.

Jo sat at the Fieldings' kitchen table sipping tea while she waited for Jenny to return with her 'wedding stuff'. Steph had headed back into the pub to join Nate and the rest of the team as they celebrated their first win of the season. Jo had begged off accompanying her, citing 'secret bridesmaid's business' as an excuse. The thought of another possible encounter with Ryan was more than she could bear.

Nothing much had changed in this room since she was last here. The aged timber table bore the scars of family dinners, football-club committee meetings and countless cups of tea. Its faded mug rings and scratches were comfortingly familiar to Jo. The antique kitchen dresser still held the precious blue-and-white china Jenny had inherited from her grandmother. Jo remembered the day an errant football, kicked by Steph's older brother Tom, sent a teacup hurtling through the air. Steph did her best to catch the cup, but it slipped through her hands and crashed onto the floor. Jenny chased Tom through the house with the broom and when he escaped to the yard she sat down on the floor and cried.

Later, after all the broken pieces were thrown away, they'd all had a laugh about it, with Jenny doing a great impression of Tom's face as he saw her coming for him with the broom.

So many of Jo's childhood memories were tied up here in this kitchen. Tomorrow she would head home to Yarrapinga, the house where she officially grew up. But it was Kallara — in fact this very kitchen — that her heart called home. It was here she'd learned how to bake fluffy scones and knit scarves for her Barbie dolls. It was Jenny she ran home to, tears streaming, when she got her first period at the age of eleven. And it was Jenny who explained the importance of safe sex, with Steph rolling her eyes in the background, on Steph's sixteenth birthday.

Jenny was the mother Jo wished she had. She loved her mum; of course she did. And she admired her too. But Katherine Morgan was not a mum you told secrets to.

Jenny's huffing and puffing brought Jo back to the present. She watched as Jenny staggered into the kitchen overloaded with books and magazines, a bolt of material and some kind of floral arrangement. 'Here, let me help,' Jo said, taking the floral piece from the top of the pile and placing it on the table.

'Sorry I took so long, love, I just wanted to make sure I had absolutely everything I need to get you up to speed. Did you bring your bridesmaid's dress to show me?'

'It's in my room. I thought I'd better show the bride first. Get her approval.'

'Pfft. If it were up to Steph she'd be getting married in a pair of jeans and a flannelette shirt. She hasn't changed a jot. Still a tomboy at heart.'

Jo grinned. 'Shall I run up to the guest room and get it?'

'No, don't worry. You can get it later. I just want to check it doesn't clash with the flower girl's dress.'

'Flower girl?'

'Ella's going to be in the wedding. Didn't Steph tell you?'

Jo shook her head slowly. 'Ella, as in Ryan's daughter?'

'Yes.' Jenny took Jo's cup and refilled it from the teapot, then poured a cup for herself. After a moment she leaned over and gave Jo's hand a squeeze. 'I know this must be hard for you.'

Jo withdrew her hand and took a sip of her tea. 'No, it's not hard. Ryan and I parted ways many years ago. I haven't thought about him in ages. I did get a bit of a shock seeing him today. I didn't realise he was back in town.'

Jenny smiled. 'Still, he was your first love. It must be...well, awkward.'

Jo nodded. 'Yes, I guess it is a little. But we're both grown-ups. I'm sure we can put aside our feelings for the sake of the bride and groom.'

'Steph's been so worried about how you'd feel. But Nate and Ryan have been mates for years and since Ryan moved home they've become even closer.'

'How long has he been back?'

'It'd be about six months, I reckon, maybe a bit longer.'

Six months! There were dozens of questions Jo was itching to ask, but she didn't want to appear overly curious about Ryan's life. She decided to take the safe route. 'I guess his mum is pleased to have him home.'

'Yes, I think that was one of the reasons he came back. Beth's not getting any younger, and I hear that she has osteoporosis, poor thing. Not that you'd know. She's as active as ever and she'd never tell you herself. You know what a private person she is.'

Jo nodded. She remembered Beth Galloway as a quiet, practical woman. Always first to be there with a pot of soup or a plate of sandwiches in times of need, Beth managed to be friendly without ever being overly intimate with anyone. At one time Jo had felt as if she was starting to crack Beth's shell, that she was getting to see the real woman beneath the public exterior. But that was a long time ago now.

'And of course he was keen to start Ella at the local school,' Jenny continued.

Jo tried to keep her face neutral at the mention of Ella but obviously failed, because Jenny reached for her hand again and gave it a motherly pat.

'You'll have your own child one day soon, love. Once you get married and start a family your relationship with Ryan will be nothing more than a distant memory.'

Jo wondered if now was the time to make her confession that the thought of having a child gave her the heebie-jeebies. 'I'm not planning on having babies any time soon,' she ventured.

Jenny nodded. 'Very wise. Good to settle into being a married couple before you add kids into the mix. There's plenty of time for you girls. You're still young. I keep trying to tell Steph that but I think she and Nate will have a baby as soon as they can.'

Jo smiled and tried to look enthusiastic. What on earth was wrong with her? Was she the only person in the world who thought reproducing was overrated? She tried to steer Jenny onto a safer topic. 'What's Ryan doing with himself? Has he set up his own veterinary practice here in the Gully?'

Jenny nodded. 'He's running a little practice from his farm.'

'Farm?'

'Yes. He and his brother Dan have bought the old Anderson place.'

'Next door to Yarrapinga?' It wasn't really a question. She knew damn well where the farm was.

Jenny nodded and went on quickly. 'It's only a small parcel of land and I expect they were looking for something not too expensive, with Ryan only just out of university. The course took him longer than he thought what with him having to raise Ella on his own.'

'Carly's gone?' Jo couldn't keep the shock out of her voice.

'Good grief, doesn't Steph tell you anything in those emails she seems to be constantly sending?'

Jo shook her head. 'Not about Ryan she doesn't. After I heard that Carly was pregnant I asked Jo not to talk about him anymore. It was just too painful to hear about how he'd moved on when I... well, I wasn't over him yet.'

Jenny smiled sympathetically. 'I understand. But I thought she would have told you about Carly. It was such a tragedy...anyway,

I guess she figured there was no use in dredging up the past when you were so far away.'

'What do you mean "a tragedy"?'

Jenny sighed. 'Let me start from the beginning seeing as Steph's kept you completely in the dark. For a long time there we didn't really hear much about what Ryan was up to. He and Carly settled in Melbourne before Ella was born. Beth likes to keep herself to herself so she never said much, not even when Carly ran off just after Ella's first birthday.'

So Ryan's relationship with Carly hadn't lasted. Jo tried to squish down the tiny bubble of happiness rising inside her. It was a ridiculous reaction. It wasn't as if she wanted him back and the collapse of any relationship was not something to be celebrated. She scrambled for an appropriate response and eventually said, 'That must have been hard for Ryan.'

'I expect it was. Seems the poor girl just couldn't cope. From what I can gather Ryan managed well enough, but it meant his degree took longer than he'd hoped. He had to drop back to part-time study for a while there. He eventually moved in with Dan and his wife in Melbourne. I don't know much more than that, except...' Jenny trailed off and looked uncomfortable.

'What?'

'Carly died three years ago.'

The shock of the statement hit Jo physically. The cup began to shake in her hand and she had to place it back on the table to avoid spilling tea everywhere. 'What happened to her?' she asked.

'She had a car accident. Ran off the road and hit a tree. Ella was in the car with her.'

'Oh dear god, how awful.'

Jenny nodded sadly. 'It was a huge shock for Ryan.'

'Had she come back? I mean, were she and Ryan together again?'

Jenny shrugged. 'I don't know. He was still living in Melbourne when it happened. He doesn't talk about it at all. Lord knows plenty of people have tried to get him to open up but he won't discuss it. All I know is that Carly died and Ella was badly hurt.'

Suddenly Jo felt ashamed. Today when she had watched Ella run across the oval she'd felt resentful of that small innocent girl. Ella's existence had taken Ryan from her, and the child's presence had reminded Jo of what she once had and what she had lost. But poor little Ella had lost so much more. 'Poor Ryan,' she said.

'Yes. He's been through a lot for one so young. But he seems to be doing well here. As well as the vet practice he and Dan are raising cattle, organic beef I believe. It seems everything's finally fallen into place for him.'

Jo could think of nothing to say. She couldn't believe she'd been so self-centred. For months after their split — years, if she was honest — she'd fumed about how quickly Ryan had moved on from their relationship. She resented Carly for taking up the space in Ryan's heart that she believed was rightfully hers. She knew her refusal of his marriage proposal had hurt him, but she hadn't wanted to end the relationship and she had told him as much. When she left he'd promised he'd wait for her. The next thing she knew Carly was pregnant.

All these years she'd secretly dreamed of seeing Ryan again and flaunting her bigger, better, happier life in his face. But today he seemed not the least bit interested in her, or her success, and now she knew why. Ryan had grown up and he'd had to face the most adult problems imaginable. She, on the other hand, was behaving like a spoiled child.

She had to let go of her childhood now. Ryan was her past. It was time to grow up.

CHAPTER
4

Jo watched her breath form frosty clouds as she waited for the kettle to boil. Last night she'd forgotten to set the timer on the heating. At dawn she realised her mistake and crept out of bed to turn it on but an hour later the kitchen was still freezing. Yarrapinga had been empty for a couple of years now and it seemed the cold had seeped into its structure, unwilling to retreat even when attacked with the full force of central heating.

Outside the property looked much the same as last time she was home. A few of the paddocks were leased out to a neighbouring beef farmer and the home paddock still had a couple of elderly ewes wandering in it. Jo paid a retired carpenter, Brian Hughes, to maintain and manage the property so it didn't get too rundown in her absence. Brian made sure the sheep were well taken care of and kept the rest of the property spick and span too.

Brian's wife came in once a month to dust, polish, remove cobwebs and generally make sure the house was clean, but there was no hiding the fact that the place was deserted. It felt more like a museum than a home.

Jo had arrived here late the day before after a lazy Sunday spent drinking tea and reminiscing with the Fieldings. Maybe it was the contrast of the empty house after the noise and frivolity of Steph's family home that made her so keenly aware of Yarrapinga's lifelessness. The rooms were just as she'd left them two years ago. In fact little had changed since she first moved to New York, but somehow the house seemed sadder, lonelier than she remembered. Some of the furniture had gone with her mother. The tapestry-covered footstool, a nest of occasional tables and the small bookcase had disappeared from the sitting room, and her mother's antique dressing table was gone as well. Otherwise the house was as it had always been.

With Daddy gone this was just a structure — bricks, timber and plaster. It wasn't a home.

For two years Jo had procrastinated about what to do with Yarrapinga. Somehow it seemed disrespectful to sell while Katherine was still alive, even though technically it was probably the right thing to do. She had power of attorney over her mother's affairs, and perhaps Katherine's interests would be better served if Jo sold the house and invested the money, but right now she was pleased she still had somewhere to come home to.

At JFK on Friday morning she'd fleetingly thought about moving back home for good. As she boarded the plane she realised that her life in New York would be very different now that she was no longer the future Mrs Zachary Carlton.

She often wondered how much of her success was due to Zach's celebrity status and his family's not inconsequential influence in the publishing industry. Somehow she'd let herself get sucked into Zach's superficial world. They moved in the same circles and had all the same friends. Once she'd said yes to Zach's carefully orchestrated proposal she began to see how small her world had become. Ironic really, that she'd come all the way to New York to escape the perils of small-town life, only to discover the world's most vibrant city could be just as claustrophobic.

Coming back home to stay had been a nice fantasy. She could write here without interruption and it would be wonderful to be close to Steph and Jenny. Realistically, though, it wasn't an option.

Especially now Ryan was here.

It would be hard enough getting through the next three weeks, trying to be courteous to each other for the sake of their friends. She dreaded the thought of partnering him at the wedding. Living next door to him forever wasn't something she could even contemplate.

Her life was in New York, with or without Zach. She had written *Hollywood Kisses* before she met him and even though her fame and celebrity status might be down to him, the book's success belonged to her. She had made a life for herself before Zach and she could do it again. In some ways she was looking forward to being back in her own little apartment, in her own funky neighbourhood. She had her writing and her blog. She wasn't short of money. And she loved Manhattan.

Thoughts of moving back to Linden Gully were just a brief fantasy, nothing more.

And that being the case, it was wasteful to keep Yarrapinga on the off-chance she might want to visit Linden Gully in the future. Once this wedding was over she couldn't foresee any reason to come back. The nursing home was 45 kilometres away in Bellington, so it would probably make more sense to stay there when she visited Katherine. And she was always welcome at the Fieldings' if she wanted to spend time in the Gully.

Now was as good a time as any to investigate putting the house on the market. She had three weeks to fill in before the wedding and may as well make good use of the time. Usually she spent every spare minute writing, but not at the moment. The current book wasn't flying from her fingers. In fact she was at a point where she was totally stuck. She figured a few weeks away from the page might be just the thing to get her creative juices flowing again. Determined to have a complete break from it all she hadn't even bothered to pack her laptop. She had to admit the lack of her daily routine was already making her feel a little antsy, but there were plenty things here in Linden Gully that needed her time and attention. Now she had no excuse to put those things off any longer. With that thought in mind Jo made a mental note to call Carter Real Estate later in the day, but first she needed to see if the old Jeep was in working order so she could get herself into town for supplies.

Ryan was busy thinking about his meeting with a potential customer as he wheeled his trolley around Glasson's IGA supermarket. Being a salesman didn't come naturally and was his least favourite part of running the farm. Generally Dan took care of this side of the business, while Ryan's job was to make sure the cattle were happy and healthy. But with Dan and Bec away on holiday it was up to him to make the pitch next week.

Fortunately, organically raised beef was a hot product right now and his customers generally took little convincing. Still, he found it calmed his nerves if he went over his sales pitch a few times in his head before a meeting, just to make sure he had all the facts and figures down pat.

He didn't see the other trolley coming around the corner until it was too late. The carts banged and he looked over at his fellow shopper sheepishly, ready to make his apology.

Bloody hell. It was her.

'Ryan! Sorry I didn't see you there. I guess I was too busy looking at everything on the shelves. Everything seems so different to home, I mean the States. You know, it's all a bit nostalgic here, seeing all the stuff I used to love like Vegemite,' Jo babbled.

Home? That was an interesting slip of the tongue. This used to be her home, back before she turned out to be some sort of precious celebrity.

At least she looked more like herself today. Her long hair was pulled back into a simple ponytail and she'd replaced those stupid heels with a pair of flattish boots. But her arms dripped with expensive-looking bangles and she was wearing a pair of gigantic hoop earrings.

The enormous sunglasses were pushed up on top of her head and they held her hair off her face so he could see her warm brown eyes. Once upon a time he could read those eyes as clearly as any map, or at least he'd thought so at the time. But today she avoided his gaze, her eyes darting around the store as she rabbited on about being sorry in that strange accent she seemed to have acquired. Who knew what she was thinking?

Suddenly he realised the chattering had stopped and she was looking at him expectantly. Was this what she wanted? Idle chit-chat in the grocery store, like they were casual acquaintances? No way. He was not going to stand around pretending that this was normal. 'Look, Johanna, don't worry about it. It was my fault. Now, if you don't mind I'm kind of in a hurry.'

'Sure, but before you go I just wanted to say...' She paused, seemingly unsure of how to proceed. After a moment she allowed her eyes to meet his.

Suddenly he knew exactly what she was feeling.

Pity. She pitied him, for god's sake.

'Ryan, Jenny told me about what happened...to Carly, I mean. I just wanted to say —'

He shook his head. No. He wasn't going to listen to this from her of all people. It was hard enough dealing with his guilt about Carly without having to listen to empty platitudes about how sorry people felt for him. 'Stop, Jo, *Johanna*. I don't want to talk about what happened. What's done is done.'

'Okay.' She didn't avert her eyes from his.

Ryan pulled his trolley back and went to move around her, but she placed her hand on his cart to prevent him from leaving.

'Please, Ryan, I just wanted to say that after what you've been through...well, you know, I don't want you to worry about what happened between us. I don't want you to feel uncomfortable around me. I thought perhaps we could put the past behind us and maybe even...'

Ryan didn't attempt to keep the scorn out of his voice. 'What?'

'Perhaps we could try being friends.'

Seriously? If the notion weren't so insulting it would be laughable. *Sorry, Ryan, you lose. Thanks for playing and as a consolation prize...*

Had she forgotten what they once had, and that she had deliberately walked away from all that? Perhaps she thought that now she was famous all her sins should be automatically absolved. Or was this guilt talking? Maybe she felt the precious gift of her friendship could make up for all the damage done.

Ryan shook his head. 'Sorry. Not interested.'

She bit her lip the way she always did when she was trying to keep her cool. 'Well, that's a shame. I hope we'll be able to at least be civil to each other these next few weeks, though, for Steph and Nate's sake.'

He nodded curtly and drew the trolley back once more. 'Whatever.'

Her face was flushed and he could see tears welling in her eyes. For a split second he was eighteen again, watching Joey struggle to keep her composure after yet another barb from one of the Gully's 'it' girls. His instinct was to comfort her.

He felt like a heel. Once upon a time he would have done anything to protect her, to ease her pain. For that reason alone maybe he should give her a pass, say what she wanted to hear and let it go. What did it really matter? There was no changing the past. They could never truly be friends but it wouldn't kill him to be civil. 'Look, Jo, I'm sorry —'

She put up her hand and motioned for him to stop. Her voice was quiet and controlled as she spoke. 'Forget it. I was only trying to be nice. To let you know that I've forgiven you for what you did and that for my part I don't hold any grudges. I know you've had it hard, being left to raise the child on your own, but Jesus, Ryan, that's no excuse to behave like an arsehole.'

What the hell? She'd forgiven *him*? Un-bloody-believable. He couldn't contain his anger. 'Are you kidding? You've forgiven me? Well that's just great, Jo. Really big of you considering you were the one that left. What was I supposed to do? Ignore the fact that you'd moved on, that you were never coming home? Was I supposed to sit here like a lonesome puppy just waiting for you to throw me a bone?'

Her eyes were wide with shock. She opened her mouth as if to speak but no words came.

It didn't matter. After seven years of holding onto this pain Ryan found himself unable to stop. 'Get over yourself, Johanna. You might be big time back home in New York, but here in the Gully you're still just plain old Jo Morgan. I'm glad you've forgiven me, really I am, but the thing is *I* haven't forgiven *you*.' He abandoned his trolley and marched out of the store without another word.

Jo leaned heavily against the shopping cart. She felt unexpectedly weak after Ryan's tirade. It was as if his anger had sucked the energy right out of her. Tears pricked her eyes and her throat felt dry and constricted.

She could not remember seeing a display of such anger, such venom, from him before. Where had it come from? It wasn't as if she was the one who had slept with someone else. Ryan had well and truly lost the plot if he thought she was the one to blame for their relationship breakdown. Clearly he'd revised history to create a version that suited him, one that made her out to be the villain and left him blameless.

She shook her head. It was so unlike him. Ryan was the fairest person she'd ever met. His sense of justice was unbelievably strong. He'd always been able to separate right from wrong and had never been afraid to stand up for what he believed in, even if it made him unpopular. And when he was wrong, he said so. He'd never shied away from apologising when he'd made a mistake.

Fate had dealt him a tough blow, and by contrast her life was peachy, on the surface at least. Of course he was entitled to feel disappointed in the way things had turned out, but the Ryan she knew would never have allowed disappointment to turn to bitterness.

Maybe she didn't know him as well as she thought.

She heard the clunk of wayward trolley wheels in the aisle behind her and sucked in a deep breath. It was bad enough that her argument with Ryan would have been heard by half a dozen other shoppers; she didn't want to add to the humiliation by looking as if she cared. Public Relations face was definitely required. For the first time ever she was grateful for all those book signings where she'd had to smile and make small talk with readers even when she had a headache or PMS. The skills learned there were definitely going to be handy in Linden Gully.

By the time Kelly Bristow caught up to her, Jo had managed to put on her most charming smile. She hoped.

'Jo Morgan, is it really you?' Kelly gushed. She leaned in and kissed Jo's cheek.

Jo tried not to look surprised at the display of affection. 'Nice to see you, Kelly.'

'I was thrilled when I heard you'd arrived in town early. All the girls are dying to see you. Of course we just knew you wouldn't miss the Wedding of the Year, but I didn't realise you'd be here so soon. Steph didn't tell anyone. Naughty thing she is, wanting to keep you all to herself.'

Thrilled? Well, that was a first. Jo couldn't remember a time when Kelly and her friends had even been mildly pleased to see her. And why on earth would Steph be updating Kelly on her movements? Steph was hardly part of the Kelly Bristow entourage. Still, now was not the time to split hairs. Kelly was a huge gossip and definitely not worth getting offside.

Jo laughed. 'Don't blame Steph. I didn't tell her I was coming. Wanted to surprise her.'

'Well, aren't you just the best bridesmaid ever? I'll bet Stephanie was thrilled.' Kelly leaned in and lowered her voice. 'Now listen Jo, I couldn't help but overhear you talking to Ryan just now.'

Jo tried her hardest to keep her face impassive. 'Oh?'

'You mustn't mind him. He's been through a lot, you know.'

Jo nodded. 'So I've heard.'

'Look, it's taken him a while to settle back into the Gully. It must have been so awful for him to lose Carly like that. So tragic. Apparently they were about to buy their own house when it happened.'

So Ryan and Carly had reconciled. Jo ignored the lump that formed in her throat as she encouraged Kelly to continue. 'Is that right?'

'I believe so. Anyway, Ryan went off the rails for a bit after it happened but he does seem to be back on his feet now,' Kelly said.

'In fact he's even started to date again. He's been seeing quite a bit of Laura Baxter.'

So that was what this was all about. Kelly was warning her off. Jo fixed what she hoped was a cheery smile on her face. 'Good for him.' She picked up a box of cereal from the shelf and threw it in the cart. 'Look, Kelly, I won't keep you. I'm sure you're very busy.' Jo edged the trolley away.

'Oh, that's okay. I've got plenty of time.' She wiggled the fingers on her left hand. 'I'm a Prescott now. I married Jeff. You remember the Prescotts, I imagine? The transport people. I'm a lady of leisure these days.'

'Congratulations.' Jo watched as Kelly's eyes flitted to her own left hand.

'Of course we all know about your engagement to Zachary Carlton. Good show, Jo. Not only have you put Linden Gully on the map with your little books but you've managed to snare yourself a big fish at the same time. You've done us proud. Who says us country gals can't mix it with the best? I mean, he's not just a famous actor, his family are considered New York royalty, aren't they?' Kelly didn't wait for her reply before she went on. 'Good grief, you're Linden Gully's answer to Princess Mary. A fairy tale come true.'

Jo laughed inwardly. Once she would have given anything for Kelly's approval. She had spent countless nights staring up at her dorm-room ceiling at boarding school, thinking about ways to impress Kelly and her friends next time she was home.

These days Kelly's approval was not only unnecessary but unwelcome.

'Is your fiancé here with you?'

Jo shook her head. 'Zach's very busy filming a new movie at the moment. Of course he would have loved to come to the wedding — he's dying to meet all my friends here. But it's just not possible right now.' A loud ringing from Jo's oversized handbag took her attention. She rummaged for a minute before locating her phone. Too late. The noise stopped just as she glanced at the screen. 'Sorry Kelly, that was my agent,' she lied. 'I'd better call her back right away, while I've got a good signal.' Jo opened her missed calls and clicked on Steph's name, quickly putting her phone to her ear.

'Hi Lydia, how are you?' Jo said loudly.

'Talk soon,' Kelly mouthed at her as she pushed her near-empty cart away.

Jo waved at Kelly as she walked away.

Steph was laughing on the other of the phone. 'Either you've dialled the wrong number or you are up to no good, Johanna Morgan.'

'Option two. You know me well, Lydia,' Jo said, aware that Kelly was probably still listening.

'Just like old times,' Steph said. 'By the way, I'm going into Belly today to look at flowers. Thought you might like to tag along.'

'Oh absolutely. I can find time for that. We definitely have a lot to discuss.'

'Linden Gully vultures circling already?'

'Yep. Got it in one. Very astute, Lydia. See you soon.'

CHAPTER
5

Ryan lowered the last hay bale into place and yelled above the tractor noise. 'How's that?'

Nate gave the thumbs-up signal and gestured for him to take the tractor back to the shed. Ryan eased the old girl up the boggy hill and into the equipment shed.

He was halfway back to the homestead on foot when Nate caught up to him and gave him a good-natured slap on the back. 'Good work, mate. Steph will be stoked when she sees all the work we've done setting up for the hens and bucks do.'

'It'll be a great night. I've ordered all the grog, so hopefully the girls have got the food under control.'

'Don't worry about that. I reckon Jenny will make enough stuff to feed an army. Speaking of grub, I'm starving. Come on up to the house and I'll see what I can rustle up. And I reckon we've earned ourselves a cold one.'

Ryan grinned. 'Cup of coffee and a sandwich will do me. I'm back on dad duty in a couple of hours.'

'No worries. I'm having a beer though. Steph's gone to Bellington with Jo. Wedding stuff. Something to do with flowers and shoes. So I might just have me a quiet one before they get back and all the wedding palaver starts up again.'

At the mention of Jo's name, Ryan looked down at his boots. Seeing her again was the last thing he needed. One confrontation for the day was plenty, thanks very much. 'Jo's coming here?' He tried to keep his tone casual.

Nate shrugged. 'Dunno, mate. Maybe.'

They approached the house in silence. At the back door Nate stooped to pull off his mud-caked boots but Ryan hesitated. 'I might take a raincheck on that cuppa. I've got a few things I should do before Ella gets home.'

Nate made a couple of clucking sounds. 'Chicken.'

'What?'

'You. You're high-tailing it out of here because you're scared Jo might show up.'

Ryan grimaced. 'I'm not scared, alright? It's just that I saw her this morning at Glasson's and it didn't go so well.'

Nate raised his eyebrows. 'Really? Look, I'm sure they won't be back for ages yet. Steph had an appointment with the florist, then they were doing something to do with shoes. I also heard coffee and cake mentioned. I can't see them being back before five. Come on in and have something to eat. Steph will have my head if she finds out you did all that work shifting bales and I didn't even feed you.'

Ryan shrugged. 'Yeah, alright, but if she turns up I'm heading for the hills.'

Nate laughed. 'I'd like to see that.'

Neither of them spoke for a few minutes while Nate busied himself filling the kettle and grabbing the ingredients for a sandwich out of the fridge. Ryan sat at the kitchen table, flicking through the local paper while he waited.

It was a comfortable silence. Nate had been there for Ryan during the worst times of his life: first as a kid, when his dad died, and more recently when Carly was killed. But talking about feelings had never been their way. Nate had shown his support simply by being there.

He'd kicked a footy with Ryan in the hospital grounds while they waited for Ryan's mum to emerge with news of his dad. And he'd gone to Melbourne to sit on a barstool and watch as Ryan wiped himself out after Carly's death. He'd made sure Ryan got home without incident and they'd never talked about that night since.

More recently he'd run alongside Ryan as he pounded the dirt roads around Linden Gully in search of freedom from the grief and guilt that he felt over Carly's death. Nate was always there. He had Ryan's back on the footy field back in the day and he had it now. Neither of them needed any words to know that.

Nate dumped a loaf of bread on the table, and spread out fresh butter, cheese and some leftover sliced lamb from the fridge. 'Help yourself,' he said. He set a couple of plates down on the table before heading to the stove to remove the boiling kettle. Nate kept his back to Ryan as he said, 'You know, I think we should talk about this Jo situation.'

Ryan didn't answer immediately. He waited for Nate to bring the coffee and sit opposite him. 'Oh yeah?'

'Mate, I know this is uncomfortable for you, and believe me, it's not a picnic for me either, but I just need to know...is there going to be a problem?'

'How do you mean?'

'Is there going to be a problem with you and Jo being in the same room? I mean, you mentioned you saw her and it didn't go so well. I don't want to be a pain in the butt about this, but I'm wondering how you two are going to manage over the next few weeks. It's not just the day of the wedding. There's the hens and bucks do and god only knows what else before the big day. How are you going to go?'

Ryan exhaled audibly. 'To be honest, mate. I don't know. Don't worry, I won't do anything that will spoil the day for you and Steph, but I honestly didn't realise how hard it would be to see her again.'

'Why's that? You're not still...' Nate trailed off, unable to finish the question that Ryan did not want to contemplate.

'No, of course not. Too much water under the bridge for anything like that. It's just, you know, awkward.'

Nate leaned back in his chair. 'I'm sorry about all this. The last thing we want to do is cause you more grief. Look, if you want to step down from the job as best man I'll understand. I'm sure Tom would be happy to step in on your behalf.'

'No way!' Ryan shook his head vigorously. He wanted to say all the things he felt. He wanted to let Nate know that he appreciated all the times he'd been there for him and now it was his turn to reciprocate. Instead he said, 'You're not getting rid of me that easily. Jo and I will have to work out a way to be in the same room without tearing each other's heads off.'

'Are you sure?'

'Yeah I'm sure. Don't worry, I'll fix it. Promise.'

'You girls go ahead. I just want to catch up with Sarah over at the newsagents while we're in town. I'll meet you at the cafe in five minutes.' Jenny turned on her heel and started walking before Steph had time to protest.

'There goes half an hour at least,' Steph said.

Jo smiled. 'It doesn't matter. I'm dying for a coffee. Plus I can't wait to have one of Green's vanilla slices. It's one of the things I crave when I'm in New York.'

'Don't they have vanilla slices over there?' Steph had a look of mock horror on her face.

Jo shrugged. 'Not that I've noticed, but even if they do, no ordinary vanilla slice can live up to the world-famous Green's.'

When Steph pushed open the door to their favourite coffee shop, Jo was taken aback. 'It's all changed,' she said. The fluorescent green vinyl padded booths were gone, and in their place stood rustic timber tables surrounded by modern white chairs. Large industrial light fittings dangled from the ceiling and a stainless-steel counter had replaced the old Laminex one. Jo felt somehow cheated. 'I liked it better the old way,' she said.

'Times change, Jo. Things move forward, even out here in the sticks. But don't worry, the cakes are as good as ever. I promise you won't be disappointed.'

Steph was right about that. The vanilla slice was heavenly and, thanks to the installation of an up-to-date coffee machine, her latte was impeccable too.

'Okay, I've fed you and given you caffeine, now you need to spill,' Steph said as Jo licked the last traces of icing from her fingers.

'What do you mean?'

'What's up? You haven't been yourself all day. And you haven't explained that weird phone conversation we had this morning. I'm not buying the jetlag excuse, so you can forget about trying that one, and I'm not taking "nothing" as an answer either.'

Jo wrinkled her nose. 'Sorry, I've been a little distracted all day. I ran into Ryan at Glasson's this morning. I tried to talk to him, to smooth things over between us and...'

Steph's eyes widened. 'And?'

'We ended up arguing right there in the canned vegetable aisle. I'm surprised you haven't heard already. I thought there would have been a Linden Gully Bulletin special edition by now.'

Steph grinned. 'I take it you had an audience.'

'Kelly Bristow, sorry *Prescott,* heard the whole thing. I was trying to escape her clutches when you called this morning. I'm not really sure if there were any other eavesdroppers.'

'Just Kelly is enough. You're right. She will have put out a bulletin by now.'

'The weirdest thing about my conversation with her was that she seemed to be warning me off Ryan. She reckons he's dating Laura Baxter. I'm not sure why she'd be so worried after the argument she overhead. Ryan made it quite clear he wants nothing to do with me.'

Steph shrugged. 'The popular wisdom around here is that he's never gotten over you.'

Jo laughed and shook her head. 'What on earth would give people that idea?'

'I don't know, Jo. He did take your break-up pretty badly. Everyone seemed to think the whole Carly affair was just a rebound thing.'

Jo felt the heat rise in her cheeks. 'Not you too?'

Steph raised her eyebrows. 'What do you mean?'

'This morning Ryan accused me of ending our relationship. Is the whole town under the assumption that I left him? Because that is not what happened and you know that.' She crossed her arms and leaned back in her seat.

'Calm down. I'm not taking sides. I know what happened wasn't your fault. But you know what it's like in the Gully. Everyone has their opinion and no one ever lets the truth get in the way of a good story. All I'm saying is it was a long time ago now. Does it really matter who did what?'

Jo shrugged. Apparently it was too much to expect unconditional sympathy from her best friend.

'It's none of anyone's business what happened between you. But you know how it is here, everyone gossips. It's one of the drawbacks of living in such a small place. In the absence of the truth people just make stuff up. You weren't here and Ryan has never spoken about what happened, so people drew their own conclusions.'

'And it never occurred to anyone in the Gully that their golden boy could have done the wrong thing, so everyone assumed I was the one to blame?' Ryan had always been adored by everyone in the Gully. His good looks, easy-going nature and natural sporting ability had made him popular as a child. When his father, a pillar of the local community, died so unexpectedly the town collectively embraced Ryan and his brothers. While all three boys were given love and sympathy, it was acknowledged that Ryan, the youngest son and a constant source of comfort to his mother, was the most like his dad. In the town's eyes he could do no wrong.

'I don't know, Jo. I guess people have their theories.'

'So the minor detail that another woman was pregnant with his child didn't tip anyone off to the fact that he was the one that ended it?'

Steph took a sip of her coffee and hesitated before answering. 'Honey, you rebuffed his offer of marriage, and then you left. Can't you see how that might look to people? I know you didn't end the relationship. I know that wasn't your intention and it sucks that Ryan didn't have enough faith in your relationship to wait, but he was only twenty-one. He made a mistake. A huge mistake, and one he's had to pay for over and over again.' Steph paused and looked at Jo. 'I don't think it's healthy for you to dwell on what happened. It's time to let the past go. You're engaged to another man. I know Ryan hurt you. But his heart got broken too.'

Jo averted her eyes. It pained her to admit Steph had a point.

'As for the town, let everyone think what they want. How can it hurt? Ryan lives here and you'll be gone in a few weeks. There's no point stirring up the past just to score points.'

Jo sighed. What sort of hard-hearted cow had she become these past few years? Maybe she'd somehow morphed into one of the narcissistic characters she was so fond of creating in her novels. Steph was right, of course. Ryan hadn't exactly had an easy time of it in recent years. And no matter what the truth was, nobody in the Gully was interested in having their local hero maligned. Whatever she said, people would always believe what they wanted. Hell, these days even Ryan believed that he was the wronged party. She needed to let the whole thing go.

She raised her palms in a sign of defeat. 'Yeah, I guess you're right, but Ryan seems so angry. It's like he can't bear to be in the same room with me. I'm worried for your sake, Steph. I don't want your wedding to be spoiled by tension in the bridal party. This morning I was trying to set up some sort of truce between us for everyone else's sake, but Ryan wouldn't have a bar of it.'

Steph smiled. 'Don't worry about the wedding. Nate and I aren't going to let a bit of awkwardness between the two of you ruin our day. I know it's hard for you, and Ryan too, but you are both so important to us that we can't imagine our wedding day without you.'

'And I wouldn't miss it for the world,' Jo said. 'I guess Ryan and I will just have to stay out of each other's way as much as we possibly can.'

Ryan hadn't given his conversation with Nate much thought since he'd left the farm that afternoon. He'd arrived back at the clinic to find Meg Weston waiting for him, with a very unhappy dog.

'Do you think you could take a look at Patch, Ryan? He's been scratching his ear and howling all day.'

A quick examination revealed a grass seed lodged in the dog's ear, which required removal under sedation. Fortunately for Patch it was a quick procedure and now the dog was awake and thumping his tail as Ryan did his post-op check. He rubbed the border collie behind the ears. 'Looking good, mate,' he said to the dog, and he smiled up at his trainee vet nurse, Taylah. 'I'm really happy with how he's pulled up. No temperature, no signs of infection and he's looking more like the happy fellow we normally see.'

Taylah was doing a school-based apprenticeship in the practice one day a week, but she loved the job so much that she popped in most days after school. Ryan loved her dedication, and hoped that one day she might have the confidence to go to uni and become a vet. She was certainly smart enough, but he knew her family had been doing it tough these past couple of years, and university wasn't a luxury they could afford right now. In the meantime he was trying to teach her as much as he could. Maybe if she could get a full-time job as a vet nurse she'd earn enough to bear the costs of a university education in a few years' time.

'Should I call his mum?' Taylah asked. 'Let her know he's doing better?'

He laughed. She insisted on calling all the owners 'mum' or 'dad'. 'Sure. That'd be great. Tell Mrs Weston she can come by in the morning to collect him. Can I leave you with it? I've got to race to meet Ella's bus.'

Taylah nodded and shooed him out the door.

Once he was on the road his thoughts drifted back to Nate's words and his promise to his friend that he would fix things with Jo.

Obviously Nate was worried, and Steph was too. It wasn't like his mate to have deep and meaningful conversations about anything.

In the past it had never been necessary. All problems could be solved with a kick of the footy, a run or, if things were really crook, a beer. The fact that Nate had brought up the subject of Jo meant that it was troubling him. And Ryan couldn't have that.

Their whole lives Nate had propped him up. If sorting things out with Jo would make Nate and Steph's wedding day a better one, then he would suck it up and make it happen. Just how he was going to do that he wasn't sure.

He'd been pretty brutal at the grocery store — maybe too brutal, if he was honest. Thinking back on their conversation, he realised he'd behaved like a child. She'd rejected him, and his pride was still hurt, so he'd behaved like a jerk. It was the type of behaviour he was constantly warning Ella against. 'Two wrongs don't make a right' was a frequent refrain in their house. And in this case Jo hadn't done anything wrong. Not recently anyway. How on earth could he expect Ella to know how to treat others if this was the example he was setting? He'd have to do better. Getting Jo back on side wouldn't be easy. He winced. Maybe he'd have to grovel a bit, which would pretty much kill him. But if that's what it took he'd do it. Anything for Nate.

CHAPTER

6

Jo brushed the dust from her hands and surveyed the attic with satisfaction.

Unable to shake the wretched jetlag, she'd been awake since four. At five she figured she might as well make good use of the time by taking care of some chores. She pulled out her iPad and tapped out a short blog post for *An Outsider's Guide to Inside New York*. She'd quickly organised a replacement blogger before boarding the plane, but didn't want her regular readers thinking she'd forsaken them.

Once that was done she set to work sorting through the stuff in the attic. If she was going to sell this house she needed to make sure everything was in order before she headed back to America. Now only a few dust-covered boxes were left on the shelves up here. Once they were sorted she could shut this room up for good.

She laced her fingers together and stretched her arms out in front of her to relieve her aching muscles. All the lifting and stair climbing was exhausting. Better than a session at the gym really, which was lucky seeing as she had not managed to squeeze in any other exercise since leaving home. Besides, the physical work helped to stop the thoughts and images that had swirled in her head ever since she clapped eyes on Ryan at the football field.

There was plenty to keep her busy up here. Aside from a few functional but ancient electrical appliances, the room mainly contained archive boxes — dozens of them — filled with meticulously filed papers. Strange that her mother would keep all these documents, when she claimed to despise sentimentality in all its forms. Granted there were few keepsakes to sort through. There were no baby clothes, treasured toys or tattered drawings to evoke memories and tug at the heartstrings. All of those had been discarded once they were no longer useful. But it seemed she had kept every word that had ever been written to her, or about her.

Everything from legal papers and journal articles to Jo's old school reports was meticulously filed. There was even a whole box of Christmas cards the family had received over the years. Maybe there was a sliver of sentimentality in her mum after all.

Most of the boxes were earmarked for the bin, but these last half a dozen would need to be sorted through.

Jo carefully removed the lid of a box marked *Johanna — Personal Correspondence* and pulled out a birthday card.

Darling Johanna,
  Wishing you a very happy third birthday, Princess
  Lots of love
  Nanna Lil xxx

Warmth spread through her chest and tears pricked in Jo's eyes as she remembered Nanna Lil's twinkling eyes and sense of fun. She'd been Jo's ally in the early years, before cancer had taken the flesh from her bones, the light from her eyes and, eventually, the life from her body.

Jo pressed the card to her lips. 'I miss you still, Nanna,' she whispered.

She replaced the card and pulled out a bundle of letters bound together with a perfectly tied satin ribbon. Her breath caught in her throat as she realised what these were.

Ryan's letters.

He'd written every week that she was away at school and she'd kept each one, sleeping with it under her pillow until the next eagerly awaited missive arrived. Ryan's letters had kept her sane during those long months away. His sharp witticisms about life in Linden Gully made her laugh out loud and his tender expressions of love brought tears to her eyes. Each week he sent her a lifeline, something to hold on to in the sea of despair that was her life at boarding school.

Clearly her mother had had no qualms about prising open the locked metal box these letters were stored in. The heat spread from her chest and up into her cheeks as she imagined her mother reading Ryan's beautiful words.

She pulled on the ribbon and let it fall to the floor, greedily seeking Ryan's familiar handwriting.

Dear Joey,

How are you? I hope this has been a better week for you. Those girls in your dorm sound like a bunch of infantile idiots. I reckon you should start publishing an underground newspaper to put the wind up them. You could write stuff like, "Which daughter of a federal politician secretly steals chocolate from the school kitchen?" or something like that. I'm sure you can come up with better stuff than me. You're the writer after all.

Jo smiled. Ryan had always believed in her, even before she believed in herself.

So I guess I'd better update you on this week's goings on in Linden Gully. I know I'm no Pulitzer Prize winner but hopefully my musings will give you some idea of the Gully's latest happenings (such as they are!)

Jo's laughter echoed through the almost-empty attic as she read Ryan's recount of being stuck in line at the supermarket while Mrs Kingcott gave Sarah Petersen a blow-by-blow description of her recent hysterectomy (or 'women's troubles', as Mrs Kingcott had discreetly euphemised).

He went on to talk about the Lions' chances of winning a game this season (dismal), Nate's new foal (he was there at the birth!), and Dan's new girlfriend from the city (annoying princess type).

And then suddenly he was serious.

Jo's eyes filled with tears at the memory of reading these words for the first time.

I miss you, Jo. I see you everywhere: at the waterhole; riding down Maddock's Gully; even in the line ahead of me at Glasson's. But of course you're not real, just a mirage teasing me, always just out of reach. I'm counting the days until the holidays. I can't wait to see you, to hold you, to hear the sound of your voice.

I love you.

Things had been so simple back then. She and Ryan were in love. All they wanted was to be together. During her boarding-school years he was everything to her, her reason for being.

But then they started to grow up and Jo discovered she had bigger dreams than simply being Ryan's girlfriend. She wanted to write, but to do that she knew she would have to experience life outside the confines of Linden Gully.

She picked up the box and rifled through the envelopes again. Right at the bottom of the box she found what she was looking for, a tattered envelope containing a faded computer printout. She remembered the thrill of opening that letter to discover an offer of a place at Melbourne University. It was her ticket out of this place and to her it was better than winning the lottery. The day the offer had arrived in the mail Ryan rode his pushbike all the way out to Yarrapinga to tell her the news that he'd got in to Veterinary Science at the same university. It seemed they were destined to be together.

Katherine had been less than thrilled to find that Ryan would be at Melbourne Uni too. She spent hours lecturing Jo about not wasting her opportunities, and Jo assured her that was one thing she didn't need to worry about. Her mother did all she could to make sure Jo didn't set up house with Ryan, paying for a room in the Halls of Residence that Jo rarely used. Ryan shared a house in Carlton with two other students and she'd spent most of her time there. In her youthful naivety she thought her willingness to spend every night in Ryan's bed was proof of her love. She didn't think she needed to wear his ring as a sign of her commitment to their relationship.

Sometimes she wished she could wind back the clock to their last night together. If only she hadn't been so full of herself and her own ambition. If only she'd explained herself better, given Ryan reason to believe it wasn't the end, maybe...

Maybe what? She and Ryan would be happily married and living on a farm here in the Gully with two kids and a couple of dogs, her dream of writing a novel still just that — a dream? Ryan might have settled for that life, but she feared that — just like her mother — she would have been sent slowly insane being a farmer's wife here in the middle of nowhere. And she would have blamed him eventually. Resented him the way her mother resented her father. Living in Linden Gully had killed her parents' marriage and, as young as she was when she left, she'd already worked out that history was bound to repeat itself unless she did something to break free.

She wiped her eyes and took a deep breath. There really was no time for this. She couldn't agonise over every single paper stored or take endless side trips down memory lane. At this rate the job would never be done.

Whatever was to be kept would have to be sent to New York, so she needed to be ruthless. Reluctantly she placed the letter back into the box and replaced the lid without looking at another thing. It was easier that way. The box went in the stack to be thrown away, along with the Christmas-card box, school reports and a number of other papers.

Before long only one box remained. It was sealed tight with layers of packaging tape. Jo picked at the edges of the tape but quickly realised she would need scissors or a box-cutter to get through the layers of adhesive. She brushed herself off once more and climbed downstairs to search the kitchen for the appropriate tool.

The sun streamed through the windows above the sink, warming Jo's back as she rifled through the drawers. A sudden rap on the window startled her and she dropped the can opener she was holding on her foot. 'Dammit!'

'Sorry. Didn't mean to scare you.' Ryan's voice came from outside. 'Are you okay?'

She looked up to find him peering at her through the dusty glass. What now? Was he here to berate her further for yesterday's attempt at smoothing things over? 'No. You made me drop the can opener on my foot.' She opened the door.

He appeared to be suppressing a grin. 'Again, sorry.'

She resisted the temptation to laugh, but it was hard. He'd always had that ability to disarm her with his smile. But after his performance in Glasson's yesterday she wasn't about to let him off so easily. 'What do you want, Ryan?'

He removed his battered Akubra and ran his hand through his hair. 'I've brought you something. A peace offering if you like.'

She shook her head. 'There's no need. I'm fine with the way things are. Honestly, I think we should just stay away from each other as much as possible. You made your position very clear yesterday. There's really no need for us to go over the same old ground again and again.'

He looked down, seemingly addressing his next remark to his dirt-caked boots. 'I'm sorry about that too. I had no right to speak to you the way I did yesterday. I behaved like an idiot.' He turned his head towards the front of the property. 'I wanted to do something to make it up to you.'

She followed his gaze and saw two horses tied to the gatepost. 'Horses? You brought me horses?' Surely this was some kind of joke?

'Horse, singular. The mare is for you, the gelding's mine.'

'Um, thanks for the thought, Ryan, but I don't think the doorman in my building will approve of me taking a horse up in the elevator.'

'She's not to keep, smarty-pants. She's for you to ride while you're here. I know how much you love to ride and I figured you might not get the chance to do it in New York.'

'Oh...' Jo looked out at the beautiful bay mare, unsure of what to say. She had to admit it was a thoughtful gesture. Riding had been such a part of her life here, and Ryan was right, it was one of the things she badly missed when she was in New York. But if she accepted this offer she would be establishing a tie with Ryan, and she wasn't sure that was wise.

'That's very kind of you, but I really don't think it's a good idea.'

'Why?'

Jo hesitated before answering. She knew what it would have taken for Ryan to swallow his pride and make this gesture. She didn't want to seem ungracious. 'I haven't ridden for ages. Maybe I've forgotten how.'

Ryan laughed. 'Don't be ridiculous. You're one of the finest riders this district's ever produced. You're a natural, Jo. A few years out of the saddle's not going to change that.'

She smiled at the compliment. 'Thanks, but I think you're overestimating my abilities. And anyway, I can't deprive you of one of your horses for weeks.'

'It's no sacrifice, believe me. Pepper doesn't get as much exercise as I'd like. She belongs to Bec, but she and Dan are away on holidays for a month, so poor old Pepper's getting fat.'

Jo's throat constricted at the mention of Ryan's brother and his wife. She and Bec had been close once. They'd even affectionately called each other 'sis', figuring that eventually they'd be actual sisters-in-law. These days she wasn't exactly on Dan and Bec's Christmas-card list. 'Won't Bec be peeved if she finds out you've leased her horse out...to me?'

'What she doesn't know won't hurt her. They're in Queensland and won't be back until after the wedding. Honestly Jo, you'd be doing me and Bec a favour.' He moved away from the kitchen door and gestured for her to follow him down the verandah steps. 'Just come and say hello, see if you like her. I reckon you two are a match made in heaven.' He started striding towards the gate and Jo found herself following behind.

'Here she is. Isn't she a beauty?' Ryan gently tugged on Pepper's bridle until she turned her head towards Jo.

Jo reached out her hand and placed it on the young mare's neck. 'Hello, lovely.' Pepper nuzzled her shoulder in appreciation and she couldn't help but laugh. 'She's certainly friendly enough.'

'She's lovely to ride. Very responsive. Look at her, all saddled up and nowhere to go. Why don't you take her for a quick canter?'

Jo shook her head. 'Honestly, Ryan, I wasn't kidding before. I haven't ridden for years. I think I might have lost my nerve.'

'You'll be fine. I'll come with you if you like. We won't go far. Maybe just up to the ridge and back.'

A wave of nostalgia swept over Jo. So many times she and Ryan had raced up the ridge. She always won, but she suspected that at least some of the time he let her. They'd arrive exhilarated and breathless before sliding off the horses and into each other's arms. Under the ancient eucalypt at the highest point of Mason's Ridge was their spot. It was only accessible through Jo's parents' farm, and even then only on foot or horseback, so there was little chance of them being disturbed. Many hours had been spent there, holding hands as they gazed out to the distant Strzelecki Ranges beyond and talked about their future. Occasionally they'd taken advantage of the light of a full moon and snuck out to the ridge to make love on a blanket under their tree. Jo briefly wondered if their initials could still be seen carved into the old tree's trunk.

Ryan shifted his weight from one foot to the other. 'Doesn't have to be the ridge,' he said. She noticed a hint of colour creeping into his cheeks. 'I didn't mean...I just thought...' He shoved both his hands in his pockets and looked at the ground.

Clearly Ryan did not want her getting the idea that there was any hint of romance attached to his suggestion. Obviously it was inconceivable to him that she was no longer interested in him that way. Which of course she wasn't. All these thoughts she'd been having were just a result of silly sentimentality. Packing up her childhood home had made her vulnerable to viewing her past through rose-coloured glasses.

'The ridge is fine,' she said, making no attempt to keep the indignation out of her voice. 'It's just a place. It's not like we're kids anymore, Ryan.'

'No, I guess not.' He turned and began unlooping Pepper's reins from the gatepost so Jo could no longer see his face. Was it her imagination or was that a hint of sadness she detected in his voice?

CHAPTER

7

Ryan watched Jo urge Pepper on, pushing the mare up the steep incline towards the ridge. Her long wavy hair had freed itself from the tie that had secured it into a ponytail and now it streamed out behind her like a triumphant blonde banner. He was no match for Jo's equestrian ability, even when she was riding the slightly pudgy and out-of-condition Pepper. He never had been.

By the time he caught her she'd reached their tree — despite himself he couldn't think of it as anything else — and had dismounted. Her cheeks were flushed and she was laughing.

'What took you so long, slowpoke?'

He shrugged. 'I guess I'm still no match for you. You win as usual.'

She smiled. 'Only because you let me.'

He shook his head. 'You've always been a better rider than me. Better than most people I know. You need to believe in yourself more.' He jumped down off Mack and let go of the reins. 'You can

let Pepper roam here. She and Mack won't go far, and if they start
to wander I'll just give them a whistle.'

'They come when you whistle?' Jo asked. 'That's pretty amazing.'
She smiled at him. 'I'd forgotten about your Doctor Dolittle talent.
You always had the magic touch with animals.'

Ryan grinned. 'What can I say? It's a gift.'

Jo gave him a playful shove and his pulse quickened at her touch.
'Don't go getting a big head there, sunshine,' she said.

He had a sudden sense of déjà vu. He remembered another day
when she'd gently teased him about getting ahead of himself. He
was bragging about kicking the winning goal for the Lions. Jo
laughed, gave him a push and told him he was 'up himself'. He'd
responded by tickling her. Before long the tickling had given way
to more intimate touches and they found themselves making love
under the protective branches of the gumtree.

Ryan shook his head slightly in an effort to free his mind from
the memory. He found himself edging away from her. There was no
chance of today's ribbing turning into anything more, but maybe
being in such close physical proximity wasn't the best idea. Her
voice, no longer teasing, cut into his thoughts.

'Thanks, Ryan, for the peace offering. It's better for everyone if
we can manage to get along. When I found out you were going to
be Nate's best man I thought the wedding would be awkward.'

'That's the understatement of the year. You looked like you'd seen
a ghost when you first clapped eyes on me.'

Her mouth formed that cheeky Joey grin he knew so well. 'You
didn't look too flash yourself.' The smile disappeared as fast as it had
formed. 'Seriously, Ryan, I don't want our baggage to spoil Steph
and Nate's big day. No matter how difficult this is for us I think we
should agree to put our differences behind us for their sake.'

Ryan's lips twitched into a smile. The horse had been a winner. Seemed she hadn't changed *that* much over the past few years. He still had some clue about what made her tick. 'Agreed,' he said, holding out his hand for her to shake. Her grip was firm and her handshake decisive.

The knots of tension that had gripped Ryan's neck and shoulders began to ease. Maybe Jo being here wouldn't turn out to be the nightmare he'd expected. Now that they'd cleared the air a bit, maybe he'd finally be able to stop pondering the 'what ifs' and move on with his life.

'It must feel great to finally have your degree and be running your own clinic,' she said. 'I remember how badly you wanted to be a vet even when we were kids. You were always collecting strays and nursing injured wildlife back to health.'

'Yeah, my animal-collecting habit used to drive Mum nuts.'

There was that smile again.

'Remember Stumpy?' she asked.

He grinned at the memory of the three-legged blue-tongue lizard he'd rescued and nursed back to health, much to his mother's vexation. 'Wow. I hadn't thought about old Stumpy in years. I can't believe you remember him.' It was nice to know Jo hadn't completely erased any good thoughts of him from her memory. Their pasts were so entwined it was impossible to think about any major event in his formative years without thinking of her.

Maybe this being friends thing could work.

Sure, why not? They were both adults, and a lot of time had passed since Jo's shattering refusal of his marriage proposal. Moving on had been hard in her absence, even after everything else that had happened. The thing was, she hadn't just broken his heart — she'd served up a decent blow to his pride as well. He'd thought getting married was a no-brainer. After two years of them both being in Melbourne practically cohabitating, he'd figured it was the next step. Sure, they were young, but he knew what he wanted and he assumed she wanted the same thing.

He shook his head at his own stupidity. He'd barely left boyhood behind when he dropped down on one knee and pulled out the tiny diamond ring he'd saved so long to buy. But he was a man now. It was time to act like one.

'So what about you?' he asked. 'Looks like you're living your dream too.'

She said nothing, but continued to stare out into the distance, a faraway look on her face.

'Earth to Johanna.'

She opened her mouth and then closed it, seemingly unsure of what she wanted to say. 'Sorry, I was just thinking about things back home...um, in New York.'

'It's okay, you don't have to correct yourself. New York is your home now. Is it everything you thought it would be?'

She lost the wistful look and her eyes shone with enthusiasm. 'New York is truly amazing. I can't even begin to describe it, Ryan. It's sort of like having the whole world compressed into one spot.'

'Sounds crowded.'

She grinned. 'It is, but that's part of the appeal. Everything moves so quickly. Everywhere you look something is happening. That first night, when I saw the lights of Manhattan from the cab ferrying me from the airport, I finally knew what it felt like to be alive.'

Her words stung as surely as if she'd slapped his face. He hadn't seen it back then but now he realised she'd always been marking time with him. He'd never been more than a distraction while she waited for something better to come along.

It had never been that way for him. She was his everything. In those dark years after his dad had died, when things were bleak on every front, Jo had been his lifeline, his hope, his reason for carrying on. *She* had made him feel alive.

He hated that all these years later he was still behaving like a stupid pup, waiting for her to throw him a bone. As much as he didn't want to, he couldn't help but feel wounded to hear how much better her life had become once she left him behind.

A pink tinge crept into her cheeks. 'That's not to say I don't miss here, of course. I do.'

'What do you miss, Jo? Name one thing.'

'I...I miss riding, and I miss my friends of course.'

'You never had any intention of coming back, did you?'

'That's not true.'

'Really? What did you imagine? That you'd head off to New York and write a book and then come back and live happily ever after with me?'

'I was barely twenty-one, Ryan. I wasn't like you. I didn't have it all figured out.'

The conversation was heading into dangerous territory. Maybe this friendship thing wasn't going to work after all. He'd been foolhardy to think it would. It was probably time to end this little outing before they ended up in another full-blown argument. He'd made his peace offering, been more than civil. Best to leave it at that. 'I've got some house calls to make this arvo, so I guess we really should make tracks.' He stood up without looking at her.

'Of course. I'm sorry, I didn't mean to take up your whole morning.'

'Not your fault. I was one who suggested the ride.'

Without a word she stood and walked away.

*

Jo didn't need to be told twice that she'd overstayed her welcome. She strode over to Pepper, who hadn't strayed far at all. She placed her hand at the base of the horse's mane and slid one foot into a stirrup. In one seamless movement she mounted the mare and propelled her forward. Pepper snorted her disapproval as Jo pressed her heels against her flesh, urging her to go faster down the steep decline. It was reckless, pushing an out-of-condition horse beyond her capabilities, but Jo's desire to get home, to end this too-close-for-comfort encounter with Ryan, overrode any inclination for common sense.

The wind stung her face and her hair whipped from side to side as Pepper thundered down the embankment, twisting this way and that to avoid trees and ditches. Adrenaline surged through Jo's body. Her heart thudded against her chest wall and her hands perspired despite the icy wind. As she approached the flat of the home paddock she pulled back on the reins, easing Pepper into a slow canter. Her lips stretched into a grin and she pumped the air with her fist.

'Wooooohooooo!'

Oh my god, did that ridiculous sound really come from her? Jo laughed. She couldn't remember the last time she'd felt so carefree. She pulled Pepper up so she could dismount and open the gate to the home paddock. She slid her hand down the horse's neck and patted her shoulder. Pepper's coat was slick with sweat. 'Sorry, old girl. I pushed you a bit too hard back there.' The mare shook her head, probably to rid herself of an annoying insect, but Jo chose to take it as an endorsement of their ride. 'You loved it, didn't you girl? You and I are going to have lots of fun together.'

The rhythmic sound of hoof beats came from behind as she unlatched the gate. Ryan was right behind her.

*

'Bloody hell, Jo. What was all that about?' The words came out louder and harsher than he'd intended, but dammit, the woman could have killed herself.

She shrugged as she held open the gate for him to pass through. 'Just a bit of fun.'

He ignored her gesture to ride through and dismounted instead. 'Fun? Christ Jo, you nearly gave me a heart attack.'

Jo dropped Pepper's reins and laughed. She moved towards him and placed her hand lightly on his chest. 'I think it's still ticking.'

His body responded instantly to her touch. A jolt of electricity fizzed through him. Seven years had made no difference to the chemistry between them. She still had the power to turn him on with just one touch.

His heart hammered, his pulse almost deafening as he covered her hand with his own. This wasn't right. As much as he wanted her, she was engaged to another man. Besides, what good could come of going down this path again? He had to put a stop to this before they both did something they would surely regret. He grabbed her hand firmly and removed it from his chest, but she didn't pull away.

Oh god, she was so close. He feared she'd see the beads of perspiration forming at his temple and know the effect she was having on him. He wanted so badly to kiss her.

And more, if he was honest.

Her eyes held his gaze, enticing him, daring him even, to take the next step. How the hell was he supposed to resist?

He moved even closer towards her, leaning in until their lips were so close her breath mingled with his own. 'Jo, I...' The words felt hot and thick in his throat and came out as a kind of strangled whisper.

She pressed a finger to his lips and shook her head. 'Don't —'

The buzzing of his phone stopped her mid-sentence. For a second she didn't move, but her eyes dropped.

The moment was broken.

Ryan fumbled in his pocket and pulled out the phone. 'Sorry,' he said, glancing at the screen. 'I have to take this. It's Mum.'

Jo nodded and backed away from him. 'Of course.'

'Mum, what's wrong?'

'Wrong? Why would there be anything wrong?'

'I don't know. I guess I just wasn't expecting you to call.' His eyes followed Jo as she made her way back to Pepper.

'It's nothing. I just wondered if I could get Ella from school today?'

Ella's name brought him crashing back to reality. The realisation of what he'd almost done hit Ryan like a punch in the gut. He had a life, dammit. Responsibilities. Commitments that were way too important to risk on some leftover feelings from a long-ago romance. Besides, Johanna Morgan wasn't the person he once knew. She belonged to another world. And with another man.

'Ryan? Are you still there?'

'Yes, sorry, Mum. You can get Ella if you like, that'd be great. Sorry if I sounded distracted but I'm in the middle of something. I'll call you later, okay?'

Jo had unsaddled Pepper and was walking towards him, tack in hand and a wide smile on her face. He should never have come here. Being alone with Jo was too risky. Hanging around here was only going to make matters worse. He eased himself back into the saddle, and gave her a wave. 'Gotta go,' he called, ignoring the look of surprise on Jo's face as he tapped his heels into Mack's side. 'I'll drop off some extra feed for Pepper later this arvo. No need to wait at home, I'll dump it in the shed and keep going.' He rode away without waiting for a reply. Today he'd been stupid, but through the intervention of the gods — or more accurately, his mother — he'd managed to dodge a bullet. He wasn't going to tempt fate again. From now on he'd keep his distance.

CHAPTER

8

The drive to Bellington — or Belly, as the locals had always called it — was anything but relaxing. For all Jo's complaining about crowded subway cars and smart-mouthed taxi drivers, at least those methods of transport didn't require any skill on her part. Either the Jeep was being deliberately recalcitrant or she'd forgotten how to change gears. Maddock's Road snaked around the edge of the National Park, and it took all her concentration to negotiate the twists and turns as she climbed out of the valley. It didn't help that the local sawmill drivers used this route. Meeting a log truck on the wrong side of the road would not end well.

Once she was out on the highway and safely in fifth gear, she relaxed enough to let her mind wander to yesterday's debacle with Ryan. Riding to Mason's Ridge with him had been a colossal mistake. There were too many memories there, and it seemed they'd both been swept up in some kind of stupid nostalgic belief that the mistakes of the past could be reversed.

At first it had been nice, comforting even, to slip back into the easy banter that had once come so naturally. But they'd gotten carried away and somehow managed to cross a boundary that shouldn't have been breached. They'd hurt each other enough in the past. Any type of romantic liaison, no matter how fleeting, would only serve to reopen old wounds. So why did her overactive imagination keep playing out the 'what ifs'?

She couldn't seem to help herself. Ever since their almost-kiss had been interrupted she'd been fantasising about feeling Ryan's lips on hers one more time. Last night, while suffering yet again from an attack of insomnia, she'd even entertained the idea of a holiday fling, but in her heart she knew that it would never work.

The sign to the Windmill Retirement and Nursing Home pushed all thoughts of Ryan to the back of her mind. Right now she had bigger things to worry about. Jo took in a few slow, deep breaths in an effort to prepare herself before stepping into the Dragon's Den.

Strictly speaking, the Dragon's Den was Katherine's study back at Yarrapinga. It was the joke she shared with her father, their little secret, and to this day it made Jo smile. In hindsight she knew it was his way of making it easier for her to deal with a mother who had little time or patience for an imaginative child. He never criticised Katherine, or challenged her parenting decisions, but in his own way he'd tried to show Jo that her mother's constant disapproval wasn't always warranted.

Now the Dragon and her Den had moved. Hopefully her fire-breathing days were over.

It was Jo's first visit to the Windmill. When she came home for her father's funeral it had been a whirlwind visit. She'd seen her mother at the service, of course; a carer from the home had brought her along. Katherine had been agitated all day, wailing and howling at the church and then complaining about the venue at the wake, much to Jo's embarrassment. The footy club had organised the whole thing after they'd gotten Jo's go-ahead via Steph.

'This is just so tacky. Your father will be rolling over in his grave, Johanna,' Katherine kept insisting. If he was, Jo doubted it was due to her choice of venue for the wake.

When she wasn't complaining, Katherine had been grabbing Jo by the hand and telling her to run, to get away from Linden Gully while she still could. It was disconcerting to say the least. At times she seemed calm and like her old self, but moments later anxiety and agitation would overtake her. Jo understood why her father had made the decision to place Katherine at the Windmill. Obviously he'd not been well himself, although he'd never said as much, and caring for Katherine was a full-time job.

The Windmill wasn't the dingy, prisonlike environment she'd imagined. In fact, the reception area was not unlike a five-star hotel. Pale pink overstuffed sofas faced each other in the centre of the room and a large floral arrangement adorned the glass-topped coffee table between them. Jo caught herself tapping her fingers on the marble counter in time to the muted Muzak that filled the room as she waited for the receptionist to greet her.

A woman with salt-and-pepper hair pulled into a lank ponytail looked up from her computer screen and raised an eyebrow. 'Won't be a moment.'

Jo stopped the tapping. Clearly the receptionist was less than impressed. Putting the gatekeeper offside wasn't likely to make the visit any easier, especially if the Dragon starting acting up. Jo smiled at her. 'No hurry,' she said.

The woman took her at her word and continued to type for a few minutes before enquiring tersely, 'Patient's name?'

'Morgan. Mrs Katherine Morgan.'

'And you are?'

'Her daughter.'

The receptionist stopped tapping at the keyboard and looked up at Jo. 'Johanna Morgan? *The* Johanna Morgan?'

Jo nodded. 'Um, I guess so. I mean, yes, I'm Johanna Morgan.'

'Oh Miss Morgan I'm so sorry to have kept you waiting like that. You should have said...I mean it's not often we have, you know, *celebrities* here at the Windmill.'

'Oh, that's okay. I hardly think I qualify as a celebrity.'

The woman's brow creased in confusion. 'You're the author, Johanna Morgan, the one who is engaged to Zachary Carlton, right?' Her eyes moved up and down Jo's body as if she was trying to reconcile the real-life version before her with the magazine images. 'You wrote *Hollywood Kisses* and *New York Nights*, right?' she added, as an obvious afterthought.

Jo nodded.

The woman stood up, smoothed her skirt and rushed around to Jo's side of the counter. She extended her hand for Jo to shake. 'Carol,' she said. 'I'm the office manager here at the Windmill. We've communicated via email many times.'

Jo shook her hand and smiled. 'Ah, yes, Carol, so we have. It's a pleasure to finally meet you.'

'Oh it's an honour to meet you, Miss Morgan. Fancy having Zach Carlton's fiancée right here in front of me! Of course I'm a big fan of your writing too. We've all read your books here, and we can't wait to see the movie of *Hollywood Kisses*. It'll be out soon, won't it?'

Jo tried to ignore the feeling of crushing dread she felt every time the movie was mentioned. Lydia had negotiated a great deal money-wise, but the movie rights to the book had been sold unconditionally, which meant the producers could do whatever they wanted with it. She hadn't been consulted at all about the script. When Zach brought home his copy to show her she'd opened it with great anticipation. By page fifty she was crushed. Her darkly funny, ironic book had morphed into a sex and shopping drama — the antithesis of what she'd intended. The fact that Zach had the lead role in the movie made matters even worse.

She forced herself to keep smiling. 'I believe so, although I've not had much to do with the movie.'

Carol was unfazed by her remark. 'How thrilling to have something you've written made into a movie. Your mother is over the moon for you.'

'Really?' Jo couldn't keep the surprise out of her voice. 'I wasn't sure if she knew. I write to her every week, but as she never responds I'm never really sure if she's receiving my news. As you probably know she won't talk to me on the phone.'

'The phone is difficult for her these days. She finds it confusing to talk to someone she can't see. However I know she gets your letters. I deliver her letters personally and she sometimes asks me to read them to her, which I'm, of course, more than happy to do for her.'

Jo raised her eyebrows. *Something to remember for future correspondence.* 'Are her eyes failing?'

'Oh no, it's not that. It's just, well, she has good days and bad. On her bad days, she can't...she doesn't know how...'

'She's forgotten...' Jo's words caught in her throat, '...she's forgotten how to read?'

'You didn't know?'

It shouldn't have come as a shock. Katherine was in this place because she had dementia. Of course she forgot things. But reading? Jo could barely remember a time when her mother didn't have a book or a document in her hand. She used to cook with one hand stirring the pot, the other turning the page. Jo shook her head slowly. 'I get regular reports from the nursing staff and her doctor, and I guess I should have put two and two together. It just never occurred to me that...' A lump formed in Jo's throat and she couldn't continue.

Carol looked at her and Jo saw genuine sympathy in the older woman's eyes. 'Some days she manages. In fact sometimes she's quite lucid and knows everything that's going on. Those are the days that she talks about you and tells us how she always knew you were destined for something special.'

Jo smiled in spite of her bewilderment. Destined for something special? Her mother had never said as much to her. In fact, she'd frequently predicted Jo would end up a teenage mother — or possibly a drug addict, after the time she'd caught Jo and Steph smoking behind the shed. She realised Carol was waiting for her to speak. 'And on the other days?'

'As is to be expected in these cases, as time goes on she's having more and more bad days — days when she thinks she's nine years old again, or when she doesn't know where she is or even who she is.'

Jo blinked back the tears beginning to form in her eyes. 'Clearly she's deteriorated since the last time I saw her. Do you think she'll recognise me?'

Carol hesitated. 'If she's having a good day, or a good moment, she might. Shall I take you through and we'll see?'

'Oh, there's no need for that. I'm sure you're far too busy, I can —'

'Nonsense. The receptionist is due back from her break any minute. I was just covering the front desk for her. I'll be happy to show you through.'

It seemed Carol was determined to witness the happy — or otherwise — reunion. She beckoned for Jo to follow her through the automatic glass doors. They proceeded past a large light-filled sitting room, a cafeteria-like dining room and then through a labyrinth of corridors. Most of the rooms they passed had closed doors, their nameplates the only clue that an actual person resided there. Occasionally the door was ajar and Jo caught a glimpse of a withered man or woman glancing hopefully at her and then deflating once they realised her footsteps were not going to pause at their door. This was no hotel, despite the plush lounges and grand piano in the sitting room.

Acid rose in Jo's throat as Carol stopped at a thick glass door and started punching a security code into the neon-lit keypad on the adjacent wall.

'Is this door always locked?' Jo asked.

Carol nodded. 'This is the high dependency unit. Most of the residents in here have severe dementia. They're prone to wandering, and we can't have that now, can we?'

'I suppose not,' Jo said quietly. Images of her mother swirled in her head — meticulous Katherine on Christmas morning, dressed in a pretty floral sundress, admonishing six-year-old Jo for not taking the time to open the card before ripping the paper off a perfectly wrapped Christmas gift; intelligent Katherine curled up on the couch in front of the fire, black-rimmed reading glasses perched on her nose and a copy of Margaret Atwood's *The Handmaid's Tale* in her hand; gracious Katherine serving aperitifs to a group of guests at a rare dinner party hosted at Yarrapinga.

This place, this home filled with feeble octogenarians, was not a suitable residence for the Dragon. The mother she knew was fierce and capable and certainly wouldn't be happy in a place like this. What had Daddy been thinking when he deposited her here?

There had to be another way. Jo wasn't sure exactly what the alternative might be but she knew there was no way she could leave Katherine to languish here in this repository for those who had passed their use-by date.

The glass door swung open. 'After you,' Carol said. Jo entered the unit and braced herself for what was to come.

'This way.' Once again she followed Carol down a series of corridors until she came to a halt outside a door bearing Katherine's name. Carol rapped loudly on the door and opened it without waiting for a response.

An overpowering smell of antiseptic assaulted Jo's nostrils as she took in the room that her mother called home. A single bed covered with a mauve quilted bedspread — not a choice she would normally associate with her mother — took up one wall. Under the window sat the mahogany dressing table from Katherine's bedroom at home. Nanna's hairbrush and silver comb took pride of place under the oval mirror just as they always had. The tapestry-covered footstool sat beside the bed. All the other furniture in the room was unfamiliar: a cheap-looking set of pine drawers and a large grey recliner. In the recliner slumped a tiny twig of a woman. She wore a faded pink woollen cardigan, worn at the elbows, atop a drab grey dress. A pair of grubby beige slippers completed the outfit. The woman didn't appear to notice their presence. Her head was tilted forward, her attention focused on her upturned palms, so Jo couldn't see her face properly. A faint muttering sound came from her lips but the nonsensical utterance did not seem intended for anyone but herself. There had to be some mistake. This shell of a woman couldn't possibly be her mother. For starters she looked years older than Katherine, but more importantly those were not her mother's clothes. There was no way she would be caught dead in such an unfashionable outfit. Style was pretty much Katherine's middle name. Jo looked at Carol, 'I think there's been some sort of error,' she said, struggling to keep her voice from breaking. 'This is not my mother.'

Carol's eyes radiated sympathy. 'I'm sure her appearance has changed since you last saw her. We do our best to make sure the residents are adequately nourished but many of our dementia patients experience appetite changes. Some may eat excessively and some, like your mum, eat very little. She's probably lost a bit of weight since you saw her last.'

'But her hair's grey. My mother doesn't have grey hair. And her clothes. Those are most definitely not her clothes.'

Carol nodded. 'We have a hairdresser who visits here, who will cut and colour the residents' hair, but Katherine refuses to go. It's distressing for her, so we don't force the issue. As far as her wardrobe is concerned that's a matter of practicality. With no family visiting regularly we purchase her clothes for her. They're chosen for durability, not fashion.'

'But she must have arrived with her own clothes. My father would have made sure she had her own things.'

'I'm sure she did, but that was a while ago now. Clothes wear out easily here. They're washed and dried in industrial machines. Unfortunately we can't specially launder clothes. You're welcome to take a look at what's in her wardrobe to see what she has. If you wish to purchase new clothes at any time, I'll personally ensure they get to her.'

A sick feeling settled in Jo's chest. This was her fault. Katherine looked like a pathetic little old lady because she hadn't cared enough to think about where her mother's clothes came from. Other patients probably had good daughters. Ones that came and took care of their parent's grooming and made sure they were eating properly. Not her poor mother. Katherine had raised a daughter who was selfish. One who'd been off living the high life, thinking that so long as the nursing-home bills were paid and she checked in via email every now and then, her job was done. She had no idea what the reality of her mother's life was. Jo made a silent vow that from now on things would be different.

Carol addressed the woman. 'Hello there, Katie. Look who I've brought to see you.'

Katie? Katherine Morgan despised nicknames. She made it clear to all and sundry that her name was Katherine. Not Kathy or Kath, and most certainly not Katie. Dear god, what was going on here?

The woman looked up. 'Is it tea time already?' The voice was weak and raspy but there was no doubting the identity of the speaker.

'Mum,' Jo whispered, the rarely used title slipping out unintentionally. 'Oh Katherine, it's me, Johanna.'

Katherine looked up and her lips stretched into a wide smile, one Jo was not accustomed to seeing. 'What a coincidence. I have a little girl named Johanna.'

'Katie, this *is* your Johanna, all grown up. She's come all the way from America to visit you.' Carol's voice had an unnatural singsong quality to it, as if she was addressing a toddler. No wonder Katherine chose to ignore her.

Instead the slight but cheerful woman who was apparently her mother turned to Jo. 'Are you here for a visit? I love visitors.'

Jo nodded, not trusting herself to speak just yet.

'Sit yourself down then and tell me something worth knowing.'

Jo's spirits lifted slightly. Katherine was still in there somewhere.

'I'll leave you to it,' Carol said, as Jo followed instructions and sat on the end of her mother's bed. 'If you need anything you can ask one of the carers at the station just inside the wing entrance. You can get the code to get out from there too.'

'Thank you,' Jo said. Carol closed the door behind her, leaving her alone with the stranger that her mother had become.

'Well,' Katherine demanded, 'what's your news? What brings you here?'

'I'm back home for Stephanie Fielding's wedding. I'm to be her bridesmaid.'

Katherine's face became animated at the mention of Steph's name. Maybe she was starting to realise who Jo was. She screwed up her nose in distaste. 'Pah. Don't talk to me about weddings. Silly girl. What's she thinking, throwing her life away like that? Tell me she's not hitching her wagon to some farmer?'

Jo felt her cheeks burning. 'Yes, both she and her fiancé are farmers. They plan to raise crops and run some sheep. They have a beautiful property, right near Kallara. I'm sure they'll both be very happy there.'

Katherine shook her head. 'Thank god my girl had more sense than that. She got away from this hellhole. Went off to finish her degree in America. She's a smart one, my Johanna.'

A lump formed in Jo's throat and she found herself unable to speak. The pride in her mother's voice was unmistakable. Her whole life she'd hungered for Katherine's love and approval. This was as close as she'd come.

Katherine went on, seemingly oblivious to the effect of her words. 'I was a bit worried for a while there. When she was a teenager she took up with a local lad. Nice enough boy, but no ambition, you know what I mean?'

Fortunately Katherine seemed to think the question was rhetorical and Jo was spared the pain of answering.

'He was destined to be a farmer. It was in his blood. I didn't want my girl making the same mistake I did.'

'What mistake was that?' Jo's tone was harsh but Katherine didn't seem to notice. She'd warmed to this topic and was eager to go on.

'Being stuck in a backwater with a man who thought passing comment on the weather was an in-depth conversation.'

Heat flooded Jo's cheeks at this stinging assessment of her beloved Dad. 'Surely it wasn't all bad?'

Katherine rolled her eyes. 'It was the pits.'

Anger knotted Jo's stomach. How could she have doubted that this woman was her mother? Her memory might have faded but her bitterness was as sharp as ever. 'What made you stay? If it was as bad as you say surely you could have left?'

Katherine's pale hand moved to her throat and she fingered the small gold cross that hung there. 'It was my penance,' she said. 'I'd already committed one cardinal sin. I couldn't risk another stain on my soul.'

Sin? What sin? Had her mother murdered someone or had a secret affair? The thought was both thrilling and horrifying in equal parts. Before Jo could press her further on the issue, Katherine returned to her thoughts on Jo's relationship with Ryan.

'At least my Johanna had the sense to make a life for herself.' Katherine lowered her voice to a conspiratorial whisper. 'And I played my part in making sure she didn't repeat my mistakes.'

What did she mean? Had Katherine done something to drive Ryan away? 'Really?' Jo worked hard to keep her voice casual. 'How did you do that?'

Katherine shrugged. 'It wasn't too hard. Men are all the same, you know. Full of ego. Once Johanna left for the States I just planted a few seeds of doubt in the boy's mind. That's all it took to convince him she was never coming back, that she didn't love him enough to return. Foolish boy went and sought solace in the arms of the first girl that made eyes at him. The fact that the girl got pregnant, well...' Katherine looked up at her with a satisfied smile, '...that was just the icing on the cake.'

CHAPTER

9

'Dad, you're not listening.'

Ryan put his empty coffee cup on the sink and turned to face his daughter. 'Sorry pumpkin.'

Ella rocked back on the kitchen chair and screwed up her nose. 'I told you not to call me that. I'm not a pumpkin.'

'I know sweetheart, it's just a nickname.'

'It's a baby name and I'm not a baby anymore. Anyway can I?'

'Um...' Ryan realised he had no idea what she was asking. Despite his best intentions he hadn't been able to concentrate properly on anything — not even his daughter — since yesterday's fiasco with Joey. He'd been utterly useless all day. First cocking up the client invoicing system, so that a job that should have taken ten minutes spilled over into an hour, then being late for school pick-up from the bus stop. Neither Ella nor the bus driver looked too chipper when he arrived five minutes after the official time. His profuse apologies were met with a gruff response from Bill, the normally cheerful driver. 'I've got a schedule to keep, Ryan.'

And now he was ignoring his child. Ella, clearly frustrated by his lack of attention, had pushed back against the table so that the timber chair balanced on two legs. 'Don't rock on the chair, Ella.'

She did as she was told but not before rolling her eyes and letting out a theatrical sigh. 'Well?'

'Well, what?'

'Can I wear lipstick at Steph's wedding? The girls at school say all proper bridesmaids wear lipstick.'

Ryan shook his head. 'You're not a bridesmaid, you're a flower girl and no, you're not wearing make-up.'

'That's so unfair. I bet my mum would have let me.'

Ella's words squeezed his heart. He honestly didn't know what Carly would have done in this situation. 'Look, lipstick is kind of a girl thing. It's not something I know much about. How about I talk to Gran and Steph and see what they think?'

Ella smiled, obviously confident that she had won this battle. 'Okay.'

'Now, I have a sick dog out in the clinic that I need to go have a look at. Do you want to help or are you going to go up to Gran's and get started on your homework?'

'I'll go to Gran's,' she said.

Ryan raised his eyebrows at this unexpected answer. It wasn't like Ella to turn down an opportunity to help out in the clinic. Clearly the lipstick campaign was her first priority. No doubt Gran would be well and truly lobbied for the next half hour or so. He smiled. 'Okay. Don't forget your school bag.'

With Ella safely despatched to the granny flat Ryan was free to let his mind wander back to the unfortunate events of yesterday. Could have been worse. Much worse.

At least he hadn't actually kissed her.

But the temptation to do so had been overwhelming. How the hell was he going to trust himself to be around her for the next couple of weeks?

He had to start using his head, not his heart — or other organs — to make decisions where Joey was concerned. Even if she was free to be with him, which she wasn't, she would be off home to New York in a few short weeks and he knew he didn't have the ticker for a casual fling. Not with her.

It wouldn't happen again. He wouldn't let it.

As he made his way from the house to the clinic at the end of the driveway he heard a car coming up the road. Hopefully it wasn't another client. He had all the work he could handle right now, although strictly speaking it was his own fault. The trickiest case he had at the moment was a stray labrador pup. A local kid had found her a few days back and brought her in, floppy and lethargic. It was a classic case of parvo. With no owner and no identification, he really should have euthanised her on the spot, but she'd looked at him with those big chocolate eyes and he couldn't bring himself to do it. To be honest he didn't think she'd make it through the first twenty-four hours, but the pup was a fighter and now, three days later, she was starting to look like she might make a full recovery.

The cattle grid clunked as the car turned into his driveway. It was a Jeep, and not one he recognised. Oh bloody hell, it couldn't be...

Jo pulled the car up in front of the clinic. Ryan happened to be standing right there, so there was no backing out. Katherine's words had plagued her all the way back from Bellington. She hadn't managed to get any more detail about exactly what her mother had said, or done, to convince Ryan that taking up with Carly was a good idea. Katherine's mind had wandered from the subject and there was no coaxing her back.

Suddenly everything Jo thought she knew about their break-up was turned on its head. Maybe she'd been wrong all this time and Ryan's betrayal wasn't as inexplicable as she'd thought. She'd found herself driving into Ryan's driveway before she'd had a chance to think about whether seeing him was a good idea or not. Sensible or otherwise, she had to know what had happened after she'd left Linden Gully.

Ryan stood at the clinic's entrance, his arms folded across his chest. Evidently he wasn't thrilled to see her, but that was bad luck, because she wasn't going anywhere until she had some answers.

'Hi Johanna. What can I do for you?' The words were pleasant enough but they contained no warmth.

No point in beating around the bush then. She sucked in a breath and got straight to the point of the visit. 'We need to talk.'

His gaze dropped. 'Look, if it's about yesterday, I'm sorry. I shouldn't have —'

'It's not about yesterday. We probably should talk about that too at some point, but I have something else on my mind.'

He looked up her, his brow wrinkled in concern. 'Is everything okay?'

She shrugged. 'I guess so. I've been to see my mother at the home. She told me some things. Some disturbing things actually, about things she said to you after I'd left for New York.'

'Oh, Jo. It was such a long time ago. Can't we just let it be?'

She shook her head. 'I need to know what happened, Ryan. Surely you don't begrudge me that?'

He sighed. 'You'd better come in, then. I've got work to do. We can talk while I sort some things out in here.'

She nodded and followed him through the glass sliding door into the small but immaculate clinic. Open timber shelves stocked with pet food and a few accessories lined one wall, a row of white moulded chairs sat against the other. A stack of timber pallets had been converted into a functional yet stylish reception desk. 'Wow,' she said. 'This is pretty swish. Did you do it all yourself?'

'Bec sorted out the waiting area. I didn't think I needed one, but she was insistent. Doesn't get used that much to be honest.'

Why was she relieved to hear that it was his sister-in-law and not his latest girlfriend playing interior decorator?

Get a grip, Johanna.

'The patient's out the back,' Ryan said, indicating she should follow him. He opened a door that led to a small treatment room, a fully equipped surgical theatre and finally to the animal accommodation. Excited barks greeted them as they entered the kennel room. 'Hey, girl, you're looking better, aren't you? Come and say hello to Johanna.' He unlatched the enclosure gate and a gangly black labrador bounded towards her.

'Hello there gorgeous. You don't look sick at all.'

'Not now she doesn't, but a couple of days back she was on death's door.'

Jo bent down and scratched behind the lab's velvety ear. 'Really? What's wrong with her?'

'She's had parvo, poor thing. Hasn't been immunised.'

Jo shook her head, thinking that some people shouldn't be allowed to have pets. 'Who does she belong to?'

Ryan shrugged. 'She's a stray. I doubt that she's from anywhere around here. In fact I've named her Holly.'

'Holly?'

'Yeah, Holly the Christmas pup. Happens all the time. People get these cute pups as a Christmas gift but a few months down the track when the pup turns out to be bigger and more work than they bargained on...'

Jo placed her hand on her heart. 'You mean she was dumped?' She knelt down and put her arms around the excited pup. 'Oh who could do that to you, beautiful girl?' She looked up to see Ryan grinning at her. 'What?'

'Nothing. I'd just forgotten how much you loved dogs.'

'Yeah, I really miss having a dog.'

'You don't have one, then? Not even a little chihuahua? I believe they're very popular with you celebrity types.'

Jo laughed. 'Don't be a smart arse. As much as I'd love a dog, I don't have one because I don't think it's fair to keep it cooped up in an apartment all day.'

'Fair enough.' He shook his head. 'You know I just can't imagine you over there.'

She stood up and brushed the dog hair from her jeans. 'Oh? Why's that?'

'No horse. No dog. Just doesn't seem right. You know, the past few days I keep thinking about when Tam was born. He was such a weak little foal. No one thought he would make it. But you refused to give up.'

Warmth spread through Jo's chest. He remembered. Ryan was the only person who understood how much that foal had meant to her. The only one who didn't think she was crazy for refusing to give up on him. 'You backed me up. If it wasn't for you my dad would have put him down.'

His lips twisted into a wry smile. 'I backed you up because I loved you, Joey. I didn't think Tam had a snowball's chance in hell of making it, but back then I would have tried to walk on water if you'd asked me to.'

The warmth spread up her neck to her cheeks. 'That brings me to the purpose of my visit. I need to know what happened, Ryan.

Why did you sleep with Carly so soon after I'd gone? Why were you so quick to throw our relationship away?'

He crouched down, ostensibly to pat the dog, but Jo knew it was so he wouldn't have to look her in the eye. 'You were the one who left,' he said. He clicked his fingers. 'Come on Holly, let's get you into the treatment room so I can have a proper look at you.'

Jo trailed behind him. 'I'm not letting it go that easily. Please, I know it's been a long time, but it's important to me. We've never had the chance to talk about what happened. I think I need to so I can fully put the past behind me. Maybe we both do.'

Ryan slid a soft muzzle over Holly's head. 'Can you hold her still for me? I need to take her temperature and she's not going to like it.'

Jo nodded and stepped forward to gently restrain Holly. She uttered some soothing words while the deed was done. Ryan was silent as he examined the dog, pausing to write a few notes on her chart as he went. When he was done he locked eyes with Jo. 'If you insist on going over old ground, let's at least be civilised and do it over a coffee. I'll just let Holly out for a run in the exercise yard and then we can go back up to the house. Ella's at Mum's doing her homework so we can talk freely there.'

With Holly sorted and the coffee made there was no excuse to delay the conversation any further, although why she was insisting on having it was beyond Ryan. What point was there in bringing all the hurt back to the surface? She had a new man in her life now, wasn't that punishment enough for him? Did she have to go rubbing his face in the mess from the past?

'Okay,' he said. 'What do you want to know?'

Her deep brown eyes held his gaze. 'Why? Why did you sleep with Carly behind my back?'

'Jesus, Jo, it was hardly behind your back. You'd left me. Have you conveniently forgotten that part of the story?'

'I hadn't left you. I'd gone overseas to study. That's hardly the same thing.' Her voice was steady but he sensed a simmering anger beneath the calm.

No way was he carrying the can for this. Sure he may have done something stupid, but she was rewriting history to make it seem as if she'd just gone away for a short break and he'd two-timed her in the interim. Was that really how she remembered it? If so she was delusional. 'You seem to have forgotten that you'd just turned down my proposal of marriage and...'

'And what?'

To hell with it. She wanted the truth, he might as well give it to her. 'You broke my heart, Joey.'

She had the good grace to look contrite. 'I never meant to hurt you, Ryan. I told you that at the time. I didn't want to get married or engaged just then. I was twenty-one for heaven's sake. At the time I didn't even know if I believed in marriage. It certainly never did my parents any favours. Is it really so hard to understand that I needed some time to decide what I wanted out of life?'

'I wasn't proposing that we get hitched there and then, just that we made a commitment to each other. You couldn't do that. The thing is, I knew what I wanted. I wanted to spend the rest of my life with you. I figured you wanted the same thing. I couldn't see the point of waiting.'

'We talked about this, remember? I told you I still loved you but I needed more time. You told me to take all the time I needed. That you would wait for me forever. Turns out our definitions of "forever" are somewhat different.'

The acid taste of anger rose in Ryan's throat at the assertion that he was the one who'd done the betraying. She was the one who'd left and hadn't had the courage to tell him it was over. 'When I said that I meant it. That was before I realised you were never coming back. I mean what was I to think, Jo? As far as I was concerned we were on track to getting married. We practically lived together those first two years of uni. I can barely remember a morning when I didn't wake up next to you. And we'd talked about it often enough, but when it came to making a solid commitment you ran.'

'I didn't run! I went away to study. It was the opportunity of a lifetime. We'd talked about me going, so I don't know why it was such a shock when I actually did. You were the one who encouraged me to follow my dream.'

'Because I thought I was part of that dream, but I was wrong.'

'You weren't wrong. What would make you think I was never coming back when I promised you I would?'

'Your mother told me the truth.'

Her face was ashen. 'What do you mean?'

'After you left your mum invited me to afternoon tea at Yarrapinga.'

'And you went?' Her tone was incredulous.

'Of course I went. She was your mother. I wanted her to like me.'

'But she hated you, you knew that. Why subject yourself to having tea with her?'

He shrugged. 'I guess I was gullible. I thought maybe she was coming around to the idea of me being part of your life. I don't know. I missed you. I figured she missed you too and maybe we could bond over that.'

'So what happened?'

'She made it clear to me that you had no intention of ever coming home. She told me that you would never be happy with me but that you were too soft-hearted to break up with me to my face. She said you hoped we would just naturally drift apart, that I would find someone else while you were gone and that we could part amicably.'

Colour flooded into Jo's face. 'Are you kidding me? You believed that? Come on Ryan. That's just...bullshit.'

Her anger hit him like a slap in the face. 'Of course I didn't believe her at first. But she went on and on about how unsuited we were for each other, how you could never be happy in Linden Gully and how in all likelihood if we got married that's exactly where we'd eventually end up.'

'But you knew what she was like. Surely you could see through her lies?'

'Lies? Well, that's just it. They weren't lies were they? I'm not a bloody fool, Jo. Can you honestly tell me you would have been happy to settle here with me?'

'I...well —'

He shook his head. 'You might have for a time, but Katherine was right. Eventually you would have hated me for holding you back. And anyway, I would never have taken her words at face value. She had proof.'

'Proof? What proof?

'She showed me a heap of documents and articles you'd printed out about working visas, permanent residency and so on. I knew they were yours because there were notes in your handwriting scrawled all over the pages. Just admit it, Jo.'

Her face was now beet red with anger. 'Admit what?'

'That you were leaving me and you didn't even have the courage to tell me the truth.'

'I'm not admitting any such thing, because it's not true. I made some notes about permanent residency. So what? They were for the future, Ryan. Our future. I wasn't just thinking about myself. I had no intention of staying there permanently without you.'

Ryan's gut clenched. If she was telling the truth then his mistake had been monumental, but he wasn't buying Jo's explanation. Katherine had made him believe that letting Jo go was the right thing, the honourable thing, to do. She'd told him he was holding Jo back, that she could never be happy in Linden Gully. He'd believed her because somewhere deep down in his heart he'd known there was a kernel of truth in what she'd said.

He looked into her eyes. 'But why would you do that without talking to me? And for god's sake Jo, you knew there was no way I would move to America.'

Her eyes dropped and she began to fiddle with the rock on her finger. 'I knew you weren't ready for that idea. Not then. And I didn't even know if I'd like it over there myself. It was all just forward thinking. Imagining a different future for us than the one you so clearly had your heart set on.'

'That's the whole point, isn't it? You clearly wanted a different life to the one we'd talked about.'

'You'd talked about, you mean. It was always you saying "when we get married...when we have kids..." I don't ever remember starting a conversation like that.'

Was that true? 'I don't remember you ever disagreeing with me.'

'Maybe I didn't. Maybe I had no idea what I really wanted back then, but I did know that I wanted you. I wasn't leaving you, Ryan, I was finding me. I always intended to come back.'

'But you didn't come back, did you? You stayed there and made a life for yourself.'

She swiped a tear from her cheek. 'Because you gave me no other choice. What did I have to come home to?'

Oh god, had he really let her go for no reason at all? He dropped his head into his hands. The magnitude of Katherine's deception, his gullibility and their combined consequences hit him like a blow to the chest.

All these years he'd hated her. Loved her yet hated her for what she'd put him through. And for what? She'd done nothing wrong. It was his stupid pride that drove them apart. Part of him had always refused to believe he was good enough for a girl like Johanna Morgan. So when she'd refused his proposal he'd been hurt. It seemed his doubt was not misplaced. Katherine's story only confirmed what he had feared all along, that Jo was not meant for the likes of him. She'd been pretending all this time, waiting for a better option to present itself.

Katherine had played him for a sucker.

Jo bit back the tears that stung her eyes. She didn't want Ryan mistaking her rage for sorrow, because right now every fibre of her being was consumed by a white-hot anger. It was probably misdirected. Ryan had been little more than a boy when Katherine had manipulated him out of their relationship. But dammit, he could have fought harder. Why didn't he have more faith in himself? In her?

'Look at me,' she demanded.

Ryan raised his head to meet her gaze. His eyes were bloodshot and if she didn't know better she might think he was about to shed his own tears. But Galloway men didn't cry.

Not ever.

'Joey, I'm sorry. You have to believe that I would never have slept with Carly if I'd known I still had a chance with you. I thought you'd abandoned me. As if I would risk my relationship with you for a meaningless...'

As his voice wavered her anger abated. It was as if she could read his mind. No matter what his intentions were on that night he took Carly into his bed, the result was anything but meaningless.

They'd both made mistakes. And now they had to live with them. Her desire to analyse the ins and outs of what had gone wrong all those years ago evaporated. What did it matter who was at fault? It didn't change anything. It was pointless being angry with her mother — the Katherine who had orchestrated this disaster didn't exist anymore. All this introspection was just causing Ryan more pain.

They'd loved each other once and it hadn't worked out. It was as simple as that.

CHAPTER

10

'Gran said she would tell Steph I can wear lipstick,' Ella announced as she ran into the kitchen.

'Hang on a minute, that's not what I said. I said —' Beth stopped mid-sentence. The smile disappeared from her face as her eyes met Jo's. 'Oh...sorry, Ryan. I didn't realise you were busy. Hello, Johanna.'

Jo swallowed, her mouth suddenly dry. Beth Galloway was a formidable woman and she was fiercely protective of those she loved. Once upon a time Jo counted herself among the people Beth cared about, but that was no longer the case. After the discussion she'd just had with Ryan, Jo was acutely aware of why Beth would feel some animosity towards her. 'Hello Beth. It's nice to see you.'

Beth's lips formed a tight smile. 'I believe congratulations are in order.'

Jo was momentarily lost for words.

'On your engagement. It was the talk of the town for a while there. It's not every day a girl from Linden Gully marries an

American movie star.' Jo didn't miss the look of distaste on her face. 'You're a very lucky girl.'

Right now Jo didn't feel very lucky at all. 'Thank you. And yes, I am.' The lie churned her stomach, but it couldn't be helped.

'Well...I don't want to interrupt your catch-up. I'll be off.' She looked at Ryan. 'We can discuss the lipstick agreement later.'

Ryan smiled and walked over to give Beth a peck on the cheek. 'Thanks Mum.'

As Beth left, Jo became aware of Ella, standing silently just inside the doorway. 'Hi, Ella. Do you remember me? I'm Jo. We met at the footy.'

Ella didn't answer but continued to eye her suspiciously.

'Ella, where are your manners? Answer Jo.'

Jo shook her head at Ryan and laughed. 'It's okay, Ryan. I'm sure Ella's just a little shy.'

He raised his eyebrows and opened his mouth to speak but Ella got in first.

'I'm not shy. Dad told me never to talk to strangers.'

Jo knew she had her work cut out for her. 'I see. That's very sensible. We won't be strangers soon, though. Did you know I'm going to be Steph's bridesmaid? Soon you and I will get to know each other really well. Won't that be fun?'

Ella's expression didn't change. 'I guess so.'

'Okay, missy, I think it's time you took your school bag to your room and put your uniform in the laundry.' Ryan was clearly keen to put an end to the stand-off. As Ella thumped off down the hallway, Ryan sat down opposite Jo at the table. 'Sorry about that. I'm not sure what got into her.'

'Don't worry about it. I'm not great with kids. I'm totally clueless about them and no matter how hard I try I seem to have a knack of putting them offside.'

Ryan smiled. 'That'll change soon enough.'

'Huh?'

'When you have kids of your own. It'll come naturally, you'll see.'

Was there no getting away from the baby conversation? What was it with men and babies? First Zach and now Ryan. Weren't women supposed to be the clucky ones? 'Not sure that I want to have kids.'

'Not yet maybe, but eventually.'

Jo shrugged. 'I guess so. Maybe.' God, why couldn't she just tell the truth? She knew very well that she never wanted to reproduce. She was not cut out to be a mother. Call it a genetic failing. Ryan, of all people, should know that. He'd witnessed her mother's inadequacies and insecurities first hand. 'In any case, I should go. I don't want to keep you any longer.'

'Jo...' He reached out across the table and put his hand on hers.

A jolt of electricity shot through her as his thumb gently caressed her skin. After all this time he could still turn her insides to mush. 'Yes?' she whispered.

'I'm so glad we had this talk. I know I said I didn't want to revisit the past but you were right, it was better to have things out in the open. We can both move on now, and maybe even have a real go at being friends?'

Friends. Isn't that what she wanted? Isn't that what she'd hoped to achieve — to clear the air so there would be no awkwardness, no more animosity between them? Why then did Ryan's suggestion sting so badly?

'Friends,' she said, in the cheeriest tone she could muster. She withdrew her hand and pushed the chair out from the table. 'Of course we can be friends. Now I really must be going. Lots to do. Packing up the house, bridesmaid stuff. You know how it is.' The sound of chair legs dragging on the polished timber boards filled the silence.

'I'll walk you to your car,' Ryan said.

'No, no. You go sort out Ella. I'm fine. I'll see you soon. At the hens and bucks night if not before.' She made for the door before he could protest.

Ryan watched the Jeep disappearing down the road from the kitchen window. It was as if a cricket ball had hit him in the chest. His discussion with Jo had made him realise what a total fool he'd been. He'd allowed a bitter woman to trick him into giving up on the love of his life. If he'd only had a bit more faith in Jo — in himself — his whole life could have turned out differently.

But would it have been better? Honestly, he didn't know. What he did know was that the past couldn't be changed. And if he hadn't gone off half-cocked and slept with Carly, he would never have ended up with his gorgeous little daughter. A life without Ella was not something he could even contemplate, so perhaps his mum was right when she said that things happened for a reason.

And Joey was happy. That was the main thing. For all her indignation at her mother's interference, who was to say that it hadn't turned out for the best in the long run? Being cooped up here in this tiny town would never have worked for her. She was too talented, wanted too much out of life to be satisfied with the simple pleasures that Linden Gully had to offer. At 21 he'd been too wrapped up in his own fantasies of how life would be to see what must have been blatantly obvious to everyone else.

In a way he didn't blame Katherine Morgan. She was only doing what she thought was best for her daughter. And her prediction had come true. Joey was wildly successful and engaged to a movie star. How could he have ever thought that anything he had to offer could compete with that?

No, things were exactly as they should be. But if everything had turned out for the best why the hell did he feel so damned empty as he watched her drive away?

Even with the radio's volume turned way up, Jo couldn't drown out the thoughts swirling around her head. Ryan hadn't betrayed her, not really. He'd thought it was over between them and was numbing his grief with a cocktail of alcohol and meaningless sex. Of course the sex hadn't turned out to be meaningless, but he hadn't known that at the time.

Maybe he was right in his reluctance to go back over old ground. What had it achieved? Did she feel better knowing that he hadn't just discarded her the minute she'd got on the plane, that he had loved her and that his betrayal came from heartbreak, not from ambivalence?

No, she did not.

In fact she felt worse somehow. Which was stupid. The air had been cleared between them, there was no animosity and they were free to be friends, which was for the best. Wasn't it?

Her mind wandered back to yesterday's aborted kiss, which sent the butterflies in her belly into overdrive. Would she have kissed him if the phone hadn't interrupted them? At the time the urge was overpowering and she doubted that she would have had sufficient willpower to resist.

Did she still love him?

Oh god, no. That couldn't be it. It was just being back here, talking about all this stuff. What she was feeling was nostalgia for something that had once been beautiful.

But what if it *was* more?

She allowed herself the luxury of imagining them back together. How would that work? She didn't have to go back to New York if she didn't want to. She'd promised Zach that she'd walk the red carpet with him for the New York premiere but after that she had no commitments. She could write anywhere, even here in Sleepy Hollow. There was the blog to consider. She could hardly write a blog about being a foreigner in Manhattan if she didn't live there anymore. But who knew how much longer she'd have that gig for anyway? Now that she wasn't the future Mrs Zach Carlton she fully expected her 'star power' to dwindle — thank god — but along with the loss of celebrity status would be the loss of the type of jobs that went along with it. No matter. If that happened it would give her more time to focus on her writing. And Ryan.

They'd live at his farm, of course. He'd spent years saving for his own place so he wouldn't give it up easily. That was okay. It was a nice property. The house had good bones. It just needed a woman's touch to inject a bit of warmth and style to add to its rustic charm.

Her mind's eye started with the kitchen. It was structurally okay, and the circa-1950s kitchen cabinets were actually pretty funky. A lick of paint, new chairs and some cute retro accessories and it would be perfect. She let her imagination run wild, picturing what she could do in each of the rooms. Of course she hadn't seen the entire house yet, but she imagined there were at least two bedrooms...

Her excitement escaped as quickly as the air in a popped balloon. There was one very big reason she and Ryan could never be together and that reason inhabited the second bedroom.

Ella.

Dear god, she couldn't even contemplate raising her own biological child, let alone anyone else's. Of course it could never work. Obviously Ryan was one step ahead of her.

We can both move on now, and maybe even have a real go at being friends.

Of course he didn't want anything more than friendship. He had a child. A life. He didn't need the likes of her coming in and messing everything up. What was she thinking? Ryan wasn't declaring any interest in renewing their relationship. He was simply rewriting their miserable end. Maybe they did still have feelings for each other, but that couldn't be helped. It was over. He wanted them to be grown-ups, to be friends.

Only thirty-six hours ago she'd wanted exactly the same thing, but now she wasn't so sure.

CHAPTER
11

'More cake, Jo?' Steph's grandmother slid a piece of her famous apple teacake onto a plate in anticipation of an affirmative response.

Jo shook her head and clutched her belly. 'I've already eaten too much, Nanna Dawn.'

'Rubbish. You've only had one slice and you've barely eaten anything else all afternoon. It's a kitchen tea, not a Weight Watchers meeting. What's wrong with you? Pining for your man are you?'

The CWA ladies clucked and giggled.

If only they knew. Maybe Jo was pining, but it wasn't for the man Nanna Dawn had in mind. Ever since her talk with Ryan her insides had been churning uncomfortably. She recognised it was impossible for them to be together, but now that she'd stopped feeling so angry over what had happened in their past she couldn't stop the *if only* thoughts from cluttering up her head.

She smiled at the sprightly old woman who'd been like a grandmother to her for as long as she could remember. 'Give me a break, Dawnie. I've got a bridesmaid's dress to fit into, you know.'

Steph raised her champagne glass and winked at Dawn. 'Good on you, Nanna, Fatten her up a bit. We don't want her outshining the bride on the big day.'

'I will have one of those,' Jo said, nodding her head at Steph's glass. She walked over to bench where Steph was pouring bubbly into flutes and put her arm around her friend's shoulders. 'I wouldn't worry about anyone outshining you, my friend. I've never seen a more radiant bride-to-be. You're positively glowing with happiness.' She picked up one of the freshly filled glasses and raised it in an impromptu toast. 'To Steph, the best friend a girl could have and the most beautiful bride in the world.'

'To Steph,' the ladies echoed in unison.

Steph hugged her tight. 'I'm so glad you came home early, Jo. It's wonderful to have you here to share in the excitement. I promise I'll do the same for you when your turn comes.'

Jenny raced over with her iPhone. 'Hold it right there, you two. I want to get a photo.' As she clicked away the ladies all oohed and ahhed and made noises about how cute the two brides-to-be were.

'We haven't heard anything about your wedding, Jo,' Jenny said. 'We're all dying to hear the details. Tell us all about it. We want to know all about Zach and all about your plans for the big day.'

Jo dismissed the request with a wave of her hand. 'This is Steph's day. You don't want to hear about me.'

Steph grinned. 'You're not getting out of it that easily, sunshine. I want to know just as much as everyone else. In my official capacity as the Bride, I command you to come clean.'

The guilt of deceiving her friend sat like a stone in Jo's stomach. It would be such a relief to get the truth out in the open, but no matter how much she longed to tell Steph about her break-up with Zach — and her unsettling feelings for Ryan — she couldn't. Not yet. A promise was a promise. Of course she trusted Steph, that went without saying. But over the last few years she'd learned a thing or two about life in the public eye. If Steph didn't know about the break-up she couldn't make an accidental faux pas. Besides, this was Steph's time to hog the limelight and she didn't want her mess of a life stealing even one tiny glint of that away.

'Really, there's nothing to tell.'

Jenny playfully slapped her wrist. 'Of course there is. Let's start with the date. Have you set one?'

Jo shook her head. 'Umm, not yet.'

'What about the dress?' Steph asked. 'Ooh, are you going to get it made by one of those fancy designers like, I don't know, the one who did Kate Middleton's dress —'

'Alexander McQueen,' said Dawn with an air of authority.

Jenny laughed. 'How do you know that, Mum? Anyway, isn't Alexander McQueen dead?'

'I read,' said Dawn, affecting an injured tone. 'And anyway, I meant the fashion house, not the man.'

As the ladies continued to swap bits and pieces of celebrity gossip Jo began to think she'd escaped the interrogation. She watched with affection, and a little bit of envy, the way Dawn, Jenny and Steph teased each other. The love and respect between the three generations of women was obvious. Her heart was filled with happiness for her friend and gratitude for the way the Fielding family always included her as if she were one of them. But she had her own mother and on days like this she couldn't help but feel sorrow for the relationship they never had and, now, never could have.

If Katherine didn't have dementia, if she still had the full use of her faculties, what would their relationship be like now? Would things have changed? The few times her mother had visited New York she'd turned down Jo's invitation to stay in her apartment, choosing to stay uptown at the Waldorf instead. She'd visited the apartment only once, screwing up her nose at Jo's decorating style. 'Daddy is perfectly happy to pay for some decent furniture, Johanna. I'm sure I've mentioned that before.'

'I like my furniture just fine, thank you.'

'If you say so,' Katherine sniffed.

She had been thrilled to lunch with Jo and Serena Collins, Jo's editor, though. Jo saw a whole other side of her mother that day — articulate, witty and charming. This was surely the Katherine that Daddy had fallen in love with all those years ago. She'd even managed to tell Serena that she and Jo's father were very pleased for Jo that her work would be published. It was the closest thing to a compliment Jo had ever received from her.

What would the real Katherine think of her now? Would she truly relish Jo's achievements or would she see her commercial success as selling out? Would she be thrilled or appalled that her daughter was engaged to a movie star? Would she be pleased or horrified to know that Jo had broken it off?

She suddenly became aware that Steph was trying to get her attention. 'Sorry,' she said. 'I was away with the fairies. What did you say?'

'The boys are kicking on at the pub after the footy. I reckon we should leave the ladies to do the washing up...' she flashed a cheeky grin at Jenny, '...and join them. What do you think?'

The churning in her stomach ramped up. By boys Steph meant Nate and Ryan. How could she face him feeling like this? But Steph was looking at her with pleading eyes and she knew that a refusal would seem churlish. 'Sure, why not?'

'How are you getting there?' Jenny asked. 'You've both been drinking.'

'I've only had half a glass of bubbly,' Jo said. 'I'm fine to drive. I promise I won't drink at the pub.'

'Won't drink? What fun is that?' Steph protested.

'Why don't you leave your car here, sweetheart?' Jenny said. 'I'll get Mick to drive you into town and he can come get you both later.'

Stuck at the pub with no car? Not a good idea. 'Oh no, that's really not necessary. I'm not much of a drinker these days anyway.'

'If you're sure?'

Jo ignored Steph's dagger looks and nodded. 'Of course. I'll make sure Steph gets home safely. Promise.'

'Alright, off you go then. Have fun, you two, and make sure the rest of the bridal party don't get themselves into too much trouble.'

When Jo walked into the pub behind Steph, Ryan's breath caught in his throat. Every time he saw her unexpectedly he was struck by how beautiful she'd become. The pictures in the women's magazines didn't do her justice. He feigned disinterest in all the media coverage she received, but every now and then curiosity got the better of him and he sneaked a look at his mum's latest copy of *New Idea*. The woman on the page never looked like his Joey. In the pictures she was always plastered in make-up, with her hair in some god-awful unnatural 'style'. And she always had the same stupid fake smile plastered on her face.

Tonight she was dressed in jeans and a simple white shirt. Sure, she still had the bloody enormous handbag — what the hell was she carrying around in that thing anyway? — and a pair of ridiculously high-heeled boots, but overall the look was fuss free. She looked more like the girl he used to know. As she walked towards the bar she was laughing at something Steph was saying. She tossed back her head and he remembered what it was like to watch that mane of wavy hair cascading over her bare shoulders as she moved above him.

He watched her notice him. Her eyes widened slightly and then her beautiful, natural smile disappeared and was replaced with her Hollywood one.

He downed the remainder of his beer in an effort to quell the sadness that abruptly engulfed him. He would never be over her, he could never have her, and now she couldn't even honestly look him in the eye. He raised his glass and nodded at the bartender. 'Give us another one, Steve.'

'Drowning your sorrows after the Lions' big loss, mate?'

'Yeah, something like that.'

Jo watched as he turned his back and ordered another beer. He'd seen her, there was no doubt in her mind about that. Their eyes had locked for a millisecond before he turned away. So after everything that had passed between them these last few days, nothing had changed. They were back to forced civility in company. Except that something had changed. When she'd first clapped eyes on Ryan at the footy ground — was it only a week ago? — she'd felt anger and hostility. Now she felt like her heart was breaking in two.

Nate slid off his barstool and headed towards them. He embraced Steph, planting a kiss on her lips before turning his attention to Jo. 'Hey Jo. Good to see you. Things have been so crazy busy around here that I haven't had the chance to catch up with you properly yet. Come here and give me a hug.' Before she could answer he enveloped her in a bear hug.

'Good to see you too, Nate.' Her eyes pricked with tears of happiness for her friends and a tinge of sorrow for herself. Steph was so lucky. Nate was a great guy and he clearly adored Steph. It was obvious to the world that they were meant for each other. Their love was simple and honest and completely uncomplicated. Was it wrong to be a tiny bit envious of what they had?

She gave him a tight squeeze before pulling away.

'What's wrong?' Nate asked. Obviously her eyes were still glassy.

She gave him her widest grin. 'Nothing, you big oaf. You just about squeezed the life out of me.'

Nate returned the grin and socked her in the arm for good measure. 'Let me get you a drink to make amends. What's your poison?'

'Diet Coke, thanks.'

'What? No bubbly? What about a wine or a beer? Or don't you drink beer anymore?'

She screwed up her nose. 'Out of the habit, I guess. Haven't found an American beer I like.'

'Well you won't find any sissy Yank beers here. Do you want a Crownie?'

'Nah, honestly, Nate. Diet Coke. I'm driving.'

He nodded and headed to the bar. Ryan appeared to be engaged in conversation with the bloke sitting beside him and Steph had been set upon by a couple of local girls that Jo couldn't quite place. Steph caught her eye and beckoned her over but Jo shook her head and indicated she was headed to the bathroom.

Fortunately the Ladies was empty. Jo dug in her handbag for some lip gloss and took a moment at the mirror, freshening up her face while she mentally prepared herself to go back into the bar and face a man who turned her insides to jelly every time their eyes locked. A man she could never have.

The mirror revealed bags under her eyes. Was it any wonder? Between the jetlag and the emotional rollercoaster she seemed to be on she'd hardly had a decent night's sleep since she left New York. All this emotion and nostalgia was exhausting. Since she'd been home the slightest thing would set her off. Some days she felt like she was permanently misty eyed. Her New York friends would be horrified at all this sentimentality. Over there she had a reputation for being resilient and practical. The girl most likely to bounce back. The sooner this wedding was over and she could go back to her nice stable life the better.

Except she had no idea what that life would look like once her break-up with Zach became public. She still had her blog — for now at least — and her writing. Her third book was due out in the fall and her agent was currently negotiating the sale of the movie rights to the second book. This time Lydia was hoping to secure more creative control for her but in any case money wouldn't be a problem.

Her social circle would dwindle, there was no doubt about that. Most of her friends were Zach's friends and she knew that they would fall away once they heard the engagement was off. But her other friends — the ones that she'd made at NYU, when Zach Carlton was just a face on a poster and not a fixture in her life — would still be there for her. And she certainly wouldn't miss all the Hollywood-style social events that went along with being the partner of a famous actor.

She pinched her cheeks to get some colour into them, the way Nanna Dawn had taught her when she was just a little girl. Despite all the emotional turmoil brought on by being here, she would miss her Gully friends doubly when she went back to the States. Nobody knew her the way Steph and her family did. It was hard seeing Ryan, especially now that she'd realised she still harboured feelings for him. But she wasn't going to let that get in the way of spending time with her oldest mates.

A last lick of gloss, an extra-deep breath, and she was ready to face anything.

CHAPTER
12

Ryan downed another beer as he watched her leave the bar area. Goddammit, why did he have to feel like this? It had been years. Why the hell couldn't he just get over her?

All that crap he'd given her about being friends had been a total crock. He wasn't sure who he was trying to convince when he came up with that one, because the physical reaction he got every time he laid eyes on her should have alerted him to the fact that friendship would never be enough.

There'd been other women, of course. When Carly died he had gone on a bit of bender and done things that he'd rather not think about. Booze and god knows how many women. After a couple of months of putting up with him being a total arse, Bec had called him on his behaviour. 'Ella's your child, not mine,' his sister-in-law had said. 'I love her, but she needs her dad. You need to start acting like a father, Ryan, or you'll end up losing that little girl.'

It was the kick in the pants he needed. From that moment on Ella came first. He vowed that he would never bring a woman home unless he knew beyond a shadow of a doubt that she was worthy of Ella's love as well as his own. To date no one had fit the bill.

He'd had liaisons, of course. He was no monk. But they'd been discreet affairs, where no promises were made and none sought. It was enough. Or it had been until Joey rolled back into town.

Nate reclaimed the stool beside him. 'Geez mate, steady on. I haven't seen you knock back the beers like that in ages.'

'Settle down. I've only had a couple. Are you my mum now?'

Nate shrugged. 'Don't want to have to carry you out of here, that's all. You're not thinking of driving are you?'

'Give me a break. I'm not a total tool. Johnno's giving me a lift.'

Nate slapped on the shoulder. 'You gonna be alright with...' He nodded his head towards the spot where Jo had been standing.

'Yeah, course I will, mate. It's all sorted. Promise.'

'Sweet. I'm getting a round. Do you want another beer?'

Ryan grinned. 'Am I allowed, Mum?'

'Give it a rest, would you? I take it that's a yes?'

Ryan nodded and swivelled around on his stool to look at the crowd while Nate ordered. It wasn't a bad turn-out, especially as the Lions had taken a beating this afternoon. He saw Jo coming towards the bar and couldn't help but notice the sea of heads turning in her wake. Male heads. Max Callahan stood up to deliberately block her path, and then grabbed her as if to dance. Ryan was on his feet and moving across the floor before he'd had a chance to think about what he was doing. Max twirled her around a couple of times and released her, laughing, so that she and Ryan were standing face to face.

'Are you okay?'

'Of course,' she said, still laughing. 'Just having a bit of fun.'

He nodded. 'Okay. Sometimes, Max can be a bit —'

'Ryan, it's okay. You don't have to protect me. I can look after myself. I'm a New Yorker.'

She was smiling and he knew she'd meant it as a joke, but her words cut him to the quick. It was a reminder that they inhabited different worlds these days. She was an internationally famous writer engaged to some movie-star wanker and he was just a country hick.

His face must have given him away because she started to back-pedal immediately. 'Sorry. I just meant —'

'Don't worry. I know what you meant. Forget it.'

They stood together awkwardly for a moment, neither of them able to come up with a neutral topic of conversation. Thankfully Nate arrived with their drinks, providing welcome relief from the escalating tension.

'Hey you two. How are you doing? Having fun? The old pub's going off tonight. Can't remember when I last saw so many people in here. Reckon it might have something to do with our celebrity guest here.' He looked at Ryan for confirmation. 'Am I right?'

'Yeah, could be,' Ryan said. 'They're certainly not here to look at your ugly mug.'

'Here to see me?' Jo shook her head. 'I highly doubt it. I hardly know most of these people.'

'Doesn't mean they don't want to check you out. Like it or not you're a star in these parts. You've put Linden Gully on the map, Jo. Everyone wants a piece of the action. Their little brush with fame,' Nate said.

'Surely you're used to drawing a crowd?' Ryan said.

Jo shook her head. 'Me? If I'm on my own, no way. I mean think about it, how many best-selling authors can you identify on sight?'

Ryan and Nate shrugged in unison.

'Exactly. Even big fans might not know what an author looks like.'

'But when you're with your...' Ryan trailed off. The word 'fiancé' stuck in his throat.

'Zach? Sure, sometimes he draws a bit of a crowd. But that really only happens in L.A. In New York people are pretty cool about celebrities of any type. They tend to just say "hey" and then leave us alone.'

New York, where everything, even the man on the street, was better. Frankly he didn't want to hear another word about the place. 'Maybe you should go mingle with your adoring public,' Ryan said. 'Don't let the likes of us monopolise your time.'

Nate chimed in. 'Go on. Give the people what they want.'

She shook her head and laughed. 'You two are first-class idiots,' she said, and in that moment a flash of the old Joey was visible.

Ryan and Nate heckled her until she gave in out of exasperation. She looked around to see if there was anyone she knew well enough to strike up a conversation with. She scanned the bar, looking for familiar faces, when she noticed Kelly Prescott and Laura Baxter sitting at the table over by the jukebox.

Kelly caught her staring and gestured for Jo to join them. Dammit! She couldn't ignore her without looking like a stuck-up cow. She plastered a smile on her face and made her way to their table.

'Hi Kelly. Hi Laura. Lovely to see you two.'

'Oh Jo, it's so brave of you to be out and about tonight. Come and sit down with us and relax for a minute,' Kelly said, pulling out a chair and indicating for Jo to sit.

Brave?

'Er, thanks Kelly. It is a bit daunting seeing all these people here. I have to say there's quite a few I don't know, and others who are familiar to me but I can't place them.'

Kelly and Laura exchanged a look.

'It's okay,' Laura said, smiling. 'You don't have to pretend with us. We know all about what's happened. You must be devastated. I can't believe you've had the courage to even leave the house.'

Had Laura been drinking? Because she couldn't for the life of her work out what she was on about. 'I'm sorry, Laura. I have no idea what you're talking about.'

Kelly's eyes widened and her hand flew to her mouth.

'You don't know, do you?' Laura said. 'Oh Jo, I'm so sorry. We assumed you would know by now. I mean the magazine came out days ago, but they don't get delivered here until Saturday.'

'Will one of you just tell me what's going on?'

Kelly dug into her oversized knock-off Louis Vuitton handbag and put the latest copy of *Gloss* magazine on the table. She slid it across to Jo. 'Turn to the back page.'

There, under the heading *Celebrity Gloss,* was a half-page photo of Zach kissing Kiara Blake.

CHAPTER
13

Rumours of an apparent break-up between Zach Carlton and his Aussie fiancée, Johanna Morgan, gained traction this week when Carlton was spotted canoodling with Hollywood Kisses *co-star, Kiara Blake.*

Sources say that the 'natural chemistry' that developed between Blake and Carlton on set has developed into a full-blown affair in recent days. This shot was snapped outside the Hurricane Club on Park Ave, where the couple had reportedly indulged in a romantic candlelit dinner.

The screenplay for Hollywood Kisses *is adapted from Morgan's best-selling novel of the same name.*

Mr Carlton has so far refused to comment, with a spokesperson saying that he would release a joint statement with Ms Morgan in the 'near future'.

Ms Morgan is currently visiting family in Australia and was not available for comment.

Jo slammed the magazine down so hard that Kelly jumped.

Joint statement! What bloody joint statement? She was totally blindsided by this turn of events. Why the hell hadn't Zach contacted her to give her a heads-up? Or Lydia, for that matter? Okay, it might not strictly be in her agent's job description, but she and Lydia were friends, weren't they?

'I'm really sorry, Jo. This must be absolutely devastating for you.' Kelly's words were sympathetic but Jo could see the barely contained glee on her face.

'Devastating isn't the word.' She stood up and turned to go.

'If there's anything we can do for you,' Laura said, her voice condescendingly saccharine, 'you know that we're here for you.'

'Actually there is one thing...' Jo turned back to see Laura's eyes widen in anticipation.

'Yes?'

Jo leaned over and snatched the magazine back. 'I'll take this. Thanks.' She swung on her heel and made a beeline for Ryan.

'Jesus, Jo. What did those two say to you? You look like you're ready to punch someone.' Ryan laid his hand on her shoulder. 'Seriously, are you okay?'

She shook her head. 'Not really. I want to go home. Have you seen Steph anywhere? I'm her designated driver.'

'She and Nate are playing pool with Johnno and Soph.'

Jo flopped down on the stool beside him and let out a large sigh. 'We'll be here all night. You know what she's like when she starts playing pool.'

Ryan's lips formed one of his lopsided smiles — the same smile that had made her fall in love with him all those years ago. 'Yeah, good luck prising that billiard cue from her hand.'

Jo found herself smiling back.

'Listen, you stay here. I'll find Steph and see if I can sort something else. There's bound to be someone here who can give her a lift.'

'No, no. It's okay. I can wait until she's done.'

But Ryan was already on his feet. 'I'm on it, alright? We're your mates, Jo. We look after each other. You know that, right?'

She nodded as he wandered off to find the others. While she waited, Jo stared at the diamond ring on her finger. It had always been slightly loose, something she'd been meaning to get fixed but had never got around to. Zach was always warning her she would lose it one day if she didn't sort something out. Today was that day. She removed the ring from her finger and slid it into her pocket.

In less than a minute both Steph and Ryan were at her side.

Steph slid her arm around Jo's waist. 'Ryan says you're upset. What's going on?'

There was no point keeping it a secret. If Kelly and Laura knew, chances were half the town had already been informed and the remaining half would know by morning. Jo opened the magazine to the offending page and passed it to Steph.

'Oh fuck,' Steph said. 'Oh, Jo, honey, I don't know what to say.' She slipped both arms around Jo's waist and pulled her close.

'What?' said Ryan. 'What is it? Let me see.'

Steph pulled back and raised her eyebrows at Jo, who simply nodded. Steph handed the magazine to Ryan.

'That arsehole! How could he even —'

Jo put her hand up and motioned for him to stop. 'It's not what you think —'

'Looks pretty bloody obvious to me.'

Jo shook her head. 'I'm not upset. Well, I am but not for the reason you think.' She felt her face flooding with colour. 'It's not all that surprising, really. Zach and I split up a few weeks back.'

'What?' Steph's mouth dropped open. 'Why didn't you tell me?' She folded her arms across her body. 'We're supposed to be best friends. Don't you trust me with your secrets anymore?'

'Of course I do. It wasn't that. It was Zach's idea to keep it a secret. I was the one who broke it off with him. I felt terrible, so when he

asked me to keep quiet until after the premiere of *Hollywood Kisses*
I agreed.'

Steph's mouth was set in a hard line. Obviously she was hurt.
'But you could have told me. I know how to keep a secret.'

'Oh, Steph, I know you can. It wasn't that. When I came home
and saw how happy you were I didn't want anything to burst your
bubble. I didn't want the lead-up to your wedding to be marred by
my problems.'

Steph gave her a gentle shove. 'You idiot. Your problems are my
problems. Got it?'

Jo nodded. 'Sorry.'

'Right then. Don't let it happen again.'

Ryan picked up the magazine and glanced at the photo one more
time. 'Jo, I don't get it. If you've broken up why are you so upset
about this photo?'

'I'm not upset, I'm angry. We had an agreement about how this
would play out, how we'd manage the media and so on.'

Ryan and Steph exchanged a glance and she laughed, the thin
tinny noise sounding unconvincing even to her own ears. 'I know,
I know. I sound like a tosser. But this kind of stuff is important
career-wise.'

Steph's brow creased in confusion. 'How?'

'It's in both our interests for the movie to do well. If it tanks some
of that negativity will wash up on me. It could affect future publishing
contracts, the success of the next book, whether I can sell the movie
rights and so on.' Heat crept up her neck and into her face. Spoken
out loud her concerns seemed trivial. It was hard for her friends to
understand the impact that public perception could have on her
career. Through no fault of her own her success had become closely
linked to Zach's. His star was on the rise, but now that she was being
cast in the role of discarded girlfriend she wondered how long it

would be before all her industry connections dried up. 'Look I know this probably makes me seem like some kind of high-maintenance wanker but I need to get home and see if I can contact Zach or my agent, just to see what's going on. I need to know if this story is a beat-up or if there's been any other media coverage. I'm sorry, Steph. I don't want to put a dampener on your night but I need to go.'

Steph hugged her. 'It's okay. You do what you need to do. Will you be okay on your own? Johnno said he'll give Nate and me a lift home, but I'm happy to come with you if you want company.'

'No, no, please don't worry, I'll be fine. I just need to sort this out and work out what sort of response, if any, I should make. I don't want to spoil your night.'

Ryan put his empty glass back on the bar. 'Can I get a lift with you, Jo? I've had my fill for tonight.'

He hadn't changed. Ryan was always chivalrous. He loved to play knight in shining armour to a damsel in distress. 'It's okay Ryan. You don't need to rescue me. I'll be fine on my own.'

'I wasn't trying to rescue you. I genuinely need a lift. Johnno was supposed to be driving me but looks like he's settled in for a snooker challenge. I don't want too late a night. I have a six-year-old human alarm clock to consider. So if it's not too much trouble...'

'It's no trouble, but are you sure you're not just being nice?'

He performed his old Scout salute. 'Scout's honour.'

Jo laughed. 'Sorry to have doubted you.'

Steph kissed them both. 'See you later. I'll call you in the morning,' she said, looking at Jo.

Five kilometres went by without either of them speaking. Jo's anger at Zach receded into the background the minute Ryan slammed the Jeep door shut and buckled himself in. His physical presence was making her belly do backflips.

For all her protestations to the contrary, she was glad not to be on her own. Ryan's chivalry was one of the things that attracted her to him in the first place. He was a rare find — a man who treated a woman as his equal and yet knew how to make her feel like a princess when it counted.

And she couldn't deny that he was looking particularly easy on the eye tonight. Despite it being mid-winter and freezing cold outside, the pub was always warm, often too warm. Ryan had removed his jacket inside and not bothered to put it back on before getting in the car. He was dressed in a simple white t-shirt that left his tanned muscular arms available for her to ogle. A man wearing a close fitting t-shirt and a pair of well-loved jeans did it for her every time.

When she was with Zach women often commented on how lucky she was to be with such an attractive man. She always smiled and agreed, but in reality Zach was not her type physically. Sure he had a fit, toned body and he was always beautifully groomed — hair cut just so, nails manicured, skin exfoliated. He wore suits cut from the finest cloth, tailored especially for him, and all his casual clothes came complete with designer labels. But he had the soft hands of a man who'd never held a shovel or an axe.

Zach's wit and warmth had drawn her to him at a time when she was in desperate need of company. The attraction grew out of fun and friendship. But she'd never felt the powerful physical pull that she was experiencing with Ryan right now.

To be honest it had been a while since she'd been satisfied in the bedroom. In fact, now that she thought about it she couldn't recall the last time she and Zach had made love. Their schedules had been impossible for the last month or so, and although they'd attended quite a few functions together they'd barely had any alone time. When they did get some time alone they were both so exhausted they generally just fell asleep. Lovemaking, when it happened, was quick and perfunctory rather than wild and passionate.

Sitting this close to Ryan had her imagination going deliciously crazy. Even when they were young, he'd known how to turn her on. They were each other's first and they'd grown and learned together. Ryan knew exactly what she liked and what she didn't. Would it be different now that they were older and more experienced?

As she fantasised about being held in those muscular arms, surrendering herself to a man who knew what she wanted, she was startled to realise the object of her desire was talking to her.

'Sorry, Ryan, I was miles away. What did you say?' Thank god it was dark so he couldn't see her face. She was sure it had turned beet red.

'Can I ask you a question? You don't have to answer if you don't want to.'

'Sure. Fire away.'

'This guy, Zach, did you love him?'

'I thought I did.'

'Huh.'

She knew that tone. He was holding something back. 'What?'

'Nothing.'

'Come on Ryan. You've clearly got something to say. Spit it out.'

'I don't know. It's just, well, you don't seem too cut up about the break-up and I can't help but wonder...'

'Wonder what?' Where was he going with this?

'Why you agreed to marry him. I mean you loved me, at least you said you did. But when I asked you to be my wife, you said no. And yet this guy pops the question with some cheesy YouTube gimmick and you said yes immediately.'

'I thought we'd sorted this out. I explained why —'

'You did, and believe me I'm not trying to go back there, Jo, really. My timing was bad. We both made mistakes. What's done is done.'

'So what's your point?'

He shrugged. 'I guess I'm wondering what your motive was.'

'My motive? What are you saying? Are you insinuating what I think you are? That I had some type of career motive, or...' She took her eyes off the road to look at him. 'Oh. My. God. You think I'm a gold digger.'

'Jo, watch out!'

She returned her eyes to the road to see another car coming right towards them. 'Oh shit!' During her concentration lapse the car had begun to drift onto the wrong side of the road. She managed to swerve the car back to the right side just in time. 'God, I'm so sorry. I could have killed us both.' Her hands were shaking so hard she could barely hold the steering wheel.

'It's okay. We're both fine. I think maybe we should pull over for a bit, eh? There's a clearing up ahead, in front of the old school house. You can pull over there and take a minute to catch your breath.'

Jo nodded without speaking, her concentration now firmly focused on the road ahead. In less than a minute she saw the spot Ryan was talking about and pulled as far off the road as she could get.

Once she'd switched off the engine, Ryan reached over to clasp her still trembling hand. 'Hey, it's okay.'

'I'm so sorry,' she said. 'I shouldn't have taken my eyes off the road. I just was so...I just couldn't believe you'd think those things about me. You know me, Ryan, maybe better than anyone else in the world.'

'I don't know,' he said quietly. 'I feel I don't really know you at all anymore. It's been a long time, Jo, and a lot has changed. For both of us.'

'Underneath I'm still the same girl you fell in love with.'

'Are you?' His voice was calm and measured. 'Explain it to me, then. Explain to me how you came to be engaged to a man that you don't really love. A man that means so little to you that when you see a photo of him kissing another woman your main concern is how this will affect your career.'

Anger bubbled up inside her. Part of her wanted to tell him to get stuffed. What business was it of his? But she couldn't tolerate the idea of him thinking she was some talentless gold digger, sleeping her way to success.

'I might not have loved Zach the way I should have but that doesn't mean I didn't care about him. I did. A lot, in fact. So much so that when he asked me to marry him so publicly I couldn't bear to see him humiliated and so I said yes, even though I wasn't sure about the idea.'

'But surely you could have told him afterwards?'

She sighed. 'Life's just not that simple for people in the public eye, Ryan. The whole thing took on a life of its own. There were magazine and TV interviews, a huge engagement party...'

'So you just went along for the ride and let the poor chump think you were going to go through with it? Jesus, I almost feel sorry for him now.'

'No! It wasn't like that. When he asked me I wasn't sure, but as time went on I decided why not? Zach and I had been together for a while; we were practically living together anyway. We had lots of fun, he made me laugh, you know? And I figured that was probably the best I could hope for.'

'What do you mean by that?'

'I knew I was never ever going to find anyone to totally fill my heart again. I loved Zach the best I could. I gave him everything I had left, but I never loved him the way I loved you.'

CHAPTER
14

After all these years these were the words he'd waited to hear. That she loved him, that no one else could replace him. A spark of hope ignited inside him. Maybe it was a the booze talking but he was starting to think there was a chance that things might still work out between them. The obstacles that had stood in their way yesterday seemed to be disappearing. She wasn't engaged. She didn't love someone else.

And she'd just admitted that she could never love anyone the way she loved him.

So she lived in New York. That could change, couldn't it? He squashed down the tiny seed of doubt that started to creep into his reasoning. Of course it could change. She was a writer. She could do that anywhere. It might take a bit of organisation, but it could be done.

Naturally, they would have to take things slowly. There was Ella to consider. But Jo would make a fantastic step-mum. He just knew the two of them would hit it off given some time.

Okay, back up a bit.

Thinking about Joey as the mother of his child was maybe taking things a bit too far. But maybe in time...

'What are you thinking?' she asked.

'I'm thinking about kissing you.'

'Hold that thought,' she said. 'There's something I need to do first.'

He watched as she opened the car window and then dug around in her pocket for something. After a second she pulled out her diamond engagement ring.

'What are you doing?' he asked.

'Reclaiming my life,' she said as she threw the ring out the window.

His mouth was on hers and it was as if the years had melted away. He was tender at first, teasing her with slow, gentle kisses that had her aching for more. His stubble gently grazed her chin and his strong, work-callused hands cradled her head, her hair tangled in his fingers. She couldn't help but think that Zach's carefully cultivated attractiveness was no match for Ryan's raw masculinity.

Ryan wanted her. There was no doubt about that. And the feeling was mutual. The desire she'd conjured up during her earlier fantasy returned with breathtaking urgency. She wanted to be closer to him, to press her body against his. She deepened the kiss, willing him to take the next step. Her need to have those strong hands move over her body was growing by the second.

His lips moved to her neck, brushing their way down to her collarbone and back up until they reached the tender skin behind her ear. Each ragged breath he took echoed in her ear, causing the heat between her thighs to intensify.

She groaned and slid her hand up under his t-shirt, and sucked in a breath of delight when she felt the ripple of well-defined muscle there. She let her hand wander over his taut belly and up over those magnificent pecs and back down again. All that physical farm labour was definitely paying off. Her hand came to rest at the top of his jeans.

This was sweet agony. She wanted his mouth on her breast, his hand —

'Hey, hey...' He drew back from her. 'Take it easy. If we're going to do this, let's take it slow.' He gently pushed the hair away from her face and planted a small kiss on her lips. 'I don't want to rush into anything, Joey. We need to slow down and think about what we're doing.'

Oh god, he was going to back out. She wiggled her fingers beneath the waistband of his jeans. 'What's to think about? I want you. You want me. We're both adults.'

He grabbed her hand and gently pulled it away. 'Well for starters, if we're going to make love I don't think the Jeep is the most romantic location.'

She giggled. 'I guess you're right. Why don't you come back to Yarrapinga with me? We can light the fire...' she put her hand back where it had been, this time pushing further down, '...and see what happens.'

He groaned appreciatively before once more removing her hand. 'Okay. But I can't stay. You know that, right? I need to be home when Ella wakes up in the morning.'

She nodded as she turned the key to start the Jeep's ancient engine. 'I understand.'

The last five kilometres seemed to go on forever. Neither of them spoke for a minute or two and then Ryan, obviously still plagued by thoughts of Zach, broke the silence. 'So what did happen then? Why did you eventually decide you couldn't marry him?'

Jo hesitated. This was not the conversation she wanted to be having right now, but if she avoided the question it looked like she had something to hide. 'He started to talk about kids,' she said. 'He wanted to start a family right away.'

'And you didn't want that? Surely you could have compromised a bit, got him to agree to wait a little while?'

Jo sighed. 'I guess talking about raising a family together made me really think about what I was committing to, the gravity of what I was doing.'

'So you didn't want to have kids with him? Is that what made you realise you didn't love him enough to marry him?'

'I guess I always knew it on some level. The baby discussion just brought it all to a head.'

'But you do want kids, right?'

Jo let out a long slow breath. Damn Ryan and his practical side. She was perfectly happy getting hot and heavy in the car, but his 'let's slow down' routine was leading them down a path she didn't want to follow. But this was Ryan, and she couldn't lie. 'No. I've thought about it a lot, believe me, and I don't want to be a parent.'

'Wow. I have to say I'm kind of surprised. I always imagined you'd be eager to start a family.'

'Really? Whatever gave you that idea?'

He shrugged. 'I don't know. The way you mothered all the baby animals on your farm. And you were always envious of Steph and me. You were always complaining about your lack of siblings. Plus I remember us talking about having kids one day in the future.'

'I was a kid back then. All that talk was just...I don't know... fantasy, play-acting. I guess back then I probably did think I would have kids one day. I thought that's what all grown-ups did. It didn't occur to me I would have a choice. But as I got older I realised that I didn't have to procreate. It wasn't, you know, mandatory. So I started to think maybe I wouldn't. God, Ryan, nobody knows better than you what a huge responsibility being a parent is. I just don't know that I'm cut out for that.'

He didn't respond.

'Maybe we should change the subject?' she suggested. This conversation was definitely pouring cold water on the heat that they'd generated just minutes before.

'Actually, you know what, Jo? I'm thinking maybe this isn't such a great idea.'

Her heart sank. 'What do you mean?'

'We sleep together, then what?'

'We do it again?' she laughed, trying to lighten the darkness that seemed to be descending upon them.

'I'm serious, Jo. Where can it possibly lead? You're going back to New York in a couple of weeks.'

'Does it have to lead anywhere? We're adults, Ryan. We want each other. Why can't we just let ourselves enjoy the moment? Maybe make ourselves some nice memories to replace the hostile ones we've both been harbouring these past few years.'

'A quick fuck for old times' sake? Really? Is that what you want?'

'I wouldn't put it like that.'

'Sex with no strings, then? Is that what you're suggesting?'

'Well...yes. I guess so.'

He was quiet for a moment and Jo thought perhaps she had convinced him. Eventually he shook his head. 'I'm sorry, Jo. I don't think I can do that. Not with you.'

'But I thought —'

'I'm sorry. I should never let things go as far as they did back there. I've had a few beers and my decision-making is probably not as good as it should be. Believe me, it's not because I don't want to. Right now I can think of nothing better than peeling off every piece of clothing you're wearing and making love to you all night.'

'You can do that. What's standing in our way?'

'The thing is Jo, you might be able to do this and walk away, but I don't think I can. There's too much history between us for that to work. You broke my heart once and I'm not willing to risk that happening a second time.'

He was right, of course. She knew that. It clearly wasn't a sensible choice. But sensible was overrated, dammit. She winced. Not in Ryan Galloway's world it wasn't. He was the most practical man she'd ever met. 'Fine,' she said, sounding more pissed off than she'd intended. 'I'll drive you home.'

'Jo, please don't be angry. I just want us to be okay with each other. We agreed to be friends and that's all I can offer you. Please say we're good.'

'Yes, yes, we're good.' As good as a person who was not getting the sex she had anticipated could be. 'Look, I know you're right and I know it was probably a dumb idea. I guess I just got carried away in the moment.' She laughed a little to break the tension. 'I guess you could say I've been going through a dry spell.'

Ryan shifted uncomfortably in his seat. 'I see. Well...as long as we're okay. I don't want things to be awkward between us.'

'We're fine,' Jo said, as they crossed the cattle grid at the entry to Ryan's property. 'Hunky dory. Promise.'

CHAPTER
15

After another night of broken sleep, Jo woke to the sound of rain on the roof. *Great.* She wasn't looking forward to driving to the nursing home to collect her mother as it was. Now she would have to contend with slippery roads as she negotiated the trip. At least she had a handle on the Jeep's gearbox now.

Despite the tricky driving conditions, almost every moment of the trip to Bellington was filled with thoughts of Ryan...and Zach. Last night she had been humiliated twice, by two different men in two different hemispheres. Surely that had to be some kind of record?

Of the two, the Zach problem was the least troubling, even though it had the potential to cause the more negative consequences. It was out of her control for the moment, although her agent had confirmed the worst. The story was all over the media back home and appeared to be true.

'Why didn't you let me know what was going on?' Jo had asked, when she finally got hold of Lydia.

'I didn't want to worry you until I had all the facts. I didn't think you'd hear about it all the way down there.' Frustratingly, Lydia was one of those New Yorkers who thought that anywhere outside of Manhattan was a backwater. Australia might as well be another planet as far as she was concerned. As agents went, though, she was the best. She went above and beyond the call of duty when it came to Jo's career. It seemed she'd had already found a PR firm to manage the situation on Jo's behalf.

After thanking Lydia profusely for all her efforts, Jo ended the call and made the one she'd been dreading. As she expected, Zach was not answering his phone. In a way that wasn't such a bad thing. What could she say to him? You broke our agreement to keep our break-up private? It sounded trivial even to her own ears, even though she knew his choice to go public was far more strategic — and important —than it might seem to the casual observer. In any case, the situation was as much in hand as it could be.

The Ryan problem was making her stomach clench and her head throb. It wasn't really a problem, was it? So they'd kissed. So she'd made it clear — very clear — that she was more than happy for that kissing to end with them rolling around naked on her four-poster bed. He'd said 'No thanks.' So what?

She'd propositioned him and, oh god, he'd said no. She felt her face flush. How could she have been so...so presumptuous as to think that if she offered herself he'd be unable to refuse?

It was embarrassing, but that was all. They'd go back to being cautiously friendly, as they'd agreed.

No harm done.

If that was the case, why did his rejection sting so much? Why did she feel like there was a gaping hole in her heart?

The sight of the nursing home pushed all thoughts of Ryan to the back of her mind. Earlier in the week she'd been adamant that a home visit would do her mother the world of good. She'd convinced a reluctant medical team that her mum would enjoy being among her things for the day. At the time she was full of guilt, and had the possibly misplaced idea that this would be an opportunity to spend some quality time with her mum. Who knew when she would be home again? Judging by the deterioration in her mother's physical condition, these few weeks might be the last chance she would have to see her mother alive.

The doctor warned her that it wouldn't be easy having her mother at home and she would have to watch her carefully. On the phone Jo had no qualms about convincing the doctor she was up to the task, but now, at the nursing-home entrance, slivers of doubt were creeping in.

'Look who's here, Katie,' Carol's singsong voice trilled as Jo entered the foyer. 'It's Johanna, here to take you out for the day.'

Katherine's face was expressionless. No spark of recognition lit her eyes as Jo leaned in to kiss her cheek.

'Are you ready? The car's just outside.'

Nothing. Jo's pulse began to accelerate. Maybe this wasn't such a great idea after all.

'I'll help you to the car, Katie. Lead the way, Johanna.'

No backing out now.

Once Katherine was safely buckled in, Carol handed Jo a bag of her mother's daily requirements. Jo opened the brown paper bag to see a pill bottle and — *oh dear god* — several pairs of incontinence underwear. The shock was clearly visible on her face as Carol said, 'Lately, she's had a few accidents. This is better...more dignified.'

A hard lump formed in Jo's throat as she nodded.

'She needs to take the pill with her evening meal. No later than six. And please have her back no later than eight p.m. I'm sure you understand that we run a skeleton staff on Sundays. I need her settled before the night shift comes in.'

Jo nodded her agreement. 'Of course.'

Carol pressed a business card into her hand. There was a handwritten phone number on the back. 'That's my personal number. Please don't hesitate to call me if any problems arise. I'm not officially on duty today, so I'll be off home in a minute, but I am more than happy to help out if any issues arise.'

Jo shook the older woman's hand and forced one of her Hollywood smiles. 'Thank you so much, Carol. Your personal attention is greatly appreciated.'

Katherine spoke her first words as they passed the *Linden Gully Population 390* sign. 'Where are we? What is this town?'

'Linden Gully, Mum. I'm taking you home to Yarrapinga.'

'Hole of a town,' Katherine muttered softly.

Jo wasn't sure if the comment was meant for her ears so she chose to ignore it. 'I have scones and jam for morning tea.'

Katherine perked up a little at the mention of scones. 'Homemade?'

Jo laughed. 'Yes, homemade.' Unable to sleep after the incident with Ryan, she had made several batches in the middle of the night.

'I do like a nice homemade scone.'

Luckily some things never changed.

To Jo's disappointment, their arrival at Yarrapinga didn't elicit any response from Katherine. She'd left the central heating on so the house was warm when they walked in through the back door to the kitchen. Jo plonked her handbag on the kitchen bench and put the paper bag Carol had given her on a high shelf in the pantry. 'Shall we have our cup of tea in here?'

'I'll take tea in the dining room. Thanks, dear.' The endearment was new but the insistence on every meal — even morning tea — being formal was not.

Jo nodded. 'I'll take you through.'

'No need for that. I'm sure I can find my way in my own house.'

She recognised it! Jo found herself grinning. This was a good idea after all. Maybe they'd get to have a proper conversation. She could tell Katherine about her life in New York...

'Why are you standing there grinning like a Cheshire cat, girl? I'm sure I don't pay you to stand around idly. You can make yourself useful and bring me my tea.'

Jo's heart sank at this abrupt change in mood. She had got her hopes up too soon. This day wasn't going to be easy. Then again, Katherine had never been easy.

At the sight of the china teapot and plate laden with scones Katherine's smile returned. Jo carefully placed the tray on the highly polished mahogany table. The dining-room table was her mother's pride and joy. As a child Jo knew that a single fingerprint left on the 'good mahogany' led to a stern lecture. She could only imagine what sort of punishment a scratch, no matter how accidental, might bring about.

Jo set the table with side plates and napkins, poured the tea and then placed a buttered scone on a plate and offered it to her mother. 'Jam?'

'Yes please. Aren't you kind?'

There was silence for a moment while Katherine tucked into her scone. 'Mmm, delicious,' she said as she delicately wiped the corners of her mouth with a linen napkin. 'You're a good cook. Are you married? Children?'

Jo shook her head. 'Neither.'

'Ah, very wise, very wise indeed. Marriage is overrated.'

Jo felt a pinprick of alarm. The last thing she wanted was her father's memory sullied. She offered Katherine another scone as a diversion, but Katherine shook her head.

'Oh no thanks. I've had plenty. One mustn't let oneself go. Standards are important, you know, even in this backwater town. It's very important for me to set a good example for my daughter.' She lowered her voice to a conspiratorial whisper. 'It's not as if she'll find any other decent role models in Linden Gully.'

Jo swallowed in an attempt to rid herself of the lump that was forming in her throat. 'What's she like, your daughter?'

Katherine smiled. 'Very clever, my Johanna, which is just as well, because she's too pretty for her own good.'

Too pretty? Not once had Katherine ever said she looked attractive, let alone pretty. Even when Jo was dressed in a custom-made Collette Dinnigan gown, her hair twisted into an elegant chignon and her make-up professionally applied for her school formal, the best Katherine could say was that she looked presentable.

'Being pretty is a terrible curse,' Katherine continued.

'Why is that?'

'No one ever takes pretty girls seriously.'

'Oh?'

Katherine shook her head sadly. 'I was a pretty girl once. All that brought me was trouble.'

'What do you mean?'

'I wasn't just a pretty face,' Katherine said. 'I was smart and ambitious too. I went off to university to study law. My daddy was so proud of me. "Smarter than all the boys in the street put together," he used to say.'

'And your mother?'

Katherine bit her lip. 'Mother didn't approve of me studying law. She thought it was a waste seeing as I would just get married one day anyway. She thought I should go to the local secretarial college or if I insisted on a degree, it should be teaching or nursing.'

'But you didn't agree?'

'Pfft, teaching? Or nursing? Quite frankly I couldn't think of anything worse. I knew exactly what I wanted to do.'

Jo knew the next part of the story. Her mother had met a man at university, a fellow law student, and they were expected to marry. Then during one of the semester breaks she'd travelled to Bellington to stay with her roommate's family. There she met Andrew Morgan, her roommate's brother. It was love at first sight, and after a whirlwind romance they married. Katherine completed her degree but never got to practise law.

Even though she knew the story, Katherine's candid retelling made it seem fresh and new. 'What happened when you went to university?' she found herself asking.

Katherine's eyes sparkled. 'Oh, I loved university life. It was so exciting. The course was demanding, but I coped easily, so I had plenty of time for socialising. After being closeted away at a Catholic girls' school for most of my life it was very eye opening. I enjoyed mixing with the other students. My roommate, Louise, and I were the best of friends. We had quite a large circle of friends. It was the happiest time of my life,' she said wistfully.

'And that's where you met your husband?' As a child this was Jo's favourite story. Her father would tell her how he fell in love with her mother the minute he looked into her deep brown eyes. Katherine was always less effusive, glossing over the details to explain that it was a whirlwind love affair and when Andrew proposed just three months after meeting her she was powerless to say no. Back then Jo had never suspected that her father's love was a one-sided affair. She simply thought her mother's natural inclination for understatement made her a less enthusiastic storyteller. Now, as an adult, she was well aware of her mother's lack of interest in her marriage.

Katherine frowned. 'Andrew was Louise's brother, so yes, I met him during those years. He didn't attend the university though.

He was older and already had his degree. I met him on a visit to Louise's family during a semester break.'

'And you fell in love at first sight?'

Katherine laughed. 'Good god, no. Whatever gave you that idea?' She paused to sip her tea. 'It was lust I suppose. He was good-looking and keen on me. I was flattered, I guess. We went out one night to see a band at the local pub and all the girls were fawning over Andy...'

Andy? That was a new one.

'...but I was the one he wanted. I let my pride dictate my actions. We left the pub and went for a walk along the banks of the river. It was romantic I guess, and a bit naughty, seeing as I was all but engaged to another man.'

'You mean —'

'Yes,' Katherine said with a hint of defiance in her voice. 'I did something immoral. And I didn't regret it either. Or I wouldn't have except for one thing.'

'What was that?'

'I got pregnant, didn't I? So then I was saddled with a man I didn't love and a child I didn't want.'

Jo bit down on her bottom lip in a vain attempt to stop the tears that immediately welled.

'Are you alright? You look unwell.'

'Fine,' Jo lied in the steadiest voice she could manage. 'Just something caught in my throat. I'll get a glass of water from the kitchen. Shall I put the kettle on for another cup of tea while I'm there?'

'That would be lovely. Thank you.'

In the kitchen, Jo filled the kettle and clicked it on before stepping into the walk-in pantry and pulling the door behind her. Only then did she let the tears fall.

Sure, it wasn't a total surprise that her mother was pregnant with her before she was married. She'd done the maths, or at least attempted to. Both her parents were cagey about the exact wedding date. They celebrated their anniversary — if a peck on the cheek and an exchange of cards could be called a celebration — on the second of January. But once Jo had caught a glimpse of their wedding certificate and she was sure it was dated the second of March. She knew better than to ask Katherine about the discrepancy.

It was one thing to suspect she was conceived out of wedlock and quite another to find out she was unwanted. She'd imagined her parents as passionate lovers, unable to keep their hands off each other. It was certainly the picture Daddy had painted. Now she realised she was the product of one sordid night. Unwanted and, if the truth was told, unloved by her mother. She was the cause of her mother's bitterness. Katherine's conservative Catholic upbringing gave her no choice but to carry the child and marry its father.

Jo choked back a sob. Any way she looked at it she came to the same conclusion. Her mother had never wanted her. Katherine resented having to give birth to her and raise her.

As the kettle whistled and clicked itself off Jo took a few deep breaths and used the sleeve of her jumper to dry her eyes — another thing Katherine would not approve of. As hard as it was going to be to walk back into that room and make polite conversation with a woman who wished she didn't exist, she didn't have a choice. No matter how confronting this was, she was responsible for Katherine's health and comfort today. She wasn't sure she could manage to have her for a whole day, as she'd originally planned, but she could make her some more tea and perhaps a sandwich before bundling her back off to the nursing home.

She took two fresh cups from the cupboard above the sink and then remembered the teapot was still in the dining room. Two more deep breaths and then she forced herself to face Katherine once more. 'I'm a silly billy. I forgot to take the teapot —'

Katherine's chair was empty. Jo's heart began to pound, but she told herself not to panic. Her mother was probably in the bathroom. 'Katherine?' she called.

No answer.

Jo scuttled down the hallway towards the bathroom. 'Mum! Are you okay?'

The silence was deafening.

CHAPTER
16

'Look at me, Daddy.'

Ryan grinned and snapped a shot on his iPhone as Ella trotted past on Tinkerbelle. 'Well done, pumpkin. You're doing great. Remember, sit tall like a soldier.' He watched her closely as she continued to trot around the exercise yard. Ella had a great seat for someone so young. She was born to ride and had a natural affinity with horses. Even Mack, who could be skittish at times, was gentle as a lamb around Ella. She reminded him a little of Joey when they'd first met. Back then she preferred spending time with her horses rather than with people.

He winced and rubbed his temple. The dull thud in his head — the result of last night's overconsumption — was intensifying by the minute, and thoughts of Jo did nothing to help.

Why the hell had he kissed her like that after promising himself he wouldn't get involved? Sure the booze had loosened his inhibitions, but it wasn't as if he was blind drunk. He shook his head at his own stupidity. Seven years and nothing had changed. He still wanted more from her than she was willing to give. The minute he'd discovered that there was no fiancé, he'd got his hopes up, then, when she'd thrown that ring out the window, he'd thought...well, he'd gotten ahead of himself and started to think they might have a future together. But her confession that she didn't want kids poured cold water all over that idea.

There was no doubting the chemistry between them. Jo was still attracted to him and was clearly happy to engage in some sort of physical affair for the time she was here, but she couldn't offer anything more. She didn't seem to understand that it was more than a roll in the hay to him. Being with her, feeling her soft velvety skin against his, drinking in her sweet vanilla scent, all of those things just made the knowledge that she would leave even more impossible to bear. He wouldn't do it to himself. Not a second time.

He clasped his hands behind his head and craned his neck in an effort to release some tension. Coffee and some painkillers would go down well, but supervising Ella's ride came first. They had to make the most of the break in the weather. The rain had stopped for the moment but by the look of the sky it wouldn't be long before it came down again.

'Give Tinkerbelle a rest, honey. Let her walk for a couple of laps.'

'But I love trotting, Dad.'

'I know. You can have another go in a minute, but I think poor old Tinker is a bit tired.'

'Okay.' Ella reached down and gave her pony an affectionate pat on the neck. 'Sorry girl. I was having so much fun I didn't realise you were puffed.'

The smile on Ryan's face disappeared as he realised his mobile phone was ringing. He had heard the clinic phone ringing about five minutes ago but ignored it. He didn't work Sundays unless there was an emergency. The clinic answering machine listed his mobile number, but made it clear that this was for emergency situations only. He glanced at the screen to see who was calling but the number was unfamiliar. Great. Whatever the emergency was, he hoped it didn't take him away from his lazy Sunday with Ella for too long. He answered with a sense of trepidation. 'Ryan Galloway speaking.'

'Ryan, oh thank god you picked up.' Jo's voice had an edge of hysteria.

'Jo? What's wrong?'

'I've lost Mum,' she sobbed. 'I'm so sorry. I didn't know who else to call. I tried Steph's place but no one's picking up. Her mobile is going straight to voicemail and I just don't know what to do.'

'Hey, hey, slow down. I can barely understand you. Tell me what's happened. Where are you?'

'At home.'

'At Yarrapinga?'

'Yes. I brought Mum home for a visit. I only left her alone for a minute and now she's gone. I've looked everywhere but I can't find her. She's just vanished. I don't know what to do. Oh god, Ryan, what if she's in the dam? Or the creek?'

'First of all stop panicking. That's not going help. How long has she been gone?'

'I don't know. Fifteen, maybe twenty minutes.'

'Look she can't have gone far. She'd have to negotiate several fences to get to either the dam or the creek, so I wouldn't worry too much about either of those.'

'What should I do? Who should I call?'

'Don't worry. I'll take care of all that. I'll notify the police in Belly. They'll call the SES and organise a search party if they think it's necessary. In the meantime I'll call a few mates to come and give us a hand.'

'Thank you. I'm just so worried something terrible has happened to her.' She broke into sobs again.

'It'll be okay, Jo, I'm sure. Just keep looking. I wouldn't mind betting she's still pretty close to the house. I'll be there as soon as I can.'

Jo slid her mobile phone back into her jeans pocket and went back inside the house to get her coat. It was raining again and Katherine was out wandering around in it. They had to find her soon or she'd be soaked through. If she didn't end up in the dam or under a car, she'd end up with hypothermia. How on earth had she let this happen? Her one go at showing she was capable of showing some care for her mother and she'd stuffed up. Maybe fatally.

No. She wouldn't let her thoughts go there. Talking to Ryan had calmed her enough for her to realise she needed to start thinking clearly if Katherine was to be found. She went back to the last place she'd seen her mother, the dining room. She sat in the chair Katherine had used and looked around. What was her mother looking at before she left? Had something caught her attention?

The dining room adjoined the formal lounge, which opened onto the hallway leading to the front door. Had Katherine slipped out that way? Nobody ever used the front door. To Jo's knowledge it hadn't been opened in years. It was kept locked, but with the key in it in case of fire. She got up and raced to the door. It was closed, but the 'sausage dog' draught stopper was out of place. She tried the handle and found the door unlocked. Katherine had definitely left the house this way. Jo pulled the door open and walked out onto the front verandah. Her eyes slowly scanned the surrounds, looking for something, anything, that might give a clue to her mother's whereabouts. She took in the white gravel path lined with the heritage roses Katherine had always been so proud of. The path led to an arbour of climbing roses, which framed the front gate. Her father called the arbour 'Katherine's folly' because it was so much work to maintain and useless in his eyes, but her mother had always insisted that creating a good first impression was essential.

Beyond the gate was the road, and on the other side of that hectares of untamed bush. No matter how calm Jo forced herself to be, how clearly she thought, she wasn't going to work it out. She'd never known what was in Katherine's heart or head, even when they'd shared a home. What hope did she have now? Given her mother's current mental state it was impossible to know what choices she would make.

The sound of a car diverted her train of thought. *Please let it be Ryan.* Seconds later Ryan's Patrol came into sight. She raced around the verandah to the back of the house so he'd see her as soon as he pulled up. As he began to slow the car she waved her arms and he tooted the horn in response. It was only when he came to a complete stop that she realised he wasn't alone. She squinted into the mist. Who was that sitting in the passenger seat?

'I've got her,' Ryan called as he jumped down from the driver's seat.

'What? How?' Jo's hand flew to her chest and she ran down the verandah steps. Could it be true? Had Ryan found her mother?

Ryan walked around to the passenger side and held out his hand to help Katherine down out of the four-wheel drive. 'Easy does it, Mrs Morgan,' he said. 'Take your time. There's no hurry.'

Jo rushed to her side and threw her arms around her mother, in an uncharacteristically heartfelt embrace. 'Mum,' she said. 'I was so worried. I thought something dreadful had happened.'

Katherine's skin was icy, much like her response to Jo's embrace. She did not return the gesture and her body stiffened as Jo pressed herself against her.

'Mr Galloway,' Katherine said. 'Who is this woman? Do we know her?'

Ryan smiled his most charming smile. 'Yes, Mrs Morgan, we do. This is Johanna.'

'What a coincidence.' Katherine said. 'I have a daughter called Johanna.'

Jo burst out laughing and crying at the same time.

By the time Jo had finished showering her mother and helping her into some clean, dry clothes, the kitchen was full of volunteers who'd arrived to help with the search. She feared the crowd of unfamiliar faces would be too much for Katherine, but she wasn't letting her out of her sight again. She set her mother up in a chair by the fireplace, where she could still see her from the kitchen doorway.

'Would you like a cup of tea, Katherine? And a sandwich, perhaps? It's about lunch time.'

'No tuna. I don't care for tuna.'

Jo smiled. 'What about tomato and cheese?'

'Lovely.'

'Right then. You stay put. I'll be back in just a tick.' Jo didn't take her eyes off Katherine for a moment as she moved to the kitchen entrance.

'Hey Jo. Glad your mum's okay,' said a bloke whose face she recognised but couldn't quite place.

'Thanks. Thanks to all of you for coming out to help. I'm so sorry to have spoiled your Sunday.'

'No worries,' one of the volunteers said. 'It's what we do when someone needs a hand. We look after our own. You know that.'

Jo nodded and smiled at Ryan, who had found the leftover scones and some biscuits and was now handing them around to go with the cups of coffee he'd apparently made.

Ryan grinned back at her. 'Good scones, Jo. They're worth coming out for, search or no search.'

'Ryan, would you do me a favour? Can you sit with Mum for a moment? I need to make her a sandwich and a cup of tea and I don't think she should be left alone. She seems to like you.'

'Yeah, how about that, eh? Seems I've grown on her. Look, why don't you go sit with her and I'll bring in a sandwich and a cuppa. You look like you could use one yourself.'

'Tomato and cheese.'

'Sorry?'

'Katherine wants tomato and cheese on her sandwich.'

'Righto.'

Jo cast her eyes around the room and smiled at all the kind-hearted souls who'd given up their Sunday afternoon. 'Thank you all again. My shout at the pub on Friday night.'

The room buzzed with laughter and murmurs of 'get out of here' and 'happy to help'.

'No, I'm serious. I so appreciate you all showing your concern. I'll put a tab on the bar Friday night. Everyone's first drink is on me. But right now I hope you won't think I'm being rude if I spend a little quiet time with my mum.'

Katherine seemed to have suffered no ill effects from her little adventure. In fact she looked a little more like the mother Jo remembered as she sat patiently waiting for her cup of tea, admiring her new clothes, or more accurately her old clothes. They were items Jo had hurriedly retrieved from one of the donation boxes she had packed up earlier in the week.

'How are you feeling? Are you warm enough?'

'Yes, thank you. It's lovely and warm in here. Not like our dorms at school. I can't stay much longer I'm afraid. Sister Bernadette gets peeved if any of her girls are out past curfew.'

Jo reached over and patted her arm. Katherine could no longer be held accountable for the sins of the past. There would be no explanations, no pleas for forgiveness, no joyful realisation that there was a gaping hole in Katherine's heart that only Jo could fill. Her mother was gone and only glimpses of her remained, like sepia-toned photographs found in an old shoebox. 'Don't worry,' Jo said. 'I promise I'll get you back before curfew.'

CHAPTER
17

Jo checked her phone for messages and missed calls. Nothing. Two days had passed since Ryan had come to her mother's rescue, to *her* rescue, but she'd heard not a word from him since. Her efforts to contact him had gone unrewarded. She'd made the mistake of phoning his home number rather than the mobile, calling early on Monday morning to catch him before he left to take Ella to school. Unfortunately, Beth answered the phone.

'I'll pass on the message,' she said when Jo explained she was calling to thank Ryan. And that was that. No return call, no idea whether Beth had indeed passed on the message.

Now it was Tuesday evening and Jo was fighting a losing battle with herself. Should she risk calling him? What on earth would she even say? He'd told her on Saturday night he had nothing to offer. He wasn't up for a fling. But she couldn't get that kiss out of her mind. The memory of her hands on his bare chest, his fingers in her hair as his mouth explored hers...after three nights of steamy dreams she was looking for an excuse to call him, to see him again.

What about the offer to put money on the bar at the pub? Maybe she could call to remind him about that?

No. It was only Tuesday. Way too early to be worried about Friday night. He'd see straight through that one.

She'd just have to wait until the dress fitting tomorrow night and hope that she'd see him when he dropped Ella off at Kallara. Although knowing Jo's luck, Beth would be the one bringing the kid.

But then she realised the fitting was the perfect opportunity to call Ryan. She could offer to take Ella for him. As well as giving her an excuse to call, she'd get to eyeball him in the flesh when she picked Ella up. Maybe then she'd get some clue as to how he was feeling.

When he didn't pick up her call she left a voicemail, taking care to sound light and breezy. 'Let me know if you'd like me to take Ella tomorrow night. I'm going anyway so it's no trouble.'

Ten minutes later her phone buzzed. It was him.

'Thanks so much for your offer to take Ella,' he said. 'It'll give me some time to sort out a bit of paperwork for the clinic and for the farm as well. I have young Taylah here one day a week to help out but I like to check the invoicing myself. With Dan and Bec away things have started to pile up a bit.'

'No problem. I'll pick her up at four.'

He thanked her again and said his goodbyes. There was no small talk, no personal stuff, but it didn't matter. She'd see him tomorrow. Maybe he'd even invite her in when she dropped Ella back home.

With Ryan sorted she could turn her attention back to dealing with the mess with Zach. She'd left messages and texts and even called his agent, Leon, without luck. It seemed she was *persona non grata* in Manhattan already.

She left yet another message imploring him to call before curling up in bed with one of the romance novels she'd found in the attic. They were ancient looking and had possibly belonged to Nanna Lil, but it was fascinating that Katherine had kept them. The thought of her mother secretly devouring these books was somehow both thrilling and sorrowful. Under that cold exterior her mother must have had love to give. Such a shame neither Jo nor her father ever got to see that side of her.

At six o'clock Wednesday morning she was woken from a deep sleep by her phone buzzing beside her. She answered in a trance without bothering to check the screen for details of the caller. 'Hello?' she half whispered, her voice still thick with sleep.

Zach's distinctive New York accent was the last thing she expected to hear. 'Hey babe. Did I wake you? You sound sleepy.'

Babe? She was too tired to even try to dissect why he'd chosen to use that word. She'd always hated it, even when they were together. 'It's six a.m. here.'

'Oh man. I miscalculated the time there. I thought it was later. I'm so sorry. I can call later. Go back to sleep.'

'No, Zach, wait. It's taken me days to get hold of you. You're not getting away that easily. Besides, I'm awake now.'

'Yeah, sorry about that. Everyone keeps telling me not to contact you. Let the lawyers do the talking, huh?' He laughed a little.

'Lawyers? I don't have a lawyer. Why would I need a lawyer? We're not married. This is not a divorce.'

'I know, honey, believe me I know. I was just joking about the lawyers. There's no need for alarm.' The tinge of sadness in his voice was audible despite the distance between them.

'Zach, I'm sorry, you know that, right? I'm sorry I couldn't go through with it. But you have to believe me when I say I left because

I didn't want to hurt you even more. It would have been so much harder if we'd actually been married.'

'Yeah babe, I know.'

Babe again. He was nervous. He always went into suave mode when he was unsure of himself. Something was up. 'So what's the deal, Zach? With you and Kiara? Is that for real?'

'Look, that was an accident, you have to believe me.'

'An accident? You accidentally went out with her?'

'No of course not. But I didn't see the photographer. It wasn't staged if that's what you're thinking.'

'So, it's real between you two then? It's okay if it is. You're a free man. You can date whomever you please.'

'I don't know, Jo. Early days still.'

'Where does that leave me? I guess you're not expecting me to walk down the red carpet on your arm anymore?'

'Well...your PR people and my PR people have been talking and they think it's best if we play this down. You know, no comment from either side. Don't give the story oxygen.'

'Yes, I'm aware of the strategy. I've been in contact with my agent. But I want to know about our deal. Am I supposed to be walking the red carpet with you or not?'

Zach cleared his throat. 'Chris and Leon and the PR dudes think it would be best for both of us if we stick to the original agreement.'

Best for them, no doubt. Zach's manager and agent always had an eye on the bottom line. They'd been nice enough to Jo while she was Zach's girlfriend, more than nice in fact — calling her darling and sweetheart, organising the best seats for her and her girlfriends at concerts and shows, asking her opinion about everything from Zach's wardrobe to which scripts he should read — but she'd never been under any illusion about what was truly important to them. She knew they were not her friends and that they would shaft her without a second thought if the time came when she was no longer useful. That time was rapidly approaching.

The thing was, she realised, that she simply didn't care. If Zach wanted her to walk the red carpet with him, if that would make this better for him, then that's what she would do. What happened after that didn't matter.

She was a survivor. She'd proven that to herself already. Zach didn't get her the contract for *Hollywood Kisses*, she'd done that all on her own. And she'd do it again if she had to, write under a pseudonym if necessary. Maybe she'd do that anyway. It would be a relief to start again, to be an unknown without all the baggage of her 'celebrity by association' persona.

'Look Zach, I promised you I'd come back for the premiere and all the associated hooha and I will.'

He exhaled, audibly relieved. 'That's great, Jo. Thank you. The PR people are suggesting we keep a low profile until after the movie comes out. Once the promotion's done, we can go our own separate ways.'

Poor Zach. Everyone thought his life was so perfect, but he was trapped in it. Every single moment of his life was orchestrated. No wonder he fantasised about playing happy families. Thank god she'd had the sense to get out before her life had become the same way. 'So we're playing the happy couple until after the premiere, is that right?'

'I think that's for the best. For Kiara too. We don't want her to get any unnecessary backlash. You know what the media is like over here. She's just starting out and I'd hate to see her swallowed up in all this.'

'Of course. Well you needn't worry about me. I'm about as far away from the American media as you can get. I don't think anyone will be stalking me in the main street of Linden Gully.'

He chuckled. 'I guess you're right about that. I'm sad I never got to see your hometown, though. I loved hearing all your stories about the place.'

Jo smiled. Zach was a good guy. She hoped that one day he'd find someone to love him the way he deserved. 'Well maybe one day I'll write a book about this place and you can star in the movie.'

He laughed again. 'I'd like that. Maybe I should start working on my Australian accent. How's this? *Giddaay maaate.*'

She grinned. 'Truly bloody awful and you know it.'

'More work required I guess.'

'So are we good?'

'Sure. Is it okay if I get my people to draft a joint statement? I'll make sure your PR people get input and we'll email it for your approval.'

'That's fine. But I thought we weren't giving the story any oxygen?'

'This is just preparation. We won't release it unless we're forced to.'

'Okay. That's fine.'

'Well, I'd better get going. I've got a pre-dinner function to go to, so...'

'Sure. It was nice to talk to you, Zach. I mean that.'

'Yeah, you too. Bye.'

Just like that he was gone and so was the weight that she'd been carrying around since she'd got on the plane at JFK. Zach might be hurting still but he wasn't harbouring any anger towards her. Hopefully the movie would be a big success for him and he would move on with his life. Maybe even with Kiara, although she somehow doubted that.

In any case, Zach was not plotting against her. The picture in the magazine had been as much a surprise to him as it was to her, so there was no need to stress on that front. Lydia and the PR people could deal with that now, while she got on with the business of being a bridesmaid.

She snuggled back down under the covers. Her next official bridesmaid duty wasn't till four when she had to pick up Ella. There was no need to expose her bare feet to the shock of icy floorboards just yet. She might as well enjoy the luxury of a lie-in while she waited for the central heating to come on. It wasn't programmed to start until six-thirty.

Her brain was too alert for sleep now, and as much as she tried to focus on other things, her mind kept circling back to thoughts of Ryan. He'd seemed grateful when she'd called to offer her assistance and she was hoping that meant he'd be happy to see her when she collected Ella this afternoon.

It was stupid, this new obsession with being near him. It was like being a needy teenager all over again. He'd said he couldn't do 'sex with no strings' and she couldn't offer him anything else. So lusting after him was futile. Trouble was she was kind of hooked on the adrenaline rush she got every time he was near.

Ryan Galloway had become her secret addiction.

CHAPTER
18

Jo couldn't seem to stop herself from smiling. As she drove towards the Galloway farm to collect Ella for their dress fitting, she found herself singing along to some inane pop song on the radio and grinning like she'd won the lottery.

By rights she had nothing to sing about. Her engagement was over and thousands of miles across the ocean a full-scale PR campaign was being prepared to deal with the resultant fallout. Her instincts told her no matter how much she and Zach wanted to keep things civilised there would be consequences to her leaving the relationship. She probably should care more about that, but right now she just didn't.

There were more important things to think about. Her mother had irreversible dementia and didn't recognise her anymore. And she'd just discovered she was an unwanted child. Yet Katherine's inadvertent disclosure that she wished Jo had never been born had not caused her the despondency she imagined it might. After the initial shock, it was actually quite liberating to realise that her mother's detachment from her was not personal. She didn't want any child at all. It wasn't some character flaw of Jo's that caused her mother to keep her distance. Maybe the pain would deepen with time but right now it felt as if a heavy burden had shifted.

Katherine's worsening dementia was obvious to her now. Up until Sunday's episode Jo had been worried about leaving Katherine behind when she went back to New York. But her misguided experiment in bringing her mother home had proved two things. First, Katherine had no idea who Jo was and was increasingly unlikely to remember. Second, there was no way Jo could care for her mother even if she stayed nearby. Hell, she couldn't even manage to keep her safe for a few hours. There was no doubt that the Windmill was the best place for Katherine to live out her remaining days.

It wasn't just the burden of her mother being lifted that was causing this lighter-than-air mood. It was the feeling of being among friends. It was funny, but these past few days she'd felt more a part of Linden Gully than she ever had growing up. She'd never felt as if she fitted in here, but seeing all those people streaming into Yarrapinga on Sunday, all wanting to see how they could help, had made her feel truly cared for.

As wonderful and exciting as living in Manhattan was, she'd never felt like a true New Yorker. She loved the city to bits but living there felt a little bit like being on an extended holiday. Even the title of her blog, *The Outsider's Guide to Inside New York*, reflected her non-permanent status. Suddenly it occurred to her that she'd always thought that her time in New York would come to an end.

The weekend's community effort made her realise that maybe that time should be sooner rather than later. Really, what was there to hold her in New York? She could write her books anywhere. The apartment would be easy enough to lease out. She had no pets, no real commitments.

Was she seriously considering coming back here to live?

Back to the place she'd spent years plotting to get away from?

She'd fleetingly considered it on the flight over but quickly dismissed the idea as unworkable. And once she'd clapped eyes on Ryan, her mind was made up. Just over a week ago the thought of the two of them inhabiting the same town was completely unthinkable. But now?

Her stomach flipped at the thought of his smile. He always did have the ability to make her feel as if she was the only person in the room and she'd felt that again on Sunday when he'd looked across the crowded kitchen at her.

Back when they were together he'd made her feel special. He'd made up for the lack of motherly love at home, the dearth of close friends other than Steph. She knew that in Ryan's eyes she was a star. And she could depend on him no matter what.

She couldn't help but wonder what Zach would have done if he was faced with an emergency like the one that had unfolded on Sunday. He would have called someone to help, that's for sure, paid someone if necessary. She could hear him saying, 'Whatever it costs, honey.' But she couldn't see him making her mother a cheese and tomato sandwich with the crusts cut off, or staying behind to wash the dishes and clean up the kitchen so Jo wouldn't have to on her return from the nursing home.

It was a stupid comparison. They were men from two different worlds. But spending this time with Ryan had made Jo realise it was crazy to settle for a man who didn't cherish her.

A man who didn't make her breath catch in her throat when she heard him say her name.

A man who didn't make her stomach somersault when she thought about him.

The whole idea of marrying Zach seemed ludicrous now. Even if he didn't want children it could never work. Marriage without love — real, unrelenting, overpowering love — was a hard, hollow slog. Her mother was living proof of that.

Next time she made a commitment to a man it would be with someone who cherished her.

A man like Ryan.

She wrinkled her forehead at the thought. Not Ryan, of course. She knew that was never going to be possible. She'd practically thrown herself at him on Saturday night and despite being inebriated he'd knocked her back. He'd made it clear that he wasn't interested in going back over old ground. But even if he was interested, if he inexplicably changed his mind, how would it work? He had a daughter. She didn't want kids. End of story.

She pulled into the Galloways' driveway, turned the ignition off and took a deep breath, but her attempt to calm herself down was useless. Her stomach continued to swirl with butterflies of anticipation at the thought of seeing him again. This was getting ridiculous. She couldn't sit here forever. They were expecting her and had probably heard her car pull in. If she didn't hop out soon they'd start to wonder what was going on.

One more deep breath and she was out of the Jeep and bounding up the verandah steps.

She knocked out a playful rhythm on the front door and plastered a cheerful smile on her face, in attempt to disguise the fact that her heart was pounding double time inside her chest. The door swung open and Beth stood there, not smiling, holding Ella by the hand.

'Hello, Johanna. Thank you for offering to take Ella to her dress fitting. There was really no need. I was happy to take her.'

'It's no trouble. I had to drive right past here anyway. It was the least I could do after all Ryan's help with Mum.' She hoped that at the mention of his name the man himself might suddenly appear.

Beth's expression didn't change. 'He'd have done the same for anyone.'

'Yes, I'm sure. But still, I appreciated his help. In fact, is he here? I'd like to thank him again.'

Beth shook her head. 'I'm afraid he's busy.'

Was he avoiding her? They'd made the arrangements yesterday, so he knew what time she'd be here. He'd said, 'See you then.' Jo smiled at Beth. 'Oh. An emergency at the clinic?'

'Not an emergency, no. But he is working.'

This was going nowhere. 'Okay then. Are you ready, Ella? We're going to have lots of fun, aren't we?'

Ella looked at her with unblinking eyes and said nothing.

Jo held out her hand, but Ella ignored the gesture and walked past her towards the car.

'I'll make sure she's home as soon as possible. I know it's a school night.'

'Hang on a minute. Aren't you forgetting something?'

'Sorry?'

'You'll need this.' Beth bent down and retrieved a booster seat from behind the door.

'Oh. Isn't Ella too big for one of these?'

Beth sighed. 'No, actually. I'm not sure what they do in America, but here it's the law for children under the age of seven.'

'Oh, I didn't realise. Okay, how do I use it?'

Beth raised her eyebrows. 'It's quite simple really. You just pop it on the seat and do her seatbelt up. She knows how to do it.'

Clearly she was failing the 'responsible adult' test in Beth's estimation. 'Okay, thanks. Tell Ryan I'll take good care of her.'

Beth nodded but looked unconvinced as she waved goodbye to Ella from the verandah.

Once the booster seat was sorted and they were finally away Jo set about having a conversation with Ella. What was the hot topic of conversation among six-year-olds these days? 'How's school, Ella?' Jo winced as soon as the words were out of her mouth. It was the sort of question seventy-year-old great-aunts might ask.

'Good.'

She was going to have to come up with something better if she didn't want to drive to Kallara in stony silence. Which she didn't. For some reason it was important to her that Ryan's daughter liked her. If she was going to spend more time with Ryan...

Stop it.

Regardless of what happened with Ryan, she would be spending more time with Ella, at least until the wedding was over. It would be better for everyone if Ella liked her, even just a little.

'I saw a little pony at your house when I was there the other day. Does he belong to you?'

'She's a girl.'

'Okay. Is she yours?'

No answer. Jo glanced in the rear-vision mirror to see Ella nodding. Maybe she was on the right track. 'What's her name?'

'Tinkerbelle.'

'That's a beautiful name.'

Silence, but a glance in the mirror showed Ella was smiling. Now she was getting somewhere. 'Did your dad tell you I used to go riding with him?'

'No.'

'When we were kids, big kids in high school, we used to ride our horses together every chance we got. I had a pony when I was your age called Skeeta.'

'That's a funny name.'

'It was short for Mosquito. He was called that because he was tiny.'

'How did you ride him then?'

'Well, when I first got him I was pretty small too. When I got bigger I got a new horse called Samson and then, when I was fifteen, one of the mares on our farm had a foal. The mother got sick with a virus and she died, so I raised the foal for her.'

'What was the foal called?'

'Tam.'

'That's a funny name too. Was it a boy or a girl?'

'A boy. I called him Tim Tam, you know like the biscuit? But it ended up getting shortened to Tam.'

Ella giggled and Jo grinned at her in the mirror.

'Did you know my mum?'

She hadn't seen this one coming.

'Yes, honey, I did.' Jo searched her brain to think of something genuinely nice she could say about Carly, because she'd heard kids could sense when you were faking. She didn't want Ella to think she was a fraud. 'She was very pretty.'

'I know. I have pictures of her.' Ella was quiet for a moment. 'Did my mum ride horses with you and my dad?'

'No sweetie, she didn't.'

'Why not?'

What was the right answer here? She knew she couldn't tell Ella the truth. *Because we weren't friends. Because I never liked her. Because even if I'd wanted to my mother would never have let me associate with a girl like Carly McGregor.* 'Um...I don't think your mum had a horse.'

'You could have doubled,' Ella said. 'Sometimes I double with my friends.'

'I guess we didn't think of that.'

Ella's silence revealed what she thought of that answer.

This wasn't going to be as easy as Jo had hoped.

CHAPTER
19

As soon as they pulled up outside Kallara, Ella unbuckled herself and flung open the car door. She jumped out, ran to the house and started banging on the kitchen door before Jo had the chance to close the car doors, let alone gather up all the stuff required for the fitting. The kid was either beside herself with joy to see Jenny and Steph, or she was desperate to get away from Jo. It was hard to know which.

Jenny swung the door open and ushered Ella inside. 'Come on in when you're ready, Jo,' she called.

'Righto.' Jo opened the boot and grabbed the garment bag containing her bridesmaid's dress and her make-up case. Apparently a beautician from Bellington would be there to do a make-up trial after the dressmaker was finished with them.

The kitchen was abuzz with activity. Steph's Aunty Sue was making tea, while her cousin, Madison, complained loudly that it wasn't fair that her dress for the wedding was so babyish. 'I'm fifteen, Mum, not five. I can't see why I can't have the same dress as Jo.'

'Speak of the devil. Here's Jo now,' said Sue. 'Hello, love, how are you? Are you alright? Jenny told me about the business on the weekend with your mum.'

Jo planted a kiss on Sue's cheek. 'I'm fine thanks Sue. And Mum's okay too. She's safe and sound back at the home. I should never have taken her away from there. The doctor did try to warn me but I guess I didn't fully comprehend how much she'd deteriorated since I saw her last.'

Sue gave her a sympathetic nod. 'You weren't to know. Never mind. All's well that ends well. But what about that other business?'

'What other business?'

'Your engagement, love. What's happened there? We saw a picture in *Gloss* of Zach with another...'

'Sue!' Jenny walked into the kitchen and gave her younger sister a filthy look. 'Mind your business. I'm sure Jo doesn't need us rubbing her face in it.'

Jenny walked over and put an arm around her shoulder. 'Don't mind her, Jo. There's no need to tell us anything you don't want to.'

Jo shrugged. 'It's fine. There's not that much to tell. Zach and I have separated. As to his current love life, I really can't give you any information.'

Madison looked at her. 'I heard —'

'Maddy! You heard what I said. Mind your business,' Jenny scolded.

'Whatever.' Madison scowled and went back to checking her phone.

'Madison, could you please go and check on Ella? Make sure she's not bothering the dressmaker while she's fitting Steph's dress,' Jenny said.

'Sorry,' Jo said. 'I shouldn't have let her run off ahead like that. I guess I'm not that great with kids.'

'Don't be silly,' Sue said. 'Madison doesn't mind. Do you Maddy?'

Madison rolled her eyes but did as she was asked. Once she was out of earshot Jo looked at the older women. 'Zach and I had already split up before I arrived here, so the magazine picture was not quite the shock you possibly imagined.'

Jenny's eyes widened in surprise. Obviously Steph had been true to her word and not told a soul. 'But...you never said...I don't understand.'

'I'm sorry I didn't tell you. I was waiting until after the wedding. Everyone here is so upbeat and excited. I didn't want to spoil that. I didn't want you being careful around me, thinking that you had to spare my feelings. I thought it was easier just to wait until Steph's big day was over.'

Jenny squeezed her tight. 'That was very thoughtful of you, love, but we're your family. You can tell us anything. So how are you really? And don't you dare lie to me, young lady.'

The tears welling in Jo's eyes had nothing to do with her feelings for Zach Carlton; it was Jenny's reference to family that brought the emotion to the surface. 'I'm fine. Really I am.'

'You don't look fine.'

'Honestly I am. There's some stuff to work out with Zach, but as far as my feelings are concerned, I'm definitely not heartbroken. In fact it was me who called the whole thing off.'

Jenny pulled a chair out for and Sue plonked a cup of tea and a biscuit in front of her. Jo blinked back the tears and smiled. A cup of strong tea was considered a cure-all by these country-born-and-bred women.

'So what about this actress he's been out and about with?'

Jo shrugged. 'As far as I know that's a recent development. Who knows if they're really an item or not? "Just friends" is the story we're running with at the moment. We want to project a united front until after the movie comes out. It's better that way for both of us. So I'd appreciate your discretion, ladies. I've given Zach my word.'

'Of course,' Sue said as Jenny nodded her agreement.

Madison appeared in the doorway holding Ella by the hand. 'Steph says you're all to come in and check her out.'

'We'd better do as she says,' Jo said. 'We don't want her going all Bridezilla on us.'

Everyone, even Madison, started to laugh. Steph was possibly the most relaxed bride in the history of weddings. They all piled out of the kitchen, and rushed up the hallway to the formal lounge, or the Good Room, as Jenny was fond of calling it. It was a relief for Jo to have the focus taken away from her disastrous love life for a minute.

She heard Sue's gasp as she walked in behind her and when she saw Steph she understood why. Jo struggled to remember a time when she'd seen Steph in anything other than a pair of jeans or shorts. Her practical, tomboy best friend simply didn't 'do' dresses. Until now.

Steph wore an off-the-shoulder, floor-length gown made from soft pink silk. The bodice was fitted, showing off Steph's petite feminine form, but the skirt fell in a natural line to the floor. It was simple but elegant.

Jo's hand went to her mouth at the sight of her friend looking so beautiful. So grown up.

'Well? What are you all gawping at? Do I have a huge zit or something? Too much cleavage or what? Isn't anyone going to say something?'

'Oh Steph you are breathtaking,' Jo said with just a hint of a waver in her voice.

Jenny's eyes shone with pride. 'You are beautiful, my darling. I hope that boy appreciates the prize he's getting in you.'

Steph grinned. 'Don't you worry, Mum. I tell him that every chance I get.' A ripple of laughter went through the room.

The dressmaker cut into the merriment. 'Steph, I think we are done with you.' She turned to Jo. 'Are you the bridesmaid?'

Jo nodded. 'I am indeed.'

'Jo's dress probably won't need fitting,' Steph interjected. 'She just bought it a couple of weeks ago.'

'Fine. Maybe just try it on for me so I can have a look, Jo? I'll do the flower girl and junior bridesmaid next, so perhaps someone could help this little one with her frock?' She pointed at Ella.

'Junior bridesmaid?' Madison rolled her eyes. 'Please tell me you are not putting that in the program, Steph? I mean, how embarrassing.'

'Madison, quit complaining and get your dress on. Ella, sweetie, you come with me,' Sue said.

'Come and have a tea while you're waiting for the girls to get changed,' Jenny said to the dressmaker. 'Jo can help Steph get undressed.'

Once they were alone in the room Steph didn't waste any time pumping Jo for information. 'So, what's going on with you and Ryan? You raced off together from the pub on Saturday night looking very chummy and then Mum tells me he was at your place on Sunday even after you'd left to take your mum back to the home.'

'Nothing's going on. Saturday night he needed a lift that's all. Then on Sunday I was frantic when Katherine did her disappearing act. I couldn't get hold of you and Ryan was the only person I could think of to call. He helped out, like anyone would have.'

'Oh come off it, Jo. It's me. I've known you your whole life. I can read you like a book.'

Jo shrugged. 'I don't know what to tell you.'

'You can start with the truth.'

'Which is?'

'You're still in love with Ryan.'

Was she? Yes, there was the whole butterflies in the stomach thing going on when she thought about him, but that might just be lust. There was the constant thinking about him, the desire for his daughter to like her — and the consideration of moving back to Linden Gully, for Pete's sake.

Oh hell.

'Jo? Earth to Jo. Is that why you and Zach split up? Because of Ryan?'

She shook her head. 'No. Zach and I weren't right for each other for lots of reasons. I was never really comfortable in his world. It's so foreign to me. Plus he wanted to have kids, like, immediately. I'm not ready to start playing happy families just yet. In fact I don't know if I ever will be.' Jo finished unbuttoning the back of Steph's dress and held it open while Steph stepped out of it.

'But you do still have feelings for Ryan, right?'

'Shh, keep your voice down. I don't want anyone overhearing this conversation, least of all Ella.'

'Okay, okay. Keep your hair on.'

Jo grinned. She hadn't heard that expression for years.

'You're not getting out of it that easily,' Steph whispered. 'Are you still in love with him or not?'

Jo shrugged. 'I definitely am in lust with him, that's for sure.'

Steph giggled. 'Did you...have you done the deed?'

'No!' She felt heat rushing to her cheeks. 'Not for lack of trying, though. I practically threw myself at him when he was inebriated the other night.'

'Oh. My. God. What happened?'

'Nothing. Well, a little lip locking in the car, but nothing else. I asked him to come back to my place and at first was keen but in the end he backed out.'

'Did he say why?'

Jo shrugged again. 'Not really. Something about not revisiting the past.'

'What about Sunday? How was he? Did you kiss again? Exchange meaningful looks? Have you seen him since?' Steph wriggled into her jeans and pulled a t-shirt over her head.

'No kissing. Not that there was much of an opportunity to be honest, what with the whole missing-person saga and all. The house was filled with volunteers. Ryan was great, though. Really fantastic with Katherine. But...'

'What?'

Jo pulled her jumper over her head. 'He's been cool ever since. I called and left a message with Beth — just to say thanks — but he didn't return the call. And he blew me off today. He knew I was picking up Ella, but he made Beth come to the door. She said he was working but I got the distinct feeling he didn't want to see me.' She slipped her jeans off and placed them carefully on the back of the chair.

'So what now?'

'I don't know what to do. No, scratch that, I do know what to do. I need to stay away from him until after the wedding.'

'Oh, Jo, that's dumb. Seriously, you two were meant to be together, I just know it. You obviously still have feelings for each other.'

Jo carefully unzipped the suit bag and pulled her gown out. It wasn't a typical bridesmaid's dress. Steph wanted as little fuss as possible and Jo's choice reflected that. The dress was in a slightly deeper hue of pink than Steph's dress. It was a simple cut, drawn in slightly at the waist, with a straight neckline and long soft sleeves finished with a cuff. The hem sat just above Jo's knees. She stepped into it and turned to Steph. 'Zip me up, would you?'

Steph obliged before continuing. 'Think about it. This might be the last chance you get at making a go of it with Ryan. He was the love of your life once. Surely it's at least worth a try?'

Jo shook her head. 'I just can't see how it would work. He has a kid. I can't even imagine...I don't even know if I want to have my own kids, let alone...'

Steph looked crushed. 'Oh Jo, surely there's some way...?'

'I don't think I'm going to magically grow maternal instincts overnight, and even if I did, Ryan has made it clear he's not prepared to go there.'

'I'm so sorry for putting you through all this. When I asked you to be bridesmaid I thought you were happily engaged. I never thought bringing the two of you together would cause such angst.'

'It's not your fault. Ryan and I both made mistakes in the past. I think we are destined to be apart. It's okay. I have my life and he has his. I think being here with all of you has made me romanticise the idea of coming home for a while, but realistically my life is in New York.'

'Knock, knock. Can I come in?' The question was clearly rhetorical because Wendy, the dressmaker, was already coming through the door.

Jo shot Steph a 'shut up right now' look and Steph poked out her tongue in response. 'I'll go see if the younger girls are dressed while you sort out Jo,' Steph said.

'Hey, aren't you going to check out my dress? Isn't that one of your bridal duties?'

Steph laughed. 'You know I'm hopeless at all this wedding stuff. Okay, give us a spin. Let me check you out.'

Jo laughed as she twirled around.

'You look beautiful,' Wendy said. 'That colour is very flattering on you.'

Steph nodded. 'You're gorgeous, my friend. Any man would be lucky to have you.'

Once Wendy was done tucking and pinning and all the girls were dressed in their normal clothes, they congregated in the kitchen once again and Jenny made yet another pot of tea.

Jo glanced at her watch, conscious of the fact that she'd promised to have Ella home at a decent time. It was quarter to six already and the beautician hadn't arrived yet. 'What time is the make-up person coming?' she asked.

Jenny plonked the teapot on the table along with a small jug of milk. 'Oh, sorry, I forgot to say. She called while you girls were in there nattering away. There's been some type of mix-up, a double booking or some such thing, so she's not going to make it tonight. I told her you'd ring to reschedule, Steph.'

'Pfft, do we really need someone to slap a bit of foundation on our faces? Honestly, Mum, I can't see the point. Nate'll probably keel over if he sees me wearing war paint.'

'But the photos, Steph. You have to wear make-up or you'll look all washed out.' Jenny shot Jo a pleading look.

But Jo just shook her head. 'Oh no you don't. I'm not taking sides in this one. Either way I can't win.'

'But Jo, surely you agree that she has to wear make-up? You always look so stylish in photos. You know how important it is to make an effort,' Jenny said.

'There's an idea,' Steph said. 'Why are we paying some stranger to put goop on our faces when we've got our very own style queen right here? Jo knows all about this fashion and beauty stuff.' She turned to Jo. 'Could you do everyone's make-up on the day?'

'I guess so, if you're sure you don't want a professional?'

'Great. That's settled then.' Steph said.

Jo looked at Jenny. 'What do you think?'

'Maybe you should do a trial run, Jo? Just to be sure you're comfortable with doing it. Everyone's here, so we could give it a go now if you like.'

'I'm happy to do a trial but not tonight. I promised Beth I'd get Ella home at a reasonable time.' Jo looked across the table at Ella. 'Time for us to be on our way.'

To Jo's horror, Ella's big blue eyes filled with tears.

'What's wrong, sweetheart?' Jo asked.

'Nothing,' Ella mumbled, as a fat tear slid down her cheek.

Jo raised her eyebrows at the other women, hoping one of them might be able to shed some light on the problem, but they all just shrugged or shook their heads.

Jenny walked over and put her hand on Ella's shoulder. 'Come on, Ella. You can tell us. Is there something the matter? We can't help if we don't know what the problem is.'

'It's just...well, I really wanted to put make-up on. Dad never lets me do it at home. Gran told him it was okay for me to do it because of the wedding, but now the lady's not here and we have to go home.'

Jo's heart melted. Poor little motherless Ella. It must be hard growing up in a house without a mum or a sister to do 'girly stuff' with. Of course there was Beth, but she was a practical, no-nonsense type who'd never worn make-up or worried about fashion. Jo understood a little of what it was like to long for a mother to talk to, to borrow make-up from and confide secrets in. Katherine had been present in her life but she'd always kept her distance.

She smiled at Ella. 'You can definitely wear make-up, sweetheart. It's just I promised Gran I'd have you home nice and early. But you will definitely get to wear make-up on the big day. Okay?'

Ella nodded but her little mouth remained unsmiling.

'I have an idea,' Jenny said. 'What if I put some sausage rolls in the oven. You and Ella can have tea here, Jo, so Ryan won't have to worry about that when Ella gets home. While we're waiting for the sausage rolls to heat up you can do a little make-up trial for Ella.'

'But Beth —'

'Let me handle Beth. I'll give her a call right now to check that it's fine with her.'

Jo nodded tentatively. 'Alright. If it's fine with Beth then it's fine with me.'

Ella clapped her hands in delight. 'Thank you, Jo. This is going to be awesome.'

CHAPTER
20

Cool but courteous, cool but courteous. Ryan repeated the mantra over and over as he waited for the bucks and hens night official minibus to arrive. He squinted into the glare of the setting sun, but could see no sign of his transport to the party. As the mantra echoed through his brain, his stomach churned in nervous anticipation. Jo would be on the bus, and in all likelihood would be the only other passenger aboard at this point.

He'd successfully managed to keep his distance from her since last Sunday. It had been a challenge, especially when she'd offered to pick up Ella on Wednesday. He'd forced himself to spend time in the clinic so he wouldn't have to see her. Then he'd caught a break. An emergency with one of the Wallaces' horses meant he had a legitimate reason for not being there when she brought Ella home.

Last night he knew she would be at the pub so he'd stayed away. He usually had a quick drink with Nate and Johnno before dinner on a Friday night while his mum watched Ella, but not this week. True to her word, Jo put a tab on the bar to thank all the helpers from Sunday's search. He knew this because Nate had called and tried to persuade him to drop by, but he'd made an excuse and avoided tempting fate. He'd learned the hard way that alcohol and Jo were not a good mix.

This morning had been trickier. They had been out at Nate's place finishing up all the preparations for the evening. She had been there with Steph, hanging up decorations and setting up tables. He'd been careful not to be left alone with her and had kept their conversation limited to organisational matters like where the bar should be placed and whether they had enough chairs. Several times their eyes locked, and his heart had lurched. If only life was simple and there was a way for them to be together…but that was a fanciful thought and he knew it.

These past couple of weeks the two of them had indulged themselves in some nostalgia, but in reality they were strangers to each other now. She might be beautiful, she might make his pulse thud and his palms sweat every time he saw her, but she had a life that didn't include him and he needed to remember that.

He might have managed to keep his distance but he couldn't shake her presence altogether. He constantly found his thoughts drifting to her, as they were now, and images of her — beautiful, wildly inappropriate images — invaded his dreams. It didn't help that Ella kept throwing her name into the conversation every chance she got. It seemed Jo had cast some sort of spell on his daughter when she'd taken her to the dress fitting. Ella now thought Jo was the coolest girl in the world and couldn't stop talking about her. He'd spent the past few days coming up with excuses why she couldn't invite Jo over to meet Tinkerbelle. Apparently Ella had discovered that Jo's love of horses and riding matched her own.

After tonight there was just the wedding day to get through and then she'd be gone. And all of their lives could go back to normal.

Beads of perspiration formed at Jo's hairline as the bus drew closer to the Galloway farm. 'Is there any way we can turn the heat down in here, Bob?' she asked the driver.

'Sorry love, the heating's not on. Hope you're not coming down with something.'

Jo mopped her brow with a tissue. 'I'm fine. Must just be all the rushing around to get ready on time.' In no way was she fine. She was going have to endure hours of being with a man who turned her thoughts inside out and upside down, knowing that nothing could ever happen between them. Physically she ached for him. Ever since they'd kissed in the car she couldn't get him out of her head. Every night for the past week Ryan had starred in some decidedly erotic dreams. And the fantasies didn't end when she woke up. Even right now she was imagining his lips on hers, his strong hands gently moving over her body. She felt herself blushing. Thank god Bob couldn't read her thoughts.

The bus slowed to a stop and Ryan got on. He avoided eye contact with her, focusing all his attention on the driver. 'G'day Bob. Thanks for driving the bus, mate.'

'No worries, Ryan. Happy to help out the young couple any way I can. You know that.'

Ryan nodded. 'I reckon there'll be a slab in it for you at the end of the night.'

Bob waved him away. 'Not necessary. Take a seat and we'll be off.'

Finally he had no choice but to acknowledge her. He glanced in her direction and nodded. 'Hi Jo.' He paused awkwardly and then added with a polite smile, 'You look nice.'

'Thanks.' She returned the smile but it was wasted. He'd already turned his back and taken a seat on the other side of the bus, about as far away from her as he could manage without it looking blatantly rude.

Jo got the message loud and clear. There would be no unnecessary fraternisation tonight.

Soon the bus was filled with other revellers. Lustful thoughts of Ryan were banished as Jo fielded questions about her writing and her life in New York. Thankfully all discussion of Zach and the recent magazine debacle was tactfully avoided.

By the time they arrived at Nate's the sun had set. A collective murmur of delight rippled around the bus as the shed, all lit with fairy lights, came into view. Ryan jumped up as the bus stopped and, after giving Bob a slap on the back, was the first to alight. Jo thought he'd done a runner but then realised he was standing at the door in order to assist others to disembark. He took her hand as she walked down the bus's steps. Her body responded immediately, heat pulsing through every inch of her. She withdrew her hand as if it was scorched. 'Thanks, Ryan, but I'm fine on my own.'

He nodded but didn't respond. She made her way out into the twilight on her own.

'Jo! I'm so glad you're here!' Steph greeted her with a hug. 'How awesome does this place look? Everyone is amazed by what we've done. Or I should say what you've done. I would never have come up with all this without you.'

'Nonsense. You would have been fine without me.'

Steph shook her head. 'You know what? I wouldn't. I'm so glad you came home for my wedding. I know it hasn't been easy for you.' Her eyes darted towards Ryan, who was headed up the path towards the shed. 'But nothing about this wedding would be as special for me if you weren't here. So thank you.'

Jo squeezed her hand. 'You're welcome. I'm glad I could be here. Now let's go get us some bubbly and get this party started.'

In keeping with his 'cool and courteous' plan, Ryan had decided to take it easy on the booze. The fastest way to undo his good intentions would be to let alcohol weaken his resolve. He'd been pretty intoxicated at the pub the other night, and that had almost led to disaster. If it hadn't been for Jo's offhanded remark about not wanting kids there was no doubt he would have slept with her. He wasn't going to risk that happening tonight. The sexual tension between them might be uncomfortable, but surely it was better than allowing himself a taste of the forbidden fruit. If he couldn't have her heart and soul as well as her body he'd rather abstain altogether.

'Hey, Ryan, can I get you a Crownie?' Johnno asked in his official capacity as barman of the night.

'Nah mate, I'll just take a softie.'

'Jesus, that's a bit tame. What sort of a best man are ya?'

Ryan grinned. 'Oh man, lay off would you? I've got a lot to do tonight. Best man duties and all that. Plus Nate wants the band to play a few numbers together. We're so bloody rusty; god knows what we'll sound like. I need to keep myself a bit tidy at least until that's done.'

'Not to mention it's your job to sort out the strippers.' Johnno gave him a sly smile and a wink.

'Strippers?' Steph's voice came from behind. 'Please tell me you are not serious?'

Ryan swung around and put his arm around the bride. 'Relax, Steph. No strippers. Johnno's only winding you up. Unless...' he paused and frowned at Johnno, '...there's something I don't know about? And there better bloody not be.'

Johnno shook his head. 'Nate made me promise. Reckons it wouldn't go over too well with the ladies.'

Ryan laughed. 'Can't think why not, mate. Tell me again why it is you don't have a girlfriend.'

'Haven't you got official best man stuff to do?' Johnno replied.

'Righto, I can take a hint.'

'Actually, Ryan, I was looking for you for just that reason,' Steph said. 'We need a hand to bring some of the food down from the kitchen. Mum's loading up baskets of hot food for the girls to hand around, but there are still a couple of heavy Eskies that need to come down.'

'No worries. I'll go right up.'

'By the way, have you seen Jo? I was talking to her a minute ago, but I can't see her now.'

Ryan shook his head.

'Maybe she's in the bathroom,' Johnno said. 'She's given the bubbly a good nudge already. I reckon I've served her at least three times.'

Steph and Ryan exchanged a glance. 'Oh well,' Steph said. 'I'm glad she's having a good time. If either of you see her can you send her up to the kitchen to help.' Steph headed off in the direction of the ladies toilets while Ryan went to the kitchen.

Jenny was running a tight ship in Nate's kitchen. Half a dozen women were working in perfect unison, making sandwiches, putting hot food onto plates and then expertly packing it all into large flat wicker baskets to be transported to the shed.

'At your service ladies,' Ryan announced as he entered the room.

'Ryan!' Jenny said, looking up from the pot she was stirring. 'It's good to see you, love. Come here and give me a kiss.'

Ryan went to her side and gave her a peck on the cheek. 'What can I do to help?'

'There's an Esky in the laundry full of chilled nibblies that needs
to go down to the shed. I'll give you some platters to take with you.
Once you get down there, find Jo...or one of the other girls, to give
you a hand putting the food onto the platters.'

'What? Don't you think I can do it by myself? I'm insulted!'

Jenny laughed. 'If you're anything like my husband or son your
idea of placing food on a platter will be to throw it on willy-nilly.'

'And what's wrong with that?'

'Just get one of the girls to help.'

Steph's young cousin lurked in the doorway. 'I can do it, Aunty
Jenny.'

'Wow, Maddy, look at you,' Ryan said. 'You look so grown up in
that dress.'

Madison smiled. 'Try telling this lot that. They all treat me like
I'm five.'

'Okay Maddy, you can show Ryan where the Esky is and go
down to the shed with him, but as soon as you're done putting the
food out come straight back up here,' Jenny said. She turned to
Ryan. 'Keep an eye on her. She's only fifteen.'

Madison rolled her eyes. 'I'll be fine.'

'Nevertheless I don't want you down there without responsible
adult supervision. Once we're done in the kitchen your mum and
I will take you down there, but I don't want you swanning around
amongst all that alcohol without someone to watch over you.'

Ryan hoped Jenny hadn't caught the swear word Madison uttered
under her breath in response. 'Come on Maddy. Give a guy a hand,
would you? Don't worry, Jenny. She'll be right with me.'

Madison shot him a grateful look and beckoned for him to
follow her. Once they were out the back door she began to thank
him profusely, breathlessly gushing about how nice it was to find
someone who *understood* her. She was walking so close to him they

were practically tripping over each other's feet. No matter how hard he tried to put a bit of distance between them she stuck to his side like glue. When Ryan noticed Jo coming up the path towards them instead of feeling nervous he was actually relieved. Nothing untoward could happen in Maddy's presence and at least now he had an excuse to extract himself from Madison's juvenile attentions. 'Hey Jo, if you're coming to help, we could use another pair of hands.'

'Sure,' she said, perhaps a little too enthusiastically.

As she made her way towards him, Ryan noticed she seemed unsteady on her feet. 'Are you okay?'

'I'm fine. Fantastic. Couldn't be better,' she burbled. 'How about you?'

'I'm fine too.' He took her by the elbow to help steady her. 'If you're going to help, you might want to put that down.' He took the champagne flute from her hand.

'Don't be such a wowser, Ryan. Give it back.' She reached over and grabbed the glass from his hand. 'Here. I'll finish it so I don't have to carry it.' She downed the remainder of the glass in one gulp.

Madison looked on with...was it fascination or admiration? Ryan wasn't sure, but he did know that Jo wasn't the best company for a fifteen-year-old right now.

'Hey, Maddy, be a sport and take Jo's empty glass up to the kitchen for me?'

'But —'

'I'd really appreciate it. Maybe we can have dance later on when we're finished helping out with food. Please?'

'Alright,' Madison said begrudgingly. She took the glass and Ryan watched until he was sure she was safely at the back door.

'So, what do you need help with?'

Ryan turned to face her. 'We need to take this food down to the shed and put it on platters. Jenny seemed to think the platter arrangement needed a woman's touch.'

Jo stepped forward and placed her hand on his chest. She leaned forward and he could smell her lemon-scented shampoo. Her hand slid down his chest. 'Like this?' she whispered.

'Jo!' He grabbed her hand and pulled away.

What the bloody hell was wrong with her? It wasn't enough to humiliate herself once with Ryan by throwing herself at him — she'd just gone and repeated her mistake.

And he'd rejected her. Again.

She headed off down the path without him. This was the reason she rarely drank. Alcohol made her unbelievably stupid. No more bubbly tonight. She'd done enough damage as it was. Now she just needed to avoid Ryan for the rest of the night. If she could get to the shed and get lost among the crowd she'd be fine. Ryan would be unlikely to seek her out and even if he did, he could hardly bring up matters of intimacy — or indeed non-intimacy — in such a public forum. She just needed to get through tonight. Once the party was over there would be no need to see him again until the day of the wedding.

'Jo? Jo! Please wait up.'

So much for that plan.

'Ryan, just leave it alone, okay? I'm sorry. I should never have touched you. I'm a bit tipsy and being silly.'

'You never could handle your liquor. Remember that time we got Brad Gleeson to buy us a bottle of Bacardi and we rode up to the ridge to drink it?'

Despite her discomfort, Jo couldn't help but smile. 'Yeah, I remember. I reckon we were about sixteen.'

'Two swigs and you were smashed.'

'I think it was a bit more than two.'

'No, it wasn't. I remember because the bottle was almost full and I had to leave it behind when you decided you were going to race Tam down to the river. You were like a madwoman.'

'I made it without incident, though.'

'And then you threw up on me when I finally caught up and persuaded you to dismount.'

'Not one of my finer moments, I'll admit.' She sighed. 'Nor was that, back there. Once again, Ryan, I'm sorry.'

He reached over and took her hand. She didn't resist. 'It's okay. It's not that I didn't like it. Your touch...' He bowed his head and exhaled audibly. 'Jo you do things to me that no one else can. But we have no future together. You know that, don't you?'

'Of course I know that, Ryan. But the wedding has made it impossible to stay away from you and I can't help how I feel.' She hoped Ryan hadn't noticed the waver in her voice.

'Me either,' he whispered.

Her heart soared. He felt the same way. 'So what do you propose we do?'

He shrugged. 'I guess we just have to try to ignore our feelings. You'll be gone soon, back to your life in New York. After the wedding we can go on with our lives like before.'

But life would not be the same. Everything had changed. Who knew what her life would be like now that she wasn't one half of the Zach Carlton show? While Ryan's life would go on as it had before the wedding, her life had been turned upside down. She was looking into an uncertain future and all she had to look back on was the knowledge that she had made a colossal mistake in giving up on the man she loved. Didn't she at least deserve to have a good time while she was here? Surely there was no harm in creating some happy memories to take back with her?

Ryan gave her hand a squeeze. 'What are you thinking?'

'I'm thinking that just because we don't have a future doesn't mean we can't be happy right now.'

He shook his head. 'Oh, Jo.'

'Think about it, Ryan, before you dismiss the idea. What have we got to lose? We're already both miserable. We know how we feel about each other and we know we can't be together despite that. I don't see how giving in to our desire will make that any worse. In fact, I think it will help. At least we can look back on this time we have together with fondness. Maybe being together and living the moment will give us the closure we both need to move on with our lives.'

Her features were soft in the moonlight, giving her an aura of fragility. As she spoke of giving in to desire he fought back an overwhelming urge to take her in his arms then and there. Was she right about closure? Would being together for a handful of days be enough to heal the gaping wound the two of them had created? 'I don't know. As much as I want you, Joey, I'm afraid my heart won't stand up to having you and losing you again.'

'Do you honestly think we could feel any worse than we do right now?'

Maybe she had a point. The past couple of weeks had been torture. And there was no end to that in sight while she remained in Linden Gully. Even when he couldn't physically see her, the knowledge that she was there — in his town, sleeping in a bed just up the road from his own — was driving him batshit crazy.

What difference would it make if they spent the time together, making up for lost time, creating some memories to hang on to when they were forced to part? Surely that was better than denying their feelings and avoiding each other?

He was justifying his actions to himself, but so the fuck what? This was the woman he loved. In a week she would be gone and he would be miserable. Why the hell should he be miserable right now?

As he pulled her towards him he knew they were playing a dangerous game but he no longer cared.

CHAPTER
21

The second she felt Ryan's lips on hers Jo knew there was no going back. There was an urgency in his kiss but it was more than that. It was capitulation. This was different to when they'd kissed in the car. Then he'd been holding back. He wanted her but she sensed his fear. Not any more. With each touch of his lips, each caress of her skin, he was giving himself to her. He was surrendering to a force greater than both of them. Jo knew that this time Ryan would not back away.

'Come here,' he whispered, leading her away from the path that led to the shed, and into the lemon grove, which was far more private. Before she had time to speak he was kissing her again, his lips moving from her mouth to her neck and back again. She gasped as he lifted her hair and kissed the nape of her neck. Her audible appreciation elicited a low chuckle from Ryan. 'You still like that?' he whispered.

She let a small moan of approval as his lips returned to her skin, now working their way from her neck to her décolletage. She shrugged off her denim jacket, heat flooding her body despite the chill in the air. She pressed herself against him and quickly discovered his desire matched her own.

This. This was love. It was the total, all-consuming, real deal. She'd tried to stop it, to avoid it, to pretend it didn't exist. But she couldn't. The power of what she felt for Ryan, what they felt for each other, couldn't be contained. The only way to circumvent it was absence. While ever they were near each other their desire would overpower everything else. It was totally different to the sensible, suitable, appropriate arrangement she'd had with Zach. It made no sense and it couldn't last, but it was real.

Champagne and all this emotion didn't mix well. Jo felt her legs buckle beneath her. She was saved by Ryan's embrace; his strong arms quickly moved to encircle her waist, steadying her.

'Hey, are you okay?'

She rested her head on his chest and nodded. 'I'm fine. It's just the bubbly.' *And my heart beating double time.*

'Jo,' he whispered. 'It's impossible to be near you without wanting to touch you, to hold you, but —'

'No!' Jo shifted her weight so she could look at his face. 'Don't say you can't do this or that it's a mistake. I can't take any more of this "yes, no, maybe" crap. It's obvious we can't stay away from each other. I need you, Ryan. I need to get whatever the hell this is out of my system. Don't worry, I know there's no happily ever after for us. That's not what this is. It's not about the future, it's about making amends for the past. I need closure, Ryan, and I think you do too.'

'Whoa. Steady on. Who said anything about a mistake? I was just going to say I don't think it's a good idea to pursue *closure* right here. What if Jenny or one of the others sees us? Someone's bound to come along any minute now.'

'There's plenty of more private places around here.'

'We're not teenagers anymore. I don't want to scramble around in the bushes. I want to make love to you properly. In a bed. With the lights on.'

She pressed her cheek against his chest. 'That sounds nice.'

'Right now I think we should get back to the party. It won't be long before we're missed and I don't want to set tongues wagging.'

Jo laughed. 'Let them talk.'

Ryan pulled back just a fraction. 'I'm serious. I don't want people getting the wrong idea about us. I have Ella to think about.'

She nodded. He was right. It wouldn't do either of them any good to have the town gossips on their case. 'Okay. But promise me you're not going to change your mind.'

In response he pressed his lips against hers and kissed her slowly, reigniting the heat in her lower belly.

After a moment he pulled away. 'What was that?'

'What?' she asked.

'I heard something. Sounded like someone walking through the bushes over there.'

Jo turned to look in the direction Ryan indicated but could see nothing out of the ordinary. 'You're jumping at shadows. It was probably just a possum or maybe a rabbit.'

'Maybe. Come on. Let's go down to the shed before someone misses us.'

Jo grasped hold of his hand. 'Tell me you're not chickening out? It has to be tonight, Ryan, I can't bear to wait any longer.'

He nodded. 'After the party. Mum has Ella for the night so I can come home with you if you like. You'll have to drive me back early in the morning, if that's okay?'

'Of course. What about Bob? Won't he suspect something's going on if we both get off the bus at Yarrapinga?'

'Bob's not one to gossip. He'll keep his thoughts to himself.'

'If you say so.'

'Okay, sounds like a plan then. Now, we'd better retrieve the Esky and get that food down to the shed pronto. Jenny will have my hide if it's not down there soon.'

Jo sighed. The thought of prising herself away from Ryan wasn't one she relished, but he was right. If they were absent from the party for much longer questions would be asked. At least she didn't feel quite so tipsy now. 'I think I'd better start performing my chief bridesmaid's duties a bit more proficiently. Right now I seem to be letting the side down.'

Ryan stroked her hair. 'I think we'd better give each other a wide berth for the rest of the evening.' His hand moved from her hair and he trailed a finger down her spine.

Jo's skin tingled with delicious anticipation as he hand came to rest at her waist. He pulled her close again and kissed her.

'You're not making much of a case for avoidance,' she said.

'It's unbearable being close to you and not being able to touch you. I'd prefer to keep my distance until we're free to do whatever we want.'

Jo laughed. 'I was only teasing. Let's get this food sorted and then go our separate ways.

'Here's something to think about while you're playing the perfect bridesmaid.' He nuzzled her neck, trailing kisses from her earlobe to her collarbone.

Jo shivered involuntarily before giving him a gentle shove. 'Stop it. We're never going to get back to the party at this rate.'

He laughed and let her go.

Somehow Ryan managed to get through the small talk and dodge the endless appeals from his mates to 'just have one beer', and he even succeeded in making a half-decent toast to the bride- and groom-to-be. But all the time his mind was elsewhere. Part of him couldn't wait for the party to end so he could finally get Joey alone and bring to life the fantasy scenes that regularly invaded his dreams. But there was hesitation there too.

It was true that they couldn't seem to stay away from each other, and true that they both needed to resolve their feelings for each other before they could move on. Was a fling really going to fix anything? Or was it just asking for trouble?

There was no point in kidding himself that it was just sex. It could never be that, not with her. But it couldn't make anything worse than it already was. He'd tried to stay away from her, tried to protect his heart, but the fact was it was too late. The moment he'd seen her walking towards him at the footy ground his carefully constructed life had come crashing down around him. There was no protecting himself from what he felt for her. He loved her. He would always love her. If he couldn't have her forever wasn't it fair enough to enjoy the time they did have? When she left he would be shattered, but eventually his life would slide back into the gentle rhythm he was accustomed to. Last time he'd been so angry it had crippled him. Maybe this time the memory of what they'd shared would ease the pain of losing her.

'What's up with you, princess?' Nate said, slapping him on the back. 'We're supposed to be partying and you look like you have the weight of the world on your shoulders.'

'Just thinking about a few things I need to take care of.'

'Well, stop thinking. It's time to rock'n'roll.'

Ryan laughed. 'Rock'n'roll? Jesus, mate, that's a bit retro isn't it? How many have you had?'

'Come on. Grab your guitar. It's time to give the people what they want.'

*

Jo had just returned another empty platter to the house when Steph came running towards her. 'Hurry up,' Steph said breathlessly, 'or you'll miss it.'

'Miss what?'

'The boys have got the band back together. They've been rehearsing for months. They're going to play.'

'Are you serious?'

'Deadly.'

Jo had briefly wondered about the raised platform at the back of the shed when they were setting up for the party. Nate had been vague, saying only that it might come in handy for 'speeches and stuff'. She had put it down to Nate being a bloke and not knowing too much about organising a party. Now she realised he'd had a big plan all along.

The band had started when Nate and Ryan were in Year Eleven as part of a school music project. Jo remembered Steph joking that Nate thought he was going to be the next Dave Grohl, but in reality they were never very good. Ryan sang lead vocals and Nate played the guitar. Max was the bass guitarist and they'd had a couple of different drummers over the years. Ryan could sing well enough and Nate played a mean guitar, but they'd always spent more time mucking around and laughing than doing any serious rehearsal. They'd given the whole thing away by the end of Year Twelve.

But now here they were. Jo couldn't stop herself from grinning. This was likely to be hysterical.

Without any formal introduction Nate struck the first chord and a cheer went up around the shed. They launched into an enthusiastic rendition of John Mellencamp's 'Small Town' and had the whole party up singing and dancing within minutes.

Jo laughed and turned to Steph. 'Maybe it's the bubbly talking but they're better than I remembered them being.'

Steph nodded. 'They've practised a lot, particularly over summer. Once footy season started they slowed up a bit, but they're still getting together and jamming as often as they can.'

'Really? I'm surprised. What's brought all this on?'

Steph shrugged. 'Ryan was still pretty low when he first came home. Nate was racking his brain trying to think of things that might help him climb back out of the hole. He tried cricket, but it was too hard for Ryan to commit to training, you know, with Ella and also setting up the practice. Then Nate came up with the idea of the band. Ryan wasn't too keen at first but eventually Nate talked him round. Now look at him.'

Ryan certainly seemed to be enjoying himself. He was belting out the lyrics and pumping a fist in the air. Jo grinned at this unbridled display of joy. It took her back to a happier time, when they were free to be with each other without complications.

Tonight, at Yarrapinga, she planned to celebrate all that was good about their past and finally replace their unhappy ending with a happy one. If they couldn't have happily ever after, they at least deserved to have some happiness right now.

CHAPTER
22

Ryan was having a ball. He'd forgotten how much fun it was to play in front of a real live audience. And they could hardly have asked for a more appreciative crowd. The band was never going to produce any hit records or go on any world tours but that didn't stop their friends and family from singing along and dancing like crazy as they played. At the end of each song they were met with rapturous applause and he had to admit it felt damn good.

Joey was right up the front near the stage. He'd watched Steph drag her there halfway through their first number. She was smiling up at him, singing along and dancing like she was having the time of her life. This night was turning out a whole lot better than he'd expected. He'd imagined the evening as something to be endured, an event where he'd have to carefully avoid her or, even worse, exchange awkward pleasantries for the sake of the bride and groom. But instead here he was having the most fun he'd had in ages and she was looking up at him without a trace of pity in her eyes.

And later?

He'd better not think about that while he was up on stage. Not unless he wanted the audience to cop an eyeful of...best not to go there.

As they finished a well-received version of Lee Kernaghan's 'Boys from the Bush', Nate stepped forward and took the microphone from Ryan. 'Thanks for your support, everyone. As an audience you guys totally rock.'

A huge cheer went up from the crowd.

'A few months back, when I knew we'd be having this night to celebrate our wedding, I decided I wanted to do something really special for my beautiful bride-to-be, Steph.'

A collective 'Aw' reverberated around the shed.

'Steph, the song we're about to play will never feature on the charts. You'll never hear it on the radio, but I hope you'll love it anyway, because I wrote it just for you.'

As the crowd clapped and cheered Ryan looked down to see Steph, the least sentimental girl he'd ever known, wiping a tear away with the back of her hand.

'Of course,' Nate continued, 'we all know my singing is total crap...'

Laughter and nods from the guests this time.

'...so I've asked Ryan here to sing on my behalf. But I want you to know, Steph, these words came straight from my heart and they're for you.'

Nate stepped back and strummed the opening chords, which was Ryan's cue to start singing.

> *My whole life you've been there*
> *I've known you forever and before*
> *Baby, you're my one and only*
> *You'll always be part of me*

The song might have been written for Steph but they described Ryan's feelings for Jo perfectly. He could barely remember life before he knew her. She would hold a place in his heart forever, even if he never saw her again once the wedding was over.

His eyes sought her out as he sang Nate's heartfelt words. As their eyes locked it was as if she could read his thoughts and an understanding passed between them. What they'd had together had been perfect and it deserved to be honoured as such. Tonight they would celebrate that love. Then, hopefully, they could both move on.

Jo knew that Nate had written the song. It was for Steph, not her. And yet...it felt as if Ryan was singing words directly from his heart to hers. Was she just imagining it, conjuring up the emotions she wanted him to feel, or did he really mean those words he was crooning while looking into her eyes?

You're my soul, my heart, my home.

A pang of regret stabbed at her heart. *Home.* This was her home, here with Ryan. She'd made a huge mistake by leaving all those years ago. She'd grown up hating Linden Gully, blaming the town for her unhappy childhood. She'd thought leaving here would make her happy. But all these years later and all that distance hadn't made any difference. She was still chasing happiness.

First she had thought it would be enough just to get away from Yarrapinga, away from her mother's critical eye. Then she thought being published, having others read her work, was the salve that would soothe her soul. But it wasn't enough. The hole inside her was still there. She was still unfulfilled. She thought being an international success would make all her dreams come true. But she was wrong. No matter how many books she sold, how many talk shows she went on, how many red carpets she walked down, it was never enough. She needed more and now she realised why.

All this time she'd been looking for the wrong thing, in the wrong places. She'd had the keys to happiness in her hand seven years ago and she'd thrown them away.

Now it was too late.

The anticipation of sharing a delicious night alone with Ryan was tarnished by the knowledge that he should have been hers forever. If only she'd said yes.

Tonight had to be special. She would make sure of it. It had to make up for the pain she'd caused Ryan in the past. But it wasn't just Ryan she was thinking of. She needed this too. The memory of tonight had to be enough to carry her through when she was back in New York on her own once more.

She blinked back tears as the song ended. Steph put an arm around her. 'Hey. What's wrong?'

Jo socked her in the arm. 'Nothing. Just a bit sentimental about seeing my two best buddies all lovey dovey, that's all. I'd better make sure I put the waterproof mascara on for the big day, otherwise I'll be a mess.'

Steph grinned. 'Who would have thought old Nate could be so bloody romantic, eh? That boy is sooo getting lucky tonight.'

'Steph!' Jenny's voice came from behind them. 'That is way too much information. I'm sure Jo doesn't want to know about your bedroom activities. I know I certainly don't.'

Jo and Steph burst out laughing. 'Actually, Mum, it's not too much information for Jo. In fact —'

Jenny put her hands over her ears. 'That's enough! I don't want to know, quite frankly. In any case I came over to say I think you and Nate should say a few words, thank people for coming and so on. I think some of the older guests will be keen to make a move soon. Bob reckons he'll do a run with the bus in an hour so I think we'd best get any formalities over with.'

Steph nodded. 'Righto.' She signalled to Nate, who jumped down off the makeshift stage for a moment.

Jo realised Ryan had left the stage too. She turned to find him standing right behind her.

'Hey.'

'Oh hey yourself. That was a great set. You guys have improved heaps since the last time I heard you.'

'Yeah?'

Jo nodded. 'Yeah. I really enjoyed listening to you, especially that last song.'

'Pretty amazing that Nate wrote that, huh? I mean who would've thought? Didn't know he had it in him.' Ryan averted his eyes. 'You know, in some ways that song reminded me of you...of us.'

She reached out and gently touched his forearm. 'Me too.'

He looked into her eyes once more and gave a tentative smile. 'Should we...wanna get out of here?'

'We can't just yet. But I just heard Jenny say that Bob's doing a run in the bus in an hour.'

'I don't know if I can wait that long.'

'Well, I'm afraid you'll have to. Bob's our transport home.'

Ryan shook his head. 'Doesn't have to be. I haven't been drinking. I'm sure Nate would let me borrow one of his cars.'

Jo shook her head. 'We're in the bridal party. We can't just disappear early. It's rude.'

Ryan shrugged. 'I'm sure Steph and Nate won't care.' He nodded towards the stage area. 'Looks like Nate's getting ready to make some sort of speech, god help us. Let's wait until that's done and then you can make up some type of excuse. Tell Steph you've got a headache or something. I'll offer to drive you home. Simple.'

'I don't think so. I'm the chief bridesmaid, I can't leave the party early.'

'It's nearly ten-thirty, Jo. I've waited so long for the time when I could have you in my arms again. I don't want to waste another minute.'

His honesty disarmed her. She would make it up to Steph, and it wasn't as if this was the actual wedding. In any case she'd barely seen her friend all night. Everyone wanted a piece of the bride. 'Okay. But not until after the speeches.'

Nate's voice boomed out of the microphone. 'Alright everyone. Apparently it's not enough to write an awesome song. Seems there's some expectation that I'll say a few words as well.'

Laughter rippled around the shed. As Nate continued, thanking people and praising his bride-to-be, Jo and Ryan stood side by side, almost touching but not quite. A current of anticipation surged between them. After what seemed like an age Nate finished and stepped aside, only for Steph to take the microphone.

Jo blushed at the words of thanks directed at her.

'I'm so grateful to have my best friend — my very busy and super-famous best friend, I might add — here by my side to share this very special time with me. Jo, your presence means the world to me. Thank you for taking time out of your hectic life to be here.'

As the guests applauded, Steph beckoned for her to join them on the stage. She carefully negotiated the crude stairs that Nate had knocked up out of packing crates and pallets the day before. Once she was on the timber platform, Steph stepped forward to embrace her and then nodded to Nate, who brought over a huge bunch of yellow roses. 'These are just a little something to say thank you for being here.'

A lump formed in Jo's throat. 'There's nowhere I'd rather be,' she said, ignoring the bemused look on Ryan's face.

After being forced by the crowd to make her own speech, there were lots of tears and hugs before she finally was allowed to leave the stage.

Ryan helped her down the wonky steps. Once she was safely back on solid ground he whispered, 'Now all the formalities are over we can sneak off. You go make your excuses to Steph and I'll talk to Nate about a car.'

'Are you kidding? After all those things Steph just said I can't go running off on her.'

Ryan moved her to the quiet spot at the side of the stage area. 'It's hardly running off,' he said. 'You've spent the best part of the past two days with her and it's now nearly eleven o'clock.'

'I know but —'

'Jo, please. This may be our only opportunity. It's hard for me to get away during the week and I imagine you'll be at the bride's beck and call from now on. Tonight may be our only chance. I'm not going to beg you. It's your call.'

As much as she didn't want to hurt Steph's feelings, Jo could not risk losing one last chance to be with Ryan, to put things right between them. 'Okay. I'll go tell Steph I have a headache.'

Ryan didn't give her a chance to think twice. He turned on his heel and went off to find Nate the second the words were out of her mouth.

'Steph,' she called, 'can I have a word.'

Steph turned and smiled. 'Just going to have a word to the DJ about cranking up the music. About time you and I hit the dance floor, don't you think?'

Jo shook her head. 'I've got a killer headache. Must be all the champers I had earlier. You know I can't hold my liquor.'

'Do you want a headache tablet? Mum always has half a pharmacy stocked away in her handbag. I'll ask her.'

'No thanks. I think I'll just head home. You know, sleep it off.'

Steph's smile faded in obvious disappointment, but she didn't argue. 'Of course. How are you getting home? Do you need Bob to take you?'

Guilty heat flooded into Jo's cheeks. 'Er, no. Ryan has offered to drive me.'

A look of confusion crossed Steph's face. 'Didn't he come on the bus too?'

'Um, er, yeah well the thing is...' Lying to Steph was impossible. She just couldn't do it. 'Look, Steph, promise you won't breathe a word of this to anyone, but...'

'Oh. My. God.' Steph's eyes lit up in delight. 'I knew it! You two are getting it on, aren't you?'

'Shh! Keep your voice down.'

'Well?'

Jo nodded and Steph clapped her hands together. 'Don't get too excited. It's not like we're getting back together or anything, it's more...'

'What?'

Jo shrugged. 'I don't know to be honest.'

Steph squeezed her arm. 'Go,' she said. 'And don't worry, I won't breathe a word to anyone.'

CHAPTER
23

Back at Yarrapinga, Jo's bravado began to fade. They'd bounced home, Ryan testing the suspension of Nate's old ute on the potholed gravel roads. They'd laughed and congratulated themselves on making the perfect getaway. But now Jo sat on the edge of her bed, her arms covered in goosebumps and her stomach a tangle of nerves. The exuberance brought on by her overconsumption of alcohol had vanished and she was yet again wondering if this was a good idea.

Ryan seemed to share her trepidation. He stood awkwardly in the doorway apparently unable to make up his mind on whether to join her or not. Eventually he came to sit beside her on the bed. 'This is weird, huh?'

Jo nodded.

'Look, I don't want to push you into anything you're not comfortable with. If you've changed your mind, I totally understand.'

Jo exhaled loudly. 'I want to, Ryan, more than anything. I'm just wondering about afterwards. I mean can we both handle this? Will it make things even worse between us? I don't want us to go back to hating each other, or not talking to each other.'

He took her hand. 'I think it'll be okay, so long as we both understand what this is. For my part, I understand that being here with you tonight, no matter how wonderful it is, won't change anything. Your life isn't here anymore. I respect that.'

Jo bit her lip and tried to quell the wave of sadness threatening to envelop her. Her life wasn't here, but was there anything left for her in New York?

'And I have my own life, my daughter, to consider,' Ryan continued. 'So if we do this, it has to be with the knowledge that it ends when you leave Linden Gully. This will be a beautiful end to our relationship, not a new beginning.'

Was this what she wanted? An ending? Was there any other choice?

'I want us to have that perfect ending, Jo. When I think of you I want it to be with fondness, not anger or regret.'

He was right. A beautiful ending was better than this continual unresolved tension between them. If she couldn't have him forever — and she knew she couldn't — then this tender finale would be the next best thing. 'I want that too,' she whispered.

He gently tucked a loose strand of hair behind her ear and looked into her eyes with a gaze so intense Jo felt he could see into her soul. When his lips touched hers, the last tiny shred of uncertainty dissolved. As Ryan's arms encircled her she was overcome by a feeling she hadn't experienced in a long time. It wasn't love; it was more than that. Right this second there was nothing missing from her life. She was whole. This was where she was supposed to be. Finally, she was home.

Ryan woke to the familiar sound of a kookaburra laughing. He rolled over and was momentarily startled to find a warm body in the bed beside him.

Joey.

His mouth stretched itself into a smile at the memory of what had taken place in this bed the previous night. Their bodies had not forgotten how to be with each other and had easily melded together as if they were two parts of the one whole. And yet, it was different from before. The last time they'd made love they were not much more than two kids. Their lovemaking had been sweet and tender, almost shy. Now Joey was a woman. She knew what she wanted and wasn't afraid to ask for it.

His desire for her was so great he'd hardly been able to contain himself when she'd peeled her clothes off slowly, seductively, performing a mini striptease for him. The old Joey used to hide herself under the covers, but she'd clearly grown into a woman who was comfortable in her own skin.

Once he'd shrugged off his own clothes, he drew her close. He couldn't get enough of her, his hands gliding over her soft flesh, his mouth trailing kisses down her neck as he inhaled her vanilla and honey scent. He was on a mission, but she had evidently decided she was the one who would direct the action in this scene.

'Not so fast,' she said. She slipped out of his embrace and pushed him back onto the bed. 'I want this to last.'

He didn't argue as she teased him with her lips and tongue, bring him almost to the point of ecstasy, but stopping just short of the crucial moment. As he groaned with pleasure, she took his hand and placed it on her breast. He felt her nipple harden against his palm as she whispered, 'My turn now.'

He grinned. This new, take-charge Joey was turning him on in ways he could never have imagined. 'Yes, ma'am.'

He took a breast into his mouth and flicked her nipple with his tongue, earning himself a moan of pleasure for his effort. His hand slid down over her belly and in between her legs and he discovered that her desire was as great as his own. She writhed against him as his fingers found the sweet spot.

'Oh god, Ryan, I want you,' she panted. 'Now!'

He smiled. It was his turn to do the teasing. His lips followed the path his hand had taken. Soon she had her hands in his hair and was pushing against him, moaning and calling his name.

'Ryan, stop or I'll...oh god!' She shuddered against him, her orgasm unstoppable. After a moment she opened her eyes and grinned sheepishly. 'Sorry about that. I couldn't help myself.'

He returned her smile. 'Don't worry. We've got all night.'

Now a new day had dawned and Ryan wished they could have last night over and over again. He'd told her it would be a beautiful ending to their relationship. A memory that they could go to.

And that's all it could be.

But being with Jo last night hadn't satisfied him at all. Rather than quenching his thirst for her, making love had awakened a deeper longing. She'd always be the one for him. His soul mate, if you believed in that kind of thing. But their moment had passed.

The kookaburra's cackling grew louder and Jo stirred beside him. 'Is it morning already?' she asked, her voice husky from sleep.

'Afraid so.'

She sat up in bed and looked down at him through her tangled bed hair. 'Do you have to go?'

'Soon.'

She nodded and turned away from him.

He reached for her. 'But not just yet. It's still early. Ella won't be up for a while.'

She covered her mouth with her hand as he drew her close. 'I need to brush my teeth.'

He nuzzled into her neck and slid his hand over her deliciously bare skin. 'Now?'

'You won't want to kiss me with morning breath.'

'Don't be stupid. I lo— want you, just the way you are.' He covered her mouth with his own before she could protest further. He'd very nearly let the L-word out. If they were going to make this snatched time work for them it didn't pay to complicate matters with talk of love.

He turned his attention to the matter at hand — the soft, warm body beneath him.

CHAPTER
24

Ryan was in the shower when Jo's phone began to ping. She frowned, assuming it was her agent, or maybe even Zach. Who else would be texting at this early hour?

Steph, that's who.

> *Morning Sunshine!*
> *Call with all the goss ASAP.*
> *I'm up.*
> *BTW Nate wants to do a recovery BBQ.*
> *Kicking off @ 11.*
> *S xx*

Ryan appeared in the doorway, a towel wrapped around his waist. Despite their recent — very satisfying, thank you very much — bedroom antics, Jo felt a flicker of desire flutter low in her stomach at the sight of his naked torso. She smiled at the memory of that perfect male body on top of her own and then shook her head. He was going home. To his child. Their little tryst was over, at least for the time being.

'What are you shaking your head at?' Ryan asked.

'What? Oh, nothing. Something Steph said. She just sent me a text. Apparently they're having a recovery barbecue.'

'Yeah?'

She nodded as Ryan dressed himself in last night's crumpled clothes. 'I'm going to go.' She averted her gaze, not wanting him to sense how eager she was to hear the answer to her next question. 'What about you?'

He shrugged. 'I guess I should. I'll need to go home and check on the animals in the clinic. I've got a few other jobs to do too, but I reckon I should be able to organise Ella and be back at Nate's by lunch time.'

'You're bringing Ella?'

Ryan's brow creased. She sensed the question bothered him. 'Of course I'll be bringing her. Jo, you know we can't be playing the happy couple in front of other people, right? Especially not Ella.'

Jo bit her lip. Of course she realised that.

Ryan, now fully dressed, bent down and kissed the top of her head. 'I'm sorry. I wish there was another way, but I don't want Ella to be confused by any of this.'

Jo fought hard to keep her disappointment from showing. It wasn't as if she expected last night to miraculously change things between them, but having Ryan spell out their relationship — or rather their *non-relationship* — so bluntly burst the bubble of happiness she'd been floating in for the past eight hours or so. 'Sure, I understand.'

Ryan's lips sought hers for one last tender kiss and then he stood. 'I'd really better go. See you at Nate's?'

Jo nodded. 'Yep. See you there.'

*

The winter sun warmed Jo's back as she sat on a hay bale licking the last of the sauce from her fingers. Charred sausage encased in white bread slathered with tomato sauce was a staple of the Aussie barbecue and a delicacy she hadn't had the opportunity to consume in quite some time.

'Is there room on there for me?' Steph asked.

Jo wriggled over and patted the space beside her. 'For that tiny behind? I reckon so.'

Steph squished down beside her, momentarily silent as she devoured her own barbecue snag. As soon as the last bite was swallowed down she poked Jo playfully in the ribs. 'Okay, spill. I want all the details.'

'Shh! Someone will hear you.'

'Settle down. Nobody's listening.'

Jo glanced over at the handful of blokes gathered around the barbecue. It was only just midday and many of last night's revellers were yet to appear. Some were no doubt nursing hangovers and others couldn't spare the time away from their farms, so for now at least the gathering was quite small. And Steph was right. So far they were the only two women present and the blokes were far too interested in talking about the footy to be taking the least bit of notice of their conversation. Ryan and Ella were nowhere to be seen. Maybe he'd changed his mind about coming, afraid she would fawn all over him in public.

'Okay,' she said, 'but keep an eye out for Ryan. He's paranoid about other people finding out.'

Steph's brow creased in obvious confusion. 'Why?'

Jo shrugged. 'He doesn't want to confuse Ella, which is fair enough I guess. It's not like I'm about to become a permanent fixture in his life. Besides, as far as everyone else is concerned Zach and I are still engaged.'

'Yeah, good luck selling that story around here. I'm pretty sure most people have already written him off.'

'Maybe, but I can't risk being seen in public with Ryan. I gave Zach my word I'd keep up the façade until after the New York premiere.'

'What exactly is going on between you and Ryan? I know you both and neither of you is the type to go in for a fling.'

Jo raised her eyebrows and Steph's eyes widened.

'Really? Hot and heavy, huh? So last night...I take it you did more than talk?'

'Oh yeah. Much, much more.'

'What do you mean, "much, much more"? Oh. My. God. More than once?'

Jo felt heat rushing into her cheeks. 'A lady never tells.'

Steph giggled, obviously enjoying Jo's embarrassment. 'So it was good then?'

'Steph! I'm not going there, okay?'

'I don't think you need to. I think an encore performance speaks for itself.'

Jo grinned. 'Not to mention the matinee.'

'What? Johanna Morgan, I'm shocked!' Steph nudged her with an elbow. 'No wonder he hasn't fronted yet. You broke him.'

'I highly doubt that.'

Steph chuckled. 'So you think there's plenty more where that came from?'

Jo shrugged. 'I have no idea. We didn't really discuss future liaisons.'

'So no plans for a meet-up after the barbie? A little afternoon delight?'

'No. Not that I'd say no to that, it's just I'm not sure whether Ryan saw last night as a one-off or if...'

'Let me get this right. You do the wild thing — more than once — with the love of your life but you don't know if it will happen again? And you have no idea where the relationship is going?'

'Oh, I know where it's going, alright. It's going nowhere.'

'What makes you so sure of that?'

'How can it go anywhere, Steph? We live on different continents. Anyway, neither of us wants to take it any further. It ends when I go back to New York. That much I know for sure.'

'I don't believe you. I know you, Jo. And I know how long it took you to get over Ryan. I can't believe you'd sleep with him again unless you thought there was a chance of the two of you getting back together.'

Jo folded her arms across her chest. As much as she didn't want to argue with Steph, she didn't like the way this conversation was headed. 'I didn't think you'd be so judgemental, Steph. Since when did it become a crime for two consenting people to have a little adult fun together?'

'Oh, sweetie, I'm not judging you. I'm worried about you, that's all. If you and Ryan are okay with a bit of "adult fun" as you call it, that's fine. I'm just surprised, I guess, and I don't want to see either of you get hurt. Are you sure you know what you're doing?'

Jo sighed. 'It was supposed to be goodbye.'

'What do you mean?'

'We decided to give our relationship a happy ending, a proper farewell if you will.'

Steph was quiet for a moment. 'I guess I can understand that. I mean I understand the two of you wanting to have something positive to look back on.' She placed her hand gently on Jo's forearm. 'But, geez, Jo, isn't it a bit dangerous? Aren't you scared that being together again like this will make it harder on you both once you go back home?'

'I don't know. It's hard anyway, you know? I mean seeing Ryan again like this has made me realise just how shallow my relationship with Zach really was. You just said Ryan is the love of my life and you're right about that. I've never loved anyone else the way I loved him, and if I'm totally honest with myself I'm not sure that I ever will. It doesn't matter whether I'm sleeping with him or not. That fact doesn't change.'

'So do something about it. What's stopping you from being with him?'

'Well, for starters, there's the small fact that he lives here and I live in New York.'

'Big deal. You can change that if you want. I mean, what's keeping you there now you and Zach have split up? You can write your books anywhere.'

'I have other commitments too.'

'You mean the blog?'

'Yes. Well, that's one of them. I can hardly blog about being an Australian in New York from here, can I?'

'So you'd put a weekly column ahead of a lifetime of happiness?'

'It's income, Steph. I have to make a living. God only knows how the new book will sell. And I don't have another contract in the pipeline.'

'You're a star, Jo. Everyone loves your books. I'm sure you'll have no problem selling your next book.'

'Don't be so sure. Being Zach Carlton's girlfriend didn't hurt me at all as far as signing contracts went. Now that we're no longer an item I'm not sure I'll have publishers knocking on my door. The blog brings in a regular income, and right now I need it.'

'That's bullshit, Jo.'

'Excuse me?'

'That's not a reason to stay in New York. You could easily get work here. Yarrapinga's essentially yours now so you'd have somewhere to live. Money isn't a reason to stay in New York. And New York isn't the reason you can't be with Ryan. So tell me the truth. What *is* keeping you apart?'

Jo exhaled, letting out some of the pent-up tension she'd been hanging onto. Steph could always see through her. There was no point in holding anything back. 'Ella,' she said.

'That sweet little girl? Are you kidding me? I know you said you weren't sure about having kids but really, who is? It's a gamble for everyone but you don't see many people regretting that decision, do you?'

My mother did. Jo couldn't say the words out loud. Not even to Steph.

In the absence of a reply Steph continued. 'Jo, she's a good little kid. I'm sure once you get to know each other a bit better ...'

'It's not her per se. Ella's a nice enough little kid, from what I've seen of her. But she's Ryan's kid, not mine.'

Carly's kid.

'I don't want to be a step-mum. In fact I don't want to be a mum at all. That was one the issues between Zach and me. He wanted kids and I didn't.'

'Jo, I didn't realise...' Steph's voice was quiet. 'I always thought you'd make a great mum.'

'Not everyone wants kids, Steph.'

Steph was quiet for a moment while she digested that statement. It seemed as if she'd never considered the fact before. 'Okay, maybe not everybody does, but back to you and Ryan, who's to say if you get together that you have to be Ella's mum? You wouldn't necessarily have to live with her.'

'What do you mean?'

'If you and Ryan were to give it a go there's nothing to say you'd have to live together. You've got Yarrapinga and he's got the farm. You could move back home and just take it as it comes.'

This was not an option she'd considered. All her fantasies over the years had been of her and Ryan living and working together, waking up side by side. Conducting their relationship from two separate addresses wasn't part of the plan.

Steph took her silence as tacit agreement. 'Ha! There you go. Problem solved.'

Jo slowly shook her head. 'I don't know, Steph. I don't know if Ryan would go for that. I think eventually he'd want more. I think we both would.'

'You should think about it, Jo. Kids grow up eventually. It seems silly to throw away what you and Ryan have without even trying.'

CHAPTER
25

After a long morning ride where she and Pepper had given each other a thorough workout, Jo figured she'd earned a cuppa. She guessed it wouldn't be too long before Steph called wanting to know if she'd had any more thoughts about her relationship with Ryan. She might as well grab herself a hot drink in preparation for the onslaught.

At first Steph's idea about coming home and living at Yarrapinga had seemed ludicrous. But then Ryan arrived at Nate's and smiled at her across the fire pit and her insides turned to mush. No other man had ever come close to making her feel the way Ryan did. Maybe it was worth giving Steph's idea some thought.

While the kettle boiled Jo stood at the sink and looked out the kitchen window. It was almost ten o'clock and yet the paddocks were still tinged white with frost. When she'd saddled up Pepper earlier she'd been reminded of her first winter in New York. One December morning she'd woken to find a blanket of snow had enveloped the city overnight, transforming the gritty streets into a magical fairyland. She was mesmerised by the sight and totally unprepared for the reality of living in it. Her fashionable black leather boots and thin woollen coat were no match for the sleet, snow and ice.

These days she was a pro, with a range of boots and coats for all conditions. This trip home she hadn't bothered to pack her warmest coat despite the fact that she was here in the middle of the Australian winter. Linden Gully's winters were mild compared to what she'd become accustomed to.

She crossed her fingers and said a quick prayer — more out of habit than any real belief — that her thoughts about Australia's mild winters wouldn't jinx the weather for Saturday. She wanted Steph's big day to be absolutely perfect. *Please God, no rain, no icy winds.*

The sound of her phone trilling interrupted her thoughts. That would be the bride now, calling for her debrief.

Jo grabbed the phone off the kitchen counter and was pleasantly surprised to see Ryan's name on the screen.

'Hey there, you. This is a nice surprise. I thought you were flat out at the clinic all day today.'

'Yeah, I was, but things have changed.'

Jo's heart leapt. He'd cleared his schedule for her. 'Great. Maybe we could —'

'Sorry, Jo,' he cut in. 'This is not a social call.'

'Oh.' She hoped he couldn't hear the disappointment in her voice.

'I'm really sorry to ask this but I need a favour.' There was no warmth in his voice. It was obvious something was wrong.

'Is everything okay?'

'I'm calling from the hospital in Belly. Mum's had a fall and we had to call the ambulance.'

'Oh god, that's terrible. Will she be alright?'

'I hope so, but the initial assessment from the doctor is that her hip's broken. She's in X-ray at the moment getting that confirmed. I'm not sure what will happen from here. I can't seem to find anyone who knows whether it means she'll have surgery today, but that would be my guess. The doctor will let me know once she's back from her scan. In any case I don't want to leave her on her own.'

'I understand. How can I help?'

'I need someone to pick Ella up from the bus and look after her until I get home. Normally I'd ask Steph or Nate or even Jenny but I know how busy they are this week.'

Jo winced. Babysitting was not something she excelled at. Ella was a nice enough little kid and they'd had fun together at the dress fitting — once the kid thawed out — but she wasn't sure she was ready to tackle a whole afternoon by herself with a child. How on earth would she entertain her? Or feed her? Jo realised she didn't have the first idea of what little kids ate. But Ryan was asking for her help. She could hardly refuse. 'Um, I guess so...I mean, of course.'

'Are you sure? You sound a little hesitant.'

'I'm sure. Sorry I was just, um, a little distracted by a passing car.' Jo rolled her eyes at the pathetic excuse. She plastered a smile onto her face even though she knew Ryan couldn't see it and made an effort to sound more enthusiastic. 'I'm happy to help. Where should I meet the bus?' She listened carefully as Ryan gave her directions to the bus stop and instructions for Ella's care for the rest of the evening.

Once the call ended Jo set about opening and closing every cupboard in the kitchen, in search of child-friendly food. Who was she trying to kid? There was barely any food at all, let alone anything exciting enough to tempt a six-year-old. She would have to head into town.

She pulled her phone out again and sent Steph a text.

Wanna meet @ pub for lunch? Have to shop but can b there @ 12.30

Fingers crossed Steph would have a break in her endless schedule of pre-wedding jobs. Jo could use her advice on entertaining Ella. In fact, maybe she could even bribe Steph into giving her a hand this afternoon, just for an hour or so, to help her ease into the role.

Her phone vibrated with Steph's response.

Sorry m8. Off to c celebrant with Nate. Tied up all arvo. ☹ *Talk soon.*

So much for that idea. She'd have to sort this one out on her own.

At three-thirty, Jo carefully parked the Jeep on the verge of Longford Road as instructed by Ryan and waited for Ella's bus to come into view. She was ten minutes early. Being late wasn't an option. Ryan would never forgive her if she messed this up.

After a few tense minutes of wondering if she was in the right spot, the bus finally came into view. It rumbled to a stop just behind her Jeep and she heard the hiss and clatter of the door opening.

Ella gave her a shy smile as she jumped down the stairs. Jo smiled back and gave the bus driver a quick wave of acknowledgement as the door closed behind the child. 'Hi Ella. I'm picking you up today.'

'I know. My dad called the school to tell me. He wanted me to know because usually I'm not allowed to get in a car with a stranger.'

Stranger? Obviously the magic she'd worked with the make-up had worn off. This kid was a hard nut to crack. 'Well, I'm not really a stranger, am I? You and I are friends.'

Her little brow creased in concentration. 'I guess so. But I'm still not allowed to get in a car with anyone except Dad, Gran, Uncle

Dan, Aunty Bec, Jenny, Nate or Steph,' she counted the names off on her fingers. 'Unless Dad says it's okay.'

Jo nodded. 'Fair enough. But your dad did say it's okay to come with me, right? So we should get going.'

Ella nodded.

'Here, give me your backpack and I'll throw it in the back.'

Ella did as she was told and then climbed up into the back seat. 'Where's my booster seat?'

Bloody hell, the booster seat. She hadn't even given it a thought. It was too late now. The bus had gone, there was no one else around and she certainly couldn't leave the kid standing here on her own while she went to Ryan's place get it. In any case, the seat was probably in Ryan's car in town.

'Sweetie. I don't have a booster seat, but I'm sure you'll be fine if you sit in the back with your seatbelt on. We don't have far to go.'

Ella jumped out of the car and shook her head vigorously. 'I'm not allowed in a car without a booster seat.'

Jo let out an exasperated sigh. 'Ella, I'm sorry but we don't have a choice. I don't have a booster seat and there is no other way of getting home. Hop in the car, please, and put your seatbelt on.'

'No. My dad says I'm not allowed.'

The afternoon had barely started and already it was a nightmare. 'Please sweetie, I'm sure your dad won't mind just this once. He asked me to pick you up and he knows I don't have a booster seat, so I'm sure he won't mind. This is what we call an exception to the rule. Sometimes in an emergency we have to bend the usual rules.'

Ella's baby blue eyes looked up at her from under long dark lashes. 'Is Gran going to die? Is that why it's an emergency?'

'Oh, honey, no. Your gran will be just fine, I'm sure. I just meant that we have no other way of getting home. I can ring your dad if you like and you can ask him what he thinks.' She'd hoped to get through the afternoon without having to call Ryan — she didn't wanting him thinking she was incompetent — but it seemed there might be no other choice.

Ella smiled. 'Okay. That's a good idea.'

Jo pulled out her phone and scrolled down to Ryan's number. She pressed 'call' but nothing happened. Damn it! There was no signal out here. 'I'm sorry, Ella, but I can't get my phone to work out here.'

Ella made no move to get in the car. This cajoling thing was getting her nowhere.

'Ella, you need to get in the car, right now. I'm in charge of you this afternoon and we are playing by my rules. Hop in and put your seatbelt on.' Jo's heart thumped in her chest as she spoke the words. If this didn't work she was screwed.

A scowl settled on Ella's face but she did as she was told. It wasn't the start to their afternoon that Jo had hoped for but at least the kid was safely in the car. Perhaps the best she could hope for was to do no harm. The way things were going friendship seemed too much to hope for.

Ella didn't speak during the short drive back to Yarrapinga. Jo turned the radio up and sang her heart out but when she checked in the rear-vision mirror there was no hint of a smile on the kid's face. If ever there was proof that she wasn't cut out for raising kids it was in the disdainful expression on Ella Galloway's face.

Once they were safely back at Yarrapinga, Jo let out an inaudible sigh of relief. They'd managed to get here sans booster seat — when had they even become a thing for school-aged kids? She certainly hadn't had one and she didn't know anyone who had. She couldn't remember ever seeing one in the States. But then when would she? Her life was completely child-free. None of her friends had children. She barely even noticed kids in New York.

As Ella dumped her backpack on the kitchen floor she noticed the child's eyes widening at the afternoon tea she'd left laid out on the table. Now that she looked at it there was rather a lot of food — far too much in fact for just the two of them, but she hadn't been sure what Ella would like so she'd bought a variety of treats.

She'd made a platter of cut-up winter fruits and bought a number of different flavoured yoghurts to accompany them. There were chocolate biscuits, blueberry muffins and, on a whim, she'd made fairy bread, although was more for herself than Ella. Any excuse to indulge in her childhood favourite was a good one.

'Are we having a party? Who's coming?' The scowl had all but disappeared.

'Um no, no party. This is just for us.'

'Wow. That's a lot of food. Are you a really big eater?'

Jo laughed. 'Sometimes. But I think I might have gone a bit overboard with this afternoon tea. I wasn't sure what you'd like so I got a lot of different things. We don't have to eat it all.'

Ella eyed the Tim Tams in the middle of the table. 'Dad doesn't usually let me have chocolate biscuits if it's not a party.'

'Well, you know what? Maybe this is a party after all.'

'How can it be a party for just two people?'

Jo shrugged. 'It's not the amount of people that matters, it's the occasion, the reason for celebrating.'

'What is the reason for the party?'

'Um…' Jo stalled for a second while she thought. 'This is the first time you've been to my house, right?'

Ella nodded.

'Okay. Let's make it a Welcome Party then. It's a party to welcome you to my house.'

A large grin spread across Ella's face. 'That's a great reason for a party.' She dragged out one of the bentwood chairs and sat herself down.

Jo sat opposite and smiled. This was more like it. Maybe the afternoon wouldn't be as terrible as she feared. She looked on with satisfaction as Ella helped herself to two pieces of fairy bread and a biscuit. 'Would you like a drink? I've got cordial in the fridge.'

'Yes, please.' Ella munched away on her biscuit for a bit before looking up at Jo with a puzzled expression on her face. 'You're not like other grown-ups,' she said.

'Aren't I?'

Ella shook her head. 'You're more fun.'

Jo's heart swelled. Maybe she wasn't as bad at this kid stuff as she thought.

'And,' Ella continued, 'you're not all fussy about rules and stuff like that. Most grown-ups are always going on about being responsible and stuff, but you don't care about that. You're kind of like a big kid. It's really cool.'

Jo's optimism deserted her. Even a six-year-old could see she was faking it. She tried to salvage something out of Ella's words. At least the kid thought she was fun.

'Is that why you don't have kids?' Ella asked, as she licked chocolate from her fingertips. 'Because you like having fun too much?'

Jo shrugged. 'I guess. When you're done eating maybe you'd like to play outside?'

'What about my homework?'

'Oh, yes, after you've done that of course.'

Ella grinned. 'You really don't know anything about looking after kids, do you?'

Jo slowly shook her head. She was fooling no one here.

CHAPTER
26

Jo lifted the ancient pushbike from the hooks holding it to the shed wall. The purple frame was slightly rusted, and the fabric flowers adorning its plastic basket had faded, but otherwise it looked in pretty good nick. The shed had always been Dad's domain. Katherine never ventured into it, which was fortunate. Her childhood bike would otherwise not have survived her mother's penchant for purging all items no longer required.

Of course the tyres were flat. Her eyes scanned the workshop area for a pump. It took a minute but eventually she discovered a ratty cardboard box labelled 'bike bits' with several bike pumps and a few puncture kits inside.

'Here we go,' she said to Ella. 'This is my old bike. I reckon once we put some air in the tyres she'll be perfect for you.'

Ella looked unsure. 'It's pretty old.'

Jo grinned. 'Yeah, but I'll bet it still works perfectly.' She gave the pedals a spin. 'See? Nothing wrong with it.'

Ella shrugged as Jo got to work pumping up the tyres.

'Want to give it a whirl? You can test it out in the driveway while I watch. If it works okay then you can ride wherever you like so long as you don't go near the road.'

'Okay. Where's the helmet?'

'Um...' Jo sighed in defeat. Her old helmet had probably been consigned to the scrap heap years ago. 'I don't have one, sweetie.'

'I'm not allowed to ride without a helmet.'

Another failure. When did raising kids become so complicated? She didn't remember there being so many rules and regulations when she was little. From the time she was a toddler she'd been allowed to play by herself in the garden near the house. As she grew her freedom increased. Her mother's main instruction had been 'Be home by dinnertime'. Booster seats and other safety equipment hadn't been a feature in her adventures.

What on earth was she going to do with Ella now? The homework was done, they'd exhausted the drawing and colouring options and frankly she didn't have a clue what else to try. The kid didn't seem too keen on amusing herself and Jo was fresh out of ideas.

She felt her patience wearing thin. It wasn't Ella's fault, she knew that, but it seemed the kid had been wrapped in cotton wool. Would it really kill her to ride the bike around the property without a helmet? She'd done it, Steph had done it, Ryan had done it too goddammit, and all of them had lived to tell the tale. All this fuss was ridiculous. An example of...what was the term? Hovering? No, helicopter parenting, that was it. It would do Ella good to toughen up a little. 'You don't need a helmet to ride on private property, Ella, only if you are riding on the road.'

The child looked unsure. 'Gran always makes me wear a helmet. She says, "Better safe than sorry".'

'Well honey, I don't have a helmet. I rode this bike around here for years and I was perfectly safe. My bet is you will be too. But it's up to you. If you'd rather we went inside and did more colouring in...'

Ella shook her head vigorously. 'Don't you have any other toys? Or maybe some videos we could watch?'

Jo shook her head. 'This is it, kiddo. Take it or leave it.'

Ella bit her lip and looked longingly at the bicycle.

Jo felt a twinge of guilt at coercing the child into disobeying her family's rules. Poor kid, she was just trying to do the right thing and it was selfish and immature to expect her to do otherwise. Seemed like the bike was a no go. 'Okay, kiddo, forget the bike. Let's think of something else. What do you usually do after school?'

'Ride Tinker.'

Of course! Why hadn't she thought of this before? All they needed was some type of head protection. It didn't necessarily have to be a bike helmet. 'Hang on a minute, Ella, you've given me an idea. Maybe I can find my old riding helmet. I think my dad kept all my old pony-club trophies out here in the shed, maybe he kept my riding gear too.'

Ella looked at her blankly.

'You can use my old riding helmet instead of a bike helmet. Do you think that would be okay?'

A grin spread across Ella's face and she nodded enthusiastically.

Jo scanned the shed for likely storage places, but all she saw were boxes of tools, car and tractor parts, tins of paint and cans of motor oil. Maybe Katherine had talked Dad into throwing all his keepsakes away or...she suddenly remembered the loft. When she was ten Dad had built a mezzanine loft — more like a wide storage shelf than an actual loft — at the back of the shed. He told Katherine it was for extra storage space but Jo knew he kept things up there that he didn't want her to know he had. Katherine hadn't liked to admit it, but she was terrified of heights.

Jo dragged the extension ladder to the rear of the shed and propped it up against the mezzanine floor. As soon as she set foot on the floor her heart lurched. Childhood treasures that she had thought long gone littered the small storage area. 'Oh Dad,' she whispered. He was such a softie.

'Did you find anything?' Ella called from below.

'Not yet, but I'm sure it'll be here. Just give me a minute.' Sure enough there was a tattered cardboard box labelled 'Pony Club'. Jo pulled the carton open to find every rosette, sash or trophy she'd ever won, along with an old pair of jodhpurs, and — yes! — her old riding helmet. 'Got it!' she called down to Ella.

The helmet turned out to be a little large on Ella's tiny head but Jo adjusted the straps the best she could. 'What do you think? Will it do?'

Ella grinned and nodded her approval.

'Come on then, let's get you up and running before it gets too dark to ride.'

Ella was right at home on the bike. She took off with ease, racing down the long driveway at high speed. 'Stay away from the road,' Jo called after her, but she needn't have worried. Ella executed an expert turn a full ten metres before she reached the crossover. Jo stood watching her manoeuvres for a few minutes until her phone vibrated in her pocket. There was a message from Lydia.

Heads up. Photo of u kissing unknown all over social media. Please call to discuss. Photo to follow.

What the...?

Her phone buzzed again. There on the screen was a photo of her and...*oh my god*...Ryan. They were wrapped in each other's arms, their lips locked in what was unmistakably a passionate kiss.

Shit! How the hell had this happened? She looked carefully at the photo. It was taken Saturday night at the bucks and hens night. Who on earth would have taken this? And how had it gotten on social media? There were no paparazzi here in Linden Gully. It had to be someone at the party.

Surely none of their friends would do this? Her thoughts went to Kelly and Laura. They were both there on the night, and neither woman was a fan of hers, but she couldn't believe either one of them would stoop to something so low. Laura had spent much of the evening making eyes at Ryan, finding numerous excuses to be in his presence. Surely if she'd seen them kissing she wouldn't have behaved so warmly towards him?

In any case, how the photo ended up online didn't really matter. It was done. What mattered was what happened next. She covered her eyes with her hands for a moment and tried to think. How would Zach respond to this? He'd probably think she'd gone back on her word and was using this as some sort of payback for the Kiara mishap. Or maybe this had come from Zach's camp. Maybe they'd paid someone to follow her, to catch her out and now they were using the photo of her with Ryan to prove she was the bad guy in this scenario.

Her throat constricted.

Ryan.

He would be furious. He'd been so adamant that no one could know about their liaison. It was only a matter of time before everyone in town heard about the photo — if they hadn't already.

She needed to talk to Lydia right now, so they could formulate a plan. She needed to put a stop to this, to limit the damage as much as possible. Despite it being two-thirty in the morning in New York, Lydia was clearly awake.

Jo glanced up at Ella as she whizzed by on the bike. Riding around should keep her occupied for a few minutes more at least. She'd be fine if Jo ducked into the house to make the call. The kitchen had the best mobile phone reception of anywhere on the property and the driveway was clearly visible from the kitchen window so it wasn't as if she'd be leaving her unsupervised.

'Hey, Ella, I'm just zipping inside for a minute. Will you be alright?' Jo called.

Ella nodded and waved without stopping.

'I'll be in the kitchen if you need me.'

Ella rode on without responding and Jo watched her until she disappeared behind the house as she followed the path that led to the disused chook shed.

Once inside Jo urgently punched Lydia's number into her phone.

'Jo. I've been waiting for your call.'

'God, Lydia. Things must be bad if you are texting me in the middle of the night.'

'Middle of the night? Oh, honey, I'm not in New York, I'm in L.A. for the rest of the summer. It's only eleven-thirty here. But you're right. Things aren't looking great for you here. That photo is everywhere, honey. And I've had half a dozen calls for quotes already.'

'Zach?'

'Nothing from his camp yet. I guess they're biding their time, working out their strategy. He's publicly denied having an affair with Kiara, trotting out the "just good friends" line. But that was a few days ago. I haven't seen or heard anything since this latest photo came out. It's still Sunday night here and I only saw the photo a couple of hours ago, so I expect more will come out in the morning.'

'Can we shut it down?'

'Unlikely. The only way to pour water on it is if Zach's people don't want it to run and I have no idea what their take will be. They may just decide that painting Zach as the broken-hearted, wronged party will work for them. Let's face it, as far as the movie goes any publicity is good publicity. The producers couldn't care less about how it's come by. And as far as Zach is concerned, he's their star.

They have a lot riding on him. Right now they need him to be their golden-haired boy. No one wants to see him as the bad guy.'

'Well, technically they're right. Zach isn't a bad guy. He hasn't done anything wrong. I'm the one who left. And I'm the one who's been caught kissing another man.'

Lydia laughed. 'Come on, you don't really believe that, do you?'

'What?'

'That Zach's a good guy?'

'Of course I do. I agreed to marry him for heaven's sake. I'm the one that couldn't go through with it and the reasons for that have nothing to do with Zach being a bad person.'

'Oh, Jo, I love that sweet trusting nature of yours, really I do, but sometimes you can be so naive I want to shake you. All these years in New York and you're still just a simple country girl at heart.'

'Lydia, what the hell are you talking about?'

'Zach's been screwing around on you, since…well, forever.'

Lydia's words hit her like a punch in the gut. 'What? No. That simply can't be true.'

'Sugar, I'm so sorry. I thought you knew.'

'What would make you think that?' Jo could hear the edge of hysteria creeping into her voice. She took a deep breath and tried to calm herself as Lydia replied.

'In all the time I've known you, Jo, you've never once said that you loved Zach. Even when you got engaged you were pretty matter of fact about the whole thing. I just assumed you two had an arrangement. It's not uncommon among Hollywood types like Zach.'

'But why…I mean he asked me to marry him. Why would he do that? If he wanted to screw around, why didn't he just dump me? I don't get it.'

'His family. Can you really see the Carltons being happy with their son married to some Hollywood starlet? You were the perfect match for Zach in so many ways. Young, pretty, respectable and unknown. No rehab or jail stints in your past. No trailer-trash relatives in your closet. My guess is they had you picked as good breeding stock.'

Acid rose in Jo's throat as she let out a bitter laugh. 'Like a prize cow.'

Lydia sighed. 'I'm sorry, Jo. Are you okay?'

Okay? No she was definitely not okay, but it had nothing to do with Zach and his philandering ways. Sure, she felt foolish for having believed the lies he'd fed her. And she was pissed off at all the wasted guilt and remorse she'd felt after breaking off the engagement. But she'd get over that.

There was far more at stake right here in Linden Gully. Any hope of a proper reconciliation with Ryan would be off the table the minute he saw that stupid photo. And the only reason the photo was making a splash online was because of her relationship with Zach. Now it turned out it had been a game all along. She was just a pawn being used by a man and an industry that didn't give a toss about her.

Enough. She was done with the whole damn thing. Zach, the movie, even her next publishing contract if it came down to it. She didn't want to live in a world where she had to schmooze the right people to get her books published. Hell, she'd been doing okay before she met Zach, and she could start again if she had to. She wanted no more part in this whole pathetic celebrity charade. Zach could make what he liked of the photo, say what he liked, paint her any way he wanted to. She simply didn't care. She wouldn't march to the beat of his drum anymore. And he could forget any scenario that had him walking hand in hand with her on a red carpet. That simply wasn't going to happen.

Jo caught a glimpse of Ella's curly hair streaming in the wind as she rode past the kitchen.

Everything she cared about was right here in this little town. Maybe, if she did everything right, if she explained everything the right way, if she spent time with Ella and earned her trust, then just maybe Ryan would get over having his face plastered all over the internet. Maybe one day he'd let her back into his heart. Maybe they could make things work, just like Steph had said. But even if they couldn't, she wasn't going to leave Linden Gully with Ryan hating her. She had to fix this.

'Jo? Are you still there?'

'Sorry. I'm here. Just lost in thought for a second, that's all.'

'Honey, try not to worry. I've left a message for Kendra at the PR place and I'm sure she'll get back to me first thing. In the meantime my advice is sit tight and say nothing.'

'Okay, thanks, Lydia. I really appreciate you handling all this. I know it's not strictly in your job description.'

'Anything for my favourite client. You take care of yourself now and I'll be in touch as soon as I know more.'

Jo put the phone back in her pocket and stood staring aimlessly out the window for a moment. Surely things had to start looking up. She laughed at the thought. It wasn't as if they could get much worse, right?

CHAPTER

27

To tell Ryan or not? That was the question. Of course she would have to tell him eventually, but was now really the right time? She didn't want to add to his troubles while he was worried about his mother's condition.

There was a chance he would never even hear about it. Ryan wasn't a social media user. He wasn't on Facebook — she knew this from years of surreptitious searching for his profile after she'd had a few wines — and she'd heard him remark to Steph that Twitter was 'for twits'. He didn't read gossip magazines either, so the only way he would find out was if someone told him.

Which would happen in about five minutes flat around here.

There was no getting out of it. She'd have to tell him when he came to collect Ella.

Where *was* Ella? Jo peered out the kitchen window and realised she hadn't seen any bicycle action for quite a few minutes. Maybe Ella was exploring the back garden, which was fine. A little adventure on her own wouldn't do her any harm, but Jo had forgotten to tell her not to go into the old chook shed. It hadn't been used for years and had fallen into a state of disrepair. Last thing she needed was the kid stepping on a rusty nail or cutting herself on an old bit of corrugated iron.

Jo swung open the kitchen door and stepped out onto the back verandah. She had a clear view of the front yard, the driveway and the home paddock, but Ella was nowhere in sight. 'Hey, Ella,' she called as she descended the verandah steps. 'Where are you?' No answer came and Jo called again as she followed the gravel path that wound its way behind the house and led to the veggie patch and chook shed. 'Ella. El-la. Where are you?'

And then she saw her.

Ella was on the ground, the bike beside her, and she wasn't moving.

All the way in the ambulance Jo prayed to a god she hadn't believed in since she was twelve years old. Ella was falling in and out of consciousness and Jo's gratitude that the child was alive was tempered by the fear of what sort of damage she may have sustained. What if Ella died? Or if she had permanent brain damage? How could she live with herself? How could she ever face Ryan again? The ambulance officers were noncommittal, saying only that it was 'possibly' a bad concussion, but Ella would need scans to rule out a more serious head injury. The fact that they'd immobilised Ella, strapping her tiny body to a back board, was also concerning. The ambos insisted it was routine procedure, but their expressions were grim and Jo feared they knew more than they were letting on.

She tried to call Ryan over and over without any luck. The signal was poor in patches and then, when it picked up and she managed to get through, her call went straight to voicemail. Maybe he had his phone turned off inside the hospital.

Jo fought back tears, trying to put on a calm, brave face for Ella in the moments when she was lucid. She'd already failed this little girl spectacularly. The least she could do was keep herself together enough to provide the child with a modicum of comfort.

'Hey sweetie, how are you feeling?' she asked when Ella opened her eyes, but Ella didn't respond. She stared off into the distance as if Jo wasn't even there. And then her tiny body began to jerk unnaturally.

'Oh god! What's happening?' Jo cried.

'She's seizing,' the ambulance officer in the back called to his colleague driving. He turned his attention to Jo. 'You need to calm down and be quiet. Stay in your seat.'

'Are you okay back there, Steve?' the driver called.

'Yeah.'

'Let me know if we need to pull over.'

'She's coming out of it already,' Steve replied. He looked at Jo. 'Is the patient epileptic?'

Jo shrugged. 'I'm sorry, I really don't know. I was just babysitting her for a couple of hours.'

'Well, it will be helpful for the doctors to know that information. They'll need to know her history, if she's on any medications, that sort of thing. Have you been in contact with the parents at all?'

Jo shook her head. 'No, her dad isn't answering his phone, but he'll be at the hospital. His mum is having surgery.'

Steve nodded without taking his eyes off Ella. He was monitoring her pulse.

Jo went back to her silent prayers, which were probably futile. Why on earth would God listen to her? But hopefully he had a soft spot for Ella.

After what seemed like an age the ambulance finally pulled up out the front of Bellington Hospital. 'We're taking her in through

Emergency,' the young ambo said. 'You said her dad was here at the hospital, right?'

Jo nodded.

'Best go find him then. There'll be paperwork to fill in. Medicare details and the like.'

'Yes,' Jo said, her heart sinking. Imagining Ryan's reaction to the news of Ella's injury was making her feel queasy. She gave Ella's hand a squeeze. 'I'm just going to get your dad, Ella. Won't be long.'

Ella didn't appear to hear her, or maybe she didn't understand what Jo was saying.

Oh God, please let her be okay.

Ryan was in the patient lounge, making himself a much-needed cup of tea when he saw Jo walking towards him. For a split second his mood lifted — she'd come to be with him, to cheer him up — and then he remembered she was supposed to be caring for his daughter. 'Where's Ella?' he asked.

Jo's mouth was unsmiling, her eyes glassy. 'She's here. In Emergency.'

'Did you leave her there unsupervised? God, Jo, she's only a little kid. You can't just leave her to her own devices.'

'No, Ryan, you don't understand.' Jo's face drained of all colour. And then he knew.

He broke into a run, barking at Jo as he pushed past her. 'What happened?'

Jo ran after him. 'She had a fall. I think she must've hit her head.'

'You think? What do you mean you think? Why weren't you watching her?'

'I'm sorry. I didn't think...Ryan, honestly she was only on her own for a minute. I'm so, so sorry.'

Ryan glanced at the elevator bank briefly, before deciding to take the stairs. The old lifts in this place were notoriously slow. Jo trailed behind him. He could hear her panting through her sobs. 'Is she conscious?'

'Sort of. She keeps drifting in and out.'

Ryan cursed under his breath. Why the hell had he left Ella with Jo? She'd said she was hopeless with kids but he didn't want to believe that. Now his daughter, his beautiful precious little Ella, was paying the price for his lack of judgement. Again.

When he reached the ground floor he began to run again, not caring whether Jo was keeping up or not. He pushed through the Emergency doors and rushed to the triage desk. 'Ella Galloway,' he said. 'Where is she?'

'Are you a relative?' the triage nurse asked.

'I'm her father.'

'Right.' The nurse clicked on the keyboard for a moment. 'Mr Galloway is it?'

Ryan nodded.

'I need to take a few details before I can let you see your daughter.'

'Can't that wait? I just want to see my little girl.'

'Mr Galloway the best way you can help Ella right now is to give me as much information on her medical background as possible. It will only take a few minutes and as soon as we're done I'll call one of the nurses to take you through.'

Ryan exhaled impatiently. He knew he had no choice but to play by the hospital's rules. 'Okay.'

'Is there anything I can do?' Jo's voice came from behind him.

He glanced back at her tear-stained face and a tangle of emotions — pity, anger, disappointment — fought to make their way to the surface. There was no time to deal with this now. 'Just go home, Jo. You've done enough for one day.'

Jo stood shivering outside the hospital entrance. The darkness took her by surprise and she checked the time on her phone. It was just after six-thirty. Great. The last bus to Linden Gully left hours ago. Not that it mattered, because she didn't have the money for a ticket anyway. When she'd jumped in the back of the ambulance she'd given no thought as to how she'd be getting home. She had no money, no wallet and no coat. All of which would have come in handy right about now.

Hot tears stung her eyes as she contemplated her options. She had no choice but to call Steph or Jenny to collect her. But they'd want details and she didn't know if she was up to relaying what had happened. If only Ryan had chosen one of them to care for Ella instead of her. The anger — no, it was worse than that, *contempt* — in his voice had shaken her. Not that she blamed him, of course. He had every right to feel that way. She wished there was something she could do, some way she could support him, but right now she was the last person he wanted to see.

She realised that someone should contact Nate. With Beth in hospital and Dan still away, Nate was the closest thing Ryan had to family. There was no other option. She'd have to let Steph and Nate know what was going on. Hopefully Steph could drop Nate at the hospital and pick her up at the same time. As the fine misty rain began to dampen her hair, she swiped at the tears with the back of her hand and took a deep breath before dialling Steph's number.

When Steph answered with a chirpy, 'What can I do for you?' Jo's tenuous composure crumbled.

'Steph, I need your help,' she sobbed into the phone.

CHAPTER
28

'Daddy, how come Gran hasn't been to see me?'

Ryan rubbed his temples in an attempt to dull the pounding headache that was threatening to split his skull. He'd had no sleep at all. The night had been spent waiting as Ella had been wheeled in and out of different areas of the hospital as the medical staff carried out various tests. She was stable right now, thank god, but the doctors were keeping her in under observation for another twenty-four hours. The doctor in charge was consulting a paediatric neurologist at the Royal Children's Hospital in Melbourne. The nursing staff assured him that they'd know more this afternoon and that the doctor would be in to speak to him as soon as possible.

'Gran's in the hospital too, honey, remember? She fell over and hurt one of her bones.'

'But's she's okay, isn't she?'

'Yes, of course, sweetheart.' He plastered what he hoped was a reassuring smile on his face. 'Don't you worry about Gran. She'll be as good as new in a couple of weeks. If you're better tomorrow I'll take you upstairs to see her.'

Ella pouted. 'I feel better now. Why can't I go home? Tinker will be missing me.'

'Tinker will be fine, sweetheart. Taylah is looking after her and all the other animals in the clinic while you're here.'

'But why do I have to stay here? My head isn't even sore anymore.'

'I know sweetie, but we need to be sure everything is perfectly fine before we take you home. The doctors need to double check a few things, that's all.'

'Why do they need to check? I'm okay, Dad. Really I am. I can do a handstand to prove it, if you want.'

'No. I do not want. You need to stay in bed, young lady. Am I making myself clear?'

Ella's bottom lip dropped in response to his stern tone.

He gave her hand a quick squeeze and smiled. 'Sorry pumpkin, I didn't mean to sound so grumpy. I just want you to get well as soon as possible. I know you feel okay but you've had a nasty fall and your body needs some rest so it can heal properly.' Hopefully it was as simple as that. There was no skull fracture or bleeding, thank heavens, but not all the tests had come back yet and Ryan was beginning to fear there was something the doctors weren't telling him.

'It's so boring in here.'

'I can get someone to bring in your DVD player from home if you like.'

Ella nodded. 'Dad, can you ask Jo to bring it?'

If Jo were the last person on earth he wouldn't ask her. Yesterday's babysitting fiasco had brought his priorities into sharp focus. What was he thinking having Jo look after his child? All this was his fault, not hers. She'd made it very clear that she didn't like kids and had no idea what to do with them. Yes, he'd needed help with Ella but there were plenty of other people he could have asked. He'd had an ulterior motive. A tiny part of him had hoped that by spending time with Ella, Jo would fall in love with his daughter. Despite his brain knowing their relationship was impossible, his foolish heart had still harboured hope. Not anymore.

'Dad?'

'Jo's pretty busy with the wedding. Besides, she doesn't have the keys to our house. I'll ask Taylah to bring it in.'

'But I want to see Jo. I want to tell her all about the X-ray machines and I want to say thank you for looking after me in the ambulance. I was really scared, Dad, but Jo kept talking to me and telling me I would be okay and she was right.'

Ryan sighed. 'We'll see, okay? I have no idea what Jo's plans are for the day so I can't make any promises.'

'Mr Galloway?'

Ryan turned to see one of the nursing staff standing in the doorway. 'Yes?'

'Dr Riley has finished consulting with the team at the Royal Children's Hospital. He'd like to speak with you.'

'Now?'

The nurse nodded. 'If you'll follow me, I'll take you to him.'

Once he was seated in Dr Riley's office, the older man wasted no time in announcing a diagnosis of epilepsy. Ryan stared blankly at the doctor, trying to make sense of what he'd said.

He wanted to say something, to ask the questions he knew he should be asking, but all moisture had left his mouth and his tongue felt like bark inside his mouth. He cleared his throat and opened his mouth but still no words came.

The doctor poured some water into a glass and passed it to him. 'I understand this is a shock,' he said, 'but Ella's condition is manageable. She'll need to go to Melbourne for more tests and to see the neurologist there, but I'm sure it will just be a matter of getting the medication right.'

Finally Ryan found his voice. 'Will she be on medication forever? Don't kids grow out of this sort of thing? I mean that's what we thought the last time...'

'She may need medication for life and she may not. Epilepsy is an unpredictable condition and affects each individual differently. You'll know more after you've seen the specialist in Melbourne. My suggestion is to write a list of all the questions you have and take those with you. Don't be afraid to ask anything. Ella's health and care are important. There are no silly questions.'

'Why now? I mean, did the fall bring it on?'

The doctor shook his head. 'There's no way of knowing for sure, but considering her medical history it seems unlikely. There's no evidence of head trauma. Initially the paramedics thought she was concussed but what they were seeing was some disorientation after the seizure. My best guess is the seizure caused the fall, not the other way around. You mustn't blame yourself. The seizure couldn't be stopped. There was nothing anyone could have done.'

Ryan rubbed his face with his fingertips. The unfamiliar sting of tears assaulted his eyes and he covered his face with his hands so the doctor wouldn't see. Mixed in with the fear of what was happening to his little girl was a twinge of guilt about the way he'd spoken to Jo yesterday.

None of this was her fault. If there was anyone to blame it was Carly. Or more to the point, himself. He should never have let Ella get in the car with her all those years ago. He'd wanted to believe Carly had changed, but she'd been as reckless as ever. It seemed Ella would be paying the price for his lack of judgement for the rest of her life.

His composure now recovered, Ryan lifted his head and looked the doctor in the eye. 'Sorry. I'm a bit overwhelmed by all this. I thought we'd overcome this hurdle, that it was part of Ella's past. It's hard to believe we're back where we were three years ago.'

'I understand. But try not to worry too much. Ella is stable now and she appears to be completely healthy in every other way. She's responding well to the drugs we have her on. With medication she may never have another seizure.'

Ryan held out his hand to shake the doctor's. 'Thanks doc. Best get back to her, I guess.'

Jo busied herself packing boxes at Yarrapinga. All thoughts of staying on in Linden Gully were now banished. There was no way Ryan would consider a relationship after what had happened and she couldn't blame him. The look on his face last night had been one of utter contempt.

And she deserved it.

If ever there was any doubt about her decision not to have children it was now completely wiped away. Parents devoted their entire lives to looking after their offspring. She hadn't even been able to tear herself away from her own stupid problems for a few minutes to provide the necessary supervision.

Even if Ryan could somehow bring himself to forgive her, Ella's fall had brought into sharp focus exactly why she and Ryan couldn't be together. Clearly she didn't have a maternal bone in her body, so playing happy families was out. But it was now clear that Steph's plan of living in separate houses and 'dating' wouldn't work either. Ella would always be Ryan's first priority, as she should be. He would always be torn between the two of them.

And that wasn't fair on anyone.

As she taped closed another carton, she contemplated what would happen after Steph and Nate's wedding. There was nothing for her here, so she might as well book her flight back to New York.

Thank goodness she hadn't followed Zach's advice and sub-let her apartment. It was the only home she had now.

When she'd first moved to New York her West Village studio provided her with a much-needed haven from the bustling city beyond. It might have been small but she'd made a happy little nest there. She'd decorated the walls with collages made from magazine cuttings and made the place cosy with scatter cushions, throws and curios she picked up at junk stores and markets. What the apartment lacked in size it more than made up for in personality. Initially, when she was studying at NYU, her parents had paid the rent, but once she had an income of her own she'd taken over the payments. Even after the success of the book, when she could afford to move somewhere bigger, more upmarket, she chose to stay. She loved her neighbourhood as much as she loved her little home.

Zach was horrified the first time she'd taken him there. He paced the tiny apartment asking, 'Are you sure this is it? Surely there's another room somewhere you're not telling me about?' At the time she'd laughed and told him how lucky she was. Lots of the friends she'd met at NYU were living in even smaller studios that shared a bathroom with the other tenants on their floor.

As their relationship developed she spent less and less time there. In the end most of her clothes were housed in the walk-in wardrobe of Zach's Upper East Side apartment. In fact, other than what she'd packed to come to Australia, pretty much all of her clothing was still there. Unless Zach had thrown it out, which wouldn't surprise her in the least. Especially now that the photo of her locking lips with Ryan was out in the world.

The photo.

Jo's stomach churned. Obviously yesterday had not been the time to tell Ryan about the photo, and in fact all thoughts of it had vanished from her mind from the moment she'd found Ella lying motionless beside her bike. But she would have to tell him sooner rather than later. It would be better for him to hear it from her than finding out through the local grapevine or, even worse, some random paparazzo turning up on his doorstep. Jo winced at the thought.

For the first time ever she welcomed Linden Gully's remoteness. It was unlikely that even the most intrepid reporter would trek all the way out here on the off-chance of catching her kissing an unknown farmer. Not when there was already an image out there, albeit a fuzzy one. But still, Ryan should be prepared, just in case.

She was startled by the sound of her phone alerting her to a text.

Ella would like to see u.
Visiting hrs @ 2pm.
Pls let me know if u can make it.

A wave of nausea overcame her and she gripped the back of a chair to steady herself. Had he forgiven her? The text wasn't particularly warm or friendly, but he wanted her to visit, so surely that was a good sign?

Or maybe he wanted to berate her in person for her carelessness. Jo looked at the text again in an attempt to decipher Ryan's state of mind, but it was useless. She wouldn't know until she arrived at the hospital whether he was feeling in a conciliatory mood.

Jo let out a breath she only now realised she'd been holding. What did it matter? Even if Ryan could find it in his heart to forgive her mistake there was still the matter of the photo to overcome. She feared two blows in quick succession would be more than he could bear.

Nevertheless she owed it to him and to Ella to front up at the hospital.

Will be there @ 2.
Hope Ella is feeling better.
Looking forward to seeing you both.

CHAPTER
29

Ryan could hear Ella's laughter floating out into the hallway as he made his way back from a quick visit to his mother in the surgical ward. He glanced at his watch and realised that while he'd been stuck chatting to Mrs Perrin — and the half dozen other people who'd stopped him to see how his mum was doing — it had already gone two o'clock. So unless he was mistaken that would be Jo eliciting Ella's merriment.

His heart began to pound. She said she'd come and she had, so maybe she wasn't too pissed off at him. Nevertheless, he steeled himself for an icy reception. He'd been a complete arse yesterday and, as it turned out, without cause.

He paused just outside the entrance to the ward and watched the two of them for a moment unobserved. It seemed Jo was painting Ella's nails and his daughter was sporting some type of fancy hair accessory that he'd never seen before. 'Hey you two, looks like you're having fun.'

'Jo's doing my nails, Dad, and she brought her hair straightener so she can do my hair.'

Jo glanced at Ryan nervously. 'I hope that's okay? With Beth in hospital too I thought Ella might be up for a bit of girly attention.'

Ryan flashed her a conciliatory smile. 'Are you suggesting I don't know my way around a hair straightener? Pass it over and I'll give it a go.'

Jo laughed as Ella cried, 'No way! Don't let him have it, Jo. He's hopeless at doing hair.'

'Hopeless? Well, I'm offended.'

Ella giggled. 'Sorry Dad, but you are.'

He sat beside the bed silently for a while as Jo continued to fuss over Ella. It hit him, not for the first time, that despite the fact that Ella had a loving home she was missing out on some of the things that other little girls took for granted. He knew his mother did her best but she was the parent of three boys, so she was in unfamiliar territory with Ella. Practical, no-nonsense Beth had never been one to fuss over her appearance, so a child like Ella, one who loved tutus, lipstick and nail polish, was foreign to her.

Jo was so good with her. She seemed to get all this girly stuff in a way neither he nor his mother could. Right now she was fixing Ella's dark mane into an elaborate hairdo while discussing which sort of lip gloss his daughter preferred. Ryan saw a light in Ella's eyes that she usually reserved for her beloved pony.

'Have you tried chocolate?' Jo asked.

'Chocolate lip gloss?'

'Uh huh.'

Ella shook her head. 'I didn't know you could get chocolate. That sounds awesome.'

Jo nodded. 'In New York there's this shop around the corner from my place and it sells all sorts of great make-up, hair products and perfume.'

'Like the chemist in Bellington?'

Jo laughed. 'Kind of, except that you can't get medicine or bandages or anything like that. It just sells beauty products.'

Ella's eyes widened. 'Wow.'

'Yep, it's pretty amazing. Anyway, they sell this chocolate lip gloss there that looks and tastes divine. When I go home I'll send you some.'

'Really? Do you promise?'

Jo smiled. 'Of course.'

The 'up-do' now complete, Jo sent Ella off to the bathroom to admire her handiwork.

Ryan cleared his throat. With Ella out of the room it was time to make amends for yesterday's outburst. 'Thanks, Jo, for all of this. You've really made her day.'

'It's the least I can do. I'm so glad to see her looking so well. I was so afraid she had a terrible injury. I can't begin to tell you how sorry —'

Ryan held up his hand and indicated for her to stop. 'Please, Jo, don't say any more. I'm the one who needs to apologise. I'm so sorry for the way I spoke to you yesterday. I had no right to be so awful, especially after all the care you'd given Ella.'

'But I let her get hurt. I didn't mean to, honestly. I watched her on the bike to start with and it seemed like she was a pro. I only left her for a couple of minutes, I promise. I took a phone call from my agent. I can't tell you how much I regret that. I just didn't realise...I'm...you know, I'm not great with kids.' She was talking a mile a minute and her face had blushed a deep red.

Ryan got up from the armchair and went to her. He put his hand on her arm to reassure her. 'Shh. You did nothing wrong. I let Ella ride her bike in the yard all the time. Exactly the same thing would have happened if I'd been watching her.'

Jo shook her head. 'I doubt that.'

Ryan looked deep into her eyes. 'Honestly, Jo, it would have. The fall didn't cause Ella's symptoms yesterday. There's a bit of a story behind this...' he glanced towards the bathroom, '...but I can't risk telling you all of it right now. Basically Ella's been diagnosed with epilepsy. The doctors think she had a seizure yesterday and that's what caused her to fall, not the other way around.'

Jo gasped. 'Oh, Ryan, that's awful. She'll be okay though?'

He nodded. 'I think so. She has to go to Melbourne to see a specialist, but the paediatrician here seems to think she will be fine. It's just a matter of getting her on the right medication.'

'That sounds promising, but still it must be an awful shock for you.'

'Yes and no. As I said there's a bit of a story behind all this, but I can't risk Ella overhearing. Can I please make dinner for you to apologise for my behaviour yesterday? I'd like to explain why I reacted the way I did.'

Jo smiled at him with her eyes. 'I would love that. Tonight?'

He shook his head. 'Can we make it tomorrow night? Ella isn't being discharged until the morning, so I'll be staying here tonight, but I'd love you to be there for her welcome-home dinner. If it suits you we can eat early and then you and I can talk once Ella's in bed.'

'Sounds great, I'm pretty sure there are no essential bridesmaid duties tomorrow night. Oh... do you think Ella will still be able to be in the wedding? She's looking forward to it so much.'

'I can't see why not. I'll double check with the doctor before I make any promises to her, but I'm pretty sure she'll be able to walk down the aisle with the rest of you on Saturday.'

'That's a relief. I'd hate to see her miss out.'

Ella came skipping out of the bathroom and made a beeline for Jo. She threw her little arms around Jo's waist. 'I love my hair, Jo. I really, really wish you could live near my house forever so you could come and do it all the time.'

Ryan watched Jo's eyes moisten at Ella's words.

She bent down to return Ella's embrace. 'That's a lovely thing to say. Thank you, Ella.'

'It's true,' Ella replied. 'I like doing hair and make-up and stuff with you. And if you stayed living next door we could go riding together.'

'I would love that, but after Steph and Nate's wedding I really do need to go home. I have an apartment in New York and all my things are there.'

'But you could go and get your stuff and come back right?'

Jo struggled to come up with another compelling reason for going back to America. The kid had a point. Other than some clothes and a few knick-knacks there was nothing waiting for her in Manhattan. She'd been home for less than three weeks but it felt like a lifetime.

Home.

She smiled at the word. Three weeks ago she'd thought of Linden Gully as anything but home. Somewhere along the line that had changed. Every day she'd spent here had chipped away a little of her New York shell and for the first time ever she was beginning to feel like she belonged. Nevertheless she couldn't stay. She couldn't bear to live in the town, seeing Ryan on a regular basis and knowing they could never be together.

He'd made it quite clear he wasn't up for anything more than a fling, or *closure* as he was calling it. And despite his assurances that Ella's fall was not her fault, yesterday's events had only served to reinforce her belief that parenting was not for her. The threat of losing Ella had been way too real. She couldn't imagine how parents lived with that type of risk on a daily basis.

'As much as I love it here, Ella, I really can't stay. But you know what? We can still be friends and we can still talk to each other all the time.'

'On the phone?'

'Maybe, but I have an idea that might be even more fun.'

Ella looked sceptical. 'Really?'

'Do you have an iPad at home?'

'Yeah. Dad has one but I'm not allowed to use it.'

'Maybe if you asked Dad nicely he'd let you FaceTime with me every now and then. I could show you my apartment and all the shops I was telling you about. Would you like that?'

Ella looked over at Ryan. 'Can I, Dad?'

Ryan scratched his head and pretended to consider the request.

'Pleeease Dad? Pretty please?'

'Well, I can hardly refuse when you put it like that.'

Ella grinned. 'Awesome. I can't wait to see that shop you told me about.'

Jo smiled. 'I know you'll love it. And don't worry, I won't forget to send the lip gloss.'

'Knock, knock. Can I come in?'

The three of them turned as one to see Taylah standing in the doorway.

'Hey Taylah. Come on in,' Ryan said.

'Special delivery of one DVD player.'

Ella's eyes lit up. 'Did you bring any DVDs?'

'Sure did,' Taylah said.

As Ella's attention turned to the bag of goodies Taylah had brought in, Jo took it as her cue to leave. 'I really should be going,' she said.

Ella stopped rifling through her DVDs. 'Do you have to?'

'Afraid so, kiddo, but I promise I'll see you soon.'

'Jo has agreed to come over for dinner when you come home from hospital, so you'll see her then, okay?' Ryan said. He looked at Jo. 'I'll walk out with you. You don't mind sitting with Ella for a minute, do you Tay?'

Taylah shook her head. 'Of course not.'

Jo gave Ella a quick hug. 'See you tomorrow, kiddo.'

Ella returned the hug and planted a kiss on Jo's cheek. 'Bye, Jo.'

Once they were out of Ella's earshot Ryan began to speak. 'Thanks for agreeing to come today. Not just for my sake but for Ella's. She's really taken a shine to you.'

Jo felt a bubble of happiness welling inside her. She'd never expected Carly's daughter to win her heart, but somehow Ella had managed to do just that. 'She's such a sweetheart. It's impossible not to be taken by her. I'm really glad she likes me too.'

As they rounded the corner and headed towards the elevators Ryan reached for Jo's hand. Startled, she stopped and turned towards him, her eyebrows raised.

'Sorry,' he said, withdrawing his hand. 'I didn't mean to make you feel uncomfortable.'

'I'm not uncomfortable, you just surprised me that's all. I came in here thinking you were never going to speak to me again, let alone be...affectionate.'

'Yeah. I am truly sorry about that. I really lost it yesterday. I was just so afraid.'

'It's okay. I understand. Well, as much as someone without any kids can. I guess most parents would feel the same way.'

Ryan shook his head. 'As I said before there's a bit more to it than just being worried about the accident. It's a really long story and one I would like to tell you over dinner tomorrow.'

'Of course. There's really no need to explain further but I'm happy to listen if there's something you want to get off your chest.' There was actually something she needed to get off *her* chest.

Now was probably the time to tell him about the photo. She should tell him — his image was out there and he had a right to know — but she just couldn't bring herself to sully the moment.

Another day probably wouldn't make that much difference. He was holed up here at the hospital for the moment and had little contact with the outside world. Besides, it had been almost twenty-four hours since Lydia broke the news and so far the story didn't seem to have much traction. Maybe Zach's people had decided to bury it for some reason, or maybe no one gave a toss who Johanna Morgan was kissing. In any case, there was probably no pressing need to worry Ryan with the details right this minute. It could wait until tomorrow.

She checked to see no one was looking and then leaned in and kissed Ryan on the cheek, her skin brushing against his unshaven chin. She grinned and ran a finger along his jawline. 'You can keep that.'

'The stubble?' He ran a hand over his chin. 'Really?'

'Very sexy,' she said as she headed off to catch the lift. 'See you tomorrow.'

CHAPTER
30

Ryan wheeled the cart aimlessly up and down the aisles of Glasson's supermarket. Why the hell had he offered to cook? He wasn't totally hopeless in the kitchen — he had meat and three veg down pat — but this dinner needed to be special, and fancy wasn't part of his repertoire.

His gut clenched at the thought of sharing the truth about Ella with Jo, but he had to do it. There was no way forward for them if she didn't know the whole story. And he'd come to realise developing a proper relationship with Jo was something he wanted more than anything.

The whole 'closure' scenario that the two of them had bought into was a total crock. Making love to her had just strengthened the feelings he'd been trying to quash all these years. He'd tried to convince himself it was physical, pure lust, and that his desire would recede when she left. But when he saw her with Ella, the two of them chattering and giggling together, he saw the possibility for something much more.

And then he knew.

This time he would fight for her.

So an amazing dinner was in order to set the scene. And wine. Maybe sparkling wine? She was probably used to drinking some swanky French Champagne. He grimaced. Not much bloody hope of sourcing that at the pub's bottle shop.

'Ryan, are you okay?'

He swung around to find Mrs Clemmens from the butcher's shop staring at him. 'I'm fine thank you, Mrs C. How are you?'

'I'm well, thanks. Is there a reason you're pulling faces at the produce? Is there something I should know about the carrots?'

'What?' He looked down at the bag of carrots in his hands. 'Oh. No, the carrots are fine. I was just miles away. I'm trying to work out what to cook for dinner tonight. I'm cooking for a friend and I think her tastes might be a little fancier than mine.'

Mrs Clemmens nodded sagely. 'I'd heard you and the lovely Miss Morgan might be a bit of an item. Good on you, Ryan. You deserve some happiness. I know some around here had it in for Johanna because of her mother, but I've always liked her.'

So the Linden Gully grapevine was buzzing with speculation. Somehow the fact didn't bother him as much as he thought it would. If things went to plan maybe they'd all have something to talk about. 'Oh, it's nothing like that Mrs C. Well, what I mean to say is it's a thank-you dinner. Jo was looking after Ella when she fell sick. The dinner is to thank her for taking such good care of Ella.'

'How is Ella? Poor little mite.'

She's fine. In fact, she's at home now with her friend Gemma. Gem's mum is watching her while I do a quick shop so I really should —'

'Lamb.'

'I'm sorry?'

'If you want to impress her you can't go past roast lamb. She's been living in America and I believe the quality of lamb over there is inferior to ours. A nice roast is sure to impress.'

'Mrs C, you're a lifesaver!' He bent over and kissed the bemused middle-aged woman on the cheek. Ryan didn't know whether she was right about Australian lamb being superior, but he did know that a roast dinner was something he excelled at.

'When you've grabbed some veggies pop over to the shop and tell Ed I sent you. He'll fix you up with a lovely little leg. And after that you might like to head over to the bottle-o for a nice drop of red to go with it.'

'Way ahead of you, Mrs C. I'd better fly!'

Jo threw yet another top onto the bed. It was just a casual dinner, for heaven's sake. Why on earth was she having so much trouble deciding what to wear? It was a dinner at home so formal attire wasn't required and yet jeans and a t-shirt seemed too sloppy. She wanted to show Ryan she appreciated all the effort he was going to.

She pulled out a baby pink cashmere jumper — three weeks ago she would've called it a sweater — as she contemplated the night ahead. Ryan had things he wanted to talk about. He'd said he needed to be honest with her about something, although she couldn't imagine what.

But it wasn't Ryan's disclosure she was worried about. She had to tell him about the photo. Lydia had phoned earlier and reported some mild interest in the story. It hadn't run on the news sites or in any of the papers, but a few of the gossip blogs had picked up on it, so there was still a chance that some twit would try to get a comment from Ryan or, even worse, snap candid shots of him and Ella.

She couldn't wait any longer. She had to tell him tonight.

Maybe, if she explained it properly, he would understand. After all, it was hardly her fault. And he'd been so understanding about Ella's fall. She'd expected him to refuse to speak to her ever again, but here he was cooking her a conciliatory dinner. Maybe he'd take this latest development in his stride too. Perhaps the photo wasn't the big deal she was making it out to be.

She didn't want to leave Linden Gully with him hating her again. The rollercoaster of emotions she'd experienced these past few days had reinforced how important Ryan was to her. If they couldn't be together as a couple she could live with that. It hurt to know that after this week he would no longer be part of her everyday life, but she also knew that in time the pain would heal.

They'd missed their window, that one perfect moment in time when it could have worked between them. Now their relationship didn't just affect them. There was a child to consider. Ella had already suffered more than her fair share of angst in her short life. She'd lost her mother. She'd been uprooted from her home more than once and now she'd been diagnosed with a serious medical condition. She didn't need to add an incompetent stepmother into the mix.

The crazy thing was, if ever there was a kid that could make her change her mind about becoming a parent it was that sweet little girl. When she'd first looked at Ella all Jo could see was Carly. She was ashamed to admit — even to herself — that she'd judged an innocent six-year-old by the sins of her mother.

She, of all people, should have known better. The whole time she'd lived in Linden Gully that had been her fate too. She'd never fitted in here because people had been quick to judge. They'd assumed she was a carbon copy of her cold and distant mother.

Now that Jo had spent time with Ella she could see her for herself. And she liked what she saw.

But like and love were two different things.

Just because she liked the child didn't mean she could give her unconditional love, the type of love required to be a good parent. Jo knew what it was like to grow up with a mother who didn't know how to love. There was no way she would risk having Ella grow up in a house like that.

And that was that. She and Ryan could never be.

But after all they'd been through these past few weeks she couldn't bear the thought of him hating her again. She crossed her fingers and hoped he wouldn't take the whole photo fiasco too badly and their plan of bringing a happy conclusion to their relationship would not be jeopardised.

Settling at last on the pink jumper with a pair of dark denim jeans, Jo dressed herself in record time — being late for dinner wouldn't be a good start. She pulled on her tan leather boots, smeared her lips with strawberry lip gloss and grabbed her keys.

Fingers crossed.

Ryan prodded the meat with a fork, releasing a trickle of pink juice into the roasting pan. The meat was done to perfection. If he removed it now there would be just enough time for it to rest before the veggies were done.

Hopefully Jo would be on time. Ella was bursting to see her. If she arrived right on six as planned there'd be time for the girls to socialise while he made the gravy, which should keep Ella happy.

His two favourite girls together.

He smiled at the thought. Hopefully after tonight there would be a lot more times like these to come.

They'd all have dinner together and then, once Ella was in bed, he could sit down with Jo and tell her everything.

His resolve to fight for a relationship with her had not dampened overnight. In fact, if anything it had grown stronger. She was amazing with Ella, and Ryan knew that Jo's warm heart was big enough to embrace his little girl.

There were obstacles, he couldn't deny that. But this time he was determined to work to overcome them. He wouldn't lose Joey again. He couldn't.

A loud knock at the door prompted an excited squeal from Ella. 'I'll get the door, Dad.'

Before he'd had time to answer, he heard the click of the doorknob and Jo's voice drifting down the hallway.

'Hey, Ella. How are you? You look great. What a pretty dress.'

'It's my party dress. I wore it just for you.'

'Really? I'm honoured. Here, I brought you a little welcome-home present.'

Ryan made his way out into the hall in time to see Ella discarding pink wrapping paper onto the floor.

'Oh!' she gasped. 'Dad, look! It's a jewellery box.'

A lump formed in Ryan's throat. He knew exactly what it was. He'd given Jo the music box as a gift to take back to boarding school at the end of their first summer together.

Ella flipped open the lid and gasped again as the little plastic ballerina popped up.

'Wind the key,' Jo said.

Ella did as instructed and Ryan watched in delight as her eyes widened when the ballerina began to twirl to the tinny strains of 'Unchained Melody'.

Ryan sought Jo's gaze and when their eyes met he smiled. 'I can't believe it still works.'

Ella looked up at him, her brow creased in confusion. 'What do you mean?'

Jo crouched down so that she was at eye level with Ella. 'This is a very special music box. I've had it since I was sixteen. Your dad gave it to me.'

Ella's eyes widened. 'Did you, Dad? Was it a birthday present?'

Ryan cleared his throat. 'No. When we were kids Jo didn't go to the same school as me. She went to boarding school. Do you know what that is?'

Ella nodded. She wrinkled her nose and looked at Jo. 'That must've been horrible.'

'I have to admit it wasn't great,' Jo said.

'That's why I gave her the music box. So she would always remember that she had friends here in Linden Gully who were thinking about her.'

'And that's why I want you to have it now, Ella. When I go back to New York you can open up the box and listen to the music and remember the fun we've had together.'

'That's really cool. I love it. Thanks Jo. I'm going to go and put it on my desk right now and put all my special treasures in it.'

As Ella trundled off down the hallway Ryan motioned for Jo to follow him into the kitchen.

'Wow, something smells good. Do I detect the aroma of lamb roast?'

Ryan nodded as he uncorked the red. He hadn't planned on drinking this early in the evening but after seeing the music box he needed something to put him back on an even keel. 'Yep. I have it on good authority that Australian lamb is the way to a young lady's heart.' Sheesh. Did he really just say that? If he wasn't careful he'd send her skittering back out the door.

But Jo laughed and nodded as he held up a wine glass in query. 'On whose authority?'

'Mrs Clemmens.'

'Well, the butcher's wife would say that, wouldn't she?'

He grinned. 'I guess so.' He gulped a mouthful of wine and lowered his voice. 'Thanks for giving Ella the music box. I can't believe you kept it all these years.'

'It's lucky it survived Katherine's many purges. I have so few things left from my childhood. But Dad knew how special this was to me. I found it packed away with a few other precious bits and pieces in the loft of his shed.'

'No one could accuse your mother of being sentimental.'

'That's for sure.'

'In any case, I'll make sure Ella looks after it.'

'I know she will Ryan. That's part of the reason I gave it to her. She's such a sweetheart.'

There. He knew it. He knew that given enough time Jo would come to love Ella as much as he did. It seemed his little girl had already started to chip away at Jo's heart.

CHAPTER
31

Ella held out her plate and smiled her best 'daddy's girl' smile. 'Can I have another piece of apple pie?' She paused momentarily before remembering her manners. 'Please?'

Ryan shook his head and laughed. 'I don't think so, missy. You've had a big dinner and an enormous serve of pie already. Aren't you full?'

Ella shrugged. 'Not too full, and Gran's apple pie is my favourite dessert.'

'How about we put it in the fridge and you can have it for dessert tomorrow?'

She pouted her protest but didn't argue. 'Okay.'

'Come on, I'm going to run the shower for you. Time for you to get ready for bed.'

'Dad, no! I want to stay and talk to Jo.'

'Honey, you've been sick. You need your sleep.'

'It's not fair, I —'

'Hey, Ella,' Jo interrupted, 'how about this? What if you go get ready for bed and then I'll come in and read you a bedtime story when you're all tucked up. Does that sound like a plan?'

The smile returned to Ella's face and she nodded enthusiastically.

Ryan shot Jo a grateful look. 'Well come on, miss. Let's get a move on. We don't want to keep Jo waiting.'

Once Ella was in bed Ryan gave her a kiss and left Jo to it. Ella had a large pile of books at the ready, which he figured would give him ample time to take care of the dishes and to go over what he wanted to say to Jo. Again.

He couldn't keep the truth about Ella to himself any longer. Telling Jo was a risk, but there was no avoiding it. He wanted her to share his life, and Ella's life, and that meant no secrets.

He and Jo had screwed up big time seven years ago. They'd kept things from each other. He wouldn't make the same mistake twice. This time everything would be laid bare — for better or worse.

He covered the leftover pie and placed it in the fridge, loaded the dishwasher and popped the kettle on while he listened to the sound of muffled giggling from the bedroom. He was tossing up whether to rescue Jo when he realised the only sound he could hear was the tinkling of the music box. Jo's footsteps in the hallway followed soon after.

'I thought I'd have to come and save you. Ella can be mighty persuasive when she wants something,' he said as Jo appeared in the doorway.

'I know how to deal with fans,' she said with a wink.

'Ha. Sorry I doubted you. Is she asleep?'

'Not yet, but she's not far off.'

'Good, because there's something I need to talk to you about. Do you want another glass of red?'

Jo shook her head. 'Not for me, I'm driving, but you go ahead.'

Ryan resisted the temptation to quell his apprehension with alcohol. A clear head was needed for this conversation. 'Nah, I've had enough. I probably should stay under the limit in case Ella needs to go back to the hospital.'

An expression of concern settled on Jo's face. 'Is that likely?'

'I don't think so, but I don't want to take any chances. Once she's seen the specialist in Melbourne we'll have a better idea of what we're dealing with. That's partly what I want to talk to you about.' The kettle clicked off, momentarily diverting their attention. 'I'll make us a cuppa, eh? The fire's going in the living room. Why don't we head in there and get comfy on the couch? What I've got to say might take a little while.'

She nodded her agreement in silence.

Once they were settled on the couch Ryan took a deep breath and started. 'So you know about Carly's death, right?'

'I heard she was killed in a car accident.'

'Yes, she was, but she wasn't the only person in the car. She had Ella there with her.'

'Jenny did mention that.'

'I figured you would have heard. Linden Gully's grapevine still works as well as ever.'

She smiled but said nothing, encouraging him to go on.

'So maybe you didn't hear some of the other details and I want to fill you in on those now.'

'Ryan, it's okay. You don't have to tell me —'

'Actually I do. In any case I want to.'

She sank back into the couch and took a sip of her tea, indicating she was ready to listen.

'Ella was injured. Very badly injured. She wasn't in a car seat and as a result she got thrown around in the accident. She suffered internal injuries and a fractured skull.'

Jo's hand flew to her mouth.

'The injuries were so severe we weren't sure she'd pull through, but she's a gutsy little kid. She was in ICU at the Royal Children's for over a week, but she made big improvements every day. Unfortunately though, one of the side effects was that she started to have seizures.'

'You mean she's been epileptic ever since the accident? Oh my god, Ryan, why didn't you tell me? How could you let me look after her without telling me something like that?'

'Hang on, hang on. It's not as simple as that. When she was in the hospital after the accident she was put onto an anticonvulsant medication. The seizures stopped. The medication was continued for 12 months and then she was slowly weaned off. She's never had another seizure until this week. I always knew there was a possibility the seizures would return, but as the years went by I guess I became a bit complacent. I promise you, I would never have put you, or Ella, in that position if I'd known what was going to happen.'

'It must be very worrying. Especially when you thought she'd made a full recovery.'

He exhaled, and allowed his body to relax a little. 'Yeah, it is a bit. I'll feel better when I've spoken to the specialist and have a clearer picture of what we're facing. Thank god it's treatable, though.'

Jo slid over so that her leg was touching his. Under normal circumstances that would be enough to get his blood pumping, but not tonight. Tonight there was something bigger at stake. He stood up. 'There's more, Jo, but I just need to double check that Ella is sleeping. I can't risk her overhearing what I have to say.'

Jo stood too. 'Do you want another cuppa? I'll make it.'

'Yeah, thanks. That'd be good.'

He padded down the hallway in his socks, hoping not only to find his daughter sleeping but also to brace himself for the discussion to come. He was risking everything by telling Jo, but there was no other way forward.

After satisfying himself that the steady rise and fall of Ella's chest was proof of her slumber, he made his way back to the living room. Jo handed him a steaming cup of coffee. He took it but didn't resume his place on the couch. Instead he went and stood by the fireplace. Better if there was some space between them.

She looked up at him expectantly. 'You said there was more?'

'I need to explain to you why I reacted the way I did at the hospital.'

'You've already apologised for that. I understand, truly I do. You were worried. I'm sure any parent would do the same.'

Ryan shrugged. 'I don't know about that. In any case I lashed out at you and I shouldn't have. I was really angry at myself, if the truth be known.'

'Yourself? Why? Ella's fall wasn't your fault. There was nothing you could have done.'

'I don't know. I guess seeing her in the hospital like that brought it all back to me — the car accident, I mean. It was my fault she was in that car. I should never, ever have let Carly have her unsupervised. That girl just wasn't fit to be a mother. It wasn't her fault, she never knew any better, but I did. She convinced her case worker that she'd changed, that she was well, but I should have known better than to leave Ella alone with her.'

'Case worker?'

'I'm not sure how much you know about our relationship.'

'Not much. Just that Carly left when Ella was little.'

He nodded. 'Twelve months old. Ella wasn't even walking. Carly just couldn't cope with the relentless nature of being a mother. Looking back I think she had postnatal depression, but we were both so young and I didn't know about stuff like that then. She started drinking, quite a lot. I was trying to work and to study part time but it got so bad I was afraid to leave her alone with Ella. I told her she needed to get help or I would report her to the authorities. And so she left.'

'Oh god, that must have been terrible.'

The bitter taste of guilt rose in his throat. 'You know what? At the time, I really didn't care. It was a relief not to have to worry about her. I didn't chase her, didn't check up on her. I just set about caring for Ella and making her life as stable and carefree as it could be. I figured Carly was big enough to look after herself. If I could change that now...'

Jo shook her head. 'I'm sure you did the best you could.'

'Did I? I don't know. Sometimes I think that it was my fault that she drank. Maybe it wasn't that she couldn't cope with the baby, maybe it was because I didn't love her. Worse than that I resented her because...'

'She got pregnant?'

'No, I never blamed her for that. I resented her for something she had no control over — she wasn't you.'

'Oh Ryan.' Jo rose from her seat and moved towards him but he gestured for her to stop. The last thing he wanted right now was her comfort. There was still a long way to go and he was afraid if he wavered this time he might never garner the courage again.

'Jo, no. Please, I need you to hear me out.'

Jo settled back into her seat. 'Go on.'

'Whatever the reason, she left. And I didn't really care that much. Ella and I were fine on our own. Bec and Dan helped me out and Mum did what she could. I managed to keep my studies up and work a bit as well as taking care of Ella. Then when she was almost three, Carly turned up out the blue. Said she was better and she seemed to be. She wanted to come back to live with us, but I wasn't ready for that. To be honest I wished she'd stayed away. I was angry, Jo. I didn't want her to swan back in and mess up our lives.'

'I can understand that.'

'Well Carly couldn't. She was pissed off. She started making noises about getting a lawyer and seeking custody of Ella. I panicked. I didn't want it going to court. I was afraid of losing custody.'

'But surely that wouldn't happen?'

He shrugged. 'Who knows? I wasn't prepared to take the risk. So I made a deal with her. Access to Ella, twice a week, supervised by me or one of my family. At first she was happy with that but after a while she wanted more.'

'She wanted to see Ella on her own?'

'Yes.'

'And you let her?'

'Not at first. But she did seem better, more stable, and Ella loved spending time with her. The day of the accident I had an opportunity to observe a rare surgery at the veterinary hospital in Werribee, but Bec wasn't around and I needed someone to care for Ella. I rang Carly and asked her if she could watch Ella for a few hours. I had no idea she would take Ella in the car. I left her the car seat, just in case, but I stressed to her it was only for emergencies. When I thought about it later I realised she probably had no idea how to fit it. I should have put it in her car before I left. I really didn't think...'

'What happened in the car? Was the accident her fault?'

Ryan inhaled deeply. Fault. It was such a subjective word. And it wasn't like he hadn't played the blame game over and over in his head. He'd railed at Carly, been furious with her and cursed the day she'd walked back into their lives. But in the end he'd accepted that the responsibility for Ella lay squarely at his feet.

'The autopsy found she had a blood alcohol reading of .07. She shouldn't have been driving. It happened at eleven o'clock in the morning. It never occurred to me that she was still drinking. She seemed so much better.' He paused to look at Jo.

Her face and her body language radiated empathy. 'You mustn't blame yourself. You wouldn't have let Ella stay with Carly if you thought she was in any danger.'

He shook his head in protest, but didn't argue the point. It was more important to get this next part out. 'Jo, what I'm about to tell you is strictly confidential and I hope you'll respect that.'

'You don't have to tell me anything you're not comfortable sharing.'

'I want to tell you.'

She nodded. 'Okay. You have my word I will keep whatever it is to myself.'

This was it. If he told her there would be no going back. He took a deep breath and launched into it. 'After the accident, Ella had massive injuries. The doctors tested her blood type in case she needed a blood transfusion. She's not the same blood type as me.'

Jo was silent, obviously not seeing where this was going.

'Ella's blood type is B. Carly's was A. I'm an O.'

Comprehension dawned on Jo's face, but she waited for him to say the words.

'Long story short. Ella's not my daughter.'

CHAPTER
32

Ryan's words hit Jo like a punch in the gut. How could Ella not be his? It simply made no sense. 'What the hell are you talking about, Ryan?'

'Biologically, Ella's not mine. Her blood type makes it impossible.'

'I get that bit, but if she's not yours why is she with you?'

'She might not be biologically mine, but I raised her. She's still my daughter.'

'But why did you stay with Carly in the first place? Was it to spite me, Ryan? To hurt me? To make me give up on you? Because if that's what it was, it worked. I couldn't compete against a woman who was pregnant, could I?'

'My decision had nothing to do with you, Jo. When Carly told me she was pregnant I was devastated. I knew I would be tied to her in some way for the rest of my life. It was like a jail sentence. But I had to accept the consequences of my actions. I had no idea Ella wasn't mine until after the accident.'

'You're saying Carly tricked you into believing she was pregnant with your child?' Confusion and anger caused her voice to rise.

'I honestly don't know. Maybe she thought I was the father or maybe she knew I wasn't. I don't know and none of us will ever know now.' Ryan turned his back and toyed with the fire, prodding a log with an iron poker and sending a shower of orange sparks up the chimney.

When he turned back to face her she could see the defiance in his eyes. 'Even if she did know, even if she did deceive me, I was the person she chose to be the father of her child. I will always honour that.'

Jo didn't know how to react. She'd given up all hope of a relationship with Ryan when she heard about Carly's pregnancy. Finding out the whole thing was quite possibly a lie was almost too much to bear. They'd thrown their relationship away and been apart all these years because of something that wasn't even true. Her head was spinning. It was too much to process. 'So who is her real father? Where's he in all of this?'

Ryan shook his head. 'I don't know. That secret died with Carly. There have been attempts to trace him but they were unsuccessful.'

'Attempts by who? Who else knows this?'

'No one.'

'No one? You mean you haven't told the authorities...who the hell do you notify about this sort of thing anyway? God, Ryan, you can't keep something like this a secret. Can you?' She had no idea. Was it illegal to keep a child when you knew she wasn't biologically yours? Was that why Ryan hadn't told anyone?

'No. Of course not.' There was a hint of irritation in his voice. 'I've consulted a lawyer, several actually. As soon as I made the discovery I sought legal advice. The attempts to find Ella's biological father were part of the legal investigation. I just meant I haven't told anyone else yet.'

'Not even your mum?'

'No.'

'But why?'

'Because it's none of anyone else's business. I didn't want anyone else telling me what I should or shouldn't do. I'm Ella's dad. I've always been her father, no matter what any blood test says. I'm taking steps now to make her legally mine. The adoption will make sure that no one can ever dispute my claim to her or take her away from me. I'm not interested in what other people, even people in my family, might have to say about that.'

Jo's indignation at the injustice of it all dissipated. Of course Ella was Ryan's daughter no matter what the blood tests said. And Ryan was not the type of man to walk away from his responsibilities. His loyalty was one of the things she loved most about him. 'Adoption?'

'Yes. I'm in the process of formally adopting Ella. My name is on her birth certificate, so technically I don't need to adopt...it's a bit of a legal grey area to be honest. But if there was ever a dispute and it could be proved I knew about her blood type, then that might not go well for me. After discussing the options with my lawyer I decided it was the best course of action. If I chose non-disclosure I'd be living under a cloud. I'd always be worried about being found out and Ella being carted off by the authorities.'

'Could that happen?'

'Highly unlikely. Still, I wanted to make sure that no one could ever take her away from me. When she's older I'll tell her the truth. I want her to know that I chose to be her dad. I wasn't tricked into it. I want her to know she was wanted.'

Jo's heart swelled and her eyes moistened with emotion. 'So the adoption isn't complete?'

'Almost, but not quite. There's been a lot of red tape. It's a complicated situation and it's taken some time. Carly's parents had to be consulted and I was very worried they might not give their approval, but they did and now we're almost there. It should all be completed by the end of September.'

'So it's a done deal?'

'Pretty much. But I'm still edgy about the whole thing, worried that something will go wrong at the last minute. That's part of the reason I reacted so badly at the hospital. It was fear, not just of losing her in some accident, but fear of having her snatched away from me due to perceived negligence.'

'Oh Ryan. I had no idea. I'm so sorry.'

He came and sat beside her on the couch again. 'It's not your fault, that's what I'm trying to say. None of what happened was your fault. My fear of her being taken away is probably an irrational one, but until the final papers are signed I'm going to be on edge about things like that. My reaction at the hospital was out of line, but after what I've told you I hope you have a better understanding of why.'

Jo put her hand on his thigh. 'Ryan,' she said gently, 'you are a fantastic father. Anyone can see that. Ella is a great little kid, and that's coming from someone who isn't particularly fond of little kids. I'm sure you don't have anything to worry about.'

He nodded. 'You're right, I'm sure.'

'I'm glad you told me but I'm not sure why you did.'

Ryan grasped her hand and looked deep into her eyes. 'I don't want there to be secrets between us, Jo. I don't know what will happen with us in the future, but I do know that the only way forward is for us to tell each other the truth. Always.'

Future? What future? Their future was hopefully a few more delicious hours in the bedroom followed by a fond farewell. A happy ending. Wasn't that what they'd both agreed to?

'Jo, in the spirit of full disclosure I have to tell you something else.' He paused for a second and took her other hand in his. 'I love you and want you to be in my life forever.'

Jo's pulse began to thud in her ears.

'I want you to be part of my life, Jo. Part of our lives, mine and Ella's. She might not be biologically related to me but she's my daughter in every way that counts. If we're ever going to be together I need you to understand that Ella is part and parcel of that, no matter what. I'll never do anything to jeopardise that relationship.'

Jo wanted to stop him, to say something about how she loved him too, but parenthood was a risk she just couldn't take. He was looking at her with such hope and tenderness in his eyes and she knew she was about to break his heart all over again. When she opened her mouth it seemed full of sand. No words came.

Ryan filled the silence between them. 'After I saw you with Ella yesterday I knew that I had to try to make a go of it with you. I think we were destined to be together. No one affects me the way you do. It's been seven years and I still catch my breath when I see you. My heart still hammers like I'm a nervous teenager every time we touch. When I see you playing with Ella my heart is full and I know that if I could have that vision in my life every single day, my world would be complete. If you still love me, and I think you do, I can't see why we can't be together. Ella's already fallen in love with you. We could be a family, if that's what you want.'

He loved her.

Not *had always loved her*, or *part of him would always love her*. He loved her. Right here. Right now. For a few seconds she allowed herself to revel in the elation of hearing those words said out loud.

Was he right? Was there some way that this could work? Should she go against her instinct and give it a go?

In the absence of her reply, Ryan continued. 'I know you said you don't want kids, but I see the way you are with Ella. I know we could make it work somehow. I can't bear the thought of you leaving, Jo, and I think you feel the same way.'

Jo's stomach somersaulted. Why was she fighting this? The only man she'd ever really loved was in front of her, telling her they'd find a way to make it work. Surely it wasn't that simple. Or was it?

'I don't know…I don't know what to say. It's complicated.'

'I don't need an answer from you right now. I know this has come out of the blue and that I've probably overwhelmed you by dumping everything on you at once. But I couldn't let you leave again without telling you how I feel. I want to fight for us this time, Jo, and I'm prepared to do whatever it takes.'

He leaned in and softly kissed her. She closed her eyes and luxuriated in the kiss. As his mouth gently moved over hers, Jo was tempted to ignore all the reasons why this wasn't a good idea and just say 'yes'. Why the hell not? He loved her, he wanted her and she loved him too. Wasn't that all that mattered?

As she pulled back gently and opened her eyes she caught sight of Ella's doll, naked and discarded under the coffee table. Her fantasy came crashing down around her. Being with Ryan was just that — a fantasy. Him saying the words 'I love you' didn't change their situation. Her elation evaporated and was replaced with regret. What did it matter if they loved each other? It didn't change the fact that there was a child involved and she couldn't go there.

'Ryan, I think you know I love you. But I'm not ready to be a mother.'

'I'm just asking you to consider the idea. I think we can make a go of it. We can take it slow if you like. What if you stayed on for a bit after the wedding, moved back to Yarrapinga for a while? We could see each other, you could spend time with Ella, see how the two of you get along. I mean, we probably couldn't move in together immediately anyway, not until after the adoption's finalised. But there's no reason we couldn't spend time together. If things go well then we can take the next step when all three of us are ready.'

A whirlpool of emotions swirled in Jo's head. Wasn't this exactly what she'd wanted, what she'd fantasised about? What the hell was stopping her? She was being handed a second chance at happiness here. She should be grabbing hold of it with both hands. 'What then? What if it all goes well and we decide to move in together? I'm scared, Ryan. What if I turn out to be like my mother? Ella deserves better than that.'

Ryan pulled her in and held her against him. 'I have no fear of that happening. Ella is the most precious thing in the world to me. Do you really think I would be asking you into our lives if I thought there was even a remote chance of you not being up to it?'

'How can you be so sure?'

He released her and pulled back a little so she could see his face. 'The fact that you're even thinking about how a potential relationship could affect Ella shows me you're made of the right stuff. Honestly, Jo, no parent has all the answers, no parent is perfect. Do you think I get it right all the time? Because I don't. Every parent is just making it up as they go along, doing the best they can. Part of the reason I told you about my situation with Ella was to show you that biology has absolutely nothing to do with being a parent. Showing up is what counts. You just have to be there each day and do the best you can.'

Every part of her wanted to give in and say the words he wanted to hear, but she needed some time to think it over. This was a huge decision, one she wouldn't be rushing into. 'I want to believe you, but I just don't know what to say to you, Ryan. It's a lot to contemplate.'

He nodded. 'I know. Like I said, you don't need to give me an answer right now. I just wanted to be honest with you, Jo. Last time you left we held things back from each other. I didn't want to make the same mistake twice.'

He'd laid his soul bare before her and told her things that he'd been keeping secret for years. That couldn't have been easy. Now there was something she needed to tell him, and after all he'd just said it wasn't going to be easy. With Ella's adoption not finalised the matter of the photo being in the public domain would probably weigh heavily on him. Hopefully he'd understand that it wasn't her fault. She kissed him gently and placed her hand on his cheek. 'I do love you, you know. No matter what I decide I want you to know that.'

He nodded. 'I know.'

'I have something I need to tell you too.' She paused for a beat to steel herself against the disappointment she was about to see in his eyes.

'Oh yeah? What's that?'

The shrill sound of the phone ringing saved her from having to reply.

Ryan glanced at his watch. 'Jesus, it's nine o'clock. Who rings the landline at this hour?' He jumped up and ran to the kitchen to answer it.

Moments later he was back, his face pale and his expression tense. 'That was the hospital. It's Mum. Seems she's running a high temperature. She's picked up an infection. They've put her on strong antibiotics but...'

'What?'

'It doesn't look good. There's a real chance she won't make it through the night.'

'Oh Ryan.'

'I need to go to her. I hate to ask this Jo, especially after what I put you through last time, but could you possibly —'

'Stay with Ella? Of course I will. You don't need to ask. Just go.'

He pulled her close and hugged her tight. 'Thank you. I'll keep my mobile on, so you can call me if you're worried about anything at all. I'll be back as soon as possible.'

'Don't worry. I promise I'll take good care of her.'

CHAPTER
33

The tiny grey-faced woman lying in Intensive Care bore little resemblance to Ryan's mother. For as long as he could remember his mum had been a formidable presence in his life. No matter what happened to her, no matter what life threw at her, she bore it all with a smile on her face. Now she looked small and helpless and Ryan felt like a child again.

Surely this wasn't the end? Not when things had been going so well for her. For the first time in her life she'd been able to relax a little. All her sons were settled — they'd completed their studies and had careers they loved. Dan and Bec were happily married and were planning to start a family of their own. Having them on the farm had brought Beth great pleasure. Two of her boys and her granddaughter on the same property was a dream come true for her. And Patrick might be in London, but he and Georgie were always coming home for visits, and they were planning to move back to Melbourne at the end of the year.

And now, there was the possibility that Jo might join their family — if things went the way he hoped they would.

Beth had loved Jo once. She admired her strength and independence. She had never said much about the Morgans, but he knew his mother was less than impressed with Katherine's distant parenting method. It had made her fiercely protective of Jo. Beth had treated her as a member of the family, the daughter she'd never had. So when Jo left him broken hearted, Beth's grief was twofold. She mourned for his loss and for her own.

This time around his mother hadn't allowed herself to get close to Jo. He understood. Hell, he'd gone down that same path to begin with. But every minute he spent with Jo just reinforced the fact that there was no protecting his heart from love. No matter how hard he tried, he couldn't not love her. It was a fact, pure and simple. If she didn't love him back, didn't love him enough to give them a chance at working things out, he'd be heartbroken all over again. But if he let her go without telling her how he felt, without doing his best to convince her that they were destined to be together, he'd regret it for the rest of life. In general he wasn't a gambling man, but this was one of those times when there was no other choice but to roll the dice and see where they landed.

If he got lucky and Jo stayed, Mum would be happy for him and he just knew she'd let Jo back into her heart.

A touch on the shoulder made him jump.

'Sorry, didn't mean to scare you.' It was one of the nursing staff. Sarah? Sally? Something like that.

'It's okay. I was in another world. How's she doing?'

'She's stable for now. Her temperature's dropped a fraction and has stayed the same for the past two hours, which is a good sign. Ideally we'll start to see some improvement soon. The next couple of hours are critical.'

Ryan's chest tightened. 'So she's not out of the woods yet?'

'Not yet, I'm afraid. But don't give up hope. She seems like a fighter.'

'Yeah, she's a tough old bird, aren't you Mum?' Ryan's phone vibrated in his pocket. He grabbed it and checked the screen. It was a text from Patrick. Ryan held up the phone to the nurse. 'It's my brother, Patrick. He lives in London. When I called him earlier I didn't know anything much. He's asking if he should book a flight home?'

She shrugged. 'I can't tell you or your family what to do, but I can say that the next few hours are the critical ones. If she continues to improve, then things are looking up. If not, then the likelihood of a good outcome starts to diminish.'

'If you were me, what would you tell him?'

'Look, he's not going to make it here in the next few hours so I think the sensible thing would be to tell him to hold tight. We'll know more by the morning.'

'Right, I'll text him to let know to wait a few hours and I'll call him as soon as I have any news.' Ryan started texting as he spoke.

'Just the two of you, then? No other siblings?'

'There's actually three of us. My other brother lives with us at the farm but he's away in Queensland at the moment. I called him already. He'll be on the first flight home tomorrow. But then he'll have to drive from Melbourne so we won't be seeing him until tomorrow night, I wouldn't think.'

The nurse smiled. 'Good thing you're here then. You look exhausted, though.'

'Yeah, it's been a rough week. My little girl has been in hospital too, so I haven't a decent night's sleep for a few days. But no worries. I'll survive.'

'Your mum's sedated, so she'll be out of it for a while. Don't be afraid to get a little shut-eye. I promise I'll wake you if there's any change.'

'Thanks. I might see if I can grab forty winks.' As the nurse quietly slipped out of the room Ryan took her advice and balled his jacket up to use as a pillow. Slowly his jumbled thoughts began to ease as his body succumbed to exhaustion and sleep overtook him.

Jo whiled away the hours mindlessly flipping through the TV channels and texting Steph. She didn't disclose any of her conversation with Ryan to her friend, focusing instead on Beth's situation. She wasn't ready to hear Steph's opinion on her current dilemma. Not yet. She needed some time to think this through on her own before involving anyone else. Thank goodness Steph was no princess. She'd responded to the news that Jo might not make tomorrow's bridesmaid's lunch without a hint of disappointment. Her only concern was for Ryan and his mum. If she was worried about any potential disruption to her wedding plans, her texts certainly didn't reveal it.

Jo stared at the infomercial for some stupid exercise machine. It must be getting late if this was the best thing on TV. She glanced at her phone. It was after midnight and there'd been no word from Ryan so far. Looked like she was here for the night. She stifled a yawn, flicked the TV off and wondered where Ryan kept the spare linen. Sleeping in his bed wasn't a good look, not with Ella here, so she figured she might as well make herself up a bed right here on the couch. She slipped her boots off and padded down the hallway as quietly as possible, in search of a linen closet. Obviously she wasn't as stealthy as she thought because halfway up the passage Ella's voice pierced the silence. 'Dad! Dad! Come here. Dad!'

Jo raced to Ella's room. A tiny nightlight illuminated the room and Jo saw the little girl sitting upright in bed, tears streaming down her face. 'Honey, what's wrong? Are you sick?'

'I want my dad.'

'I know sweetheart, but Dad's not here right now. He had to go out for a little while.'

'To see a sick horse?'

Jo faltered. She hated to lie, but she really didn't know anything about Beth's condition and it wasn't really her place to tell Ella anyway. Her instincts told her to keep quiet, at least until she'd had a chance to talk to Ryan. 'Something like that, yeah.'

'Gran usually looks after me when Dad has to go out.'

'I know sweetie, but Gran's in the hospital.'

'Yeah, I know.'

'Are you okay? Do you need a drink or something?'

Ella shook her head. 'I had a bad dream. I dreamed Tinkerbelle ran away.'

'Oh, that's awful, but you know Tinker is safe and sound in her stable right?'

Ella sniffed. 'I guess, but it gave me a fright. She's my friend. I don't want to lose her.'

'Tinker would never run away, honey. She loves you. Now, how about you snuggle back down under the covers and get some sleep?'

'When I have a bad dream Dad always hops into bed with me and stays until I go back to sleep.'

'I can stay here with you until you fall asleep if you like.' Jo looked at Ella's expectant face. It seemed the kid wanted more. 'Or, if you really want me to I can hop in with you for a little bit.'

Ella threw back the covers. 'Yes please, Jo. Come on, get in.'

Jo carefully slid in beside Ella's warm little body and was surprised when Ella threw an arm over her belly.

'You smell good, Jo. Sort of, I don't know...like a mum.'

Jo stroked Ella's hair in response. 'Shh,' she said hoping Ella wouldn't hear the tremble in her voice. 'You go to sleep. I won't go anywhere, I promise.'

She felt Ella's slender body relax and curl into her side. As the child's breaths became deep and rhythmic, Jo found her own breathing keeping time. This really wasn't so bad. In fact, it was kind of nice.

She tried to remember a time when she'd shared a bed with her mother and came up blank. If she cried out in the night it was Daddy who answered her call. He was kind enough, but would never have climbed into bed with her. Even if he'd thought of such a thing, which was unlikely, Katherine wouldn't have approved. It wasn't long before she learned to deal with her fears by herself.

Her heart swelled as she recalled Ella's words. 'Like a mum.' Was there any higher praise from a child? After a shaky start Ella had let her into her life and was now embracing her as if she was already part of the family.

Maybe she could do this. She and Ryan weren't even officially together and already she'd bonded with his child. She still wasn't sure about the whole idea of kids in general, but Ella wasn't any old kid. She was Ella, lover of horses and lip gloss and sparkly shoes. Fairy princess one minute, fearless warrior riding a magnificent steed the next. She was adorable and intelligent and sweet and occasionally exasperating.

And Jo was falling in love with her.

CHAPTER
34

'Wake up, sleepyhead. It's morning and you have a child to go home to.'

Ryan opened his eyes groggily, taking a second to remember where he was.

'Rise and shine.'

His senses came to life as suddenly as if he'd had a bucket of ice-cold water thrown in his face. 'Mum! You're awake.'

'Of course I'm awake. It's morning.'

He pulled himself out of the vinyl armchair and went to kiss her. 'Oh Mum, I was so worried about you.'

'Pfft. You should know better, Ryan. As if I'd let some trifling infection beat me. Really, I'm insulted you think so little of me.' But she smiled and pulled him in for a hug.

'How are you feeling? What can I get for you?'

'I'm feeling much better and you can get me nothing. Honestly, being in hospital is better than being in a five-star hotel. I've never been so spoiled in all my life. All I have to do is press this buzzer and a nurse comes running.'

He grinned. 'So this was the plan all along, huh? Break your hip and get an all-expenses-paid holiday. I'm onto you now.'

She winked. 'Just don't dob me in to the nurses on your way out.'

'Out? I'm not going anywhere just yet.'

'Oh yes you are. Where's my granddaughter? Who's looking after Ella?'

'She's at home. Jo's with her.'

Beth frowned. 'Oh, I see. Was that really wise, Ryan? You don't want Ella getting the wrong idea.'

'First of all, I didn't really have a lot of choice. Jo happened to be there when the hospital called and all I was thinking about was getting here to see you.'

Her face softened. 'Oh love, I understand. I just don't want to see you or Ella get hurt, that's all.'

'I love her, Mum. That's the simple truth. I'm hoping she'll stay on here in Linden Gully and, well, one day I hope to make her my wife.'

Beth shook her head. 'Ryan, she's not the marrying kind, that girl. Don't get me wrong, I understand why you love her. I loved her too, once upon a time. But mark my words, she won't settle in this town, not even for you,' she said.

'It's not her fault, not really, but there's a piece of her missing. God knows that mother of hers never let up on telling her she wasn't good enough. A person hears that often enough and they start to believe it. That's what sent her scampering off for the bright lights of New York, you know. She's trying to prove to everyone, to herself I guess, that she's worthy. Trouble is when you're that broken inside there's not enough success in the world to fix you.'

'You don't know her now, Mum. I think she could be happy here. Happy with me.'

'Well, maybe I'm wrong and I hope I am. I just don't want to see you get hurt again.'

Ryan leaned in and kissed her again. 'I don't want that either, Mum. But I can't let her go back without giving it a go. Please tell me you'll support me no matter what happens.'

'Ryan Galloway, as if you need to ask that question. Now please get out of here and go home to your daughter.'

'Okay, okay. I'm going.'

As he waited for the elevator his phone beeped. It was Jo's response to his text that he was on his way home.

Can't wait.

Ryan couldn't stop grinning. This might just be the best day of his life. Mum had dodged a bullet and was well on the way to being her usual no-nonsense self, and maybe, if he was lucky, Jo would tell him her answer was yes. He had no reason to believe she'd do any such thing but her text had him cautiously optimistic.

On his way out of the hospital he made a couple of quick calls to his brothers, to let them know the good news. Dan was still at Coolangatta airport, so he was lucky to catch him. 'Honestly mate, Mum's much better. There's no need to rush home,' he reassured his brother. It wasn't easy but he convinced his older brother to stay and enjoy the last few days of his well-earned holiday.

Patrick was relieved to hear the good news but insisted he and Georgie would come home anyway. 'I'll be back next week. I just want to see Mum and make sure all's well. I've got some leave owing to me so I might as well take it.'

'Righto, mate. I'll see you then.' Ryan smiled as he ended the call. It would be great to have the Galloway clan back together again. And hopefully he'd have some good news to share with them all by then.

'Hey, Ryan. You're looking pretty happy with yourself mate.'

He turned to see Joel Simmons, a bloke he'd gone to high school with, standing right beside him. Ryan thrust out his hand to shake Joel's. 'Hey Simmo. Good to see you. How're you doing?'

'Never better. How about you?'

'Can't complain.' He eyed Joel's uniform. 'You working here now?'

'Yeah, I'm the NUM — sorry, nursing unit manager — in Emergency. Just up here grabbing a drink from the vending machine. Ours is on the fritz downstairs. What brings you here?'

'My mum, actually. She's in ICU.'

'Oh man, I'm sorry to hear that.'

'Don't be. She's on the mend. I expect she'll go back to the surgical ward soon.'

'Ah, that explains why you're looking so chipper. Thought it might have been something else.'

Ryan laughed. 'Yeah? Like what?'

'I dunno. Maybe something to do with the fact that you've pinched a girl from one of those movie-star wankers. You sly dog, you. I know Jo was your high-school sweetheart and all but it must feel pretty damn good to know that she still prefers you over that Hollywood pretty-boy.'

Every muscle in his body tensed. How the hell did Joel Simmons know about Jo? 'What the...? Joel, I've got no clue what you're on about.'

'Come off it mate. It's splashed all over the internet. My missus showed me a photo on one of those Hollywood gossip blogs.'

'Jesus.' Beads of sweat began to form at his temple. 'Can you remember which one? I mean have you got a web address?'

'Jeez, mate, I dunno. Just google her name and I'm pretty sure you'll find it. Are you okay? Sorry, Ryan, I assumed you knew. I would never...'

Ryan nodded but didn't stick around to hear the rest of Joel's apology. He gave a quick wave as he headed for the stairwell. 'Gotta go, mate. Catch you soon.'

He flew down the stairs, taking them two at a time. This had to be some kind of mistake. She knew how much he'd wanted to keep their relationship private. Surely she wouldn't have done anything to jeopardise that?

In the hospital foyer he kept his head down, desperately hoping that he'd make it back to the car without seeing anyone he knew. Once he'd safely closed the car door he pulled out his phone and typed Jo's name into the search engine.

And there it was.

A close-up photo of the two of them locking lips.

Oh fuck.

How could he be so bloody stupid? He'd trusted her. He loved her and he thought she loved him too. But if she loved him how could she let this happen? There had to be an explanation.

He looked at the photo again. It was taken at Nate's place during the bucks and hens night. She'd been all over him, pushing him to kiss her. Was she in on this? Was it some sort of publicity stunt?

No.

He couldn't believe that. Maybe she didn't know about it either. But how could she not? She was always looking at that bloody phone of hers, checking her texts, posting on Facebook, twittering or tweeting or whatever the hell you called it. Surely someone in that massive network of hers would have put her onto the fact that there was a photo circulating of her kissing some random bloke? And if that was the case, why hadn't she said anything to him? Especially after everything he'd told her last night. Didn't she realise how damaging something like this could be for him? The last thing he needed was to be tangled up in some sordid celebrity scandal right at the time he was supposed to be signing Ella's adoption papers.

Ella. Oh god. What if she saw this? What if one of the kids at school got hold of it?

He needed to get back home and get to the bottom of this monumental stuff-up. Now.

'What comes next?' Jo asked.

'I have to clean my teeth and then you brush my hair,' Ella replied.

'And that's it? We're ready to go to the bus stop.'

'Yep. Jo, do you think you could do a braid for me? Dad can't do them.'

'Of course, honey.'

'Awesome! Wait til Annabelle sees me. She'll be so surprised.'

'Hurry up and do your teeth, then, so we have enough time.'

Once the teeth and hair were sorted and the school bag checked and rechecked, Jo bundled Ella into her car. This time there was no argument about the car seat. Maybe she should invest in one of those if she was going to stay. Okay, maybe she was getting ahead of herself now, but after spending the night here with Ella, Jo knew that she was prepared to, no scratch that, *wanted* to give this being a family thing a go. She wasn't sure how it would work. Maybe they'd take it slowly, as Ryan had suggested, but she'd made up her mind. When Ryan returned she would tell him her answer was yes.

As they approached the bus stop Ella piped up from the back seat. 'Who's picking me up?'

Jo smiled. 'I'm not sure, honey. Either me or Dad. Don't you worry, I promise one or both of us will be here.'

She pulled the car over to the side of the road and helped Ella out just as the bus approached. 'Have a great day, sweetheart,' she said and planted a kiss on the top of Ella's head.

Ella grinned up at her. 'Thanks. You too.'

Jo waved as the bus pulled out and then pulled the Jeep into a U-turn. It'd been quite a morning. She had to admit she was proud of her achievements so far today. Ella was safely on the school bus in correct uniform. She'd eaten a good breakfast, had a healthy lunch packed in her school bag and was sporting a pretty awesome hairdo. Seemed she was getting the hang of this parenting thing already.

Ryan had sent a text at around seven to say Beth was on the mend, which was a huge relief. And now Ryan was on his way home and she was going to be there to greet him.

In her underwear.

She smiled at the thought of his surprise when he found her in bed waiting for him. First she would tell him she loved him, that she would always love him and that she was going to find a way for them to be together. They could work out the details later. The important thing was that it was what they both wanted.

Then they would make love. After, while he slept, she'd cook for him, maybe lamb and veggie soup — she'd have to see what was in the fridge — and bake some cookies for Ella to eat when she got home from school. They could greet the school bus together. A perfect end to a perfect day.

Of course there was still the photo to contend with. But with every day that passed it was becoming less of a story. A middle-of-the-night phone call to Lydia once Ella was peacefully asleep had confirmed that Zach's people were doing everything in their power to kill the story. A statement on Zach's website claimed there was doubt about the authenticity of the photo. The quality was pretty poor so maybe people would believe that.

In any case, if she and Ryan were going to be together now, what difference did the photo make? Surely he realised everyone would know about them soon enough. Hopefully Ryan would see reason. He was bound to feel annoyed at having his privacy breached, but he could hardly blame her for that. And hopefully his joy at her answer, plus the extra surprise she was planning, would outweigh any negative fallout over the photo.

She parked the car near the house and raced back inside. A glance at her phone told her she probably had twenty minutes before he arrived. Plenty of time to call Amanda, the one friend from boarding school she still kept in touch with. Hopefully Manda would have the information she needed in order to surprise Ryan. She was buzzing with anticipation of his excited reaction.

After all her indecision and worry, spending last night with Ella had put everything into perspective for her. Suddenly life seemed simple. She was in love and she was loved. What else was there?

Jo cleaned the kitchen table and put away the breakfast things as she chatted to Amanda. Everything her friend had to say was positive and she promised to email all the information to Jo as soon as their call was over. Once their goodbyes were said she headed into Ryan's bedroom and pulled the covers back on his king-sized bed. She just had time to shimmy out of her jeans and jumper and slip between the covers before she heard Ryan's ute rumble across the cattle grid.

Her stomach flipped in anticipation as two thuds signalled his boots being removed and dumped on the verandah. The front door slammed as he entered the house.

'Jo? Where are you?'

'In here,' she called.

The look on his face when he saw her was not what she'd imagined. His lips were set in a hard line, his brow creased into a frown. 'What are you doing in bed?'

'Ryan. Sorry. I just thought we could —'

'I don't think so, Johanna. I think you should get dressed.'

'Okay.' Jo's heart thudded against her ribcage. Was he angry? What had she done? 'Ryan, is there something wrong? I'm sorry I got into your bed without asking. I can assure you I didn't sleep in here. I didn't do anything to give Ella the wrong impression.'

He raised his eyebrows. 'Is that so?'

What the hell was going on here? 'What do you mean by that?'

He held up his phone and there it was — the photo. Why hadn't she told him last night when she had the chance? 'I can explain. Well, actually I can't really. I'm as pissed off about this as you are.'

'Just get dressed would you? Then we'll talk.' His voice was calm but cold. He turned his back and left the room as she pulled back the covers.

She threw her clothes on willy-nilly, not bothering to check if buttons were properly fastened or if her hair was okay. When she was done she found him sitting at the kitchen table. He looked up expectantly as she walked over and took the seat opposite him.

'Well? Care to explain this?'

Fear made her lips tremble. 'Ryan, please. You're overreacting. This is not my fault.'

'Who took it, Jo? How did it happen?'

'I honestly don't know. Maybe it was someone at the party.'

'You really expect me to believe that? There's no way any of the people at that party would do something like this to me. They're my friends. I trust them.'

Blood rushed to her cheeks as fear was replaced with anger. 'And you don't trust me?'

'I want to trust you, Jo, but I don't see how this could have happened. If you didn't have anything to do with it, why didn't you tell me about it? You clearly knew it was out there.'

'I was going to. Last night, in fact. But then you hit me with all the stuff about Ella and then you were gone...'

'Come off it, Jo. You knew how important it was to keep this relationship private for Ella's sake. After what I told you last night I would have thought that you'd understand it's not just about my feelings, it's about keeping her in my care. Jesus...' He visibly paled. 'What else is out there? Is there anything else I should know?'

She shook her head. 'Not that I know of. Ryan, you have to believe me, I had nothing to do with this. And anyway, I thought you wanted us to be together? What difference does it make if people see a photo of us kissing?'

'It matters because as far as the world is concerned you're an engaged woman. It matters because it puts me in the middle of a Hollywood scandal and leaves me and my child open to scrutiny that we could well do without, but most of all it matters because you lied to me. You kept something from me, even after I told you the most intimate details of my life. I don't know what to think. You say you had nothing to do with it, but how do I know that? I can't trust anything you say anymore. Jesus, after everything I said about honesty...'

'Ryan, you have to listen to me. I want to be with you. I'll do whatever it takes to fix this.'

He shook his head sadly. 'I'm sure you mean that, Jo, but I don't know anymore. I love you, and part of me will always love you, but maybe we're just not meant to be. We haven't even started yet and look where we're at.'

'Ryan, this is just a road bump. It's not a big issue.'

'Maybe not in your world, but it is in mine. Your life's too big, too complicated for me. This incident has reminded me that you're a celebrity. This little town, a simple little life with me and Ella, will never be enough for you.'

'That's not true.' She didn't try to stem the tears that were running down her face.

'I'm sorry, Jo, but I can't risk it. It's one thing for you to break my heart but I can't let you do that to Ella. I won't let you.'

CHAPTER
35

The Jeep's tyres skidded on the gravel driveway as Jo pressed down on the accelerator. The sooner she got away from here, the better. Her cheeks burned with hurt and humiliation and she could barely see where she was going through the tears.

Once the farm could no longer be seen in the rear-vision mirror she pulled over to the side. She laid her head on the steering wheel and sobbed.

It was so unfair. She'd come here wanting nothing more than to be a good bridesmaid and escape the limelight for a bit. She hadn't sought Ryan out, hadn't even known he was here. And then, when against all reason she found herself falling for him all over again, she'd fought those feelings, told herself it could never work. Okay, so sleeping with him had been foolish, but he was the one who insisted they could have more. She'd doubted him, but he'd been convincing and then, oh god, that little girl...she'd fallen in love with Ella almost as much as her dad.

She thought she'd found it. Her place to call home. Where she finally belonged. Now it had been torn from her grasp before she'd had the chance to properly take hold. And despite what Ryan thought, this time she'd played no part in her downfall.

In her heart she'd known all along that the photo would upset him; she realised that's why she'd put off telling him. But she didn't expect the white-hot fury she'd just witnessed.

In a way, she didn't blame him for being angry. In light of what he'd told her last night she understood his fear. But the photo wasn't her fault. If only she could work out who'd snapped it and, more to the point, who'd uploaded it. Half the people at that party were unlikely to even use social media, let alone know how to upload a photo to Twitter. Of the people who were more likely to be tech savvy, she couldn't imagine who would do such a thing. Ryan was still a golden boy in these parts. No one would do something deliberately to hurt him. Unless one of the guys thought it was a good practical joke?

She swiped at her eyes with the backs of her hands, before searching her handbag for some tissues. Sitting here bawling her eyes out wasn't going to help. She glanced at her phone. It wasn't even ten o'clock. There was still plenty of time to have the special bridesmaid's lunch she and Steph had organised, if Steph hadn't made other plans already. She pulled out her phone and scrolled down the contact list, jabbing at Steph's name as soon as it emerged.

'Hey you,' Steph's voice chirped down the phone. 'I wasn't expecting to talk to you this morning. I believe Beth's making a good recovery. Thought you and lover boy might be having a little celebration.'

'How'd you know about Beth?'

'Grapevine. What's wrong with you? You sound like you've got a cold or something. Don't you dare get sick before my wedding. I simply won't have it.'

'Don't worry, I'm not sick.'

'Have you been crying? What's going on there?'

'I'm fine. Well, not totally fine, actually, but I can tell you the details of that in person. Have you still got time for lunch today?'

'Absolutely.'

Jo picked at her Caesar salad while Steph wolfed down a burger with the lot. When the last bite was gone Steph wiped her mouth with the napkin and patted her stomach. 'That's better. I was totally famished.'

'No pre-wedding jitters spoiling your appetite then?'

'Nup. All good. I mean what's there to be nervous about, really? I love Nate and he loves me. We're going to stand up and say that in front of a whole bunch of people who love us to bits. I can't think of anything better really.'

Jo couldn't either. 'I'm so happy for you both.' Try as she might she couldn't stop the tears pooling in her eyes.

'Jo, I'm so sorry. I can't believe I'm waffling on about love after what's just happened.'

'Don't be stupid. You're getting married the day after tomorrow. You're allowed to be happy, in fact I think it's probably expected. It's me who should be apologising. All I wanted when I came home was to be here for you. Instead you're the one propping me up.'

'Now you're the one being stupid. It's been wonderful having you here. And I love that we can still tell each other everything. I want to be here for you Jo, wedding or not. Honestly, I don't see what all the fuss is about. It's just an excuse to have a party and wear a frou-frou dress.'

Jo laughed through her tears. 'Your dress is hardly what I'd call frou-frou.'

'It's tizzy by my standards. Anyway, my point is, just because I'm getting married doesn't mean I don't want to listen to your problems. I've missed our chats so much, Jo. Skype just isn't the same thing.'

'I miss them too. More than you know. Since I've been home I've realised that my relationships in New York are kind of shallow. I've got plenty of friends, people I can meet for a drink or go to a club with, but no one I can really talk to. No one I trust.'

'Come home then. What's stopping you?'

'You know, early this morning I really thought that was a possibility, but now...how can I come home with Ryan living up the road? Linden Gully is such small place. We'd be in each other's faces all the time. I couldn't bear it.'

'Surely this latest fiasco will blow over? I mean from what you've told me I can understand Ryan being a bit pissed off — you know how private he is — but it's not that big a deal. He'll get ribbed by some of his mates and whispered about by some of the school mums for a week or two. You know what it's like. Next week there'll be some new gossip spreading like wildfire.'

Jo had told Steph the whole story on the drive to Bellington. Well, almost the whole story. She'd left out the part about Ella not being Ryan's biological daughter. That wasn't her news to tell and besides, she'd given him her word. 'Hmmm, I don't know. He seemed pretty angry to me. I can't see him cooling off any time soon.'

'Maybe because he thinks it was you who uploaded it. If we could only work out who the real culprit is then surely Ryan would see sense.'

Jo shook her head. 'Believe me, I would love to know who did it, but I have no idea. I guess I could spend some time online later today and see if I can trace it back to the original upload, but if the photo's gone viral — which it seems it has — it'll be like looking for a needle in a haystack. And I have no internet connection at Yarrapinga. I've been relying on the 3G on my phone. Bit useless for something like this.'

Steph signalled the waiter. 'Do you want another coffee?' she asked.

Jo nodded. 'Sure. It's not like I have anywhere else to be.'

'Same again, thanks,' Steph said to the hovering waiter, before turning her attention back to Jo. 'Wouldn't it be easier if we just looked at who was there that night and used a process of elimination?'

'I've tried that and come up with zilch.'

'Maybe you don't know everyone as well as you think you do. I don't suppose you've got anything useful like a pen or a bit of paper in that gigantic handbag of yours?'

Jo grinned. Steph saw handbags as a utility, not a fashion statement. 'As a matter of fact I have both.'

'Good. Give them here. Let's make a list, shall we?'

For the next thirty minutes Steph carefully recorded every guest present at the party and gave an honest, and sometimes withering, assessment of each one's character. By the time they'd finished their coffees, they'd exhausted all possibilities. They were no closer to an answer but Steph's descriptions had at least given Jo a laugh. 'I think we should reconcile ourselves to the fact we're never going to get to the bottom of this one,' she said.

'I'm not giving up that easily. I'll work it out eventually, mark my words. And the person who's responsible better get their running shoes on when I do.'

'Honestly, Steph, I don't even know if it matters. Clearly Ryan doesn't trust me. He told me I broke his heart when I left for the States. I guess I have to take responsibility for that. I kept telling myself our break-up was his fault, that he jumped into a relationship with Carly the minute I hopped on the plane. But the truth is I was the one who left. I was scared. Scared of marrying a country vet and then resenting him for holding me back. Scared of becoming my mother.'

'Oh Jo, you are not Katherine, not by a long shot.'

'Yeah, I know that now. But back then.... anyway, Ryan was right to feel betrayed when I left. I've recently discovered my mother had a hand in making him believe I wasn't coming back. And I had no right to expect him to wait.'

'All that's in the past. Let's worry about right now. You two are destined to be together. If I believed in all that astrology claptrap I'd say it was written in the stars.'

Jo smiled. Steph had always teased her about her belief in things of a mystical nature. 'I think maybe we missed our chance at happily ever after. Ryan hasn't fully recovered from what I did to him all those years ago. He doesn't trust me. And if I can't prove that someone else uploaded the photo I don't think there's much chance of convincing him otherwise.'

Usually Fridays at the clinic were fairly relaxed. Ryan always kept the morning free so he and Taylah could catch up on administration and tidy up the treatment room. When there was time he tried to spend some time teaching her some basic procedures, like taking temperatures, suturing and the like. But this morning he was in no mood for teaching.

'Where's my stethoscope?' he snapped.

'I put it on the trolley in the exam room, I'm sure of it,' Taylah said.

'Well, it's not there now.'

Taylah's face bore a shocked expression at his raised voice as she left the reception desk and rushed past him into the examination room.

Seconds later she was back. 'Is this what you're after?' She held up the stethoscope.

It had been there all along. Ryan's shoulders sagged and he tried to let go of the tension he'd been holding onto since yesterday.

'Yes. Thanks Tay. Sorry for being so snappy. I'm just having a really crappy day.'

Her face took on its normal sunny appearance. 'That's okay. It's not like you at all, though. Hope everything's alright?'

'Yeah, nothing dramatic.' *Only that my heart is broken and it's my own damn fault.* 'Just having one of those days.'

Taylah nodded and went back to entering data into the clinic's computer. She was a good kid and had turned out to be an enormous help in the clinic. She didn't deserve to have her head bitten off for no reason. Clearly he wasn't fit to be around people right now. 'Hey, I think I'm going to take a quick drive over to the Craigs' farm to have another look at that lame horse they've got. I'll go to the Ag store and pick up a bit of feed while I'm out. We haven't got anyone booked into the clinic for a couple of hours have we?'

'No. Actually, no bookings until the Findlay kelpie at four.'

'So you'll be right here for a bit? I'll be back after school pick-up to see Mrs Findlay's dog.'

'No worries.'

He whistled for Neddy, one of Dan's cattle dogs, who flew from his sunny spot on the verandah and bounded into the back of the ute. 'Wanna come for a ride, mate?'

Ryan couldn't help but smile at the wide grin on Neddy's face.

Once they'd crossed the cattle grid he allowed himself to wallow in the injustice of this morning's events. He couldn't stop thinking about that bloody photo. It was tangible evidence of the moment he'd relented and handed Jo his heart on a platter.

She'd vehemently denied having anything to do with its upload to the web, and maybe that was true, but he hated that there was a nagging doubt that he couldn't shake. Last night his imagination had run wild with ideas about what might have happened. The more he thought about it, the more convinced he was that she had *something* to do with it. Clearly she didn't snap the shot herself, he'd remember that, but maybe she'd had some involvement. He couldn't think of another explanation. No one else at the party had any motive to hurt him this way.

He couldn't quite work out how she'd gotten someone to take it. He hadn't noticed anyone unfamiliar at the party. But then again these Hollywood types knew how to get things done. Maybe she'd paid off some dodgy paparazzo to hide in the bushes all night. Yeah, that was probably it. Come to think of it, there'd been that noise in the bushes that he'd commented on and Jo had laughed it off, telling him it was a possum.

In the cold, hard light of day, he realised that this idea was a bit far-fetched and there was most likely a more simple explanation, but he hated that his imagination had gone there. Surely that wasn't a good sign? He wanted to be able to take Jo at her word, to trust her, but what if he did and then he turned out to be wrong? He had Ella to think about, and there was simply too much at stake.

As he pulled up outside the Craigs' place his phone began to ring. He went to silence it, expecting it to be Jo, but saw Steph's name flash onto the screen. As much as he wasn't in the mood to talk, he thought he'd better take it, just in case she needed something done urgently for the wedding.

'Hey Steph.'

'Hey yourself. What are you up to?'

'I'm up at the Craigs' place, checking on one of their horses.'

'Oh.'

'Did you need something?'

'Yeah I was hoping to grab you for a quick coffee and a talk.'

So she'd heard already. He really didn't need to listen to Steph pleading Jo's case. 'Sorry, but I've got a pretty full day. After this

I've got to head into town for some supplies and then I'm going to see Mum.'

'How about if I come to the hospital? I'd love to say hi to your Mum and then we can grab a quick coffee afterwards.'

He hesitated. 'Steph, I'm sorry, but if this is about Jo, I don't want to hear it. Just leave it alone, alright?'

'It's not about Jo, well not all about her. It's about the photo.'

'Steph, I really —'

'Look, Nate and I are getting married tomorrow and I don't want my maid of honour and the best man looking daggers at each other all day.'

'I promise that won't happen.'

'I know it won't after what I've got to show you. Now quit being difficult and do what I say. I'm the bride you know, so you have to. It's in the rulebook.'

He couldn't help but chuckle despite his reluctance to see her. Obviously she wasn't giving up. 'Okay, okay, you win. But let's not do the hospital thing. I'm sick of the sight of that place this week. And I'm sure you don't really want to make a special trip to Belly just to see me.'

'I will if I have to.'

'Steady on, I'm not trying to weasel out of it. I can drop by your place on the way if you like.'

'Nah, not a great idea. It's freakin' wedding central here. Mum's out of her tree. I'll meet you at the bakery for a coffee instead. Text me when you're done at the Craigs'.'

'Okay.'

An hour later they sat opposite each other with a couple of overly foamy lattes and a pile of cinnamon donuts between them.

'Thanks for coming, Ryan. I wouldn't have insisted if it wasn't important.'

'Shouldn't you be doing some sort of wedding stuff?'

She shrugged. 'Not really. Mum's got it under control. Truth is I'm happy to be out of the place for a bit. I have to be back by four, though. Jo's arriving then so we can do the make-up trial.' She screwed up her face in distaste.

'So I'm guessing what you have to say is pretty important, seeing as you used your "I'm the bride" card to get me here.'

'Yeah, sorry about that. Look, I'll cut to the chase. I know who uploaded the photo and it wasn't Jo.'

'What? Who the hell…?' How could this be true?

'Now before you get all bent out of shape I need you to promise me you'll listen to the whole story and not start ranting and raving like a lunatic before I'm done.'

'Yeah alright, but I —'

'I mean it, Ryan. Just listen to the story and then you can have your say.'

He nodded and picked up his coffee to stop himself from interrupting her. Steph could be formidable when she wanted to be.

Steph stirred her coffee and used her teaspoon to lift some of the foam from the top of her coffee. 'It was Maddy. It was an accident, or so she says, and I believe her. But even if it wasn't, you have to know that Jo had nothing to do with it. She had no idea the photo had been taken and the first she knew about it was when it started to go viral. Maddy's made a full admission.'

Ryan shook his head and plonked his coffee back on the table. Maddy was just a kid. 'Why on earth would she do something like this?'

'Apparently you and Jo "blew her off" at the party.' Steph used her fingers to indicate quotation marks.

'I…we didn't, it was just —'

'Hang on, let me finish. She said you palmed some job off on her so the two of you could be alone. She was pissed off. She's a teenage girl, Ryan. You might not have meant to upset her but in case you haven't noticed she's had the hots for you for about six months now. You ditching her for Jo would have been a big slap in the face for her.'

'Oh god. I had no idea.'

'Apparently she decided to follow the two of you to see what was going on.'

'But why take a photo? I don't get it.'

Steph shrugged. 'It's what they do isn't it? Kids, I mean. It's how they communicate with each other. Maddy can't seem to do anything without recording it on her phone. Anyway she said she never meant for it to go viral. She sent it in a Snapchat to a friend. It was never meant to go any further than that.'

'Snapchat? What the hell is a Snapchat?'

'It's kind of like instant messaging, but whatever you send isn't permanent. It disappears after the other person has read it. That's why Maddy thought it'd be safe to send.'

'If it disappears how did it end up all over the internet?'

'Apparently the friend took a screenshot and saved it. She sent it to another friend and someone, somewhere along the line, uploaded it to Instagram. Maddy doesn't know who, or if she does she's not saying. I guess that's not so important anyway.'

Ryan covered his eyes with his palms and began to rub them. Bloody hell, this was a total mess.

'Maddy's so remorseful, Ryan, not to mention embarrassed. She knows she owes you and Jo an apology, but I said I'd break the news to both of you first, so it wasn't such a shock. Honestly, she didn't mean to cause you such grief.'

'So Jo knows?'

Steph nodded. 'Yeah, I told her as soon as I figured it out. But she didn't think you'd take her calls, so I volunteered to let you know.'

'How did you figure it out?'

'Jo and I were talking about it yesterday and I made a list of all the people at the party. Maddy's just a kid. Neither of us thought to put her on the list. When I got home she was there with Aunty Sue. She was playing with her phone, snapping selfies and posting them on Instagram. It suddenly occurred to me that she might be the one.'

'So you confronted her?'

'Yep. Got her on her own under the guise of secret bridesmaid's business and just flat out asked her. She broke down immediately and confessed. Apparently she's been worried sick about the whole thing but was too scared to say anything.'

'Poor kid.'

'So you're not mad at her?'

Ryan shrugged. 'It was a dumb thing to do, there's no doubt about that. But she's just a kid and it was a mistake. I know we all did some pretty stupid things when we were kids.'

Steph grinned. The relief on her face was obvious. 'I'll let her know she doesn't need to worry about you throttling her then.'

'Can't say the same for Jo.' Maddy wasn't the only one who needed Jo's forgiveness.

'I'll handle Jo. You know, I happen to know she's at home right now if you wanted to see her for any reason.'

Seeing Jo wasn't high on his list of priorities right now. He needed breathing space to figure out what he wanted. 'Good to know.'

'So are you? Going to go see her?'

Ryan leaned over and gave her a gentle sock to the arm. 'Mind your own business.'

Steph put on a mock serious face. 'It is my business. I'm the bride, remember?'

'I could hardly forget, what with you mentioning it every five minutes.'

'Well?'

He stood to go, gathering the last of the donuts up in a napkin. Steph raised an eyebrow. 'They're not for me, they're for Neddy. He's waiting in the ute,' he said.

'That's not what I meant.'

Ryan sighed. 'I've got to go see Mum, Steph. I'll see you tomorrow when you're in your bride get-up.'

Steph screwed up her face. 'Gawd, don't remind me. I don't know where it's written that the bride has to wear a dress. I would have been happy in jeans, but...'

'You'll be a gorgeous bride, I'm sure.' He leaned over and kissed her cheek.

As he went to pull away Steph grabbed him by the hand. 'You know the best wedding present I could ever have would be to see my two best friends happy. You and Jo are meant for each other. She loves you, Ryan, and I know you love her back. Stop complicating things and let yourself be happy.'

CHAPTER
36

Ryan stood at the kitchen window waiting. He heard Jo's old Jeep approaching before he saw it. She'd be walking in the door in a minute or two.

'Ella,' he called.

His daughter appeared in the doorway, her eyes shining with excitement. 'Yes?'

'Do you have everything you need to go to Steph's?'

'Yep. I've double checked just like you told me.'

'Jo will be here to collect you soon. I think you should go out and see Tinker to say goodbye. She'll miss you.'

'Good idea, Dad.'

'There's a carrot in the fridge if you want to give her a treat. Take your time. I'll make Jo a cup of coffee while she waits.'

'Okay, thanks.' She swung open the fridge door, grabbed the carrot and was skipping down the back steps just as the Jeep turned into the property.

Would she be angry? He wouldn't blame her. He hadn't given her a fair hearing. So now it was time for an apology from him and to settle things between them before Nate and Steph's big day.

The Jeep pulled up and he watched her getting out of the car. She stopped to fiddle with her hair before approaching the house. She was nervous. He knew how she felt.

He opened the kitchen door before she'd had a chance to knock. 'Hey Jo. Come on in.'

She gave him a tentative smile. 'I'm just here to pick up Ella. Steph asked me to.'

'Yeah, I know. She called me.'

Jo gave him an apologetic look. 'Sorry. She's just trying to help.'

'Yeah I know. And in a way she is helping. I wanted to talk to you before the wedding anyway. Clear the air.'

Jo looked around. 'Where's Ella?'

'I sent her out to say goodbye to Tinkerbelle. I wanted a moment alone with you so we could talk.' He nodded towards the kitchen table. 'Sit down. Can I get you something? Tea? Coffee?'

She shook her head, but took a seat at the table anyway.

He sat opposite and cleared his throat. 'I'm sorry to launch into this without prelude, but I'm not sure how long Ella will be and I don't think either of us want her to overhear.'

Jo nodded. 'I understand.'

'I'm sorry for blaming you about the photo. I know now it was Maddy. All I can do is offer you my apologies and hope you can forgive me.'

The tension in Jo's face lifted and she smiled widely. 'Of course I forgive you. I completely understand. I'm so happy we have this cleared up.' She extended her hand across the table.

Ryan's throat constricted. Looking at her so happy and expectant made what he had to say next almost impossible. The last thing he wanted to do was hurt her, but he had to be honest. He gave her hand a quick squeeze and then released it and leaned back in his chair. 'Jo, I'm sorry, but this doesn't change anything.'

Lines of confusion creased her brow. 'I don't understand.'

Ryan took a deep breath in and then exhaled slowly before answering. 'I think we have to accept that no matter how attracted we are to each other, how much we care for each other — and I do care, Jo, really I do — we just can't make this work.'

'No...' Her voice was unsteady. 'I don't accept that. I thought Steph explained. I didn't have anything to do with that photo, Ryan. I would never put you in that situation willingly and I would never, ever do anything to hurt or embarrass Ella.'

'I know that. I do. But don't you see? We don't trust each other. You lied to me by omission. You knew about the photo but didn't tell me —'

'Because there wasn't a good time. Ella was sick and then there was the crisis with your mum...'

'If you'd trusted me, those things wouldn't have mattered. You would have found the time.'

'And if you'd trusted me you would have known I had nothing to do with the upload of that bloody photo.'

'Exactly. But I don't trust you. I want to, but I'm not there yet. I think my reaction to the photo proves that.'

Jo bit her lip and her eyes glistened with unshed tears.

'I'm sorry. I'm not trying to hurt you, but it's the truth. We've hurt each other in the past and while the wounds might have healed over, they've left some scars.'

'But in time...'

He shook his head. It wasn't as if he hadn't considered giving the relationship time to work itself out. Last night he'd thought of nothing else, but after a sleepless night he'd come to the conclusion that it was too big a risk to take. For him and for Ella. 'If things were different, if I didn't have Ella to consider, then maybe we could give it a go. But as it stands I have too much to lose. I can't afford to take a gamble on something that, let's face it, is anything but a sure thing.'

She blinked back the tears. 'I might go see if Ella's almost done.'

His heart lurched. This was it. She wasn't going to fight it. He'd made the right decision but that didn't mean it felt good. 'Jo, you know I love you. It's just not the right time for us. I wish things could be different but —'

She stood up and shook her head. 'Just stop. I don't want to hear any more. You've obviously made up your mind. So that's that. We just need to get through the next twenty-four hours or so without causing anyone else grief.'

'Joey...'

'I'm going to get Ella. Can you put her bag and the booster seat in my car, please?' Her eyes were dry and her expression emotionless.

'Are you sure you're okay to drive? You seem a little...'

'What? Angry? Pissed off? Well, that's because I am. Angry at myself, that is. I knew right from the start that it was foolish, dangerous even, to let myself get involved with you again, and yet I did it. I'm a bloody idiot. But don't you worry. I'll get over it. And as for being fit to drive, do you really think I would do anything to put that precious little girl in danger? You might not have noticed, Ryan, but I happen to care about Ella. Quite a lot, in fact.'

Before he had the chance to respond she'd slammed the back door behind her.

Luckily Ella was so excited about having her nails painted and all the other girly things that were planned as part of the wedding-eve festivities she didn't notice anything was amiss. Jo knew that despite only being six years old Ella was an astute child, so she was careful to keep the conversation light and airy.

'What do you think we'll have for dinner?' Ella was asking. It seemed a reply was not required because she babbled on without a pause. 'I hope it's something nice. Maybe there'll be fairy bread, because it's sort of like a party. I love fairy bread. It's my favourite thing to eat, but Gran says it's only party food, and Dad always takes notice of what Gran says.'

This one-sided conversation continued all the way to Kallara. Ella required no more than the odd one-word response from Jo before verbalising the next thought that crossed her mind. At another time this would be highly amusing, but right now Jo was simply relieved that Ella hadn't noticed anything was wrong.

Unfortunately, hiding her distress from Steph and Jenny was not as easy. Jenny took one look at her and immediately ushered Ella into the living room. 'I've got a special job for you, Ella,' Jenny said. 'Sue and Maddy are putting rose petals into little bags so the guests can throw them over the bride and groom after the ceremony. Do you think you can help?'

Ella nodded enthusiastically as Jenny opened the door to reveal Maddy and Sue sitting on the floor surrounded by cellophane bags, baskets of rose petals and ribbons. Maddy's face turned a deep crimson when she noticed Jo looking at her. They would need to talk, but not now. She needed time to cool off a bit first.

'Jo, you look like you could use a cuppa. Come and sit at the table and talk to me while I make us all one,' Jenny said.

'Stuff the cuppa, it's my wedding eve. I think that deserves a drink. Bubbly anyone?' Steph said from behind her.

Sue shook her head. 'Not for me. Not yet anyway. I'll be in for a cuppa when we've finished this lot, though.'

Jenny shut the door, while Steph went to the fridge. 'What about you, Mum? Are you having one?'

'Just a smidge. I need my wits about me tonight. There's still a lot to do. And don't you girls go silly either. The last thing we want is a hungover bride or bridesmaid.'

'We'll be good, Mum. I promise. Although I'm not sure I can say the same about the boys. I noticed Nate putting a slab in the fridge before I left.'

Jo collected three champagne flutes while Steph expertly removed the cork from the bottle. The resulting pop silenced them all momentarily.

Once Steph had poured and they'd all taken a seat Jo raised her glass, 'Here's to you, Steph, my lovely friend. May you and Nate have happiness always.' To her dismay a tear slid down her cheek and plopped onto the table.

'Thanks, but what's with the waterworks?'

Jo shrugged, not trusting herself to answer.

'I knew there was something up from the minute you came through the door,' said Jenny. 'We have no secrets in this house my girl, you know that. Out with it.'

'I'm in love with Ryan.'

Jenny and Steph exchanged a glance.

'Yes,' said Jenny. 'Now tell us something the whole town doesn't already know.'

Jo managed a weak smile. The whole town? Really? Was it that obvious? 'He's told me there's no hope for a future together. I don't know why I'm so upset. Until a few days ago I was the one saying it could never happen.'

'Why?' asked Jenny. 'I mean why did you think it could never happen? If you've broken up with Zach and you have no ties in the States, why couldn't it work?'

'Because of Ella,' Jo whispered. 'I was afraid I wouldn't be a good stepmother, that I wouldn't love her enough. I was worried I would turn out like my mother.'

Jenny folded her arms across her chest. 'Now that's just plain ridiculous. You are nothing like your mother. Well, not in that respect anyway. You inherited the best bits of both your parents, I have to say. And you've turned out to be a fine young woman, Jo. Don't let anyone tell you otherwise.'

'Thanks Jenny. I can always rely on you to sing my praises.'

'I meant every word I just said.' Jenny took a sip of sparkling wine and smiled but Jo saw the moisture in her eyes and her heart swelled. Why had she ever worried about knowing how to love a child? She'd had the perfect role model right in front of her all these years. Jenny had been more of a mother to her than Katherine ever had. Ryan was right. Biology truly played no part as far as love went.

'You obviously changed your mind about becoming a stepparent then, if you were considering making a go of it with Ryan,' Steph said.

Jo nodded. 'Over the past few weeks I've gotten to know Ella and I've come to care for her very much. I still don't know about the whole having a baby scenario — maybe that part's not for me — but I do know loving Ella would never be an issue.'

'You told Ryan all this, right?' Steph said.

'Not really, I was going to tell him on Thursday morning. I was all set to declare my undying love.' She paused to smile at Steph's raised eyebrows. 'But then he came back from the hospital fuming about the photo and I never got a chance.'

'Oh, love, you have to go to him and tell him. You can't leave things like this,' Jenny said. 'He loves you. Anyone can see that. He's just afraid of being hurt. Poor bloke really hasn't had much luck with relationships. You left him once before and then there was all that terrible business with Carly.'

Jo shook her head. 'I tried to talk to him just before. He says he doesn't trust me.' She swiped at the tears now streaming down her face.

Jenny moved to sit beside her. She put a comforting arm around Jo's shoulder. 'This is not the Johanna Morgan I know. The girl I know and love is the most determined and resourceful creature on earth. She never lets obstacles stand in her way, no matter how huge they might seem. All is not lost. Not yet. You need to pour that drink down the sink right now and go to him. Find some way of convincing him that you're in it for the long haul. That you won't let him or Ella down.'

'I don't know what to say to make him believe me. Maybe he's right. Maybe we've missed our moment and it's all too late.'

Steph put her champagne glass down in front of her and looked Jo in the eyes. 'You know Ryan better than anyone in this world. Surely there must be something you can think of to make him change his mind?'

Jo didn't move a muscle but her brain suddenly kicked into overdrive. Maybe there *was* one thing that would convince him. Surely it was worth a shot? At this stage there was nothing left to lose. 'Jenny, can I use your office computer? I need to print an email.'

Jenny's eyes lit up. 'Of course honey. You go right ahead.'

'Steph, what time were the boys heading over to Nate's?' Jo asked.

Steph glance at her watch. 'Not for another hour, at least. Macca's coming from Melbourne for the wedding. Nate had to go pick him up from the train in Belly at five, so I don't reckon they'd be back before six. It's very likely that Ryan won't be leaving home for another half an hour or more, if that's why you're asking.'

'It is. I just need to print something out first.'

'Well what are you waiting for,' Jenny said. 'Get cracking.'

Five minutes later Jo was heading out the door, clutching half a dozen sheets of paper to her chest. 'I'm so sorry to be running out on your wedding-eve celebrations, Steph. I'm a dud maid of honour. I promise I'll be back as soon as I can.'

'Don't be ridiculous. I said this to Ryan earlier and now I'm going to say it to you — the best wedding gift Nate and I could receive would be to see our two best friends happy. And by happy I mean with each other. So go work on my wedding present and take all the time you want.'

'Thanks. Take care good care of Ella while I'm gone, and Steph...'

'Yeah?'

'Wish me luck.'

CHAPTER
37

Ryan was in the clinic when he heard the vehicle thundering over the cattle grid. He frowned. Someone was going too fast. He wasn't expecting anyone. All the appointments were done for the day and he'd sent Taylah home half an hour ago. Best check out who it was. Maybe someone had an emergency and needed help bringing the animal inside. He opened the clinic door and walked outside.

Bloody hell.

It was Jo.

What now? Oh please God, not Ella. He shook his head to dismiss the thought. If anything had happened to Ella Jo wouldn't have wasted time driving here, she would have phoned. So what was she doing here?

She skidded to a halt near the pathway that led to the clinic, jumped out of the Jeep without hesitation and started running towards him with a sheaf of papers in her hand.

What the hell? He'd made it clear that this thing between them was over. He knew she was pissed off but he hadn't expected to see her again until the wedding and he'd assumed that by then everything would be cool but civilised between them. Now she was running towards him like a madwoman. He definitely hadn't seen this one coming.

'Ryan,' she called as she got closer. 'Thank goodness you're still here. We need to talk.'

'I'm just about to head off to Nate's place. Can this wait?'

She shook her head. 'I know Nate's gone to Bellington to get Macca and won't be back until six, so don't think you can blow me off that easily.'

'Okay. I guess you'd better come on up to the house then.'

She shook her head. 'No. I'm not going inside that house again, not until you want me there. I can say what I have to say right here.'

He recognised the fiery determination in her eyes. It was the look she got before every gymkhana. The one that said 'take me on if you dare'.

He shrugged. 'Have it your way then.'

'Earlier today you told me you didn't trust me. I'm here to tell you that you can.'

'Jo, we've been over this.'

'No. You've had your say. Now I'm having mine.'

Obviously she wouldn't be happy until she'd said her piece. It was probably better to let her get it off her chest without interruption. 'Go on then, you have my attention.'

'I get that I hurt you when I left last time. I understand that I broke your heart. And you know what? You were right. I was hedging my bets. I wasn't ready then to make a commitment. When you got Carly pregnant — or thought that you did — I let myself off the hook. It was easier to blame you for being disloyal than to face up to the fact that I didn't know what I wanted.' She paused as a clap of thunder sounded above them.

'Looks like a storm's coming. We really should go inside.'

'No. I can't. I can't go back in that house unless it's what we both want. The next time I cross that threshold I want it to be with you. For us to be together.'

God, she was making this so damn hard. 'Jo, please...'

'Let me finish.'

He nodded for her to continue. Best get this over with before the rain started. It was bad enough that his throat had gone completely dry and his head had begun to pound. He didn't need to get soaking wet as well.

'When I left here it wasn't about you, it was about me. I never felt comfortable here, or anywhere for that matter. I needed to know who I was, get comfortable in my own skin. Back then I never let anyone in. I was too afraid of rejection to really put myself out there. I blamed the town for pigeonholing me, for believing I was a younger version of my mother, but I see now that it was my own fault. Partly, at least. I never gave anyone any reason to believe anything different about me.'

'But we were close. You let me in.'

She nodded. 'Yes. You were different. But we were just kids really.' She hung her head. 'I didn't know if you would be enough. I didn't want us to turn into my mum and dad. I didn't want to resent you,' she said. 'But now I realise how wrong I was. After all these years I've finally figured out where I belong. Where I make sense.' She looked at him. 'It's here, Ryan, with you and Ella.'

'Jo, I want to believe that more than anything on earth. I know you think that's what you want, but how do I know you'll feel the same way this time next year, or next week for that matter?'

'Because now I know who I am, what I want. I love you, Ryan. I understand what loving you means and I don't just accept it, I embrace it. I embrace you, I embrace Ella and all that comes with being in your lives. I live for school drop-offs and pick-ups, for helping out at the clinic and on the farm. I look forward to spending time with your mother, your brothers and their families. I can't wait to head out to the footy on Saturday arvos and the pub on Saturday nights. I love you and I love Linden Gully. Please let me come home.'

A flash of lightning lit the darkening sky as Ryan considered her heartfelt speech. He wanted to believe her, to take her in his arms and tell her they never had to be apart again. But in the end these were just words. Eloquent words, he'd give her that, but she was a writer and she was used to manipulating language to suit her purpose. Was she really ready to give up her New York life for plain old Linden Gully? How long before she changed her mind?

'I know what you're thinking. Where's the proof? Well, don't worry. I've come prepared.' She shoved the fistful of papers into his hand. 'Read these.'

'What are they?'

'Read them and see.'

He glanced down at the top sheet. It appeared to be a printout of an email exchange between Jo and a woman called Amanda Briggs.

A quick scan of the content revealed that Amanda Briggs was a lawyer and Jo was apparently consulting with her on the topic of adoption. What the...? He flipped to the next page, which contained general information about adoption of children by stepparents. The next few pages were filled with legal mumbo jumbo, precedents about adoption, custody and the like.

'I don't understand.'

'Manda is a friend of mine from boarding school. She's a family law specialist.'

'And?'

'I called her on Thursday morning, when I was waiting for you to come back from the hospital. We had a brief discussion about your situation. Don't worry, I was discreet. I didn't give her personal information about you or Ella, not even your first names. In any case, anything I said to her will be kept in the strictest confidence. I asked her a number of hypothetical questions, relating to adoption of a child by a stepparent.'

The first fat raindrops began to plop onto the pages he held. 'You would consider that?'

'Of course I would. Obviously only if it was something Ella wanted and...'

'And?'

'Well, you and I would have to be married first.'

As the heavens opened and rain began to bucket down Jo stood perfectly still and looked into his eyes. It was then he realised she wasn't going anywhere.

Jo's pulse thudded in her ears. She could hear it over the roaring wind and intermittent rolls of thunder. He wasn't saying anything. This was it. She had nothing else. Nothing left to give. If he walked away now it would really be the end. Forever.

Slowly, deliberately, he moved towards her, never taking his eyes off hers. They stood for a moment face to face, his hand slowly caressing her cheek as the rain washed the tears from their faces. Suddenly, before she had the chance to protest, he scooped her up into his arms.

'What are you doing?' she laughed.

His answer brought fresh tears to her eyes.

'Carrying you over the threshold of your new home.'

CHAPTER
38

The overnight rain was cause for great concern in the wedding household, particularly from the mother of the bride, who fretted and fussed and eventually resorted to praying for an end to the rain. It seemed no amount of calming or cajoling from Jo, or indeed the bride herself, could talk Jenny down.

'Mum, we have a marquee the size of a circus tent. We'll have the ceremony in there if need be.'

'Yes, but it's not designed to withstand a hurricane.'

'The weather report says clearing showers,' Jo ventured, giving Steph a cheeky wink. 'No hurricanes are mentioned.'

Jenny had thrown her hands in the air, tutting and clucking, before heading into the office to check the online forecast one more time.

In the end the worry was unfounded — either that or the prayers were successful — because as the happy couple exchanged vows on a purpose-built deck beneath Steph's favourite gumtree the sun poked its head through the clouds.

Just as the celebrant said those magic words, 'You may kiss the bride,' Ella tugged on Jo's hand. 'Jo. Look there's a rainbow.'

Jo's gaze left the kissing couple for a moment to take in the sky. Ella was right. A faint rainbow stretched out behind them. It was a perfect backdrop to a perfect day.

She joined in the applause for the kiss and stole a glance at Ryan. He was looking mighty fine in his classic black dinner suit. Jo made a mental note to encourage a similar type of attire at their own wedding, which, according to Ryan, would be taking place as soon as legally possible.

She didn't want to wait either. Now that she'd decided where she wanted to live the rest of her life, she wanted to get on with it as soon as possible. But it wasn't only that. The sooner they were married the sooner she could apply to adopt Ella. Amanda had already told her that she and Ryan would need to be married for at least two years before her application was likely to be successful.

They didn't need a big fancy wedding. In fact she'd be happy with a simple registry-office affair, but once word got out around here she doubted that would be possible. And denying Ella the chance to repeat her starring role as flower girl seemed kind of mean. So they'd do something simple at home and, knowing this town, they'd have plenty of help.

The sun slipped behind the clouds again and a few sprinkles of rain tickled her face.

'Everyone into the marquee,' Macca called, apparently revelling in his first official task as master of ceremonies for the day. Ryan appeared at her side. He scooped Ella up and sat her on his hip and took Jo by the hand. 'Shall we, ladies?'

Ella giggled and nodded. 'Let's go.'

Once they were seated at the bridal table and all the guests had taken their places, Macca stepped up to the microphone. 'Ladies and gentlemen, welcome to the wedding reception of Mr and Mrs Andrews. Steph and Nate, please stand up and take a bow.'

The bride and groom obliged as the guests showed their appreciation for the newlyweds with a round of thunderous applause.

Macca gestured for the crowd to quieten down before he continued. 'Tonight we're going to run with a slightly altered program to your usual wedding. At the bride's request we are going to get all the formalities out of the way right away so we can, in Steph's words, "Get on with the party". So without further ado, I'm going to call on the happy couple to take their places on the dance floor for their first dance together as a married couple. Ladies and gentlemen, please give them a round of applause.'

The guests all stood and applauded as Steph and Nate twirled awkwardly around the dance floor to Ben Lee's 'Gamble Everything For Love'.

Ryan caught Jo's eye and smiled. 'Great song,' he said.

'Maybe it's an omen,' she replied.

'Jo, when do we get to dance?' Ella asked.

'In a minute, honey. Macca, the man with the microphone, is going to ask the bride and groom's parents onto the floor in a minute. After that he'll call on Daddy and me. You listen to him and when he calls your name you can come onto the floor and Daddy will dance with you.'

'Who will you dance with then?'

'I'll be okay. I'll have a little rest.'

As she spoke Macca called for the parents to join Nate and Steph. Jo was thrilled to see Jenny looking so relaxed and happy as she and Mick moved expertly around the floor.

'Ladies and gentlemen please give a warm welcome to our maid of honour, Johanna Morgan, partnered by the best man, Ryan Galloway.'

Ryan took her by the hand and led her down to the wooden dance floor he and Nate had constructed weeks before. He pulled her in close and she noticed he was wearing some sort of cologne. 'You smell gorgeous,' she said.

He grinned. 'Thought I'd better make an effort. Now I've got you I don't want you losing interest.'

'No chance of that.'

'Happy?' he whispered.

'Unbelievably.'

Macca's voice boomed over the song, 'Now we have our junior bridesmaid, Madison Keating, partnered by her dad, John, and our gorgeous little flower girl, Ella, who'll join her dad, Ryan, on the dance floor.'

Ella skipped to join them. Jo released Ryan's hand so he could take Ella's, but Ella shook her head and grabbed Jo's hand. 'Don't go Jo. I don't want you to be by yourself. I don't mind sharing.'

Ryan smiled at Ella and took Jo's other hand. The three of them formed a circle and began to dance. 'Welcome home, Joey,' Ryan said.

EPILOGUE

One year later...

'I see you're in the *Woman's Day* again, love.'

Jo grabbed the paper-wrapped package of sausages Mrs Clemmens plonked on the counter and slipped it into her cotton shopping bag. 'Yeah. They did a photo shoot when I was down in Melbourne for the book launch.'

'You look lovely in the photos, Jo. I'll bet young Ella was impressed.'

'I don't know about that, Mrs C. I think she was a bit miffed she had to stay at home and go to school while I was there. But I've promised her I'll make it up to her.'

'What have you got in mind?' The older woman passed Jo her change and rested her ample body against the counter. Clearly she was ready for a chat.

Mrs Clemmens was what Katherine would have termed a 'nosy parker'. Once upon a time Jo would have brushed off her questions but these days she welcomed them as part of life in Linden Gully. Over the past year Jo had slowly come to realise the enquiries about her life came from a place of genuine interest and, in Mrs C's case, pride. Jo was one of Linden Gully's own and her success was the town's success.

From the moment she and Ryan announced their relationship — with that very public kiss at Steph and Nate's wedding — the town had drawn her into its loving arms. They'd even protected her when that TV reporter came sniffing around, looking for a story.

She'd been naive, thinking the photo of her kissing Ryan would just disappear without a ripple. First there was that hack of a reporter from the local TV station and then a couple of other suspicious visitors to the town, all of them snooping around, asking questions. But they'd got nothing. No one — not even Kelly Prescott or Laura Baxter — would talk. The story died down pretty quickly in the end. She'd gotten lucky. A big scandal involving the local member of parliament had definitely helped to push her story out of the news cycle.

'Earth to Jo.'

'Sorry Mrs C, I was away with the fairies.' Jo lowered her voice slightly. 'She doesn't know yet, so keep this under your hat, but when I go to America for the book tour in September, Ryan and Ella are coming too.'

Mrs Clemmens raised her eyebrows and then gave her a conspiratorial wink. 'Don't worry, love, your secret's safe with me. Wow, America, eh? I'm sure she'll be thrilled. So how long are you going for? Who'll look after Ryan's practice?'

A smile twitched at the corners of Jo's mouth. She should have known Mrs Clemmens wouldn't be satisfied until she had all the details. Not that it mattered. It wasn't as if she was in a hurry to leave the butcher's shop. It was still early and she had a leisurely day ahead. After working her butt off for the past few months she'd finally submitted her fourth novel to the publisher yesterday. She figured she deserved a day off. When this morning's grocery shopping was done she planned to drop in at Steph's for a cuppa and a catch-up. With the baby due any day now, Jenny and Nate were insisting the new mother-to-be had to stay home and rest, which was driving poor Steph nuts. Jo had promised to bring cake and gossip.

'We'll be gone for a month,' she told an attentive Mrs Clemmens. 'Ryan was a bit worried about leaving the practice for so long, but he's managed to find a locum to handle any emergencies. Between Dan, Bec and Beth, the farm will be fine.'

Mrs Clemmens nodded her approval. 'It's wonderful how Beth's come on since her hip replacement. I saw her the other day over at the CWA hall and she looked fit as a fiddle.'

'Yeah, she's made a full recovery now, thank goodness. We rely on her quite a lot, but she seems to love helping out.'

'I'm sure she does. She'll miss you all while you're gone, though. A month seems such a long time. How will Ella cope being out of school for so long?'

'She'll be fine. She's a bright little thing and she'll only miss two weeks of classes because we're going during the school holidays. I'm sure she'll catch up.'

Mrs Clemmens nodded as Jo spoke.

'We're packing quite a lot into that month. The book tour starts in LA so we can take Ella to Disneyland and Universal Studios while we're there. We're visiting San Francisco and San Diego too. I think Ella will love the San Diego zoo. We have ten days in New York and then, on the way home we'll have a few days in Hawaii. You never know, Ryan might even give surfing a go.'

Mrs Clemmens clapped her hands in obvious delight. 'Now I'm envious. Sounds like the trip of a lifetime.'

Mrs Clemmens was right about that. It was a wonderful way to celebrate the first anniversary of Ryan's signing of the adoption papers, as well as serving as a belated honeymoon. She supposed most newlyweds wouldn't want to take a child away with them, but Jo wouldn't have it any other way. She was especially looking forward to spending time in New York showing Ryan and Ella all her favourite parts of the city. She couldn't wait to see Ella's face when she saw the vast array of toys in FAO Schwarz, or the Ferris wheel in Toys R Us.

Ryan was nervous about his first visit to the 'Big Apple' — and he kept calling it that even though she'd told him no New Yorker ever would. Despite his distaste for big cities she knew he would marvel at the open space provided by Central Park, and he'd be impressed by the view from the top of the Empire State Building. Who wouldn't? She'd bought tickets online for a Yankees game and hand-picked some restaurants and diners where she hoped he'd be blown away by the food and the friendly service. And, of course, they'd visit her old neighbourhood so Ryan could meet some of her friends from her NYU days.

The last time she'd visited the States, almost a year ago now, she'd reluctantly gone alone. It was impossible for Ryan to travel at that time. His mother was still recovering from her fall and he was waiting to sign those all-important papers that would make Ella irrefutably his.

Ella begged to go along, and nothing would have made Jo happier than to grant her request. She would have loved to take Ella to the premiere of *Hollywood Kisses* because at least then one of them would have been happy to be there. But Ryan didn't think it was a good idea for Ella to travel so far when her epilepsy diagnosis was still so new. And as much as she wanted to share New York with her, Jo really didn't want Ella exposed to all that stupid media scrutiny.

So she walked the red carpet by herself.

Zach was there with Kiara on his arm, and they were the darlings of the paparazzi and the crowd. Jo had been played by him, made to look as if she'd been having an affair all along when really it was the other way around. Not that she cared anymore. Ryan's identity hadn't been revealed — he was referred to as her 'Australian mystery man'— and that was all that mattered.

Her split from Zach made front-page headlines in the week before the premiere, so Jo could have chosen to stay away. There was no need to keep up the pretence, and she owed Zach nothing. But she needed to go back to New York to pack up her things and tie up a few loose ends, so she figured she would hold her head high and walk the red carpet anyway. This was the movie of *her* book after all. Why shouldn't she be at the premiere?

Still, it hadn't been easy and she'd been more than a little relieved when she'd stepped on board the aircraft to go home. Back to her family, where she belonged.

The bell on the butcher's door tinkled, indicating a new customer's arrival. Jo put a finger to her lips to remind Mrs Clemmens not to share her secret and the older woman gave her a reassuring nod.

'Good morning, Mrs Irvine,' Jo said, as she backed away from the counter.

Elderly Mrs Irvine smiled and returned the greeting before turning her attention to the meat on display.

'Well, I'll leave you to it Mrs C,' Jo said. 'Thanks for the sausages. They're Ella's favourite.'

Mrs Clemmens smiled as she waved her goodbye. 'You're a good mum, Jo. Ella's lucky to have you.'

'I'm the lucky one,' Jo said, and she stepped out into the winter sun.

ACKNOWLEDGEMENTS

My heartfelt thanks go to:

Kate Cuthbert for believing in this book, and all the team at Harlequin for being so great to work with.

Amanda Knight for being my sounding board, my critique partner and a wonderful friend.

Carmen Vicos and Catherine Evans, for reading countless drafts. Your comments and support helped me coax the scribble into a story. Without you this book wouldn't exist.

My editor, Kate James, for helping me to shape this into a much better book than it would have been otherwise.

Georgina Penney, for providing the right advice at exactly the right time.

My lovely writing friends, Delwyn Jenkins, Janette Radevski, Jennie Jones and Rachael Johns, for your friendship and support.

My family and friends, especially my sister-in-law, Tracie, and brother, Dean, who sing my praises every chance they get, and my friend, Fiona, who is still by my side after forty years of friendship.

My beautiful nieces, Georgie and Sophie, for helping me with Ella's character.

All my AWSOM buddies. I love being part of this diverse and dynamic group. You all rock!

Romance Writers of Australia. I'm so grateful for the ongoing support and professional development this amazing organisation provides.

My fellow Escape Artists. What a welcoming and supportive group of people you are. I love working alongside you all.

My book club. Thanks for being such an awesome cheer squad. Special thanks to Kelly for your friendship, support and encouragement (and all the bubbles!).

Shannean and Alison for your expert legal advice.

All my Facebook and Twitter friends and followers. I can always depend on you guys to help me out with a name or a tricky bit of research. I really appreciate the interest you show in my writing. Thanks for sharing the journey with me.

All the readers who take the time to write a review or email me their thoughts about my books. I love hearing from you and your support is what keeps me going. Thank you.

My wonderful husband, David, and my three beautiful sons, Charlie, Will and Alex, for sharing me with my characters. I love you all xx.

And Millie and Lulu, for getting my writer's butt out of the chair and out of the house every day!

talk about it

Let's talk about books.

Join the conversation:

 on facebook.com/harlequinaustralia

 on Twitter @harlequinaus

www.harlequinbooks.com.au

If you love reading and want to know about our authors and titles, then let's talk about it.